DEFY

THE BLADES OF ACKTAR

BOOK THREE

DEFY

TRICIA MINGERINK

Sword & Cross
Publishing

Published by Sword & Cross Publishing
Grand Rapids, MI

Sword & Cross Publishing and the Sword & Cross Publishing logo
are trademarks of Tricia Mingerink. Absence of ™ in connection with
Sword & Cross Publishing does not indicate an absence of trademark
protection of those marks.

Cover by Ashley Joy Illustration
Ashleyjoyillustration.com

Edited by Nadine Brandes
Nadinebrandes.com

LCCN: 2016908060
ISBN: 1-943442-02-9
ISBN: 978-1-943442-02-7

To my fans: Congratulations, you survived *Deny*'s cliff-hanger!

Books by Tricia Mingerink

The Blades of Acktar
   Dare
   Deny
   Defy

Character List

Abigail Alistair – third child of Lord and Lady Alistair. Friend of Brandi's.

Blane Altin – one of Respen's Blades

Blizzard – Leith's horse

Brandi Faythe (BRAN - dee) – Renna's younger sister. Her full name is Lady Brandiline Faythe.

Esther Alistair – fifth child of Lord and Lady Alistair

General Uriah Stewart – general in the Resistance army

General Wentle – general in King Respen's army

Ian McCrae – Resistance member

Jeremiah Alistair – fourth child of Lord and Lady Alistair.

Jolene Lorraine – Lady Lorraine's daughter.

King Leon Eirdon (ee - EAR - don) – the former king killed by Respen

King Respen Felix (REH - spen) – king of Acktar. He was the lord of Blathe.

Lady Annita Faythe – Renna and Brandi's mother. She was the sister of King Leon.

Lady Eve Alistair – Lord Alistair's wife

Lady Paula Lorraine – lady of the town of Sierra

Leith Torren (LEETH TOR - ren) – former Blade, now on the run

Lord Hector Emilin (EHM - ih - lihn) – lord of the town of Dently, killed by King Respen

Lord Henry Alistair – lord of the town of Walden

Lord Laurence Faythe – Renna and Brandi's father

Lydia Alistair – second child of Lord and Lady Alistair. Friend of Renna's.

Martyn Hamish – one of Respen's Blades. Leith's former friend.

Queen Deirdre Eirdon (DEER - dree) – the former queen killed by Harrison Vane

Quinten Daas – one of Respen's Blades

Ranson Harding – one of Respen's Blades

Renna Faythe (REHN - nuh) – The lady of the town of Stetterly. Her full name is Lady Rennelda Faythe (REHN - nehl - duh).

Shadrach Alistair – Lord Alistair's oldest son

Location List

Acktar (AHCK - tar) – a country mostly made up of flat prairie

Nalgar Castle (NAHL - gar) – the capitol of Acktar

Eagle Heights – the Resistance base

Stetterly (STEHT - er - ly) – a town near the Spires Canyon

Walden (WALL - den) – a town near the Sheered Rock Hills

Uster (UH - ster) – a town near the Spires Canyon

Sierra (see - AIR - uh) – a town on the prairie between Walden and Nalgar Castle

Sheered Rock Hills (SHEERD) – the mountain range that forms the northern border of Acktar

Spires Canyon – the canyon that forms the eastern border of Acktar

The Ramparts – the section of steep cliffs that border the Waste

The Waste – the desert on the eastern side of the Sheered Rock Hills

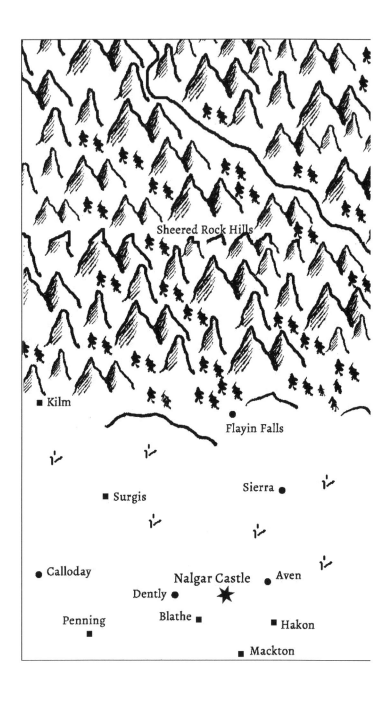

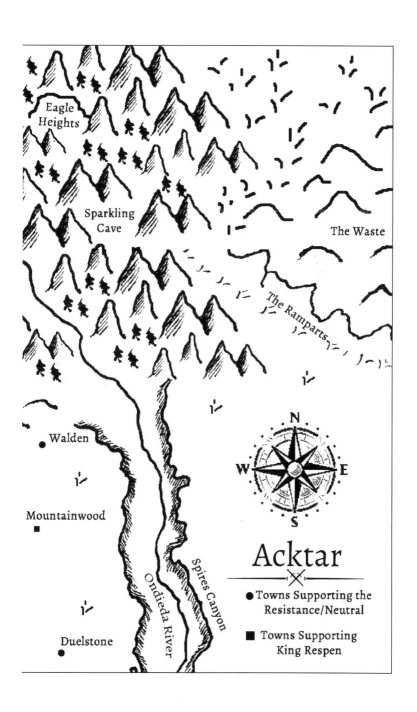

Eagle
Heights

Sparkling
Cave

The Waste

The Ramparts

N

W   E

S

Walden

Mountainwood

Ondieda River

Spires Canyon

Duelstone

Acktar

⚔

● Towns Supporting the
   Resistance/Neutral

■ Towns Supporting
   King Respen

And the Philistine said, I defy the armies of Israel this day; give me a man, that we may fight together.

Then said David to the Philistine, Thou comest to me with a sword, and with a spear, and with a shield: but I come to thee in the name of the Lord of hosts, the God of the armies of Israel, whom thou hast defied.

This day will the Lord deliver thee into mine hand...that all the earth may know that there is a God in Israel. And all this assembly shall know that the Lord saveth not with sword and spear: for the battle is the Lord's, and he will give you into our hands.

- I Samuel 17:10, 45-47

1

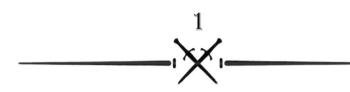

Leith Torren had left Brandi's sister behind to die. No matter how much Brandi had kicked and screamed, Leith hadn't let her go. He'd picked her up and carried her away. And that *wasn't* all right, no matter how much Leith whispered it in her ear.

This wasn't how a rescue was supposed to work. Leith was supposed to charge into Nalgar Castle, fight off the guards, and ride away with both Brandi and Renna. That's how things always worked in stories. God always provided a way for the good guys to escape. God had told Noah to build an ark. He'd sent His angels to protect Daniel.

But Renna had been left behind. Uncle Abel and Aunt Mara had been executed. Brandi curled against Leith's chest. His arms kept her steady as Blizzard loped through the darkness, the dawn breaking in front of them.

Why had Leith left Renna behind? Brandi had tried to understand. Really, she had. But surely Leith could've tried harder. He could've done *something*.

But he hadn't. And Renna had been left behind. What would Respen do to her? Would he kill her? Why wouldn't he kill her? After all, it's what he'd planned to do. What if Renna was already dead?

No. She couldn't be dead.

How long had they been riding? They didn't stop. They didn't sleep. Whenever Leith slowed their pace to let the horses walk, he, Shad, Jamie, and the four rescued trainees swung down from their horses and also walked. But Brandi didn't move.

Brandi closed her eyes and rested her head on Leith's shoulder. Maybe Leith would think she'd fallen asleep.

She couldn't sleep. Her chest ached. Her head filled with the sights and sounds of death. She couldn't even cry.

Apparently, she didn't fool Leith. He hugged her tighter. "Just a little farther, then we'll stop."

She forced herself to nod. The horses needed a rest. She could feel Blizzard's exhaustion in the jagged way his hooves pounded the ground. He'd carried two riders for most of the way. She'd ridden with Shad Alistair, heir to Walden, for a few miles and with Jamie Cavendish, Leith's former trainee, but not enough to make up for the long miles Blizzard had run with both her and Leith on his back.

Not that she was happy with any of them at the moment.

Blizzard surged up yet another slope, legs straining, nostrils flaring. Saliva flew from his open mouth, joining the sweat running down his sides and legs. They entered a mass of boulders, like the ruins of some long ago giant's castle.

Leith halted Blizzard and swung down. "We'll rest here."

The trainees slid off their horses but remained in a group, as if they didn't dare so much as twitch an eyebrow without permission.

Leith glanced at Jamie and tipped his head at Brandi. Brandi suppressed the urge to roll her eyes. As if she couldn't tell that Leith had just ordered Jamie to keep an eye on her in case she tried something crazy.

Not that she wasn't thinking about it.

Leith and Shad headed toward a large boulder. Probably to take a look around.

Brandi twined her fingers in Blizzard's mane. Between her legs, his sides heaved. If she knew the way, she'd take up the reins, wheel Blizzard around, and charge back to Nalgar Castle.

But she couldn't do that to Blizzard. He'd given them his all to get them away. She couldn't ask anything more from him. Besides, she didn't have a plan to rescue Renna. Not yet, anyway.

Not that Leith had done any better, and he'd had a plan. Instead, he'd mucked it all up and left Renna behind where Respen could kill her.

As Jamie swung down from his horse, Buster, Brandi sighed. She probably should get down too. Blizzard deserved to get a good rub down. She eased her leg over Blizzard's back and slid to the ground. Her gaze snagged on a rock at the base of one of the boulders.

She stiffened. That rock. This place. She'd been here before. This was the same den of boulders they'd stopped at briefly after Leith and Jamie had faked her and Renna's deaths, and their bloody nightdresses were buried under that rock.

A lot of good that plan had done. Here she was, right back where she'd started, but without Renna.

What were Shad and Leith so busy looking at? She scrambled up the boulder and spotted them at the crest, lying on their stomachs and peering over the edge. From here, she could see that the boulder balanced on a tall promontory. The Sheered Rock Hills loomed all around them but fell into the rolling prairie down below.

She used the boulder to boost herself into the lower branches of a scraggly pine. It swayed a little with her weight. Far below, the dark shape of a building jutted from the prairie in the pre-dawn haze. It took her a moment to recognize the tan stone of Walden Manor. The black maze of wooden barricades, dirt mound, and dry moat surrounded the manor.

But surrounding that...Brandi's pulse beat in her throat. A sea of dark shapes with lines of white tents sprawled around Walden Manor. Respen's army. Hearing Respen taunt her and Renna about it was one thing. Actually seeing it surrounding Walden, a place she'd called home for several months since having to flee her home town of Stetterly, was another.

Leith's voice carried to her. "They haven't fallen yet. Maybe they'll be able to hold out. It looks like the army's settled in for a siege."

Shad remained silent and still, staring at his besieged home. Lord Alistair, Shad's father, was down in that manor. Brandi swallowed. Lord Alistair had been so nice to her and Renna when they'd stayed at Walden these last few months. Why did she have to lose him too?

He was going to die. That much was certain despite Leith's attempt at reassurance. Sure, Lord Alistair and his men had held out against Respen's army for three days but that didn't mean they could hold out forever. Who knew when help would arrive? If it ever did.

Brandi dropped to the ground and trudged back to Blizzard. The horse had waited long enough for a rub down. She set to work untying Leith's bedroll and saddlebags. As she reached for the saddle's girth, Leith appeared at her side and beat her to it.

She scowled and stepped back. She didn't need his help. She could handle this on her own.

Leith set the saddle on the ground and rested his hands on her shoulders. His grip was firm enough that she couldn't pull away. She huffed, crossed her arms, and met his gaze.

The journey had tousled his black hair. His forehead creased as he stared at her with eyes as green and bright as cornstalks. "Renna's safe for the moment. Respen won't hurt her."

"How do you know that? He was going to kill us." Brandi's throat squeezed. What if Respen had already killed Renna? Or worse, tortured her. Renna wasn't strong enough for that. How would she ever manage being alone at Nalgar Castle?

Leith held her gaze. "No Blade has ever escaped, much less betrayed Respen and lived. He can't let me get away or he'll lose his hold on the rest of the Blades. And right now, as long as we escape the Blades, Renna is his only means to lure me back."

Brandi cocked her head. It'd cause a ton of problems for Respen if the Blades stopped fearing him. After all, look at Leith and Jamie. The moment they stopped being afraid, they turned on him.

Leith squeezed her shoulders, his eyes begging her to understand. "I never would've left Renna behind if I thought I was leaving her to die. You know that, right?"

After a moment, Brandi managed a nod. If she hadn't been so mad, she probably would've seen it sooner. She shouldn't have doubted him. He'd done a lot—lied to King Respen, joined the Resistance, taken a knife in his shoulder, broken his friendship with Third Blade Martyn Hamish—to keep Renna safe. Of course he wouldn't stop now.

If running away was keeping Renna safe, then that's what Brandi would do. For now.

She glanced at Jamie. He rubbed a handful of dry grass across Buster's drenched back. The sweat turned the buckskin's fur into the same color as wet sand. "Will the Blades be hunting Jamie? He's an escaped Blade now too. And the trainees?"

"Yes, though I'm the one Respen will want the most." Leith straightened but kept one hand on her shoulder. "Go rest. I can finish with Blizzard."

Brandi pulled away from him and shook her head. "I'm all right. I can take care of Blizzard." She jabbed a finger at the trainees huddled in a group. The oldest boy couldn't be much more than ten and the youngest maybe eight. "I think they need someone to reassure them that they're safe. They're still looking at you like you're the First Blade."

Leith grimaced but he headed toward the trainees. They shrank away from him. He knelt and spoke in a low voice.

Hopefully they'd listen. Leith still looked like a Blade with his black clothes and knives strapped all over his body, but he wasn't a bad sort. When he wasn't dragging her away from her sister, that is.

Martyn, on the other hand...Brandi ripped two handfuls of grass and scrubbed them along Blizzard's back. She wouldn't mind biting his shoulder. Or giving him a good kick in the shins or somewhere else more painful. He was the cause of all their problems. If he hadn't captured her and Renna, dragged them to Nalgar Castle, and stopped

Leith's rescue, she and Renna would already be at Eagle Heights, safe with the Resistance and away from Respen.

The stalks of grass turned into mush in her hands. She grabbed another few handfuls and kept scrubbing. When Blizzard was as dry as she could make him, she hobbled him.

She plopped crosslegged on the ground and nibbled on the bit of dried meat Leith handed her. Of course it'd be dried meat. It seemed to be the only thing Blades ate.

Jamie laid out her bedroll near her. His brown hair stuck out in several directions above blue eyes that studied her.

She opened her mouth to argue. She wasn't some simpering, helpless ninny who needed someone else to set up her bedroll for her.

Jamie shook his head. "Just rest. If you can."

She snapped her mouth shut. Arguing sounded like too much work. Exhaustion pressed against her skull. Perhaps she could close her eyes for a few minutes. Surely she was too tired to dream.

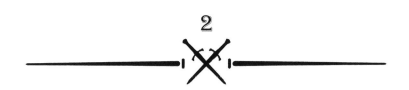

2

Leith leaned against a boulder, but he couldn't rest. He should. He hadn't slept the entire ride from Nalgar Castle and very little the night before that. But his stomach knotted too tightly. He'd assured Brandi that Renna was all right, but did he believe it?

If only he could turn Blizzard around now and return for her. But what good would it do? He'd simply be captured and take away Respen's one reason to keep her alive.

And Martyn. What had Respen done to him? What punishment had he suffered because Leith had succeeded in rescuing Brandi? How much did he hate Leith now?

Shad slid down the boulder and dropped to the ground next to him. "I can take your watch if you'd like. You look done in."

Leith shook his head. "I can't sleep. Might as well do something useful while I'm at it."

"She'll be all right." Shad patted Leith's shoulder, but his mouth remained in a tight line. He looked about as sure of those words as Leith. "Don't worry. Once we arrive at Eagle Heights, the Resistance will help. We'll rescue Renna."

Leith leaned forward, resisting the urge to jump up and pace. The Resistance couldn't let Renna remain at Nalgar Castle. She and Brandi were the last of the Eirdon line. They were daughters, and not sons, but they were all Acktar had.

Leith might not be able to do much for Renna right now, but the Resistance would aid her. The mysterious Leader, whoever he or she was, would rally the Resistance to rescue Renna. All he and Shad had to do was get to Eagle Heights safely.

Easier said than done. Respen would send the other Blades after them. How much of a lead had Leith gained on the Blades by pushing everyone so hard? Half a day, if that.

If the Blades caught up...if they captured or killed him, Renna would die. Respen no longer would have any reason to keep her alive.

He had to focus on that goal, not on the ache in his chest. He'd failed to rescue her, but he wouldn't fail her again. He'd get to the Resistance at Eagle Heights. They'd mount a rescue, and Renna would be saved.

"How far is Eagle Heights?" Leith waved at the mountains stretching north above them. How long would Renna have to stay at Nalgar Castle? What would Respen do to her in the meantime?

"A week's hard riding, though we're going to take longer." Shad nodded at the trainees. "They won't be able to keep up a hard pace for long. And my mother, Jolene, Lady Lorraine, and everyone else who left Walden before the attack are waiting for us in the meadow, and they'll be traveling with us to Eagle Heights. I'm the last one left in Acktar, besides my father, who knows the way."

Leith raised his eyebrows. "What would they have

done if we'd run into more trouble than we could handle?"

"A Resistance scout was bound to pass through eventually to check on the situation in Acktar, so they wouldn't have waited forever." Shad shrugged. "What do you want to do when we get there? Do you have another change of clothes?"

Leith ran his hand over the knives strapped across his chest over his black shirt and trousers. He did have his set of prairie tan clothes in his saddlebags. He could slip back into his role of Daniel, a peasant farmer.

But he was done with lies, even that one.

Perhaps he could change out of his black clothes and take off his knives and tell them that he was a Blade once he was in their camp. But somehow, even doing that much felt like a lie. Like he was tricking them into taking him in, only to reveal the truth later.

"I don't want to continue lying." Leith leaned his head against the stone behind him. "Besides, they already know you have a Blade on your side. Some have even seen me from a distance. It's not like they'll attack me once you explain."

"They'll be wary. You won't be accepted as one of them." Shad's hand closed around his sword's hilt. "And whatever you choose now, that's how you'll enter Eagle Heights."

He could enter Eagle Heights as any other Christian peasant fleeing Respen. He'd be welcomed, befriended. Or, he could remain a Blade. It wouldn't matter if he'd turned to their side. The thirty-seven marks on his right arm gave them plenty of reasons to hate him.

"No more lies. If that means I enter Eagle Heights as a Blade, then so be it." Leith stood and dusted off his trousers. "Doesn't look like anyone else is sleeping either. Let's push on."

Leith held out a hand. As he pulled Shad to his feet, Shad winced and pressed a hand to his side. A bright spot of red seeped through his shirt.

"Your wound. It's bleeding again." Leith frowned. Shad had been wounded while pretending to be former First Blade Harrison Vane shortly before they left for Nalgar Castle. Leith had tended it, but they hadn't taken the time to stitch it.

Shad shook his head. "It's fine. Nothing to worry about."

Should Leith press him to get it stitched? Leith could do it if he had to. He eyed Shad's shirt. The red spot wasn't growing, and the wound hadn't been that deep.

Shad sighed and unbuckled his sword belt. "Fine. You get the others moving, and I'll wrap a fresh bandage over it."

While Leith saddled a horse for the two youngest trainees, he glanced over his shoulder at Shad. From what he could see, the scab had broken open at one corner. Nothing serious, but the ride ahead of them might tear the scab open worse.

Leith boosted the two youngest trainees, boys of only eight, onto the horse. They gripped the reins and stared at him. So silent. Still so scared.

If only Renna was here. She would've been able to give them the kindness they needed. Leith had rescued them. He'd assured them they were safe now. But he was still their former First Blade. They didn't trust kindness given by him.

He shook his head and helped another trainee onto a horse. He hadn't trusted kindness when he was nine either. Not until Renna had given so freely when he'd hadn't deserved it.

Leith strode to Blizzard and tossed the saddle onto

his back. *Renna*. How could he possibly think about leaving her behind? It'd be two, almost three weeks at the earliest before he could return. How could he abandon her for that long?

He had no choice. He could return to Nalgar Castle now. He might even be able to sneak into the castle and find her. But she'd be well guarded. The bait in a trap. And once Leith was caught, both of them would die.

More than that, Renna was Martyn's responsibility. Martyn had fought Leith once. He'd do it again to keep Leith from rescuing Renna. The only way for Leith to rescue Renna by himself would be to kill Martyn.

Leith couldn't do it. Was that wrong of him? Should he be willing to kill Martyn if it meant he could rescue Renna? He'd once betrayed Martyn and risked his life. But back then, Shad and Lord Alistair had assured Leith that they'd do everything in their power to make sure Martyn didn't get killed.

If only there was a way to rescue both Renna and Martyn. But Martyn remained too loyal to his duty. It'd take more than mere words to convince Martyn to turn on Respen.

The Resistance. It was their only chance. Even Martyn wouldn't resist an army. Perhaps, somehow, Leith could rescue Renna and Martyn with the Resistance's help.

Brandi trudged to Blizzard. When Leith knelt to give her a boost, she scowled and shoved past him. "I don't need help."

Leith stood and handed her the reins. He shouldn't let her actions hurt. He had dragged her away from Renna.

With Brandi settled on Blizzard, Leith saddled a brown horse they'd taken from Nalgar's stables. Earlier, one of the other trainees had ridden it. But Blizzard needed a rest from carrying two riders, and doubling the youngest trainees wouldn't tire their horse.

After he swung into the saddle, Leith sidled his horse closer to Brandi. "What's this horse named?"

Brandi shrugged. "I don't know."

Leith gripped the reins. Not the answer he'd been hoping for. Had he left both sisters behind in Nalgar Castle? "Well, he's a horse. He needs a name."

"Big Brown." Brandi's voice remained as flat as a river boulder.

What would it take to get the old Brandi back? He hung his head. Renna. That's what it would take. But how long would it be before he could reunite Brandi with her sister?

Shad led the way deeper into the Sheered Rock Hills. Leith eased into the rhythm of the unfamiliar horse beneath him. Last time he traveled this trail, he'd had Renna behind him. He'd been confident—too confident— in the knowledge he was sending her to safety.

He glanced at Brandi. She swayed in time with Blizzard's strides, her face blank, her eyes cold. What sort of pain was she feeling now? How much would it hurt her to reach the meadow tonight, the last place they'd all been together and happy only a few weeks ago?

Leith caught sight of Jamie also studying Brandi. Their gazes met, and the tight line of Jamie's mouth probably mirrored his own expression. Leith tipped his head toward Brandi, and Jamie nodded. Perhaps if Leith couldn't help her, Jamie could.

The day stretched into long hours and still longer miles. Night had fallen by the time they reached the ridge overlooking the mountain meadow, its edges screened with thick pines. A pinprick of light flickered between the branches.

13

Leith drew in a deep breath, realized he gripped the hilt of one of his knives, and dropped his hand to his thigh.

As they drew closer, low voices murmered through the pines. To their right, a stream gurgled, and the small waterfall churned in a muted roar.

"Halt." A voice like that of a girl or young boy growled from somewhere in front of them. "State your names before I put an arrow in your chest."

"Jolene, it's me. Shad." Shad held out his arms away from his weapons.

"Shad?" Something rustled. A dark shape dashed from the trees. Shad barely had time to swing down from his horse before the figure slammed into him. "You're all right?"

Leith glanced away. His chest ached. Renna had greeted him like that, right before he'd left her behind.

Shad finished murmuring to Jolene and turned to the rest of them. "Let's join the others."

He led the way through the tree line. Leith hung back, letting everyone else pass him. When Shad stepped into the firelight, Lady Alistair leapt to her feet, followed by Shad's sister Lydia. They hugged Shad so tightly he winced. Lady Lorraine remained where she was, though a smile twitched the corner of her mouth.

Leith didn't belong here. The moment he stepped through the trees, the guards would panic. Lady Lorraine and Lady Alistair would eye him with suspicion.

Shad tugged Brandi into the firelight and explained how Renna had been left behind at Nalgar Castle. He introduced the Blade trainees. Lady Alistair smiled, wrapped her arms around the youngest two, and pulled them closer to the fire. At least they would be welcomed and cared for.

"And the Blade?" Lady Lorraine rested a hand on the knife in her belt. "Where is he?"

Leith stepped through the pines into the firelight. The guards jumped to their feet, hands reaching for their swords. Lady Alistair paled. Lydia gaped and pressed her hands over her mouth as if she couldn't believe that the peasant farmer she'd encouraged to pursue Renna was also a Blade.

Leith forced himself to stay still. He couldn't blame them for being wary. How could they reconcile Daniel, the person he'd pretended to be, with a former killer?

"It's all right. This is Leith. He's on our side." Shad glanced around at the circle of faces. His gaze stayed on the guards. "You trained with him. You can trust him."

The guards took their hands away from their swords, but none of them relaxed their stance.

Leith hung his head. Even now, while on the run and no longer a Blade, he couldn't outrun his past.

Jolene glanced at Shad, straightened her shoulders, and stepped forward. "I believe we have a little venison left if you're hungry."

Leith nodded and sank onto one of the logs circling the fire. Two of the guardsmen shifted away from him, leaving a yard gap between him and the next person.

Shad plopped onto the log. "We're traveling, and for once, I don't have to do the cooking."

"Don't be so sure about that. So far, I've done the hunting and helped with the cooking. Tomorrow is your turn." Jolene handed him a plate. She turned to Leith and held out a second plate. Her smile remained in place, though it had tightened to something forced. "How was Renna? When you saw her?"

Leith took the plate and inhaled the rich smell of the

chunk of roasted meat. Would Martyn make sure Renna had something to eat? Or was she being fed moldy bread and water in Nalgar's dungeon? He cleared his throat. "Scared." Except at the end, where she'd remained behind so Leith could escape with Brandi. "But brave."

On a log a few feet away, Lydia leaned forward. When Leith glanced at her, she looked away and toyed with a piece of bark.

Leith might've been worthy of Renna as Daniel the peasant farmer, but he wasn't as a Blade.

He forced himself to eat the venison on his plate and ignore the way the guards flinched every time he picked up a knife to cut another bite.

As he finished, Brandi dumped her plate on the pile of dirty dishes and strode away. Lady Alistair hurried after her and laid a hand on her shoulder. Brandi shrugged it off and stalked into the dark in the direction of the stream and waterfall.

Leith set his plate aside, but before he could climb to his feet, Jamie dropped his dishes and headed into the trees after Brandi. Probably just as well. Jamie might be able to help Brandi more than Leith could right now.

He rested his elbows on his knees. He had to rescue Renna, if only to bring back Brandi's smile.

3

Renna undid the laces holding the splint on her left leg and rubbed her fingers along the bone. When she pressed on the small fracture, pain shot through her leg. At least the swelling had gone down and the bone no longer throbbed.

What did she expect? That her bone would heal in two weeks? She might be able to start putting weight onto it in a week or so, but it'd be another three to four weeks before it'd be fully healed.

Three to four weeks. What would happen to her in that time? She couldn't run or escape. Leith promised he'd return for her, but when? Did she want him to? Respen would use her as bait to trap Leith. Better for him to remain somewhere out there, free, than try a useless attempt to rescue her.

Renna leaned her forehead against her arms. Brandi and Leith had been gone only a day. She'd have to be stronger than this to survive the weeks—perhaps months— she'd have to spend at Nalgar Castle alone.

No, not alone. God was with her, even here. She couldn't let go of that or she'd crumble.

Why had God left her here? Why couldn't He have used Leith to rescue her? Surely God must have some purpose for her at Nalgar Castle. Some reason that she had to stay.

How could she find that purpose while locked in the dungeon and unable to walk?

The door rattled. Two guards stepped inside, grasped her arms, and yanked her to her feet. She cried out and blinked at the spike of pain. They dragged her up the dark stairs.

Where were they taking her? Her stomach clenched. Where was Martyn Hamish? Last time she'd been taken out of this cell with guards instead of him, she'd been forced to watch Uncle Abel's and Aunt Mara's executions.

Her breath hitched. Was she being executed now? No warning. No taunting. Just dragged out and killed?

No. Respen made it clear she was bait for Leith. He needed her alive to lure Leith back to Nalgar Castle. But that wouldn't prevent Respen from torturing her. She shuddered. She didn't have the strength to endure torture.

They hauled her out the door of the North Tower. She squinted at the brilliance of the summer sunlight reflecting off the cobblestones of the courtyard. Heat waves shimmered against the Great Hall. She tipped her head to the pale, sun-burnt sky and gulped a breath of the hot air. As hot as it was, she should enjoy these short minutes outside before she was dragged back into the dungeon or inside to face Respen's taunting.

Thankfully, no wooden block waited in the courtyard as it had the day Uncle Abel and Aunt Mara died.

Where were they taking her? She hop-skipped as fast as she could between them. When she stumbled, the guards lifted her from her feet and carried her by her arms. Crossing the courtyard, they entered under a stone archway into a long passageway. At the far end, she glimpsed the green of the grass-covered Queen's Court.

They were probably headed to see King Respen. Renna braced herself to face him again. What did he have to gloat about this time?

But midway down the passageway, the guards dragged her to the left to another arched opening in the wall instead of to the right and up the stairs to Respen's chambers. They stepped onto the end of a wooden bridge. Below her, a moat—nothing more than a dry ditch at this time of summer—surrounded the Blades' Tower.

Martyn strode across the bridge toward them, his blond hair waving in wild curls. His eyes remained hard. His mouth pressed into a line, bracketed by deep grooves. "I'll take her from here."

The guards dropped her arms and shoved her. Renna caught herself on the wooden railing as both legs buckled. She hauled herself onto her good leg.

Martyn spun on his heel and strode back toward the Blades' Tower. "Come."

She bit her lip and hopped forward, using the wooden railing to steady herself. The guards remained at the end of the bridge, preventing her from doing anything other than follow Martyn's order.

She reached the door to the Tower and managed to catch it before it swung shut behind Martyn. Why was she being taken here?

No choice but to go forward. She heaved the door open and hopped inside. For a moment, she saw only deep blackness broken by orange pinpricks of light. As the door grated shut behind her, her eyes adjusted to the darkness inside the windowless room.

19

Several long tables filled the space around a central chimney with openings for fires on either side. Candelabras spaced along the outer wall provided the only light. A walled nook took up part of one wall next to the dark opening for the staircase at the far end.

Martyn halted halfway across the room and motioned for her to follow.

She hopped to the nearest table and used it to brace herself. Why didn't he pick her up and carry her? He'd had no problem doing just that only a few days ago. Was he taking his anger at Leith out on her? Martyn was too tied to his duty to waste time on kindness. But he'd never been purposefully cruel either. Had he changed?

Martyn halted at the bottom of the stairs, leaned against the wall, and crossed his arms. His face had an odd, pale color in the candlelight.

As she reached his side, she blinked at the stone steps spiraling into the darkness above. How was she ever going to manage?

"Where are you taking me? Is Respen..." She swallowed. She couldn't ask. Would Respen torture her now that Leith had escaped?

"The king wants you locked in the Tower from now on."

"Why?" Why was he moving her now? And what made the Tower safer than the dungeons?

"Leith proved he could break into the dungeons too easily." Martyn shifted and peered up the staircase. "You're my personal responsibility."

In other words, Martyn wouldn't be able to blame incompentent guards if she escaped this time. If Leith wanted to rescue her, he'd have to go through Martyn.

Could he do it? Or was she beyond even Leith's ability to rescue now?

Footsteps pattered down. A boy dressed all in black rounded the corner and tromped down the last few steps. After a glance in Renna's direction, he faced Martyn, clenched his right fist, and thumped it across his chest. "The room is all set."

Which room were they putting her in? How many stairs would she have to climb? But at least this was simply a change of rooms. Not a torture session.

Martyn jabbed his thumb at Renna. "Help her up the stairs."

The boy, a Blade trainee, grimaced, his nose wrinkling. Renna sniffed. She did smell a little rank. She hadn't had a chance to bathe in nearly a month.

The trainee leaned away from her as she rested her elbow on his shoulder. He couldn't have been much older than eleven or twelve.

Martyn marched up the stairs ahead of them, his back stiff and straight. Renna hopped up each step the best she could, using the trainee to steady herself.

When they reached the second floor, Renna was already breathing hard. She halted for a moment across from a door marked with a number *24* over Respen's crossed daggers symbol. The next door in the hallway was labeled *23*.

Did the door numbers correspond with the Blades' ranks? If so, then Martyn's room would be near the top.

The trainee forced her to continue hopping.

At the landing on the third floor, Martyn halted and leaned against the wall. He was breathing hard, beads of sweat glistening in the shaft of light streaming through the arrow slits along the passageway.

Renna rested one hand on the wall and leaned her weight on the trainee's shoulder. She gasped for breath.

Her good leg shook. How had Leith managed climbing up and down these stairs so often? If her guess about the doors was correct, then his room would've been near the top like Martyn's.

Martyn straightened and strode down the passageway. Renna bit back a groan. As she reached the next set of stairs, she eased some of her weight onto her injured leg. Pain shivered through her bone, but not as much as before. Perhaps she'd be able to start limping around under her own power soon.

Her good leg wobbled with each stair. She focused only on the next step, the next hop. Just one more. Then another. Another.

The stone flattened into a corridor. She halted, her body trembling. She couldn't force herself up any more stairs. If Martyn wanted her on the fifth floor, he'd have to carry her.

Martyn braced a hand on the window ledge a few feet away. His head hung. His knees buckled a fraction, but his grip on the ledge kept him upright.

Something more than anger was wrong with Martyn. Renna limped, winced, and took another step forward. A cold chill swirled into her toes. Martyn's words during Leith's attempt to rescue her echoed in her head. *You know the punishment I'd face.*

What punishment had Martyn been talking about? Would Respen punish him because he'd failed to stop Leith from escaping and rescuing Brandi?

Of course Respen would. Since he couldn't punish Leith, he'd punish Martyn instead.

As she neared, Martyn pulled himself straighter. The light from the arrow slit fell across darker patches staining the back of his black shirt. Before he could stop her, Renna stretched and touched one.

Martyn whirled and backed away from her. "Don't."

Renna held up her fingers. A faint sheen of red glinted in the sunlight. "You're bleeding."

"It's no concern of yours." Martyn grabbed her upper arm.

She yanked her arm out of his grip. "Yes, it is. It's your punishment for Brandi's escape, isn't it?"

He turned away, but not before pain tightened his jaw. Renna fisted her fingers into her buckskin divided skirt. Martyn had suffered for Brandi's escape. An escape Renna made possible by tackling him. "I'm a healer. I can help you."

His brown eyes darted toward her. For a minute, she caught a glimpse of something—an ache, a longing—before shutters walled his emotions away. "No. I'm fine." He tugged her forward again. "Is that how you got to Leith? False kindness?"

"It isn't false." She bit her lip. When she'd first met Leith, her kindness had been false. But now her heart ached to help Martyn. He didn't even know how much he needed help.

Was this the reason she'd been left at Nalgar Castle? To touch Martyn's hurting heart? Maybe by showing him kindness, he'd see the source of that kindness the way Leith had.

He needed her help whether he liked it or not. Renna turned to the trainee. "Fetch boiling water, rags, bandages, and salve. Surely you keep healing supplies in the Tower."

The trainee glanced from her to Martyn, a wrinkle creasing his forehead.

Martyn shook his head. "My orders are to transfer you to your new room. That's it."

"Is Respen waiting for a report? Will you be punished if I'm not locked in some cell within five minutes?" Renna met his gaze and refused to look away. He was hurt, and someone had to tend him. He might be stubborn, but he should see the reason in that. "It's not like I'll ever be out of your sight."

"Fine." Martyn's shoulders sagged only a fraction. He waved at the trainee. "Do as she says."

Saluting, the trainee spun and clomped down the stairs.

Martyn stared in that direction for several minutes even after the trainee disappeared from view. "He's the last loyal one left. All the other trainees went with Leith."

The other trainees escaped too? Renna ducked her head to hide her smile. Of course Leith and Jamie wouldn't leave the young boys behind to be trained as killers.

She straightened and faced Martyn. "You need to lie down."

He shuffled down the passageway slowly enough that Renna managed to keep up with her hopping gait. He halted before the third door from the end. The crossed daggers symbol carved into the door with the number three at their center.

Renna cocked her head. "Are you the Second Blade now or still the Third Blade?"

He shrugged and grimaced. "Second Blade, though King Respen hasn't called a Meeting of the Blades to officially promote me."

So why wasn't he using the Second Blade's room? Renna rubbed her fingers along her skirt as she followed him inside, leaving the door open.

The arrow shaft across the passageway lit the inside of the room just enough for her to make out a few black shapes in the darkness. A knife scraped against flint a few times. A candle flared and brightened the tiny room.

An iron-framed cot took up all of one wall, a small table next to its head. Across from the cot, a basin and washtub sat on a stand underneath a row of pegs. Knives hung in their sheaths from several of the pegs while spare sets of black clothes and one set of tan clothes dangled from the others.

While the floor was tiled with stone, the ceiling was formed of large beams branching out in a wagon wheel pattern from the far wall. Wooden planks held up the stone of the floor above.

So small. So much stone. How had Leith lived in this room for four years without going insane? Perhaps Respen sent his Blades out so frequently because they would go crazy staying here.

Martyn rested one hand on the bedside table, the other against the wall. Even more color had drained from his face.

"Take off your shirt and lie down." She waved at the bed and bit her lip. Dark brown stains splotched across the blanket. How badly had he been hurt?

Martyn glanced down at himself, then back up at her.

She crossed her arms and gave him her best eye roll. Brandi would've been proud. "I'm a healer. I need to tend you. Now take your shirt off or I'll take one of your knives and cut it off."

Not that she could go through with her threat, but it seemed like something Brandi would've said. Surely Renna could at least pretend to be tough and bossy. She pressed her mouth into a frown. Did she look intimidating enough?

The muscle at the corner of Martyn's jaw flexed. He

THE BLADES OF ACKTAR

unbuckled his knives and set them on the bed within easy reach. With a grunt, he peeled his shirt over his head and dropped it on the floor. He lay down on the cot, propped up on his elbows. The muscles in his arms and shoulders remained tense.

Beneath a layer of blood, lacerations weaved across his back. What had happened to him? What would make wounds like that?

Martyn gripped the hilt of one of his knives, his other hand clasped around the sheath as if prepared to draw it.

Renna knelt next to the cot. "I'm not going to hurt you."

He flexed his fingers on his knife. "Why not?"

"You need help, and I have the skills to give it. Yes, you're a Blade, but that doesn't make a difference." She toyed with the ragged end of her blouse. "God has called me to love my enemies, and this is one way I can show that love."

He snorted. "Love. Loyalty. Friendship. People toss those words around so freely, only to throw them away first chance they get."

What turned him so bitter? Was it only Leith's betrayal or was it more than that? Renna reached out to touch his shoulder but stopped herself. He didn't want comfort from her. She had to be patient with him.

Footsteps pounded on the stairs. The trainee appeared in the doorway, huffing and carrying a tray.

Renna pointed at the bedside table. "Set the tray there. Then fetch a few more candles. I need more light."

The trainee's eyes narrowed, but he followed her instructions. As soon as he left the room, she reached for the bowl of steaming water. Wetting a cloth, she dabbed one of the slashes oozing blood.

Martyn flinched and sucked in a breath. His back

stiffened beneath her fingers. He had broader shoulders and bulkier muscles than Leith. Would he lash out at her?

No. Martyn was too controlled for that. She dipped the rag back into the hot water as the trainee returned with three more candles. He lit and placed them on the table.

"Do you need anything else, Second Blade?"

Martyn took his hand off his knife long enough to wave toward the door. "No. Run through your basic fighting moves. Return for the tray in an hour."

The trainee saluted and scurried off.

Renna washed Martyn's back as best she could. So many slashes. So much blood. "What happened to you?"

"I was whipped." Martyn's words gritted through his teeth. "My punishment."

"I'm sorry."

"No, you're not. You wish you could've gone with them."

Of course she did, but she wouldn't tell that to him. He wouldn't understand how she could be both sorry that he'd gotten hurt and sorry she hadn't left.

She wrung the cloth out again. "Why didn't you go with Leith? You didn't have to fight him."

"Yes, I did. Leith's the one who taught me that. Always follow orders, and you'll survive." Martyn swiped a hand through his thick, blond curls. "I don't understand what's gotten into Leith. He used to know the mission always comes first."

"Perhaps he found something worth risking his life for."

Martyn huffed out a breath. "He thinks you're worth risking his life?"

Warmth spread through her chest. Months ago, she would've hesitated. But what could Respen do to her at this point? He already planned to kill her. He already knew about her faith.

This was her chance to finally do something other than hiding. She had a purpose—a duty—to help the hurting souls here, starting with Martyn. "I'm not, but Leith discovered that God is worth it because God has already deemed Leith worthy in His Son, Jesus Christ."

Martyn shook his head. "That's even more outlandish than claiming he's doing this all for you."

Patience. That's what Martyn needed from her right now. Renna washed the last of the blood from his back and reached for the jar of salve. If only she had Brandi's wisdom when it came to stuff like this. Brandi had taken her time getting Leith interested in her Daniel stories before she revealed the truth in them. She hadn't tried to force everything overnight, and neither should Renna.

After spreading the salve across his back, she wrapped bandages around his torso. "There."

He pushed himself upright and swung his feet to the floor.

Renna sat back on her heels and winced at the pain that shot through her leg. "Don't get up. You need to rest."

"I'll rest after I show you to your room." He took her hand and hauled her to her feet. "Grab one of the candles. You'll want it."

Of course Martyn wouldn't rest until he'd completed his orders. After picking up a candle, she leaned on Martyn as he led her from his room, past one door, and opened the door at the very end of the hall.

Renna hopped forward. As soon as she was inside, Martyn swung the door shut behind her. A bolt scraped, locking her inside.

She held up the candle to inspect the room. An identical cot, bedside table, and washstand to Martyn's provided the only furniture in the room, though the hooks above the washstand remained empty. A bucket tucked beneath the foot of the cot while an extra candle sat on the table.

This would've been Leith's room while he was the First Blade. Had he left anything here? Maybe a hidden knife? She lifted the mattress, felt around under the cot, and checked behind the table and washstand. Nothing. If he'd left anything here, Martyn or the trainee found it already.

Set low in the wall separating this room from the Second Blade's room next door, a chip of stone wedged into a crack. She knelt, ran her fingers along the crack, and tugged on the shard. It didn't budge. But if she could pull it out, would the stone be loose? Not that it'd do any good. The hole it'd leave in the wall would be barely big enough for her hand to fit through.

It'd be something to remember, if she should need to see into the next room.

She sank onto the cot, her leg throbbing. She was a healer. She should know better than to do too much too soon after an injury.

At least she had a bed. That was an improvement. She'd miss the small dungeon window, but this room didn't reek of dried blood and death.

She brought a corner of the blanket to her nose and smelled leather and saddle oil. *Leith.*

Was he all right? Would he and Brandi stay ahead of the Blades chasing them?

They were in God's hands. She'd trusted that yesterday, and she could trust that today too. Right now she might not be able to help them, but she could pray. It would be enough

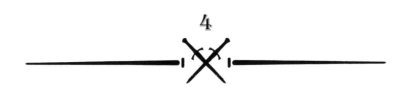

4

Leith lay on his stomach on a cliff's edge, scanning the hills laid out in front of him. The tops of pines spiked as far as he could see, broken only by jagged cliffs. At the edge of his range of vision, a rocky pass between two cliffs remained empty.

If any Blades were trailing them, Leith would spot them here. Unless they took a circuitous route that risked losing the trail and losing time, the Blades had no choice but to skyline themselves in the pass.

How far behind were the Blades? Traveling light as they were, the Blades would move much faster than the group Shad led deeper into the mountains. It'd be only a matter of time before they caught up.

Movement caught his eye. A black speck trotted through the pass, followed by another. Leith counted a total of five figures as they crossed the pass and disappeared into the trees in the valley below.

Five Blades stalked them. More than he'd hoped, but fewer than he'd feared. Still, they'd closed the distance.

Leith squirmed backwards into cover before he stood and crept to the stand of trees where he'd tied Big Brown.

The horse glanced at him before it returned to nibbling the leaves from a nearby tree. Leith patted its neck. "You appear as bored as your name."

Swinging on, he urged the horse into a fast walk up the trail left by Shad and the other travelers. With his quicker pace, he covered the miles up the rocky slopes and cedar-covered ledges and caught up with the larger group when they stopped at noon to rest the horses at the banks of one of the many streams that meandered down the slopes.

As soon as Shad spotted him, he looped his horse's reins over a log and walked over to Leith. Lady Lorrine joined them.

"What did you find out?" Shad held Big Brown's head as Leith slipped from the horse.

"We have five Blades tracking us."

"Five?" Shad gripped his sword's hilt so tightly his knuckles paled to a sickly blue-white. "I was hoping maybe three. But five?"

"It's not the end of the world. We can handle five Blades if we have to." Lady Lorraine touched the hilt of her dagger.

Shad glanced at the rest of camp, and Leith followed his gaze. Five of the guards paced around the perimeter while three more were hidden in the trees farther out. The rest of the guards lolled on the ground, some napping, others checking weapons. A maid from Walden, who'd waited until the last moment to leave, had gathered the former Blade trainees into a circle while two other maids laughed as they talked to some of the guards.

Jolene sat on a log between Lady Alistair and Lydia. All of them wore knives buckled to their waists, and Jolene wore her quiver filled with arrows. Brandi slumped on a log, eyes blank and staring, while Jamie lounged against a tree a few feet away, alternating glancing from Leith to Brandi to the knife he was polishing.

Could they handle five Blades? Between Shad and Jolene, they had more than enough arrows, and Lady Lorraine could handle herself if it came to a fight.

Did Leith want a fight? People got hurt in battles, and they had too many unskilled people along to risk forcing a fight between themselves and the Blades.

"It'd be best if we avoided a confrontation." Leith drew in a deep breath. "They're mainly after me. If I draw most of them off, you'll only have to worry about one or two."

"How do you plan to do that?" Lady Lorraine's hard gaze searched his face as if still wary of any plan he might present.

"I'll ride into the Waste."

"The Waste?" Shad gaped at him. "Surely you aren't insane enough to go in there."

"I'll be fine. I've been there before." Leith forced himself to grin. "I was the First Blade, after all."

The dreaded Waste spread to the east of the Sheered Rock Hills, a stretch of desolate, jagged rocks devoid of water. Many failed Blades fled into it. None had ever succeeded.

Shad crossed his arms. "Being the First Blade won't protect you from dying of thirst. Or a rattlesnake bite."

"No, but the other Blades won't be immune to those things either. The difference is that I'll be prepared." Leith layered steel into his voice. This was their best option. He wouldn't let Shad talk him out of it. "When I reach the Waste, the Blades following me will have two choices. They can either track me into the Waste or they can spread out along the edge hoping to spot me when I leave. Either way, I'll double back, sneak past them, and rejoin you."

"They do have a third option." Lady Lorraine arched an eyebrow. "They could give up on capturing you, turn around, and pursue us again. Then we'd face all five Blades without your help."

"I'm their main mission. They have no choice but to pursue me."

Shad straightened and met Leith's gaze. "So what do we do while you're gone?"

"There's a cave to the northwest where you can hide the women and children. You'll be in a better position to defend yourselves should the remaining Blades attack you." Leith rubbed the hilt of his dagger.

"I know the one." Shad frowned and touched his sword. "And if the Blades kill you? Or you die in the Waste?"

"If I'm not back in a week, assume I'm dead."

Not that he planned on dying. He needed to stay alive so Respen didn't kill Renna.

"I don't like it." Shad's shoulders sagged. With Lord Alistair fighting for his life in the besieged Walden or possibly even dead, the duty of leading fell on Shad. If only Leith didn't have to make the burden heavier by leaving. "We have other options."

Lady Lorraine fingered her knife's hilt. "Perhaps, perhaps not. We have to either kill or lose the Blades before we reach Eagle Heights. Unless you want to set up a pitched battle against five Blades, we would be better off losing several of them."

Leith eyed Lady Lorraine. He probably shouldn't have been surprised that she took his side. He was nothing more than a strategic asset to her.

"All right." Shad clapped Leith on the shoulder. "But

you're not allowed to die. We need our First Blade."

"You're the one I'm worried about. You're going to fall off a cliff or something without me around."

He and Shad hiked back to the rest of their group. Most looked away from Leith quickly. Still wary. Would they ever realize Leith was safe?

But, no. He was a Blade and not worthy of their trust.

While Shad and Lady Lorraine explained to the others about the five Blades and Leith's plan, Leith changed out of his black clothes and dressed in a set of tan trousers and shirt. In the treeless Waste, his black clothes would soak in the sun.

He unsaddled Big Brown and swung the saddle onto Blizzard's back. In the tough country he'd ride through, he wanted his own horse.

Sorting through his packs, he left in only the essentials. As he finished strapping on the saddlebags, Brandi wandered over to him. She carried a bulging waterskin. He took it from her and hoisted it across the saddlebags.

Brandi wrapped her arms around his waist. "I don't want you to go."

Leith hugged her tightly. If only he didn't have to go. He gripped Brandi's shoulders and waited until she met his gaze. "God willing, I'll be back before you even miss me. I'll lose the Blades, we'll get to Eagle Heights, and we'll rescue Renna."

She blinked up at him and cleared her throat. "Take care of Blizzard."

Leith grinned. "I promise. And you take care of Big Brown for me." He unbuckled the knife he'd strapped to his waist, the same knife he'd given to Renna all those months ago. Leith held it out to Brandi. "It wouldn't hurt to wear this."

She took it and nodded. "All right."

After one last pat on her shoulder, Leith led Blizzard to the edge of camp. There, Jamie leaned against a tree. He held out three canteens. "I should go with you."

Leith clapped him on the shoulder. "I'm depending on you to keep an eye on things here. A few of the Blades will continue to track this group, and you'll be the only one with enough knowledge of the Blades to help Shad stop them."

Jamie straightened his shoulders, rested his hand on his knife, and nodded. "I understand. I'll watch out for Brandi."

"Thanks." Leith tied the canteens to his saddle and swung onto Blizzard. Across the camp, Shad lifted his hand in a wave. Leith waved back, turned, and pointed Blizzard's nose east toward the Waste.

5

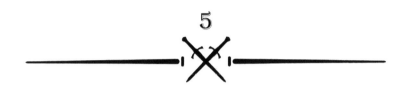

Leith had left her too.

Brandi clenched her fists to stop the tears building in her chest. Across their camp, Jolene wrapped her arms around Shad's waist. He leaned his face into her hair and pulled her closer.

Swallowing, Brandi turned away. That should be Leith and Renna, if Leith would stop dragging his feet. Was Renna all right? Or had she already broken without Brandi there to hold her together?

Why did everyone Brandi loved have to die? She'd barely known her Uncle Leon, Aunt Deirdre, and her cousins Aengus, Keevan, Rorin, and Duncan. Her parents had died not long after. Uncle Abel and Aunt Mara had been executed. Now Renna was stuck at Nalgar Castle, and Leith was riding into the Waste.

Neither of them would survive. Leith said they'd be fine, but Brandi didn't believe him. No one would be fine.

She used to believe in miracles. Nothing could hurt her and Renna. They'd be like Daniel, kept safe by God's angels no matter what the evil king did.

But perhaps they were more like Stephen. Brandi

wrapped her arms around her stomach. She'd never liked the story of Stephen being stoned to death. It didn't make sense. Why would God let Stephen die when He could've saved him?

Brandi squeezed the sheathed knife tighter in her hands. Renna hadn't been able to protect them the last time they'd been attacked by a Blade, but Renna hadn't known how to use the knife. Even if she'd had a chance, Renna wasn't a fighter.

But Brandi *wasn't* Renna.

In the dungeon when Leith had come to rescue them, Brandi had searched for a weapon and tried to fight. But she hadn't known how, and Renna kept getting in her way.

Next time, Brandi would fight back.

Strapping the knife to the sash around her waist, Brandi marched to Jamie and placed her fists on her hips. "Teach me how to fight."

"What?" Jamie tore his gaze from the trees and stared at her.

She rolled her eyes. Was Jamie deaf? "I want to learn how to fight. I don't want to be helpless while someone else protects me all the time."

That hadn't worked so well for Renna. Brandi touched the hilt of the knife Leith had given her. If something happened to Leith, it'd be up to Brandi to rescue Renna.

Jamie still gaped at her. Across the hollow, Shad ordered everyone back into the saddle. Brandi tapped her foot. She wasn't going to let Jamie move until he agreed.

His shoulders slumped. "All right. I'll teach you to fight. We'll start after supper tonight."

Brandi clenched her fists. Finally she'd be able to *do* something.

If only she could devour her supper and crawl into her blankets. Her bones ached with the long ride. Instead, Brandi followed Jamie to a dark corner of their camp under the spreading branches of a pine. Lydia glanced at her, but neither she nor Jolene tried to follow her. Not after Brandi had brushed them off in their earlier attempts. They might be Renna's friends, but they couldn't try to fill in for her sister.

Jamie crossed his arms. "First we need to work on your walk."

"What's wrong with the way I walk?" Brandi stared down at her feet. She didn't see anything wrong.

"You make too much noise." Jamie scowled. "You're too small to fight like a soldier so I'm going to teach you to fight like a Blade. To do it, you have to be able to sneak like a Blade."

"Does this make me like a Blade trainee or something? I mean, you're the Thirteenth Blade, or you were. And you're training me." She cocked her head and held up the knife. She probably didn't look as impressive as she felt.

Jamie's scowl grew. "No."

"Oh, come on. Of course I'm a Blade trainee." Brandi spread out her arms and tottered forward on her toes. That was pretty quiet, right?

Jamie scrubbed his forehead with his palm. "You're still prancing about like a horse."

She scowled. He was supposed to be helping her, not making rude comments. "Well, how am I supposed to walk?"

"Pretend the ground is sharp. Walk like you don't want to put weight on your feet." Jamie eased forward, toes first, heels afterwards. "Feel your way forward with your toes and don't put your feet all the way down until you're sure you won't snap any sticks."

Brandi tried it. After a few minutes, she kind of got the hang of it. At least, Jamie stopped looking at her like she had the feet of an ox and the brain of a squirrel. "Now what?"

"Now I'll show you a few basic things you can do if someone comes at you with a knife." Jamie stepped closer to her, a stick in his hand. He handed her a stick.

He showed her how to smack a knife away from her body and lunge forward with her own knife aimed at an opponent's stomach. By the time Brandi fell into her blanket that night, her arms straggled limply at her side while her back ached with bruises from landing on the dirt.

But for the first time since Leith had dragged her away from Renna, she felt almost happy.

6

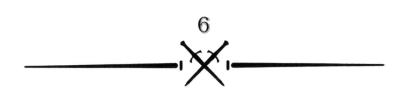

Renna eased weight onto her left leg. A flutter of pain throbbed through the bone. She gritted her teeth, limped another step, and touched the wall above the washstand. As much as it hurt, she had to grit through it. When Leith returned to rescue her, she needed to have her strength back.

The lock rattled. She stiffened. It wasn't time for Martyn to bring her meal.

She turned as the door swung open. Martyn stood in the doorway. "Come."

"Where are we going?" Renna gripped one of Martyn's shoulders. His height stretched her arm above her head.

"You'll see." He pulled her from the room. She stumbled and caught herself against the door jamb.

Why wouldn't Martyn tell her where they were going? She hopped down the hallway, leaning against Martyn. What was Respen planning?

On the second floor, Martyn halted. Renna leaned against the wall and gasped for breath. She peered at Martyn. He didn't look pale like he had before. "How's your back?"

"Healing."

He helped her hop down the last two sets of stairs and across the common room. As they crossed the wooden bridge, Renna caught her breath. They had to be heading for the king's apartments. Would Respen taunt her again? Did he have news about Leith or Brandi?

As they reached the passageway, Renna hopped toward the winding staircase to Respen's chambers. Might as well get Respen's taunts over with as quickly as possible.

"No, we're going this way." Martyn pulled her down the passageway toward the opening that spilled onto the green lawn of the Queen's Court, named for one of Acktar's queens who'd insisted she wanted grass inside the castle instead of only stone.

Renna's foot snagged on a stone. She tripped forward and set her injured leg down to catch herself. Pain shot up her shin. She cried out.

Martyn's arm wrapped around her waist and set her back on her good leg. She glanced at his face, but his eyes remained cold and blank.

A lump formed in her throat. Leith would've asked if she was all right.

As they exited the dark passageway, Renna blinked at the courtyard spread before her. A tiered fountain spat water into the sky, surrounded by a lush, green lawn unlike any she'd seen in Acktar. How much work did it take to keep this lawn so green during the height of Acktar's summer?

Martyn led her on a bluestone path that cut through the lawn, rounded the fountain, and ended at a wide, brick staircase. The staircase branched into two wings of apartments set into the outer wall of Nalgar Castle filled with lavish chambers reserved for visiting nobility.

Renna closed her eyes. Last time she'd been here—nearly six years ago now—it'd been mid-winter, the stairway decorated with pine boughs from the Sheered Rock Hills, the courtyard still and silent. She, Brandi, and their cousins Rorin and Duncan built a row of snowmen by the fountain, though Keevan had whacked their heads off with his sword.

The rest of the castle, it held few memories. She'd been too young to wander the castle alone. But this courtyard and these suites of rooms? She'd stayed here with her parents. She'd played in the Queen's Court with Brandi, Rorin, and Duncan.

"This way." Martyn tugged her up the stairs to the landing on top. The arrow slits set into the outer wall overlooked a grassy slope, the Blades' Tower off to her left.

Before she had a chance to enjoy the view of the world outside Nalgar Castle, Martyn hauled her to her right, down a short passage, and into one of the rooms above the Queen's Court.

Wood paneling covered the stone walls. A four-poster bed of some dark wood dominated one corner, a blue dress spread out on top of it. Near it, a fireplace, complete with a low fire dancing behind the grate, warmed the stones that remained cool despite the summer heat outside. On the hearth, a large tub of water wafted steam and the scent of sage into the air. Towels and soap waited on the chair set next to the metal tub.

"What's going on?" She was still a prisoner, right?

Martyn pulled away from her grip. "I'll be outside so you can't escape. Don't take too long." He shut the door behind him, the lock clicking into place.

Renna didn't move. What was Respen's game now? She hopped to the broad windows and peered out. The

Queen's Court spread below her, Respen's chambers and the Great Hall across the lawn. She scowled. Even if she could fashion a rope and climb out the window, she'd still be trapped.

The smell of warm water and soap taunted her nose, a sharp contrast to her own unwashed odor. That probably explained all this. At this point, her stench would torture Respen more than it did her. Perhaps Brandi would've tried just that, but Renna would rather be clean.

She eyed the tub, then the doorway. How long would Martyn give her? She searched the room, but none of the furniture appeared small enough for her to move by herself and large enough to prevent the door from opening.

Shrugging, she pulled all the drapes shut. She wasn't going to miss the chance for a bath. She'd just have to be quick.

She scrubbed herself until the water turned the color of rain-soaked mud. After drying, she tried on the blue dress. The silk fell in soft waves around her. The hem dragged a few inches on the ground, but the waist and bodice fit well enough. Renna checked the curved neckline. Not low-cut and revealing like she would've expected.

With her injured leg, she couldn't twirl. Instead, she swished the skirt back and forth, watching the silk flow and glimmer. What would Leith think if he could see her in this dress?

Would he even notice?

Then again, if Leith was here, he'd be too busy rescuing her to care what she wore.

She turned away from the mirror. Enough daydreams. She needed to concentrate if she was going to face Respen.

On the bed she found two smooth sticks and linen bandages. After wrapping her ankle and calf with the new splint, she brushed her hair and paused in front of the dressing table mirror. In the light filtering between the drapes, her damp hair shone with golden streaks and framed her face, now pale without its layer of dirt.

She forced herself to smile. There. She looked almost elegant, like she fit the part of Lady Rennelda Faythe, lady of Stetterly, rather than the grimy captive she'd been for the past weeks.

After attempting to gracefully limp across the room, she knocked on the door. It swung open. Martyn eyed her for several seconds before giving a sharp nod. "Let's go."

As they retraced their steps down the stairs and across the courtyard, Renna held her head high. If she looked like a lady, perhaps she'd have the courage to act like a lady.

Martyn knocked on Respen's door and was rewarded with a terse "Enter" from inside. While Martyn held the door open for her, Renna grasped the too-long skirt and did her best to hop-limp into the room.

King Respen stood in the same spot he'd been when he'd executed Uncle Abel and Aunt Mara, peering out the window into the cobblestone courtyard, his hands clasped behind his back.

In the center of the room, a table had been set up with two chairs and a blue tablecloth draped over it. Silver platters of food covered the center of the table in an artful arrangement, two candlesticks poking between them. China plates marked each spot while the silver table settings marched in neat rows on either side.

Cherry-glazed pork, buttered green beans, corn, and puffy rolls with several kinds of jams lay next to it. Her nose tingled with the smells.

Respen turned from the window and strolled across the room. He gave her a short bow and waved a hand toward the table. "Have a seat."

She stared at the food. Something was wrong. Respen didn't act this way. He must have something to gloat about. Or...she swallowed hard. "I'm not going to eat anything."

He snorted. "If I wanted to poison you, I would not waste such extravagant food to do it."

She limped to the table and allowed him to pull the chair out for her. She eyed the food. Respen did have a point. Poison wasn't his style. Too subtle. Not enough blood. Besides, if he wanted to poison her, he could do it just as easily in her cell as here.

He slipped into the chair across from her. The candlelight danced in his dark eyes and played along his shiny black hair and pointed beard. If it weren't for the evil lurking behind that gaze, Respen might've been a handsome man.

As Respen reached to spoon food onto her plate, she drew in a deep breath. She'd faced this dilemma before, when Leith had been healing in their kitchen from an arrow wound. He'd been a Blade then, and praying in front of him might've gotten her and Brandi arrested.

What did it matter now? She'd been arrested. Respen already planned to execute her. What else could he do to her?

She peeked at Respen as he dished a slice of pork onto his own plate. Was this her purpose in remaining behind at Nalgar Castle? Was she supposed to witness to King Respen, the sworn enemy of the church in Acktar?

Brandi would do it. Renna cleared her throat. Respen's dark eyes flicked toward her. A chill curled in her stomach. "I'm going to pray before I eat."

She bowed her head and squeezed her eyes shut before she could see Respen's reaction. Brandi would've prayed out loud, but Renna didn't have enough courage for that. She silently prayed for God's courage to face whatever Respen had planned for her.

When she opened her eyes, she found Respen staring at her. "You defy my expectations. I thought I had broken you of that habit by now."

"If I'd been relying on my strength, then yes, you would've." She swallowed, trying to keep her voice steady. "But God gives me the strength to persevere."

She'd always been taught that God preserved the faith of His people, that no child of God could ever permanently lose their faith. What did that mean for Respen? He'd attended the church in Blathe years ago. Had he never truly had faith? Or was it possible—however unlikely it seemed—that he'd temporarily wandered away but could regain it again?

He raised both eyebrows at her and picked up his fork. "Eat."

Lifting her own fork, she dug into the pork, beans, corn, and roll laid out on her plate. She ate small portions of each, knowing better than to eat too much rich food after her diet of bread and water for the past weeks.

When she finished, she rested her fork on the edge of her plate and leaned back in her chair. Respen had already finished his food and stared at her with his dark, flat eyes. She squirmed and met his gaze. "What do you want from me? You aren't the type to go to all this trouble unless you want something."

He tapped his fingers on the edge of the table. "I have a proposition for you, Lady Rennelda, one that I think will gain us both what we want."

What would do that? She picked up her glass. "I won't agree."

"You have not heard my offer yet." Respen's deep voice rang, as if he already knew she'd agree to whatever he had planned. "I want an end to this rebellion. You want an end to what you call a persecution, is that correct?"

She nodded. She took a sip of her water and eyed him. What was he planning?

"The Resistance, as you call it, is founded on the principle that I am not the rightful king of Acktar. I can quench their little rebellion, but it will take years of bloodshed that can be avoided. I had thought to kill you to prevent you from being a rallying point. But I have a better idea." Respen's fingers halted their tapping. "I want to marry you."

Renna choked on her sip of water. She slammed her glass on the table and coughed. When she could breathe again, she gaped at Respen. "Marry you? Why would I ever marry you?"

Her stomach churned. Marry the man responsible for her family's murders? She'd stood in this very room as he executed Uncle Abel and Aunt Mara. She gripped her glass tighter. She might throw up into it.

"It would solve my problem. Married to you, I would become the rightful king of Acktar. The claim of righteous resistance would be ripped away from the rebel leaders. A few might continue to fight me, but the majority would fall in line. The very principles they fight for now would demand nothing less." Respen stroked the tablecloth.

Her stomach heaved. Should she try to fight it or make a dash for the window? Closing her eyes, she concentrated on steady, deep breaths.

"Of course, with you as my wife, I might be willing to indulge a few of your peculiarities. I could not continue to persecute Christians if my wife was one, now could

I?" A pleased smile slunk across his face.

She bolted upright, her heart pounding. "If I marry you, you'll stop the persecution? You'll allow the churches to meet and rebuild? You won't arrest people for praying or owning a Bible?"

His smile broadened. "Yes, that would be our deal. You marry me, and I'll stop the persecution."

She trembled. Could she possibly agree to that? Marry the man who'd killed her parents, aunts and uncles, and cousins? She shuddered at the thought of being near him. As his wife, she'd have to let him kiss her…and more. He was like, fifteen years older than her. Perhaps not old enough to be her father, but old enough to be Brandi's father. Respen's son would've been about Brandi's age had he lived.

But how could she possibly say no? She'd be like Esther in the Bible, using her position as queen to save people sentenced to die. She could be a part of rebuilding the churches scattered across Acktar. Surely it was the right thing to do.

Would Respen keep his end of the bargain? What if she married him, then he didn't keep his promise?

But what would he do if she refused? He couldn't kill her because he needed her to lure Leith back to the castle. That wouldn't stop him from torturing her. Or perhaps he'd set up her execution to force Leith to return?

She had to swallow several times before she could speak without retching. "Could I have some time to think about it?"

"Of course. Something this momentous should not be done lightly." He stood, strode to the door, and opened it. "Second Blade Hamish."

Martyn stepped into the room and saluted. "Yes, my

king?"

"Return Lady Faythe to her new quarters. Instruct the servants that she is to be provided with everything she desires." Respen turned to Renna and bowed. "She is to be treated as my future queen."

She stared at him and pressed her hands over her mouth to hold in the meal she'd just eaten.

Respen's slick smile skittered chills across her skin. "You will agree eventually. After all, sacrifice is the foundation of your faith, is it not?"

As Martyn helped her to her feet, Renna's heart sank into her toes. He was right. She was called to self-sacrifice. Even if that meant marrying King Respen.

7

As the half-moon joined the stars sprinkled across the deep blue sky, Leith urged Blizzard forward. His horse picked his way down ever smaller rocky slopes. At the base of one hill, they paused by a creek. While Blizzard drank, Leith filled his canteen. Bending over, he drank as well. This was the last clean, flowing water before the Waste.

When Blizzard finished, Leith groaned as he hauled himself back into the saddle. Exhaustion pressed against his eyes, but he couldn't allow himself and Blizzard more time to rest. Three Blades had followed him when he'd split away from Shad and the others. Now that he was alone, they'd stepped up their game. They were no longer content to simply track him. Now they hunted him.

If they caught him and dragged him back to Nalgar Castle, Respen wouldn't have any reason to keep Renna alive. Leith had to ride harder. He slept only three hours at a time with a few brief stops during the day to allow Blizzard to drink and graze.

By the time the sun tickled the horizon, Leith exited the foothills and rode onto the expanse of prairie stretching between the Sheered Rock Hills and the Waste. Five pronghorns bounced over the shorn grass and far in the distance, a herd of bison flowed across the horizon. A few yards away, a prairie dog chittered a warning and dove into its hole.

Midafternoon, Leith glanced back. Three black shapes of men on horseback exited the Hills behind him. He had less than half a day lead on his pursuers. He faced forward. In the distance, a line of cliffs sliced across the prairie. The Ramparts, the entrance to the Waste.

After a few hours rest by a rock outcropping, Leith pushed Blizzard onward until they reached the foot of the Ramparts as the setting sun coated the crumbling grey ridge in orange and gold. Dismounting, Leith led Blizzard along the base of the jagged peaks. He and Harrison Vane had explored this region for then Lord Respen Felix. When they'd left, Leith had hoped never to enter the Waste again.

Leith halted before a gap in the wall of rock. This was it. The Waste.

He stroked Blizzard's nose. If only he could leave his horse here and not drag him into the desert with him. But he couldn't leave Blizzard behind. If he did that, he'd never be able to catch the horse again to return to Shad and the others after he exited the Waste. Nor would Leith put it past the pursuing Blades to hurt Blizzard if they got a chance.

A winding trail slithered between the peaks. Blizzard balked at the narrow opening, but Leith tugged him forward. The powdery stone crumbled beneath Leith's boots. Blizzard snorted and pranced nervously as his hooves sank into the dust. The grey-purple peaks jabbed the sky on either side in piles of decaying, porous rock.

When Leith placed a hand on the side of the stone next him, bits of it burst into dust against his fingers.

The gap meandered between the jagged cliffs before disgorging him onto a desolate plain. Desiccated grass poked through the ashy ground, dried husks waiting for the next rainstorm to revive them for a few precious days. To his right and left, the plain dissolved into gullies and dry washes carved in the last, barely-remembered rain. Ahead, the ground folded into trackless ridges, the last rays of the sun burning on the tips.

Leith scrubbed Blizzard's neck. "That's where we're headed, boy. Straight east."

He swung onto his horse and let Blizzard choose their path. Occassionally, a strip of dry, nearly dead prairie swathed the space between the mounds of rock. He spotted a lizard sunning itself on a rock, but it was the only sign of life. Even the breeze no longer gasped, leaving the crumbling stone aching with silence.

As darkness settled, Leith walked Blizzard forward. He couldn't ride at night. Blizzard could be injured in the shifting sands and treacherous holes. Better if Leith tested the ground first. But he couldn't take the time to stop and rest for the whole night. The Blades would push on through the darkness as they had on the prairie. Besides, at this time of year, he'd have to rest during the hottest hours of the day.

He slogged through the scraping grass and the crumbling soil. The aloof stars and later the cold moon provided feeble light for him to stumble by.

Midway through the night, Leith allowed himself a brief rest. Pouring an inch of water into his cooking pot, he held it for Blizzard to drink. His horse slurped up the water, then licked the pot, his tongue grating against the cast iron, until every drop was gone. Leith returned the pot to his pack while Blizzard craned his neck around, ears twitching as he searched for more water.

Leith rubbed the horse's nose. "I'm sorry. No more water for now. We have to make it last as long as possible."

He dug out a slice of bread for himself and munched it down, the bread sticking to his throat and teeth. Allowing himself a few mouthfuls of water, he held the liquid on his tongue, soaking, savoring, until he swallowed.

How far would he have to go to outrun his hunters? If they'd stopped at the edge of the Waste to wait for him there, then he wouldn't have to go far into the Waste before circling around and exiting the Waste through a gap to the north.

None of the Blades tracking him had traveled through the Waste before. Odds were they wouldn't spot the gap that Leith and Vane had stumbled across when they'd explored this region.

But if the Blades followed Leith into the Waste, he'd have to outlast and outdistance them as he circled around. They'd be forced to either turn around or die. In either case, Leith would be free to circle back and return to Shad without the Blades following him.

Somehow, he'd have to make his small supply of water last long enough to keep him and Blizzard alive. It was all the water he had. Even if he stumbled across water, he wouldn't be able to drink it. All the water in the Waste was contaminated with the dust and minerals from the rocks. Even boiling couldn't cleanse it.

At least he had more water than the Blades hunting him. While he was well prepared with a waterskin and three canteens for him and Blizzard, they had no warning and no time to prepare. They'd have only three, maybe four, canteens for three men and three horses.

Leith could outlast them, but he still might end up dead. The Waste could claim him just as easily as the Blades.

He blew out a long breath. His life belonged to God, even here. He wouldn't die until God's time, whenever that was. He could only pray it wasn't soon. Renna depended on him.

Pushing himself upright, he picked up Blizzard's reins and kept plodding forward, keeping an eye on the stars. He couldn't let himself get turned around. It'd waste time and allow his pursuers to catch him, and he'd be unable to find his way back to the Sheered Rock Hills.

Dawn rose with a timid hush. Leith closed his eyes at the first caress of sunlight on his face and breathed in the sweet smell of morning.

Onward. Ever onward. The miles blurred into mindless, trudging steps. Sometimes walking, sometimes riding. All around, the peaks—sliced with bands of red, orange, pink, and purple as if the stone couldn't decide which color to wear—rolled away into a forsaken landscape. The air that touched his face stank with dust and heat like the fetid breath of some poisonous beast.

Still he and Blizzard trudged onward. He wrapped his extra shirt over his head to give his face and neck some protection from the merciless sun. His nose still crinkled with burned skin.

That afternoon, Leith halted Blizzard on the eastern side of one of the slopes where the height of the peak and a stand of dried brush provided some shade. After he pulled the saddle from Blizzard's back, the horse rolled on the ground, scrubbing his sweat-soaked back against the grey pebbles. The dust mixed with the globs of sweat, covering Blizzard in a layer of quickly drying mud.

After giving Blizzard more water, Leith left him to graze on a patch of spiky grass and scrabbled up the grey-purple slope, diggings his fingers into the porous rock. At the top, he sank onto his stomach and peered back the way he'd come.

After a few minutes, two black dots trudged from a gap between two mounds of rock. At the base of the mound, one plopped to the ground, the other joining him a moment later.

They must've left one of the Blades to guard the edge of the Waste in case Leith circled back while the other two chased him. A good plan, except that Leith didn't intend to leave by that gap.

Leith slid down the slope and lay beneath the scrub brush to catch a few hours of rest before he pushed on and, hopefully, lengthened his lead until they were out of sight. This chase was no longer a sprint. It was an endurance race.

8

Brandi landed in the dirt on her rump. A stick jabbed her ribs as she sprawled on her back. "I'm never going to get this."

Jamie reached out a hand. "You're getting better. It takes time. Remember, I've been training since I was eleven."

She rolled her eyes and pushed herself to her feet. After three nights of training with Jamie, her body ached with bruises. A small cut on one of her arms throbbed.

But she couldn't give up. She had to get good enough to rescue Renna. How she planned to do that...well, the plan could come later.

She adjusted her grip on the knife, shifted her weight to the balls of her feet, and eyed Jamie. "All right. Again."

Jamie rushed at her, knife outthrust. Brandi swiveled as they'd been practicing and shoved his knife-arm away from her body. As the knife passed inches from her waist, she stabbed forward with her knife, stepping in to push Jamie off balance.

He sidestepped and smacked her hand away. She avoided his attempt to hook a leg behind one of her knees and twisted her grip on his knife-hand. He moved with her, trying to get her off balance.

She matched his move and felt Jamie's balance falter. Finally. She'd done it. She'd...

Jamie let go and sidestepped. Her momentum tossed her forward. Jamie tapped her spine with his knife.

Brandi sighed. She was hopeless at this. How was she ever going to rescue Renna if she couldn't last two seconds in a fight?

Jamie sheathed his knife. "Let's take a break from knife work for a while."

"Good, I need a rest."

"We're not resting." Jamie dropped to his hands and knees, then stretched out his legs. "We need to work on your strength."

Brandi groaned. It'd be so much easier if she was a boy and had muscles and strength and stuff. Jamie made her do exercises until she flopped on the ground, her clothes soaked with more sweat than she'd thought her body capable of producing. "I'm done."

He flopped onto the ground beside her. At least he was panting and covered in sweat from doing the exercises with her. The first day, he hadn't even been tired when she'd called it quits.

She stared at the scraps of sky visible between the tree branches. The evening twilight had faded into night, and the stars brightened to their full twinkle overhead. A crisp taste of cold and pine crackled in the air, the mountain night colder than the summer nights she had experienced in Stetterly when the darkness had only hushed the day's hot breath.

Several yards away, the fire danced to the murmer of the adults' voices, too low for her to hear what they said over the treefrogs and nightbirds.

The silence tore at her. She didn't like silence. It had worries and fears and all the things she'd spent years pretending not to feel. Forcing a lighthearted smile on her face, she propped herself up on her elbow. "Where do you see yourself in the future?"

Jamie locked his fingers together and placed them behind his head. His brown curls twined over his hands. He looked kind of cute like that, lounging on the ground with the starlight creating interesting shadows around his eyes and mouth. "Where do I see myself if we survive long enough to have a future?"

Brandi nodded. Perhaps it was foolish thinking about the future right then, but she couldn't help her curiosity. "Let's say you live. What would you want to do?"

He stared at the stars for so long Brandi wasn't sure he'd answer. Eventually, he glanced her way, two stars reflected in his eyes. "Until recently, I thought I'd be a Blade until I messed up or refused to kill, and Respen killed me. Since Leith got me out of there...I don't know. I guess I haven't had the time to think about it." He gave a long sigh and drew up one of his knees. "But, if God does have me survive, I guess I want to do something for Him. I'm not sure what, but I want to do something meaningful that helps people like me who are angry at God for a while and don't know how to make it better."

Brandi rested her head in her hands. His answer made her insides hurt. That's what she'd wanted. She wasn't a healer like Renna, but she had wanted to help people anyways. But now...she bit her lip. She was the one angry at God and didn't know how to make it better.

"What about you?" Jamie's voice sliced into her thoughts. "Where do you see yourself in the future?"

She shrugged. "On an adventure, I guess. I was always kind of restless at Stetterly. Do you know what I mean? Renna was scared of everything. I don't want to be like that. I want to go out and experience the world and travel all over Acktar."

Jamie rolled upright. "Well, your future is already here then. You're on an adventure and traveling Acktar."

Brandi sat up, tucked her knees to her chest, and hugged them. "It's not nearly as fun as I imagined."

He gave a snort that might've been a laugh had their topic been less sober. "I'm sure you didn't imagine bruises."

She felt her mouth twitch. "And I didn't imagine bugs or dirt or lack of baths." Funny how her daydreams never included aching muscles and buzzing mosquitoes. How naïve had she been? She hadn't known anything back then. The world seemed like a cheery, sunny place. But now she'd seen the darkness lurking in Acktar.

She rested her head on her knees. In the darkness of Nalgar Castle, King Respen had tempted her to doubt her faith in a way she'd never been tempted before.

And he'd succeeded. She swallowed at the tears she'd walled away the moment Leith tore her away from Renna. Trusting God used to be so easy. Sure, her parents' deaths had been hard, but she hadn't seen what Renna had. She hadn't even realized what was going on until afterwards. Uncle Abel, Aunt Mara, and Renna had taken so much of the grief for her that she hadn't had to bear the burden of it. It had just seemed easier to be the happy one and let Renna do all the worrying.

Until King Respen tore all that away from her. Uncle Abel and Aunt Mara were gone. And this time, she didn't have Renna there to bear the burden for her. She had to do it all by herself. And she wasn't sure how.

9

Renna limped across the plush rugs in her new chamber. Although she now had sunlight streaming in through wide windows and a view of the grass courtyard, her door remained locked and guards stationed before it. Her new prison might be plush and comfortable, but it was still a prison.

She paced in front of the window. What was she going to do? Should she agree to Respen's deal? Nausea gurgled in her stomach. Could she really marry Respen?

Renna squeezed her eyes shut. Her heart gave a special ache. *Leith.* What would he think if he returned to rescue her, only to find her married to Respen? She wrapped her arms around her stomach. How much would it hurt to see Leith but belong to someone else?

What would Uncle Abel and Aunt Mara have her do? Would they counsel her to accept Respen's proposal or refuse?

Renna hugged her stomach and stared past the Great Hall toward the cobblestone courtyard where Uncle Abel and Aunt Mara had died. What would they say? They'd always been willing to make sacrifices. Would they tell her to sacrifice herself to save the Christians in Acktar? But they'd also tried to protect her, so perhaps they'd say she should refuse?

Brandi would tell her to refuse. So would Leith.

But if she didn't marry Respen? The killing would continue. The church would dwindle.

Even if she was rescued and the Resistance defeated King Respen, what then? She and Brandi were the last of the Eirdon line. It'd be Renna's duty to become queen. She'd have to marry someone the country would accept as king.

A chill swirled down her arms. Leith couldn't be king. He'd hate such a visible leadership position. More than that, the country would never stand to have a Blade as king.

If Renna became queen, Brandi would have to be Lady of Stetterly. Could she handle that kind of responsibility?

Renna tugged on the end of her braid. What was she going to do? Would she end up Queen of Acktar no matter what decision she made? She could either become queen by marrying Respen or by hoping the Resistance won. Was it her duty to marry Respen and assure protection for the Christians in Acktar instead of putting her hope in a slim chance?

Either way, she'd lose Leith. And that hurt worst of all.

She couldn't stand the confines of her room any longer. She had to go outside. Leaning against the window frame, she stared at the bubbling fountain set in the green expanse below her. If only she could sit on the edge of that fountain and think for a while.

Why couldn't she? Respen had declared she was to be treated like his future queen. She marched—well, limped— across her chamber and rapped on her door.

It swung open, and a soldier poked his head in. "Yes, my lady?"

The respectful greeting gave her confidence. "I'd like to sit outside in the Queen's Court for a few hours. Would you be able to escort me there?"

The guard ducked his head. "Let me check." He closed the door. The lock clicked into place. Renna waited by the door, counting the minutes as they rolled by.

Respen said she should be treated as his future queen, but apparently she was still just as much a prisoner as she was before. She couldn't even go outside without asking the guard for permission.

Finally, the door reopened. Martyn stood in the hallway. He held out his arm. "Ready for a few hours outside?"

Nodding, she grasped his arm and let him help her down the hallway. As they started down the brick staircase, she cocked her head. Why was Martyn doing a job that easily could be accomplished by a boy with half his training and skills? "Why are you escorting me? The guard would've been perfectly capable of helping me down the stairs and watching me for a few hours." She waved down at her splinted leg. "It's not like I can escape."

"You're my prisoner and my responsibility." Martyn guided her down the last step. "If you escape, I'll be held responsible."

"But I can't escape." Not yet anyway.

"I can't take that risk." Martyn rolled his shoulders as if remembering his whipping.

Renna rubbed her fingers against the unfamiliar silk of her skirt. If she escaped, Martyn would suffer more of those horrible lashes across his back. No wonder he didn't want to take any risk in guarding her.

If Leith didn't return before her leg healed, should she try to escape on her own? Leith wouldn't have to walk into the trap that Respen planned to set for him. She wouldn't have to make a decision about marrying Respen.

But if she failed, Respen would lock her up in the Tower again and probably station even more guards around her. She'd only make it harder for Leith to rescue her.

When they reached the fountain, Renna sank onto the warm, stone wall ringing a small pool. Her injured leg already ached from that much exertion. After a quick scan of the area, Martyn retreated to the stairs and perched on the third from the bottom. He produced a knife and a polishing cloth.

Two guards stood at the arched tunnel that led to Respen's chambers and the cobblestone courtyard. Apparently, her prison had only been extended to the courtyard. The rest of the castle remained off limits.

At least she had some semblance of privacy. She could still feel their watchful eyes on her, but at least they were too far away to see her expression.

Leaning over, she dipped her fingers in the water, swirling her fingers until tendrils of current danced around her fingertips. Even in the heat of the summer day, the water remained cool as the mountain streams she and Brandi had splashed through on their journey into the Sheered Rock Hills.

Would she ever see those waterfalls again? Or venture outside the walls of Nalgar Castle? She shook the droplets from her fingers. Would she ever see Brandi again?

What should she do? The question ached through every bone, every muscle, every nerve of her body.

What would God have her do? The question rose to the surface, flowing like the water over the layers of the fountain behind her. She hadn't asked that question before. She'd based her actions on what others would do. She'd wanted to have courage like Leith or contentment like Brandi.

Her focus had turned earthward again when she should've been looking heavenward. What would God have her do?

Wait. The answer thrummed through her. *Wait on the Lord: be of good courage, and he shall strengthen thine heart: wait, I say, on the Lord.*

When was the last time she'd patiently waited for God's answer? She tended to make demands of God. Keep her safe. Keep Brandi safe. Deliver them *right now*. She didn't take the time to wait for God's answer, to learn the contentment and strength of patient waiting.

She'd asked King Respen for time. She didn't have to answer him right away. When it was time to answer, she'd know what God wanted her to do. Perhaps she couldn't find out the answer any way except by waiting.

Closing her eyes, she lay on her back on the fountain wall, one hand over her eyes, the other trailing in the water. She prayed for Brandi and Leith, that both of them would take the time to wait for God's answer instead of taking matters into their own hands.

10

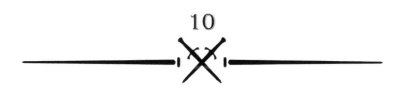

Brandi woke to a hand shaking her awake. She groaned. Her hip hurt from the hard dirt beneath her blanket. Her legs and arms shot sharp pain to her fingers and toes. Her eyelids felt glued shut.

"Time to get up." Jamie's far too cheery voice cracked her warm bubble of sleep.

She groaned again and whacked him. "It can't be morning yet." She scrubbed her eyes and shoved herself up. Jamie would only get more insistent if she delayed, and if he didn't shake her awake, Lady Alistair, Lydia, or Jolene would do it.

After she packed her blanket, she grabbed a slice of dried meat. Shad gathered their group together and herded them onto their horses. Brandi munched on her breakfast as they started riding once again. Even her jaw ached while she chewed.

Why had she thought training might be fun? It was work. And pain. And more work.

Shad led them deeper into the Sheered Rock Hills. Brandi moaned at the constant upward motion. She gave up any attempt at pride and gripped her saddlehorn instead of relying only on the strength of her thighs.

Ahead of her, Lady Alistair also gripped her horse and swayed as if wearied by so much travel. Lydia and a few of the maids fared a little better. Somehow, Lady Lorraine managed to look as tough as ever. She must've been made of steel or something.

Brandi let her body rock back and forth with the motion of her horse. She closed her eyes and relaxed. Perhaps she wouldn't fall if she let herself doze for a few minutes...

A scream ripped the midmorning air. Brandi jerked awake. Shouting blasted around her. Shad whipped an arrow from his quiver, nocked, and fired into the trees. Jolene scrambled to nock an arrow. One of the maids from Walden lay on the ground, a knife sticking from her neck.

"Get down!" Jamie dove from Buster.

The Blades had caught up with them. Brandi threw herself from Big Brown's saddle. They couldn't attack now. She wasn't ready yet.

Jamie grabbed her shoulder and hustled the two of them to the side, placing their backs to a large cedar. Brandi drew the knife Leith had given her and gripped the hilt. She kept it pressed to her side, hidden next to her. Surprise. Jamie said that was one of a Blade's best weapons.

"I saw only one Blade." Jamie flexed his fingers around the hilt of his knife. "We had two following us."

She searched the trees around them. The shouts of the guards grew farther away, as if they chased the Blade deeper into the forest. Where was the other one? If he was here, he'd be looking for her.

A black shape dropped from a tree near them, landing lightly on his feet within reach of Jamie. The Blade struck high and fast. Jamie dodged. The Blade stepped forward, using his height to push Jamie until Jamie tripped over a rock and tumbled backwards down an incline.

Jamie rolled, trying to get to his feet in case the Blade pounced.

The Blade didn't pounce. With Jamie temporarily out of the way, he wheeled and charged at Brandi.

She was his target. If he'd gone after Jamie, she would've been free to run to the others. He probably hoped to kill her before Jamie had a chance to attack again.

She gripped her knife and crouched. His knife stabbed toward her stomach. She swept it aside as she'd practiced. Her instincts carried her forward, thrusting with her knife.

He'd block her thrust. She'd practiced this a hundred times with Jamie, and a hundred times she'd had her knife swept aside.

"Kent!" Jamie scrambled at the edge of the slope.

The Blade glanced at Jamie. Brandi kept thrusting forward. Her knife met a strange resistance, a hard but soft surface that gave beneath the tip. She stumbled as the knife slid into the Blade's stomach.

He gasped and collapsed to his knees in front of her. He pressed his hands around her knife sticking from his gut. A rasping noise bubbled from his throat as he flopped to the ground on his back.

She'd killed him. A shaking sensation filled her chest, as if she couldn't decide if she should go numb or panic. Her knees locked. The world tilted, as if the mountains below her feet heaved.

"You all right?" Jamie's face cut through the black swirl dancing across her vision. His fingers curled over her shoulders, pressing into her skin. "Brandi?"

"I killed him." The words rang hollow in her ears, too flat, too small to hold the emotion they should. What emotion should she feel? She should be horrified, right? Burst into tears, perhaps bawl that she'd never do it again?

But all she felt was cold.

"I distracted him. He didn't expect a girl to fight back." Jamie gave her a slight shake. "He's not dead yet. Your sister healed Leith from a wound like that."

Brandi's eyes stole around Jamie at the man curled around his wound. Renna would've been able to tend him.

But Renna wouldn't have put the knife in him in the first place.

Brandi shook her head. "I can't. I don't know how." Nor could she stop shaking long enough to do anything.

Pounding feet crunched the dirt and pine needles. Shad's face joined Jamie's. "Did he hurt you?"

She blinked up at him. She couldn't tell him she'd stabbed someone. Jamie understood, but Shadrach Alistair, raised to protect his mother and sisters from the slightest trouble, wouldn't. Even now, Lady Alistair and Lydia huddled in a protective ring of guardsmen. None of them would consider picking up a knife and fighting back.

But they didn't have to. They weren't alone.

Jamie jumped in to save her once again. "No. We held him off."

Shad nodded and swung his gaze toward the dying Blade. "Put him near the others. We'd best tend him."

Two of the guards obeyed his order. Brandi pressed against the tree as they carried the moaning Blade past her. They were going to help him, but he'd die. Her knife had gone deep. Too deep.

Shad patted her shoulder. "You're safe. The other Blade was wounded, but he got away. I doubt he'll be in any shape to keep following us."

Brandi nodded, but she didn't feel safe. She was numb, like a part of her was bleeding out along with the Blade she'd stabbed.

11

He was surrounded by rattlesnakes. When Leith woke after sleeping through the hottest part of the day, he'd cracked his eyes open to find himself eyeball to eyeball with a large rattlesnake.

Its brown scales with darker brown splotches on its back curled only a foot away from his nose, inches from his hand. A flick of his eyes downward told him two more snakes curled near his knees and feet.

He drew in a slow breath and tried to remain calm. He must've paused near a rattlesnake den. Hundreds of snakes could be populating the area around him. Like him, these snakes had sought out shade during the heat of the day to avoid overheating.

As long as he didn't move, he'd be fine.

The rattlesnake swiveled its arrow-shaped head. Its slitted eyes stared at him while its obscene, red tongue stabbed at the air. It could taste his fear, his body heating with the suppressed urge to run. He smelled like prey.

He couldn't move, not even to draw his exposed hand closer to his body. Any movement could scare the snake into biting. There was no cure for snakebite. Even if someone had created such a thing, he was too deep in the Waste to get to medical help before he died.

Renna needed him to survive. He couldn't die here, especially not from something as accidental as a snakebite.

The snake's head hovered and swayed in front of him. Testing, searching, for the source of the fear it scented.

Leith had to calm down. He could feel a shudder building along his spine. Or perhaps it was another rattlesnake sliding along his back. His skin prickled. The muscles in his back stiffened as if prepared to fend off a snake's fangs, but he couldn't turn his head to look.

He glanced at the sky. He still had an hour of heat before the sun sank low and the earth cooled enough for the snakes to slither from their shade and seek the remaining warmth before night chilled the stone.

An hour surrounded by snakes.

The shudder built with the desire to run, to move. The minutes crawled by.

He had to distract himself from the rattlesnakes surrounding him. Anything to forget that death lurked one wrong twitch away.

Prayer. He squeezed his eyes shut to block out the image of the thick, scaly body in front of his face. Prayer kept him steady when he faced Respen. Prayer would keep him calm now.

Renna. Locked in that dark dungeon cell without even Brandi to comfort her.

Brandi. Torn from her sister and depending on Leith to return and rescue Renna.

Shad. Struggling with the burden of taking his father's place.

Jamie. Trying so bravely to have a man's courage at thirteen.

Martyn. Bitter from Leith's betrayal.

The trainees he and Jamie had rescued. Jolene and Lady Loraine. Lord Alistair and his men fighting for their lives at Walden. Were they still fighting? Or had they been overwhelmed and killed?

The air cooled around Leith. His bones ached from the stone beneath him while his muscles cramped with the tension of remaining motionless.

The snake moved. Its scales rasped against the stone. Leith cracked his eyes open. The snake's thick, ropy body thrashed in waves against the rock. A section curved over his hand, the dry scales catching on his exposed skin.

Leith's breath seized in his throat. His fingers threatened to spasm. He'd never screamed in his life, but he was tempted now.

Something brushed against his boot. His leg tensed with the reflex to kick the creature away, but his good sense stopped him.

Don't react. Don't kick. Don't breathe.

The snake's rattle knocked against his hand. In moments, it slid from the rock and disappeared into the tall grass. The other snakes followed it, congregating on a few of the rocky ledges still exposed to the sun.

Across the grassy area, Blizzard snorted and moved into a shady spot, but he continued eating. He'd been around snakes before. He ignored them, and they ignored him.

The rustling, scraping sound faded into silence around him. After searching as far as he could without moving his head, he slowly twisted his head around. When he didn't see any snakes, he eased himself up on one elbow. Nothing around him moved. He craned his neck and checked behind him. No snakes.

He curled into a sitting position and, finally, allowed himself to dissolve into shudders.

When his shakes stilled, he pushed himself to his feet. He needed to get moving. He'd lost too much time while he'd been immobile. He called for Blizzard. The horse's ears flicked. After snagging several more mouthfuls of grass, Blizzard trotted over. Leith scratched the horse's neck to reward him for coming. When the horse had relaxed until he nearly tipped over, Leith threw the blanket and saddle on Blizzard's back.

Once his horse was saddled, Leith gave Blizzard water and drank some himself. They were already down to two and a half canteens. Leith swung into the saddle and nudged Blizzard.

When they were well past the snakes, Leith halted Blizzard at the base of a tall mound. While Blizzard snuffled at the bare ground, Leith scrambled up the mound and dropped onto his stomach.

He scanned the empty, dead hills around him. Nothing stirred between the dusty purple peaks and the patches of yellow-brown grass. After a few minutes of searching, Leith slid down the mound and returned to Blizzard.

Even after the delay, he'd still managed to lose the pursuing Blades. Maybe they'd lost the trail or run out of water or been forced to give up. If they were still back there, trying to stick to his trail, they wouldn't last much longer.

No matter. Leith had accomplished his goal. He was out of sight and free to circle around. Besides, he couldn't delay turning around any longer. His own water supplies were already lower than he would've liked considering the distance he and Blizzard had to travel yet.

He pointed Blizzard's nose north to begin the arc that would take him back to the Ramparts and out of the Waste.

12

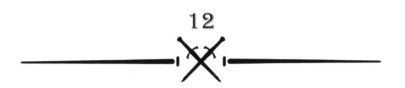

Renna resisted the urge to itch the sunburn on her nose. She shouldn't have fallen asleep on that fountain. The midday sun had fried every bit of her exposed skin red as the tapestries hanging over the walls in the king's chamber.

Across the table, Respen eyed her. She squirmed. Weakness—any kind of weakness, even sunburn—could be exploited. To cover her discomfort, she stabbed her fork into the beef on her plate.

Was Leith all right? Where were he and Brandi right now? Had they reached Eagle Heights yet? If only she had some way of knowing.

Respen's eyes remained on her as she chewed and swallowed. When he continued to stare, she tried to force a bit of Brandi's levity into her voice. "Does my sunburn look that bad?"

His eyebrows shot up. He tapped the table. "It does look…"

She reined in her smile at making the king speechless, even if it was at the expense of her looks. Respen seemed to be in a good mood. Perhaps she could ask him for a few things. "It still itches. Is there a healer in the castle that might have a salve?"

"Yes, of course." Respen's fingers stopped their tapping. "I'll have the healer stop by your room."

Renna squeezed her hands together below the table. "Actually, I was hoping I could go to the healer myself." As Respen's eyes darkened to black, she hunched and forced herself to finish. "And I'd like free rein of Nalgar Castle."

He lashed forward. Renna flinched. A scream curled in her throat.

Respen's hand stopped six inches from her face. He drew his hand back, clenched his fist, and pounded the table. "No. You think I'd let you escape."

Her heart thrummed in her throat. He'd nearly slapped her. He'd done it before. He'd come close to doing it again. "No, I wasn't trying to escape. I just want to be able to move around the castle."

Somehow, moving about the castle was important. She couldn't say how. Maybe she grasped at dandelion fuzz. But perhaps there was someone she was supposed to help in the castle. At the least, she'd have the freedom to wander the castle without having to ask Martyn or the guards for permission each time.

Respen relaxed against the chair, fingers drumming the tabletop. "What are you willing to exchange for this freedom?"

Stomach clenching, she stared at her lap. What did Respen want from her? Surely he wouldn't demand anything untoward, would he? She glanced at the meal spread across the table. "I'll have dinner with you every night." It was the most she was willing to offer.

"Accepted."

Really? Renna glanced at him. What did he have to

gain from more time in her company? Did he hope to sway her decision? Or did he, for some reason, enjoy spending time with her? Her skin prickled, and she rubbed her forearms.

Respen leaned forward, his face harsh. "But you must promise that you will not try to escape."

Promise not to escape? She swallowed and dug her fingernails into her palms. What would happen when Leith returned to rescue her? If she promised not to escape, she couldn't go with him without breaking her promise.

Or would she? Was being rescued different than escaping?

What should she do? Was her freedom to wander the castle worth the freedom she'd give up?

Wait. The words of the Psalm echoed in her mind again. *Wait on the Lord.*

Wait for rescue. Don't try anything foolish.

Perhaps escape wasn't in her future. Even if she had the skills to sneak through the gates or climb down the castle wall, she wouldn't get far, injured or not. She'd get herself lost on the prairie and probably die of thirst long before anyone found her.

Wouldn't it be easier for Leith to rescue her if she had more freedom in the castle? If she couldn't escape, she could create opportunities for rescue.

Taking a deep breath, she met King Respen's eyes. "I promise I won't try to escape on my own."

A slim smile slunk across Respen's face, though a spark remained in his eyes. His beard grew more pointed as his cheeks tightened. "Excellent. I will inform Second Blade Hamish that he is to escort you about the castle as you wish. For your safety, of course."

"Of course." She forced herself to smile. Of course Respen had seen through her scheme. He counted on Martyn countering Leith's rescue attempt when it came.

At least Martyn wasn't an unpleasant guard. He was a captive audience when she needed to talk. Maybe if she talked to him enough, his heart would soften by the time Leith returned. Perhaps this time, Martyn would go with them instead of fighting.

Would Leith rescue her before she had to make a decision about marrying Respen? She remembered Leith as she'd last seen him, black hair straggling over his forehead into green eyes that ached with pain at leaving her behind. He was the reason she played for time. More than her parents' murders, more than the nearly fifteen year age gap between her and Respen, her heart ached at the thought of marrying Respen...and not marrying Leith.

Why did it hurt so much? She and Leith had never even talked about courting, much less marriage. He'd never shown that much interest in her except his protection of her.

But her brushes with death had a way of stripping away the lies and doubts she'd told herself. She knew her heart. Somewhere along the way, she'd fallen in love with the former Blade Leith Torren.

Everything burned with heat and sunlight. Leith stumbled forward. Was he going in the right direction? What direction what he supposed to be going?

West. That's the direction he should be walking. He'd turned around to head back. When was that? Yesterday? The day before?

He had to rest. His arms and legs were shriveled,

useless husks as he plodded forward. When had he last had water? He couldn't remember. He'd given the last of the water to Blizzard.

Blizzard. Was his horse still there? Leith lurched to the side as he checked behind him. Blizzard's head drooped, the sag of his reins trailing on the ground. Leith held up his fist. He still gripped the ends of the reins.

He should rest. They shouldn't walk in the heat of the day, not without water.

But if they stopped, they'd never start moving again. They'd die where they lay.

He had to keep moving. His feet shuffled forward. A few more inches. A few more feet.

The muscles in his right leg spasmed painfully. He clutched at his leg, gasping in dust and air heavy with heat. When the cramp eased, his fingers refused to straighten from their claw-like grip.

Renna needed him. He had to keep going. He forced a foot forward. The muscles in his other leg cramped. He halted, both hands clutching at his legs. He didn't even have the strength to cry out at the pain wracking his body.

A deep groan rumbled behind him. He hobbled around as Blizzard flopped to the ground, a tortured moan ripping from the horse's chest.

Leith gripped Blizzard's bridle. "You can't lie down on me. I promised Brandi I'd take care of you. You can't die on me." He hauled on the horse's head.

A breath huffed over Leith's hand. Blizzard raised his head and tried to roll to his feet. He only managed to lift the one shoulder before he collapsed. His head flopped in Leith's hand.

Leith crumbled to his knees beside Blizzard's head, hands shaking. "I'm so sorry, Blizzard. I'm so sorry I brought us here." He pressed his forehead against the base of Blizzard's shoulder. He couldn't go on. He was as spent as Blizzard. He'd have to see Renna again in Heaven, because he wasn't going to see her again on earth.

He'd tried, but Harrison Vane was right. No one survived the Waste.

13

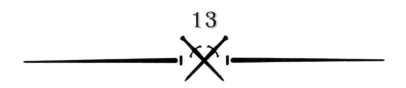

Renna limped toward the kitchen tower at Nalgar Castle. Her leg ached, but the break had mended enough that she could limp without assistance. Thanks to the healer's paste, her sunburn had healed into peeling skin.

Dark clouds gathered overhead. A raindrop splattered onto Renna's forehead. She held out her hands, palm up, and caught a few more raindrops. Finally, some rain. The farmers would be happy.

As she stepped into the kitchen's steamy interior, all activity halted. Due to her or the Blade trailing her, she couldn't tell.

The head cook, a skinny man that appeared ready to keel over from either exhaustion or fear, stumbled over and offered a stilted bow, his hands shaking. "My lady, was last night's supper not to your liking?"

Renna gave the man her best smile. "The food was lovely, thank you." She pulled herself straighter. "Today is the Lord's Day. I'd like to help out so you and your helpers don't have to work so hard today."

The cook gaped at her. "Are you sure, my lady?"

She sighed. Of course he'd fear putting the possible

future wife of King Respen to work in the castle kitchens.

But she wasn't some highborn lady not used to getting her hands dirty. She'd spent the last four and a half years washing her own dishes and clothes.

She headed for the large washtub at the far end of the kitchen across from the massive brick fireplace. An old woman, her hands crippled with age, struggled with the scrubbing cloth in her hand. Renna gently eased the cloth from her grip. "I'm not the best cook, but I'm proficient at washing dishes. I'll take over for a while so you can take a break."

"Thank you, my lady." The woman tottered a few steps away.

"Martyn, fetch her a chair." Renna waved a sudsy hand at one of the chairs tucked against the rough, wooden table in the center of the kitchen.

The cook froze, and two of the scullery maids gasped. The old woman's eyes widened. Renna bit her cheeks to stop her smile. She'd just ordered a Blade around. So what? It wasn't like Martyn would hurt her. He was her captive audience after all.

Yet would she have dared order Martyn around a few months ago? She'd changed. She could give orders now, if she had to. Did that mean she had what it took to lead? To be queen?

But she didn't want to be queen. Or lead. Or do anything besides return to a peaceful life in Stetterly. Was that even an option for her now?

Martyn set a chair behind the woman next to the fireplace. She gave him a slight nod. "Thank you, young Blade."

Renna tossed a towel at Martyn. "Make yourself useful and dry the dishes."

He clutched the towel and awkwardly grabbed the first plate. Suppressing her grin, she shoved her hands into the soapy water and dug out a pewter plate. Behind her, the normal bustle resumed. Pots clanked. The head cook dished out orders in a rising volume as he grew accustomed to the intruders in his kitchen. Meat and vegetables sizzled in a pot over the fire, emitting a savory aroma that twitched her nose.

She relaxed into the comfortable rhythm of scrubbing dishes, rinsing them, and handing them to the person next to her. It didn't even matter than the person next to her was a Blade.

What would it be like to have Leith helping her like this? If she closed her eyes, she could picture it. Stetterly Manor was gone, but perhaps they could build a small cabin instead, with large windows overlooking the stately pines of the Spires Canyon. They could wash the breakfast dishes together, laughing and splashing each other until something outside would catch Leith's eye. A deer, or perhaps a coyote, slinking through the animal trails down to the river at the bottom of the canyon.

For a moment the daydream was so real, she could smell the breeze blowing through the trees and see Leith's relaxed smile.

She plunged her hands into the sudsy water. The dishes scraped against palms. The dark, steamy kitchen wrapped around her once again. Martyn stared at her. She forced herself to shrug away the melancholy that drifted in the dust of her daydream. "Sorry. My mind wandered."

He took the tin cup from her and nodded.

She swallowed a rush of tears as she reached for an oatmeal-encrusted pot. That daydream was just that, a daydream. Either she'd agree to marry King Respen and would live forever in this castle as his queen, or she'd refuse and be used to trap Leith. Then both of them would be executed.

Or, the Resistance would win, she'd become queen, and she still could never return to Stetterly and Leith and the brightness of her daydreams.

The thought ached inside her. Why did she want a future now? For so many years, she'd been so scared of the future that she'd never wanted it to come. Now that she'd set aside most of her fear, the thought of the future taunted her with all the bright hopes that she'd never dared imagine before.

She cleared her throat and glanced over her shoulder at the old woman. "Have you worked for King Respen for a while?"

"I used to serve him at Blathe Manor back when he was Lord Felix." The old woman's curled hands rested in her lap. "Served his parents before him."

"What happened to them?" Renna scraped at the oatmeal crusted on the bottom of the pot.

The woman glanced around the kitchen, but the hubbub drowned their voices out. Only Martyn could hear them. "Killed by Rovers. I believe it was at the young Lord Henry Alistair's wedding."

Renna handed the pot to Martyn. Respen's parents had been killed in the Rover attack at Lord Alistair's wedding? That was the same attack where her parents met.

"Respen's father, now that was a hard man." The woman shook her head and rocked in the chair. "It gave Respen such a heart to help other abandoned boys. He was such a dear boy."

Dear boy? Renna reached for another pot. Somehow,

she couldn't picture Respen as a child, living under a hard father, losing his parents, having a heart. But then, Renna used to be unable to imagine the same about Leith.

Beneath Respen's cruelty, was there a hurting heart? Was it her purpose to reach it? Could she?

Not on her own, she couldn't. God was the healer of hearts. But would God use her?

She didn't know. But it was her duty to be a light no matter how God choose to use her.

This time, she wouldn't shirk. She wouldn't hide.

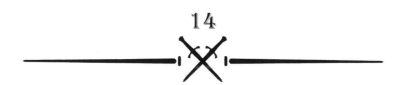

14

The sky wouldn't stop crying. If only it'd stop. Brandi didn't need another reminder that she should be crying too.

The Blade she'd stabbed had died. Shad and Jamie had buried him down the slope from where they'd buried the maid that had been killed. Brandi had watched both burials, a throb coursing through her when she saw the maid's auburn hair, a color close to her own strawberry blond.

The rain drained everyone's spirits. Even the horses hung their heads as they trudged higher and deeper into the Sheered Rock Hills. As the rain poured down on them like a constant waterfall from the sky, the trail grew slick with mud. The horses stumbled and scrambled.

Brandi pulled her cloak farther over her head. The lanolin-rich wool repelled most of the water, though some seeped into her clothing. Water cascaded from her unprotected nose and hands.

Shad shouted instructions she couldn't hear. Hopefully he'd find shelter for them soon. On the horse ahead of her, Lady Alistair shivered.

Shad shouted again and pointed. Through the grey

veil of rain, a dark hole pocked the side of the cliff ahead of them. Shad led them toward it, halted, and swung from his horse. With a motion for the rest of them to stay put, he slipped into the opening.

What if he encountered a wild animal? They couldn't afford to lose him now. He was the only one who knew the way to Eagle Heights. Without him, they'd be stuck living in this endless wilderness, wandering until they either stumbled on some kind of civilization or died.

Shad reappeared a moment later and gripped his horse's reins. He yelled something that only the people closest to him could hear. It must've been the all right signal because two of the guards led their horses into the cave. Lady Alistair, Lydia, and the four former Blade trainees followed a moment later.

The rest of their group crowded into the opening, but Brandi hung back. Getting out of the rain sounded nice, but then she'd be stuck in the same cave as everyone else. Would Lady Alistair, Lady Lorraine, or Shad try to talk to her about the Blade's death? Jamie had helped her deflect their questions earlier, but would they try again?

Jamie bumped her knee with his horse's shoulder. "It's going to be all right."

"Maybe." Brandi shrugged and glanced at the opening. Shad stood by the entrance, eyes fixed on her. Everyone except a few guards had already gone inside. Swinging down from Big Brown, she led him toward the cave entrance.

Shad gave her a smile as she passed him. "We'll be able to rest here for a while. Leith will catch up with us soon."

What would Leith think if he learned she'd killed?

Like Renna, he expected her to be happy all the time. Somehow, she didn't want to ruin the image he had of her. What if he was disappointed in her? That'd hurt worse than being stabbed herself.

She forced herself to smile and continued walking. The cave entrance was a narrow slit in the rock, the edges rounded. Big Brown balked at the opening, but Brandi tugged him forward. He ducked, his ears brushing the ceiling, and jumped as the stirrups scraped against the walls.

The entrance seemed to narrow farther. She yanked her horse another yard inside. The tunnel turned and opened up. She and Big Brown popped out the other side.

Slabs of rock piled along the walls, some rounded, some still jagged. Dry dirt created a level floor while the ceiling rose above them in a blank, orange-brown color. Someone had lit some of the candles they'd packed with them, spacing them out on top of the boulders. After all their hard work to get here, it seemed rather plain. Weren't caves supposed to be a bit more elaborate than a rocky hole in the side of the cliff? Like with crystals and fancy formations and stuff like that?

Glancing around, she tried to spot any looks sent her way. Lady Alistair and Lydia huddled under a damp blanket. Lady Lorraine had her hands on her hips as she studied the cave. Jolene perched on a boulder and worked beeswax over her bowstring and oiled the wood of her bow. Good. Maybe they'd stay so busy they wouldn't pester her.

She led Big Brown to the corner of the cave where the other horses had been tied in a line. Tugging the saddle from Big Brown's back, she draped it over a rock to dry out. Big Brown shook, flinging a few droplets into the air from his mane and tail.

Gathering the rest of her things, Brandi found an unused boulder and laid out her blanket roll and spare set of clothes. She shivered. The cool air inside the cave wrapped around her. As much as she longed to change into a dry set of clothes, everything in her pack had been soaked through.

Not that the cave provided much privacy even if she could change, though Lady Lorraine would probably change that promptly enough. She already stood in the center, dividing it into sleeping sections for the men, women, and horses.

Brandi inched into a dark corner. She didn't feel like pretending to be cheerful if Lady Lorraine assigned her a chore.

With the last of them inside, Shad led his own horse in and organized a rotation for guard duty. Several guards were sent into the rain to gather what they could find for dry firewood and fodder for the horses.

Brandi sank onto the floor in her corner and closed her eyes. Maybe she'd be able to hide in this corner all night.

Someone sank to the ground next to her. She didn't have to open her eyes to know Jamie leaned against the rock next to her. Of course *he* would pester her. He was rather good at doing that.

"Leith's going to come back."

Brandi hugged her stomach. People who left never came back. Not when they left like this, anyway. Leith wouldn't come back. Renna wouldn't come back. Brandi was all by herself. "No, he won't."

Jamie heaved a huge sigh.

Brandi waited, but Jamie didn't say anything more. Why not? Was Jamie not as sure as he sounded? Did he also think that Leith was going to die?

15

Leith woke to cold shivers on his spine. The world seemed darker than it should be. He squinted at the sloped peaks rising around him and Blizzard. The sky pressed down in a strange, blue color, like sunset but darker. The mounds of clouds rumbled as they collided.

Something cold touched his forehead. He reached up, swiped at the spot, and studied his fingers. Wet. His fingers were wet.

Water. Where did the water come from? He stared at the sky. Another drop splashed onto his face.

Rain. His mind dragged the answer from the canyon-like depths of his head.

The drops plopped down harder. He stuck his tongue out and managed to catch a few.

"Feel that, Blizzard? Rain." His voice croaked in his throat. He heaved himself to his feet, every limb shaking.

Dark clouds piled on the western horizon. More on the way. There was something he should remember about rain in the Waste. Something an old Rover told him and Vane years ago.

Lightning flashed. Thunder roared. The rain sluiced

from the sky, soaking through the shirt tied around Leith's head and washing down his face.

He and Blizzard should find shelter. He studied the hills surrounding them, their surfaces covered with widening, dark blue-gray spots. He and Blizzard lay in the gully between the hills.

A gully that'd channel the water in a flood.

He had to get to higher ground. He tugged on Blizzard's bridle. "Come on. We need to move."

Blizzard's eyes flickered open. His nostrils flared pink.

Leith knelt and pulled the soaked shirt from his head. Propping Blizzard's nose on his lap, he wrung the fabric, squeezing a small stream of water onto Blizzard's mouth.

Blizzard chomped at the water. His tongue slurped in and out between his large teeth.

When Leith had forced every drop from the shirt, he tottered to his feet and grabbed Blizzard's bridle. They couldn't stay here much longer. "Time to move, Blizzard."

Blizzard's ears twitched and his tongue continued lapping at the rain.

He and Blizzard had defied the Waste this long. He'd been ready to lie down and die, but not now. "Get up." He yanked on Blizzard's bridle and took a step back. Blizzard's neck stretched. The horse snorted louder but didn't move.

"Get up." Leith leaned backwards. "Get up."

Blizzard gathered his legs beneath him, but he didn't stand.

"Get up!" Leith took another step back. "You are *not* dying on me. Get. Up."

Blizzard groaned and lurched onto his front feet. Leith heaved as Blizzard dragged his rear legs beneath him and surged upward with his powerful haunches. He stood on shaking legs, but he was standing.

Leith patted his horse's neck, gripped the reins, and stumbled forward. The rain turned the dust into a sloppy muck that squished into his boots. The water soaking his clothes and sliding over his skin cooled his heated body. He let his mouth hang open and tilted his head toward the sky. Water trickled into his mouth, seeping into his parched tongue.

When he and Blizzard had slogged up the slope of a hill, Leith stopped. Blizzard lowered his head, snuffling at a puddle collecting in a small depression.

Leith tugged his horse's head up. Once the rain touched the ground, the harmful minerals in the dirt would contaminate it. He and Blizzard could get sick, even die, if they drank it. He couldn't risk it, even as desparate as they were.

Digging in a saddlebag, Leith pulled out his pot and set it on the ground. Rain plinged against the iron. Blizzard huffed and slurped at the water as fast as it filled.

Lightning shattered in the sky. Thunder cracked the clouds and shook the ground.

Leith knelt and opened his mouth. Rain pooled on his tongue. He relished the coolness slipping down his throat and into his shriveled stomach. The fog in his mind washed away like the dust dripping from his clothes. Rain was a miracle he'd never understood until he'd been in a place where God withheld rain, withheld life, like He did in the Waste.

When he'd caught enough water in his mouth for several gulps, he shook himself. Once the water hit the ground and became contaminated, they couldn't drink it anymore. He had to catch enough of this rain to fill his canteens and the waterskin if he could. While Blizzard still slurped at the pot, Leith pulled out his canteens and propped them between of couple of rocks. Some rain plunked through the openings, but not enough.

He searched through his saddlebags, looking for something he could roll into a funnel. His black pants wouldn't work, nor would his spoon and extra knives. Nothing in his saddlebags was both flexible and strong enough.

The saddlebags. He studied the leather top. It was both stiff enough to hold a shape and channel water, but flexible enough to be shaped. Drawing a knife, he hacked at the leather until the top came off in his hand.

Holding it up to the rain, he scrubbed it with his hand, washing away as much of the dust and trail grime as he could. The soaking turned the leather squishy and pliable in his fingers. When it was as clean as he could make it, he curled it into a wide funnel and jammed the small end into the opening of his canteen.

When he was satisfied the leather would stay, he worked at the saddlebag dangling on the other side until its top ripped away. After placing that leather funnel in the mouth of the second canteen, Leith sprawled on the ground and gaped at the sky again.

At least he and Blizzard wouldn't accidentally drink too much and make themselves sick. The downpour produced only so much water at a time, forcing them to drink slowly.

A roar rumbled in the distance, coursing along the ground instead of the clouds overhead. Leith braced himself on an elbow as a foaming torrent of blue-grey water bellowed through the gully he and Blizzard had lain in minutes earlier. The porous slopes shook with the force of the water, some giving way and sliding into the heaving mass of water.

Their hill held against the onslaught of water, only the edges crumbling. Leith leaned his head onto his hands and drank the rain.

He spent the night huddled under the saddle blanket and his cloak. He kept his pot in the open so he and Blizzard could drink their fill without touching the water stored in his canteens.

As dawn crinkled across the horizon, the rain died away. Leith wrung out his clothes and the saddle blanket. Both items were too dusty to get clean water from them.

Blizzard's ears flattened as Leith placed the wet blanket and saddle on his back and tightened the girth strap. He patted the horse's neck. "Don't worry, boy. I'm not going to ride until everything's dry."

Blizzard shook his mane and wiggled his back like he wanted to shed the uncomfortably damp saddle and blanket. Leith didn't blame him. His own clothes scratched as he grabbed his horse's reins.

He scanned the horizon. Not that he expected to see the other Blades. They'd disappeared from sight long ago. If they'd continued trailing him, they would've run out of water. Even with the amount of water they'd had, Leith and Blizzard had come within a snake's skin of dying.

Where was he, exactly? While he'd been fading from thirst, he'd lost his sense of direction. What way had Leith wandering during that time?

He faced west, placing the sun behind him and slightly to the left. As long as he headed in this direction, he'd find the Ramparts. He could follow them to the gap to the north. Once through, he'd be free to find Shad, Brandi, Jamie, and the others in the cave.

Had they arrived safely? Leith urged Blizzard forward. For a while there, thirst had driven every other thought from his head. But now his missions drummed into him. Find Shad and Brandi. Travel to Eagle Heights. Gather an army. Rescue Renna.

First, he had to find his way out of the Waste.

In the wake of the rain, the Waste thrummed with a life that had been hidden by the heat and dust. The patches of grass swelled with the hint of green while the damp earth crawled with insects and lizards coming out to feed. He stopped several times to allow Blizzard to graze on the green-tipped grass. He chewed on his own soggy piece of meat.

That afternoon, he halted Blizzard near a patch of grass and turned his horse loose to graze. He spread out the saddle and blanket on the heated boulders, keeping a wary eye out for snakes. The sun snapped up the water until nothing remained to mark the deluge of the day and night before.

When the hottest part of the day came and went, Leith saddled Blizzard and rode along a grassy slope that wound between the canyons of jagged, grey rock. The slopes displayed new patterns carved into them, spidery etchings across the layers of grey, blue, purple, and red.

A large, black shape shimmered and moved on the ground in the distance. Dismounting, Leith approached the form cautiously. A harsh cawing filled the air. A wing flapped out from the form before tucking back into the huddled mass.

Crows. Feasting on carrion.

He dropped Blizzard's reins and dashed forward, waving his arms and shouting. With a thumping of wings and raucous cawing, the crows launched into the sky. They settled onto the rocks and scrub brush a few yards away, watching him with glimmering, black eyes. The sun cast rainbows along their sleek feathers.

A mangled form lay on the ground, bits of black fabric shredded around what had once been the body of a man. Only the leather belt, boots, and knives remained intact.

Leith must've drifted more south than he'd intended. He was supposed to be farther to the north, well away from the other Blades.

It didn't matter. This Blade had died, and Leith had spotted no sign of the other one.

Grimacing, Leith eased one of the knives from the dead Blade's belt. The fading sunlight glinted on the initials *GC* etched into the hilt.

Galen Craven. When First Blade Vane and Second Blade Hess died, Craven became the Second Blade under Leith.

Leith dropped the knife into one of his saddlebags and swung back into the saddle. After Respen had learned of Leith's defection to the Resistance, Craven would've become the First Blade. He hadn't lived long enough to enjoy the rank.

Nudging Blizzard, Leith turned his back on the dead Blade. He didn't have time to give the man a decent burial, even if he had the means to chop a grave into the crumbling rock of the Waste.

As the black birds returned to their meal, a weight settled onto Leith's shoulders.

Martyn Hamish, the man he'd once considered his best friend, was now the First Blade.

16

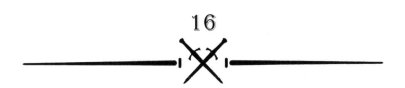

Renna swept her hair onto her head and attempted to pin it into place. She frowned at her reflection. The bun looked more like a porcupine than a tasteful hairstyle. Why couldn't her hair cooperate?

With a sigh, she took out the pins and let her hair fall down her back. Thanks to her efforts, her hair now sported frizzy crinkles.

Her door rattled. That would be Martyn coming to escort her on her morning walk. Abandoning the mirror and her attempts at doing something with her hair, she walked to the door, unlocked it, and pulled it open.

King Respen stood in the doorway, a bouquet of flowers gripped so tightly in his fist the stems squeaked.

Renna swallowed at the skittering in her stomach. What was he doing here? She'd kept her end of the bargain and dined with him every night. She hadn't tried to escape.

Had the Blades captured Leith? Or Brandi? Had Respen come to gloat?

He thrust the flowers at her. "Here."

A bouquet. Even Leith hadn't given her flowers.

No, she couldn't compare Respen to Leith. Leith had

given her a knife to defend herself. And that was so much better, right? He cared about her safety. Respen only wanted to use her either as bait for Leith or a bride to secure his crown. Nothing more.

She snagged the flowers and stepped back to gain a few feet of distance. "I need to put these in water."

Stumbling, she grabbed the glass next to the pitcher on the washstand, filled it with water, and jammed the flowers into it. She let the methodical actions keep her moving. If she paused, she might freeze. Placing the glass of flowers on the table in the center of the room, she plucked at them.

Why had Respen given her a bouquet? He never did anything without angling for something. He couldn't be trying to be romantic, so what did he want?

When she couldn't think of any more reasons to keep rearranging the bouquet, she trudged to the doorway. Respen still stood there, fingers tapping against the door frame. As she approached, he held out his arm. "Walk with me."

He was courting her. Or, at least, attempting to court her in his own fashion. Was he getting impatient with her for taking so much time to decide?

She slid her shaking fingers into the crook of his arm and let him lead her from her room and down the brick staircase. He began a slow promenade on the path surrounding the Queen's Court.

When they rounded the first corner, she gathered her courage. Last time she'd asked about his dead wife, he'd flown into a rage and hit her. Would he do it again? "What was your wife's name?"

His muscles stiffened beneath her hand. His dark eyes smoldered while his hands clenched into fists. She cringed.

Would he still hurt her, even though he was courting her?

His chest heaved in and out in a long breath. "Clarisse. Her name was Clarisse."

Renna blinked. He'd controlled his rage. Was he doing it to convince her to marry him or was she having a good influence on him? She forced herself to smile. "That's a very pretty name. She sounds like she was quite the lady."

He meandered along the bluestone path, and his eyes stared into the distance. Glimmers of something—longing, perhaps even love—flitted in his dark eyes.

Respen had killed so many people. He'd destroyed so much of Acktar. Yet he had loved, once.

Had this Clarisse loved him too? Had she understood what he'd become as she lay dying? Was the bitterness of her loss enough to turn Respen's love into such hatred? Or had his hatred always lingered there, hidden below the surface of her love for him?

The answers felt important, but how did she go about getting them? She needed to understand this man who'd taken so much from her. Was it possible to reconcile the image of him as a loving husband with the man who'd manipulated fears and weaknesses to turn boys like Leith into killers?

Respen's arm tightened beneath her hand, trapping her wrist between his elbow and ribs. She held her breath as he strode forward, eyes focused somewhere in the past. "She promised everything would be all right. She promised happiness if we followed the rules." His voice dropped into a growl. "But it didn't get her anywhere, did it?"

A chill drifted down Renna's spine. She could picture the young lady Clarisse encouraging her husband to attend church, to hold family devotions, to pray before meals. He'd do it to please her. The more he threw himself into the outward trappings of Christianity, the happier she'd become. Her happiness made him happy, but it was a false happiness, a happiness easily ripped away with her death.

Would Respen do the same thing if she agreed to marry him? Would he stop his persecution of Christians, perhaps even support the rebuilding of the churches, to make her happy?

Renna could stop the persecution like Esther did in the Bible. Surely it was the right thing to do.

If only she didn't have to marry Respen to do it. She willed her stomach to stay where it belonged. How could she even think about marrying Respen? And giving up on Leith?

Martyn stepped in front of them and thumped his right fist over his heart. "My king." He glanced at Renna before he fixed his eyes on Respen. "Fourth Blade Crossley and Sixth Blade Daas have returned."

"And?" Respen's gaze hardened. No trace of the softer, reminiscent man remained.

Martyn's eyes darted toward Renna once again. She shifted. She would've returned to her room, if Respen's grip on her arm hadn't remained so tight.

Respen tugged her closer. "I want her to hear this report."

Renna's heart crumbled. If Respen wanted her to hear, then he suspected the news was about Leith, and that kind of report couldn't be good.

Martyn cleared his throat. "Torren split from the Resistance group Shadrach Alistair is leading into the Sheered Rock Hills. Seventh Blade Kent and Tenth Blade Harding are still trailing them. Torren headed into the Waste."

Renna gasped. People only ventured into the Waste if they wanted to die.

Martyn ignored her. His fingers clenched and unclenched. "Sixth Blade Daas remained outside the Waste in case Torren doubled back while the First and Fourth Blades trailed him until Craven was bitten by a rattlesnake. He ordered Crossley to turn around before both of them died. Crossley and Daas waited for Torren to leave the Waste, but he never did. Crossley assumes that both First Blade Craven and Leith Torren perished."

Renna collapsed. Respen released his grip on her hand and let her tumble to the ground. She landed hard on the bluestone path, her knees and palms stinging. Leith hadn't survived. He'd died some horrible death in that forsaken place. No one but God even knew where his body lay.

"He assumes?" Respen's voice rumbled. "I need proof, not assumptions. Torren has tricked us too many times."

Martyn flinched. "I believe, Your Majesty, that it'd be a waste of time and effort. If Torren is dead, it wouldn't be worth sending Crossley and risk losing him to the Waste. If he's alive, the rain washed away his trail. It already washed away Shadrach Alistair's trail and prevented the Fourth and Sixth Blades from attempting to rejoin the Seventh and Tenth Blades."

Renna studied Martyn's face. Did he believe Leith was dead? The glance he sent her way held pain. His shoulders slumped.

Agony lanced through Renna's chest. If Martyn believed Leith was dead, then what hope did she have?

Respen glared at Martyn. He lashed out and grabbed Martyn's chin. The king bent his head close to Martyn. "I will listen to your counsel, my new First Blade, but tread carefully. I expect you to be an improvement over my last two First Blades."

Renna huddled on the ground. Was this what Leith had endured during his time as the First Blade? Threats. Bruises. Constant terror.

Respen flung Martyn away from him. Martyn stumbled, clutching his jaw as if the king's fingers had punched holes in his skin. Regaining his balance, Martyn saluted and strolled away at a clip that would've been a run if he'd been less disciplined.

When Respen turned to her, his eyes still burned. She gripped her skirts and tried to stop shaking. Her chest ached with emptiness, as if Martyn's words had ripped her heart out and scattered it to the breeze.

Respen's jaw tightened. He yanked her up by her shoulder and shook her. "You still love that mongrel. After all he did to your family."

She gripped his arm. Pain shot through her shoulder and neck. "You personally killed my uncle and ordered the deaths of my entire family. All Leith did was keep my parents' guards from saving them."

"And slit your cousin Keevan's throat." Respen's growl hissed across her face.

She froze. She'd known Leith must've killed one of her cousins, but she'd never asked him about it. Once she'd gotten to know him and had forgiven him for the deaths of her parents, it had seemed best to leave the past in the past.

"It was his sixth mark. He slipped into your cousin's room that night, held his hand over his mouth, and cut his throat. Your cousin didn't even have a chance to fight back." Respen leaned closer until his long, angular nose nearly brushed Renna's. "Is that the kind of man you thought he was? He might claim he changed, but I have seen him with his hands drenched in your cousin's blood."

Chills skittered across her skin. She couldn't meet his gaze and instead focused on his pointed beard. If only Leith was here. Then she could meet his green eyes, read the hurt and repentance, and banish Respen's lies.

But Leith was dead, his body abandoned to the crows.

A tear slid down her face and curled onto her chin. She swiped at it. She couldn't break in front of Respen. He'd revel too much in her pain.

Respen's lips curled. "Return to your room. I'm done walking."

Gripping her skirts, she hurried across the lawn and up the brick staircase as quickly as her healing leg allowed. She didn't stop until she slammed the door to her room behind her and leaned against it.

Leith was dead. The pain squeezed her chest and throat until she might crumble with the force of it. He wasn't supposed to die. He was supposed to escape with Brandi. Her sacrifice should've saved both of them.

Was this what she'd been waiting for? Was this God's answer to her patience? She pressed her palms to her eyes and slid to the floor. Hot tears trickled down her nose.

Why had he died? He'd fought so hard to gain his freedom from the Blades. Yet he never got a chance to live it.

She rocked, her sobs rising so hard and fast in her throat she choked on her tears. Over the past four and a half years, she'd cried these sobs too many times. The tears of loss, the final tearing. Yet this time, she had no one to hold her tight. Her parents were gone. Uncle Abel. Aunt Mara. Leith. Even Brandi was far away.

She couldn't lose anyone else. Too many people in

Acktar had already lost so many loved ones. She'd be selfish to do nothing when she could save them from this pain.

Tomorrow, once Respen calmed down, she'd tell him.

She was going to say yes. She was going to marry King Respen.

17

Brandi sat up at the babble of voices near the entrance to the cave. A guard rushed in and waved back the way he'd come. In the broad space, his hushed voiced echoed enough that Brandi caught the words "horse" and "Blade."

She reached for the knife strapped at her waist. Was the other Blade lurking outside of their cave? He'd been wounded, but no one knew how badly. Was he still hunting her?

Shad gathered a few of the guards and led them outside. Brandi stood and slipped from the cave entrance. If the Blade attacked the cave and got past Shad and the other guards, she'd face him herself. No one else would get accidentally killed because she was mistaken for Brandi.

Jamie appeared at her side and grabbed her arm. "What do you think you're doing?"

"That maid was killed because the Blade thought she was me." Brandi yanked her arm free. Jamie should know better than to impede a girl while she's preparing to fight. "I won't let that happen again."

A commotion startled a flock of sparrows to her left.

She drew the knife and faced the trees.

Was she willing to kill again? She squeezed the hilt tighter. Maybe, maybe not, but she wasn't going to run. Whatever happened, she'd face it with as much bravery as she could muster.

Shad's voice filtered through the branches a moment before he and another guard pushed through the brush, leading a horse. Dust covered the horse's dark blue-grey fur. His head sagged, his mane matted.

Blizzard.

"Leith?" Brandi stumbled forward, shoving her knife into its sheath.

The dusty shape hunched on Blizzard's back moved. Leith's green eyes peered from a gaunt and sun-blistered face. Dust covered his hair so thickly it appeared grey instead of black. His mouth cracked into a smile. "Brandi."

She hurried to them as Leith slid from Blizzard's back. His knees buckled, and he would've fallen to the ground if Shad hadn't caught him.

"Steady there." Shad looped one of Leith's arms over his shoulders. "Let's get you inside before you pass out."

Brandi snagged his other arm. "Ugh. You smell like you jumped in a river of sweat and dead animals."

"No bath. Sorry."

While Jamie grabbed Blizzard's halter, Brandi wrapped her arm around Leith's waist to steady him. His spine jabbed through his skin like a row of knives. Leith wasn't supposed to be thin and weak. He was the strong one, wasn't he? "When did you last eat?"

He tipped his head toward the sky and closed his eyes. "Two days? Three? Not sure. I ran out of food. Too thirsty to eat much."

She glanced at Leith's knives, then over to Shad's

bow. Shad and Jolene had kept them fed with fresh meat as they traveled, but Leith didn't have a bow. He couldn't even throw his knives. Short of grabbing a rabbit with his bare hands, he had no way of foraging for food himself, at least nothing that could be done while on the run.

By the look of him and Blizzard, he hadn't hung around in one spot long enough to set up snares. Had he even slept the entire time he'd been gone? The purple lines below his eyes and the exhausted sag to his body said he hadn't.

She and Shad helped Leith into the cave and over to an unoccupied nook next to one of the boulders. After giving Blizzard's reins to a guard, Jamie spread out his own bedroll. He slipped beside Brandi and eased Leith's arm from her shoulders. "Do you think you could scrounge up some of that stew we had earlier?"

Brandi nodded and dashed across the cave toward the fire they'd built. A covered pot huddled on one of the stones that contained the fire. Cracking it open, she spotted a thin layer of leftovers coating the bottom. She reached for the pot and sighed. She'd forgotten a bowl to put it in.

After she placed the cast-iron pot into the coals to reheat the stew, she raced across the cave and dug out her bowl and spoon. Returning to the fire, she grabbed the thick towel hung on a nearby rock, grabbed the pot's handle, and heaved it out of the fire.

When she returned to Leith's side with the bowl of stew, he leaned against the boulder, eyes closed. If he hadn't been talking, she would've assumed he was asleep. Shad rested a shoulder against the wall of the cave, arms crossed, as he listened to whatever Leith was telling him.

As she drew closer, Leith stopped talking and opened

his eyes. A smile creased his face as she handed him the bowl. "Thanks."

She sat down facing him and eyed his thin fingers. His skin outlined each bone and tendon as he folded his hands and prayed. Brandi fidgeted as his silent prayer continued for at least a minute. Of course, he needed to pray, but did he have to take so long? If he prayed too long, he might pass out from hunger or exhaustion before he had a chance to eat anything.

Finally he opened his eyes and picked up the spoon. He popped a bite of stew into his mouth, closed his eyes, and chewed slowly.

After he'd finished half the bowl, he glanced up at them. "What happened while I was gone? Did you get here all right?"

Shad kicked at a loose stone. "The Blades caught up with us before we reached the cave. One of the maids was killed before we wounded one of the Blades and killed the other."

Brandi flinched and stared at the ground. Hopefully Leith wouldn't ask for details. A part of her still ached at the feel of her knife plunging into that Blade and his agonized gasps as he took a day to die. She shivered and shoved the memories into the dark corner with all her other ignored memories. What would Leith think if he learned what she'd done?

When she looked up, she caught Jamie staring at her. She scowled. She didn't need him tattling on her now.

"I don't know if the wounded Blade is still following us." Shad waved his fingers toward the light streaming through the cave entrance. "I haven't seen him."

"He's still there." Leith leaned his head against the boulder. "I'll deal with him after I've rested."

Brandi rubbed her arms as another shiver stole across her skin. What was Leith planning to do? If she'd learned anything about the Blades, it was that they carried out their orders or died trying.

18

When Leith woke, he felt better than he had in days. When was the last time he'd been able to sleep until he was rested?

He pushed himself up and dragged a hand through his hair. A cloud of dust puffed, and his hand came away gritty.

Shad plopped into the dirt across from him. "About time you woke up."

"How long have I been asleep?" Leith glanced around the cave. Lady Alistair talked quietly to Lydia. The four Blade trainees huddled in a group while Lady Lorraine stood near the entrance as if standing guard. Leith didn't see Brandi or Jamie, though his view of much of the cave was blocked by a couple of large boulders. Daylight still streamed through the cave entrance, so he couldn't have slept that long.

Shad grinned at him. "The rest of yesterday and all last night."

Leith grimaced and swiped his gritty hand on his even grittier clothes. Dust billowed, covering the blanket Jamie had loaned him yesterday. "I think this blanket will need a wash."

"I'm not sure a wash would help. It might have to be burned." Shad schooled his expression into a too-serious frown. "You look and smell like something no decent scavenger would eat."

Leith didn't try to find a comeback for that one. He leaned his head against the boulder. "I came close to being crow bait there in the Waste. If that rain hadn't come through when it did, I wouldn't have made it."

"What's it like in the Waste?"

Leith ran his tongue around his mouth, still tasting the endless dust. "You've never seen dry and dead until you've seen the Waste, not even during mid-summer." He trailed off. How could he even put the Waste into words? "Not a place I want to face again."

"I'm glad you made it." Lines dug into the skin around Shad's eyes.

"Me too." What if he'd died? Respen would no longer have any reason to keep her alive. Leith would've failed in his many promises to keep her safe. He bowed his head. "One of the Blades hunting me didn't."

"And one of the Blades trailing us was killed." Shad held out a knife hilt first to Leith. "He didn't die easily. He was stabbed in the stomach."

Leith took it and turned the knife over in his hands. The initials *FK* swirled on the hilt. Farsin Kent. A quiet Blade, better at assassinations of helpless victims than actual combat. Still, Leith wouldn't wish that kind of death on anyone.

Shad clapped Leith on the shoulder. "As soon as you're ready, we need to get moving. We've delayed here long enough."

Leith bowed his head. "Understood." He had to take care of the last Blade following them before he tracked them all the way to Eagle Heights.

Jolene eased onto the ground next to Shad and held out a plate to Leith. "Shad figured you'd be hungry."

Shad grinned, and he and Jolene shared a look, like they were silently chuckling at a humorous secret. "I've been told food is rather essential."

Leith took the plate. His mouth watered with the gamey smell of roasted venison though his shriveled stomach knotted at the sight of so much food.

After eating half the slice of venison, Leith hiked to a creek and scrubbed the Waste from his skin. He dressed in his clean, black clothes and left the clothes he'd worn into the Waste where they lay. They were beyond saving.

Strapping on all his knives, he returned to the cave, grabbed his pack with his medical supplies, and retrieved the knives that had belonged to First Blade Craven and Seventh Blade Kent.

Shad reached for his bow, but Leith waved at him to stay where he was. "Best if I do this alone."

"You sure?" Shad crossed his arms. "That Blade is hunting you, after all."

"Based on the way he and Kent failed when they attacked you, he's probably one of the younger Blades. He won't attack me, not on his own." Leith hefted his pack of medical supplies over his shoulder. Which Blade was tracking them? Blane Altin? Ranson Harding? Would one of them listen to Leith given the chance? "I won't be gone long."

He slipped into the brush surrounding the cave and studied the landscape. The Blade couldn't be hiding close to the cave. Shad and his hunting parties would've stumbled on him. But he'd be someplace where he could keep the cave's entrance in sight.

Somewhere like that brushy cliff to their west. Leith eased into the dense spruce cover. He circled up and over the ridge above the cave, sticking to the shadows.

Half way, Leith had to crouch behind a tree for several minutes to catch his breath. His legs already trembled even though he hadn't hiked that far. He leaned his head against the tree's trunk. So weak. He'd better hope the Blade didn't attack him because he didn't have the strength for a fight at the moment. He prayed for strength as he forced himself back to his feet and kept going.

Thirty minutes and two breaks later, he crawled on his stomach and peered over a boulder. A black shape lay under a scrub cedar, eyes glued to the cave entrance below and to his left. Leith stalked around the boulder, easing each foot onto the pebbly ground. He came at the Blade from the right. The Blade's thatch of brown hair caught the sunlight. Ranson Harding.

Good. Leith could handle Harding. Perhaps even get a chance to help him.

Two yards away, Leith leaned his shoulder against a tree. "You should take the time to watch your surroundings, Harding. You never know who might sneak up on you."

The Blade jerked, winced, and scrambled to his feet. One hand pressed to a brown-stained tear in his shirt while the other dropped to the knife strapped to his belt. Leith rested a hand on one of his own knives. "You don't want to fight me."

Harding hesitated. Less than a year ago, Leith had been the Third Blade and Harding only the Nineteenth Blade. He was now the Eighth Blade but inherited rank didn't give him the skills to face Leith.

Harding's grip tightened on his knife's hilt. "What do

you want?" His voice cracked.

Leith moved his hand away from his knife and held up the medical kit and his canteen. "I'm here to make sure you stop following these people and to tend your wound."

Fresh blood stained Harding's shirt under his hand, but he shook his head, drew his knife, and pointed it at Leith. "No. Why should I trust you? You've probably come to kill me."

"Ranson." Leith switched to Harding's first name. "You know me better than that. I know you do. I trained you, but I was never cruel the way Vane was."

Ranson swayed, but his knife remained steady.

What had Leith ever done to make Ranson fear him like this? Nothing that he could remember, but perhaps it wasn't Leith Ranson feared. Respen and the Blades had taught him to expect a knife in the back.

Leith would have to do the unexpected. He slowly drew his knives from the sheaths across his chest and placed them on the ground. While Ranson still eyed him, he set the rest of his knives down as well.

He stepped forward and held out his hands, palm up. "I know I betrayed Respen, and I have betrayed the Blades. I know you have little reason to trust me. But I promise I'm not going to hurt you. Now place your weapons on the ground."

Ranson's knife wavered, then lowered. He laid it on the ground and added the rest of his knives to the pile.

Leith knelt and opened the medical kit. If Renna was here, she'd do a much better job, but Leith could at least do the basics. Mostly.

Ranson eased into a sitting position across from him and pulled his shirt over his head. A bloody cloth wrapped around his torso over his ribs. He tugged the bandage free, revealing a gash along his lowest rib for about six inches, deep enough for Leith to catch a glimpse of white bone in the red blood.

Leith grimaced. That wound needed stitches. He could do it, but it wouldn't be neat and tidy the way Renna's stitches would've been. But, he wouldn't ask Ranson to cauterize the wound.

Ranson shifted and stared at his wound. "I know I should've stitched it. I tried, but..."

"It's not so easy on yourself." Leith tugged out the small flask of alcohol in the medical kit. "I need you to lie down."

Ranson hesitated. "Why are you helping me? You should be glad I'm injured. You should kill me. I hunted you and hunted your friends."

Leith weighed the flask in his hand. "Last winter when I was hurt, Renna helped me when it would've been easier to let me die. She and Brandi taught me about grace and forgiveness. When I returned to Nalgar Castle, I failed to tell you and Blane and Martyn and any of the other Blades who would listen. So I'm showing you now by helping you as Renna once helped me."

Ranson studied his face for several minutes before he lay down with one arm resting behind his head.

Leith dumped some of the alcohol over Ranson's wound. Ranson flinched. He pressed his mouth shut, though a moan still caught in his throat. Leith gritted his teeth. How did Renna manage to stay so calm while tending others' wounds? Leith would rather take the wounds himself than have to watch someone else suffer.

After cleaning the wound, Leith threaded the needle with silk thread. "Perhaps it'd be better if you came down to the cave. I'm sure Lady Lorraine or Lady Alistair or Lydia could do a much better job at this."

Ranson's eyes widened as he shook his head. "No. They wouldn't want me down there. Not after Kent killed one of the girls. They'd kill me."

"No, they wouldn't. Not once I explained." Leith met Ranson's gaze. "Come with us. You could escape slavery to Respen. You wouldn't have to kill anymore."

"And be hunted, like you are?" Ranson shook his head, his brown hair thrashing against his skull.

"I'm free from Respen's orders. I don't have to kill to keep him from killing me." Leith hurt with the fear he saw in Ranson's eyes. Only God could fill that emptiness. "I don't fear Respen. God is more powerful."

Ranson stared at him. His gaze contained the same fear that had kept Leith loyal and obedient to King Respen through the bloodshed of thirty-five of his marks.

His gaze dropped from Leith's. "I can't."

Leith hung his head. Ranson couldn't shake his loyalty to Respen. He'd rather return as a failed Blade than go with Leith to the Resistance.

Leith stitched Ranson's wound closed as best he could. The jagged stitches were nothing fancy, but they'd hold well enough. He slapped some salve on it and tied on a bandage.

Sitting up, Ranson reached for his shirt and tugged it over his head.

Leith packed the medical kit, stood, and held out a hand to Ranson. "When you return to Nalgar, could you check on Renna? If you get a chance."

"I'll try." Ranson took Leith's hand.

Leith pulled him to his feet. Some of the color had returned to Ranson's face. "If that wound starts bothering you, she'll help you. All you have to do is ask."

"I'll remember. Though, I doubt I'll get anywhere near her. You know how the king is about prisoners." Ranson retreated toward his pile of weapons.

"If you get a chance, tell Blane too." Would Blane Altin be willing to listen? When Leith had trained both Blane and Ranson, those two trainees had formed a friendship as close as the one Leith used to have with Martyn.

Leith pulled two knives from his pile and tossed them to the ground near Ranson. He forced his voice to go hard. "Tell Respen I survived the Waste. Craven didn't. Don't try to follow us. We'll capture you if you do."

Gathering the knives, Ranson gave Leith a nod and hiked down the slope. A few minutes later, he emerged from a stand of trees, mounted on his horse. Leith watched from the bluff as Ranson rode south.

When Ranson reached Nalgar, Respen would know without a doubt that his only means to catch Leith was Renna. He'd tried to send his Blades, but they'd failed and would fail again now that they'd lost Leith's trail. Respen would have no choice but to keep Renna alive as bait.

How was she? Would Ranson find a way to talk to her? If nothing else, he'd be able to reassure her that Leith and Brandi had gotten away.

When Ranson was out of sight, Leith hiked down the slope, nodded at the sentries, and ducked inside the cave. He found Shad brushing his chestnut horse. Leith dug out a brush and rubbed it along Blizzard's ridged spine. Leith grimaced at how thin his horse felt below his hands. Blizzard's fur outlined each of his ribs along his sides. Still, Blizzard paused in munching on the bundle of grass to nibble at the end of Leith's shirt. Leith rubbed the horse's forehead.

"Did you find the Blade tracking us?" Shad smoothed a hand over his horse's glossy fur.

"Yep." Leith ran the brush over Blizzard's fur. "He's returning to Nalgar Castle. I'll keep an eye out, but he's gone for good."

"That'll make traveling easier from here." Shad patted his horse's neck and set the brush aside. "I didn't want to go any farther until the Blade was gone. We don't have that far to go."

Leith's stomach gave a lurch. What would happen once they reached Eagle Heights? Shad trusted him, but would the Resistance leaders? Or would they want to kill him on sight?

If even they didn't like having a Blade in their midst, they couldn't refuse to help Renna. They'd rally for her sake. That's all that really mattered.

Hopefully Renna could hold on for a little longer, and Leith would be able to return with an army to rescue her.

He brushed Blizzard until the last speck of dust from the Waste had been combed out. Blizzard finished his own pile of grass and starting on the pile of the horse next to him. That horse nipped at Blizzard, but Blizzard bared his teeth and flattened his ears. The other horse backed away.

Jamie slipped next to Leith and dumped another armful of grass in front of Blizzard. Leith rested a hand on Jamie's shoulder. "Thank you for looking out for Brandi."

Jamie scuffed his toe in the sand. "I didn't do a very good job."

Leith stopped brushing Blizzard. Something in Jamie's tone sank a stone into his stomach. Did this have something to do with the strange look Jamie and Brandi had shared the night before? Leith had barely been alert, but Brandi hadn't seemed herself. Nor had she spoken to him all morning. He'd assumed she was missing Renna, and probably still angry at Leith for dragging her away, but was there more to it?

Jamie met his gaze. "Brandi's the one who killed Seventh Blade Kent. I tried to stop him, but he knocked me to the ground. I thought he was going to kill me, but he turned to kill Brandi. He thought he could get to her before I had a chance to get to my feet and didn't expect her to use her knife."

Leith hung his head. Brandi had been forced to kill. Leith should've recognized the mixture of guilt and confusion clouding her expression. "How did she know to defend herself? I gave her a knife, but I didn't have time to show her how to use it."

Jamie's boot scuffed through the sand again. "I've been teaching her. She asked me to right after you left."

Leith's head pounded. Brandi—bubbly, carefree Brandi—had blood on her hands. That changed a person. How much would it change her?

He squeezed Jamie's shoulder. "Thanks for telling me. I'll talk to her."

Jamie's shoulders and back hunched. He'd done an admirable job of bearing a man's burden while Leith had been gone, but Leith was here to carry it now. He rested his head against Blizzard's shoulder. If he was strong enough.

19

Brandi hunched in a corner and ate her supper in silence. More venison. Of course. It seems all they had lately. If it wasn't venison, then it was elk or bison, and they really all tasted about the same.

She glanced at Jamie and Leith as they worked their way through their plates of food. In Leith's case, it was his second large plateful.

Once she'd gotten over her relief that Leith was all right, she'd avoided him. Not that it'd done any good. She'd spotted Jamie talking to him earlier. By now, Jamie had probably tattled her secret, and Leith knew exactly who had killed that Blade.

When she finished her supper, she scurried to the corner where a bowl-shaped rock formed a place to wash dishes. As she reached to scrub her plate, Leith appeared beside her. He took her plate and placed it with his to the side. "I have something I'd like to show you."

"But I have to wash my plate." She lunged around him for the dishes.

He hooked an arm around her waist, stopping her. "Trust me. You'll like this."

Shoot. Now he'd done it. What did he want to show her? Guess she'd have to go along to find out. She'd be forever wondering if she didn't.

Leith grabbed a torch, lit it, and led the way to the back of the cave. A black slit cracked the rock, gasping cold air at their faces. Brandi shivered. Shad had warned everyone to stay away from this opening to prevent people from wandering into the depths of the cave and becoming lost. "Do you know where you're going?"

Leith grinned. "I've been here several times. As long as you stick with me, you won't get lost." He stepped into the crack, turning sideways to ease though the opening. Brandi followed right on his heels.

The opening widened until they could walk side by side. The torchlight flickered over the brown, stone walls that rose in undulating rolls on either side of them. Leith remained silent as they hiked down the long tunnel.

Brandi's legs ached from the downward hike by the time the tunnel dumped them into a large cavern. Jumbles of rocks littered the floor while the ceiling rose into darkness above them. The rocks glowed pink, yellow, and green in the wavering torchlight. Brandi craned her neck back and gaped at the colors surrounding her.

The light twinkled in Leith's eyes. "You haven't seen anything yet." He led her on a winding path through the tumbled boulders until they reached a small opening set low in the wall. Leith crouched on his hands and knees and crawled into the opening, inching the torch forward to prevent dropping it.

Brandi scrambled after him. Her buckskin, divided skirt tangled around her legs. If she were a boy, she could wear trousers. They were much more suited to adventures than skirts.

The rock and soil beneath her fingers grew damp, though she couldn't see much besides Leith's silhouette ahead of her. They were still headed down, deeper into the heart of the Hills.

"We're almost there." Leith's voice echoed oddly in the confined space.

She shuffled forward until her fingertips brushed the toes of Leith's boots. The darkness pressed around her. How much rock piled on top of them? She shivered and focused her eyes on the torch bobbing ahead.

Leith scrambled and stood up. His hand reached down, and Brandi grasped it, letting him tug her to her feet. They stood in a round section of the cave. As Leith lifted the torch, the walls sparkled as if covered with fluffy balls of fresh snow.

Leith led her forward. They crunched across the crystals and turned the corner. Brandi gazed upward and gasped.

All around them, the mounds of glittering crystals rose toward a black, vaulted ceiling. Rock poured down the sides in frozen, rock waterfalls. The sparkling crystals grew around the spindly dribbles. The entire cavern flowed and glittered, orange and white, smooth and spiky.

"This is so beautiful." She turned in a slow circle. So much to take in. If she blinked, she might miss part of the otherworldly scenery surrounding her.

Jabbing the torch into the dirt, Leith led her to a rock near the center of the cavern. They both sat and leaned their heads against the rock, staring upward where the light disappeared into the vastness above them. The waterfalls of rock drooled over and through the puffs of white sparkles.

So much beauty so deep below the earth where few

people would ever see it. God had formed each of these crystals, these spindles of rock, in this unseen place. So much attention to detail simply for His own pleasure. She tried to gulp in the majesty of it but couldn't.

"Jamie told me you killed the Seventh Blade." Leith's voice was pitched so low the cavern nearly overwhelmed it.

Brandi shivered and rubbed her arms. "Yes."

"A part of you feels all shaken and scared, but another part of you feels normal, too normal. You worry because you think you should feel more shaken." Leith's eyes remained focused on the vista above them.

He'd described her jittery feelings exactly. Then again, he should know. He'd first killed years ago. She hugged her knees to her chest. "How old were you when you killed someone?"

Leith lifted his right sleeve, exposing the white scars marching in parallel lines down his arm. He touched the first scar, the one cutting across the top of his arm. "I was thirteen, younger than you. Both of the other boys Respen had raised had already killed. I was the only one who hadn't. He told me if I didn't kill my target this time, he'd kill me."

"So you killed someone." Brandi tightened her grip on her knees. She could taste the fear of being backed into a dead end gully and feeling like there was no choice but to come out fighting.

He nodded. "And became a Blade."

She rested her chin on her arms. Would she go down the same path Leith had?

Leith's green eyes focused on her. "If you hadn't killed him, he would've killed you and Jamie. If Jamie had pulled the same move you did, the Seventh Blade would've been expecting it and blocked it. You saved both your lives."

"Then why do I feel so..." Brandi squeezed her eyes shut. What word described the messiness bundled inside her? "Dirty?"

He wrapped an arm around her shoulders and tucked her head against his chest. Brandi fought the tears that came unbidden from that painful part inside her. She shouldn't cry. Not now. Not ever.

"It's all right to cry. It's just the two of us here. No one else will hear you." Leith rubbed her back. Just like Uncle Abel used to.

Her tears surged into a tide she couldn't hold back. Uncle Abel was gone. Aunt Mara. Renna. Leith was here right now, but he'd leave her eventually to go rescue Renna. He wasn't about to let her go along.

Even God felt far away. She'd never felt this distant from God before. When her parents died, Uncle Abel told her they were with Jesus in Heaven, so she set out to learn all she could. When she missed her parents, she paged through the Bible they'd given her and think about them walking the golden streets, stopping to talk with Daniel or David or one of the angels. The Bible stories were so precious because they told her about the people her parents now knew.

For some reason, it wasn't working this time. Respen had burned her Bible, and she'd lost whatever grip she'd had on her faith since childhood. Would she ever grasp it again? Faith and trust were as slippery as the fish she'd tried to catch with her fingers once. No matter how quickly she pinched her fingers, the fish always slid through, only a brief brush of scales tingling her skin.

Sobs shook her body and tore out her throat. She pressed her face against Leith's shoulder and curled her fingers into the soft fabric of his shirt. Tears burned her eyes and cheeks, but she couldn't stop them. Everything inside her poured out through her tears. Would she even have anything left when she finished?

The rush of tears ended. She tried a few more sobs, just to make sure she'd gotten everything out. When her eyes didn't prickle, she let out one last shaky breath and went quiet. She was empty, but empty was better than the pain of before.

She sniffed and scrubbed her running nose on her sleeve. After all the tears she'd shed, her eyes itched as if they'd been rubbed with dust.

"Do you know any Bible stories about people who had to fight?" Leith adjusted his arm around her back. "I don't remember any, but I still have a bunch of the Bible to read yet."

She scowled at his shirt. Did she have to think about Bible stories right now? They reminded her too much of the naively trusting girl she'd been a few months ago.

But if Leith wanted a Bible story, she couldn't refuse to tell him one.

"Well, I guess David was a fighter." Brandi's nose still drooled. She swiped at it again. "He was just a shepherd when the prophet Samuel told him he'd be king someday. When his country was in trouble, he defeated a giant with only a sling and a river pebble."

"A giant, really?" Leith's voice held something like a laugh.

"Yep. A giant. After he defeated the giant, all the people loved him. The king got jealous and tried to kill him. David had to go on the run for a few years until the other king died and David became king. He reigned for a long time and fought a lot of battles."

David was a warrior. The thought curled through her.

David fought. He killed in battle. And he was still loved by God. Another part of the story stabbed at her. "But he wasn't allowed to build God's house because he had too much blood on his hands."

"Killing always has consequences, even when you do it do defend someone else." Leith's sigh whooshed through his chest before she felt it on her hair. "What else does the Bible say about David?"

Chewing on her upper lip, she sorted through her memories. She could hear her father, his voice soft and rumbly as he perched on the edge of her bed telling her Bible stories. Relaxed and safe, she'd rarely stayed awake long enough to hear the ending. But she hazily remembered the line her father had used to end his stories about David. "David was a man after God's own heart."

She let the words filter through her, smoothing, healing. David wasn't perfect. He had the blood of battles on his hands. He'd struggled with fear and doubt and sin, but God still called him a man after His own heart.

Was she a girl after God's own heart? Probably not. Surely someone after God's own heart would feel close to God all the time. Not like she had a gaping hole in her heart where her faith used to be.

She hugged Leith and sat up. "Thanks, Leith."

He tweaked her nose and pushed himself upright. "Just returning the favor. Now let's get back to the others before Shad sends out a search party."

As they headed from the sparkling cavern, Brandi picked up a piece of the crystal-like rock and dropped it in her pocket.

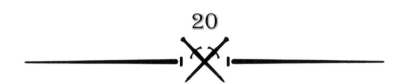

20

Renna hid her trembling hands under the table. During the salad course, she'd been working up the courage to tell Respen her decision. All she'd managed to do was tremble harder and lose her appetite.

Could he see the red, itchiness of her eyes? She'd cried herself to sleep and woke up to more tears. She resisted the urge to rub them yet again.

She couldn't do this. She couldn't marry Respen. Glancing around the room, she took in the plush surroundings, the ornate window moldings, the door to the bedchamber. This would be her home for the rest of her life. As much as she'd begun to understand Respen, and even pity him, she didn't love him.

She didn't have a choice. To save the Christians of Acktar from continued persecution, she had to marry King Respen.

Respen eyed her and her full plate. "What has you so agitated? Are you still mourning that pathetic Leith Torren?" A sneer twisted his mouth and beard.

Her heart shuddered. How could just hearing his name hurt so much? But she shook her head. Her grief for Leith was something too tender to be trampled by Respen.

Respen leaned back in his chair, one arm stretched in front of him to tap on the tabletop. "Something else has you agitated. My Blade is treating you respectfully. He would not dare do anything else. It cannot be your accommodations. You have the best room in Nalgar Castle apart from mine." His fingers halted. A smile slipped onto his face. "You have reconsidered my offer."

As she drew in a deep breath, she prayed for courage. Now was not the time to fall into her usual cowardice. Dragging her chin up, she met Respen's eyes. "Yes, I have. And I've..." She swallowed and cleared her throat. "I've decided to marry you."

"Excellent." His lips parted into a broader smile, his teeth flashing. "I will make the arrangements at once."

"Wait!" She wasn't prepared to marry him right now. She needed time. "I can't get married right away. I'll need two months at least."

He bolted forward in his seat, his elbows thumping on the table as he leaned toward her. "You still hold out hope. You dare to delay for a chance at rescue."

"No! Nothing like that." Or at least, nothing she could admit to Respen. "Leith is dead." She had to pause and swallow. She couldn't let herself break down now. "Who else would bother rescuing me? I know I'm stuck here."

That was true enough. Shadrach might want to rescue her, but Lord Alistair wouldn't allow him to do something so reckless. They had bigger concerns than her to worry about, like Respen's army, wherever it was at the moment.

His fingers drummed against the tabletop. "Then what is the problem?"

"A girl's wedding is special. I agreed to marry you,

and I want to do this right. I don't want to be hustled into the chapel wearing a dress I hurriedly grabbed from my wardrobe. I want a real wedding dress with a well-planned, beautiful wedding." If she wasn't going to marry the kind of man she'd always dreamed about, she should at least get the dream wedding. It might make it almost bearable. "Besides, you're marrying your queen. You can't do this in a rushed fashion either."

His gaze sharpened. "You are correct. A rushed wedding would look like I was forcing you to marry me. We want a joyous wedding that will prove you are my bride willingly. No one must question my right to rule."

"No, of course not." Renna struggled to keep the note of sarcasm buried deep inside her. This wasn't about her. It was about Respen quelling dissent to his reign.

"All right, my darling."

Her skin crawled at the suggestive tone slithering through his voice. His darling. When they married, she'd be his wife until one of them died. How would she survive years of marriage to Respen?

Her breathing snagged in her throat. She dug her fingernails into her palms and focused on that point of pain. She'd survive. She had to.

"You will have your wedding." Respen relaxed in his chair. "But I am not willing to wait two months. Two weeks should suffice."

Two weeks. Her throat closed. She needed more time than that. "A month. Please."

"Too long. The Resistance is too tiresome to be put off."

"Then three weeks, please." She twisted her fingers together. If she had to, she'd get onto her knees and beg. "My birthday is in three weeks. That's when I turn 18.

It'd be improper to marry me before then. Some might accuse you of marrying a child instead of an adult."

Respen scowled at her. "Fine. Three weeks. But you will be ready."

Would she be ready? How could she ever be ready to marry Respen? But she had no choice, not if she wanted to spare others in Acktar the same pain she'd experienced.

She lifted her chin. Leith once told her Respen exploited weakness. If she showed weakness now, Respen would exploit it for their entire marriage.

He matched her gaze, both eyebrows raised as he considered her. She didn't look away. After a long minute, something sparked in Respen's eyes.

Something like respect.

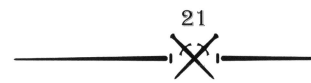

21

The monolithic cliff reared above them in a daunting expanse of grey rock. After three days of hard riding, they were deeper in the Sheered Rock Hills than Leith had ever ventured. He craned his neck upward and gaped at the mountain in front of them. "This is where the Resistance has been hiding?"

Shad halted his horse next to Blizzard. "Yep. Quite the sight, isn't it? Even if Respen found its location and managed to hike his army through the miles of rough country, it'd be nearly impossible to climb the mountain and take the fortifications."

"I guess that explains the name Eagle Heights. I should've realized, with a name like that, it wasn't some pine grove up a canyon." Leith studied the natural fortress in front of him. What other surprises would Eagle Heights hold?

Shad eyed him. "Are you sure you don't want to change?"

Leith glanced at his black clothing and knives. Even if he wanted to, he'd left his prairie tan clothes behind after he'd ruined them in the Waste. He tightened his grip on Blizzard's reins. "Yes. I'm done with lies."

He was tired of pretending to be something other than what he was. As a Blade under King Respen, he'd had to pretend he was nothing but darkness. As the peasant farmer working at Walden, he'd had to pretend he'd never been a Blade. He was done with all the pretending. When he rode into Eagle Heights, he'd be nothing more and nothing less than Leith Torren, the Blade God had rescued from darkness and made new in His grace.

If he had to face the consequences of that truth, then so be it.

"All right. I'll do my best to make sure you don't get killed on sight." Shad rested his hand on his sword's hilt, as if expecting a fight.

Leith's chest tightened. Would the Resistance allow him in? Or would they turn him away?

Nudging his horse, Shad led the way past the main escarpment to a gravel-strewn path winding between spiky pines. Leith's back itched with the feeling that an arrow might strike him at any moment. He peeked over his shoulder at Brandi and Jamie trailing behind him, leaning low over their horses' necks.

Blizzard surged up a steep section of the trail. Leith leaned forward in the saddle, shifting his weight onto Blizzard's front quarters to help him power up the slope. As they topped the rise, he eased his horse next to Shad. Ahead of them, two orange-gray towers of rock guarded a slim section of the trail.

"Halt and state your business."

Shad urged his horse two strides forward. "I'm Shadrach Alistair of Walden. I bring with me refugees seeking safety with the Resistance."

A man stepped into view on a ledge, carrying a bow with an arrow already nocked. "If you are Lord Shadrach, why do you travel with a Blade?"

Leith held still, pinning his eyes to the arrow aimed at his chest. Above him, something rustled the upper branches of the trees. Probably other guards also pointing arrows at him. If he sneezed wrong, he'd end up dead before Shad had a chance to explain.

Shad angled his horse between Leith and the bowman on the ledge. "As the Leader was informed on my last journey here, this Blade has defected from Respen and proved an invaluable aid for the Resistance. Respen has learned of his defection, and he seeks refuge with the Resistance as my father promised he'd receive."

The man disappeared from the ledge. When he returned, he kept the arrow nocked on the string, though it was no longer drawn taut. "Please wait while my runner confirms your claims."

Leith made sure both of his hands rested in view on his saddlehorn. The muscles in his back cramped from remaining so still and tense, but he didn't dare stretch out the kinks.

A man stepped beside the bowman and spoke in his ear. The bowman nodded and lowered his bow. "You've been cleared to enter. Watch Six and Seven, escort them into Base."

A thick rope uncoiled and thumped to the ground a few yards away from Leith. A second rope plummeted from a tree a little way to Shad's left. Two men slid down the ropes, leather gloves protecting their hands from rope burn. Both wore hardened leather vests and greaves. Quivers of arrows peeked over their right shoulders while their bows rested along their backs.

Leith read confidence in the bounce of their strides. These men knew their own ability to handle trouble when it came their way.

One of the men waved at them. "Dismount."

Shad called the order back to the rest of their party and swung off his horse. Leith gripped the saddlehorn and eased himself to the ground. The second of the leather-clad men not-so-subtly positioned himself near Leith, a hand on his dagger.

When everyone was dismounted and arranged in an orderly line, the guard led the way into the tight opening through the rocks. The second guard stayed near Leith.

They filed into the gap between the towering pillars of stone, walking in pairs due to the narrow pinch of the crevice. After a few turns, the crevice spilled into a broad open space on the top of the mountain. Spires of rock ringed the clearing like the battlemented walls of a castle. Fractures in the stone gaped into canyons flowing along the mountain's sides and top. All around the clearing and into the canyons, wooden cabins provided shelter for the hundreds of people that bustled in every direction.

At the far end of the clearing, a cabin—more like a manor house constructed of logs—leaned against the largest escarpment. Their escort halted in front of it. A tall, grey-haired man stepped out the door and eyed their group. Leith resisted the urge to hide behind Blizzard.

"Welcome to Eagle Heights. I'm General Uriah Stewart." The man's deep voice boomed against the rocks surrounding them. He pointed at Leith and Shad. "The Leader wants to see you two."

He led them into the large cabin's dark entry hall,

halted, and eyed Leith. "Leave your weapons here."

Shad stepped between Leith and General Stewart. "I can vouch for him. He's no more a threat to the Leader than I am."

General Stewart's hard, blank expression didn't change. "He's a Blade."

"*Was* a Blade. He isn't anymore." Shad crossed his arms and widened his stance.

"It's fine." Leith unbuckled the knives crossing his chest and handed them to Shad. "Take care of these for me."

Shad nodded and took them. At least if Shad had them, they weren't going to mysteriously disappear. Leith still needed his knives to rescue Renna.

This was the price he paid for being fully truthful about who he was. To some, like General Stewart, there was no such thing as a former Blade.

If Leith somehow managed to survive the coming war, would he always face this kind of suspicion? Would he never truly be free of his past or worthy to stand before others without someone else vouching for his character?

General Stewart shifted. A small movement, but it shouted impatience.

Leith surrendered the rest of his knives to Shad. When his last boot knife had been relinquished, General Stewart spun on his heel and knocked on a door to their left.

"Come in." A raspy voice called through the thick door.

General Stewart pushed the door open and waved Leith and Shad inside.

Shad strode into the room with Leith on his heels. General Stewart followed and planted himself with his back to the door, one hand inches from his sword.

Across the long room, a lone man stood with his back to them. His broad shoulders appeared young and strong while his blond hair had been cropped short. Candles glowed on stone pedestals at the far end of the room, but most of the space remained clad in darkness.

Leith lingered in the shadows as Shad strolled into the center of the room, gripped Leith's bundle of weapons under one arm, and bowed. "Your Highness."

"Welcome, Lord Shadrach. What news do you bring of Acktar?" The Leader's tenor voice rasped in his throat, as if it was painful for him to speak.

"Respen's armies have attacked Walden. My father and a few volunteers were besieged last time we knew." Shad's voice remained steady. "Lady Rennelda remains a prisoner in Nalgar Castle, but Lady Brandiline was rescued and brought here."

Shad paused and glanced at Leith. Leith tiptoed closer, a weight sinking into his stomach. He sensed something familiar about the Leader, something that spelled danger.

Shad tugged him forward. "The Blade I told you about, the one that defected to our side months ago, has been forced to flee Acktar."

The Leader turned. A long scar sliced across his left cheek, down his neck, and disappeared into the collar of his shirt.

The weight in Leith's stomach turned to ice. It'd been dark like this, moonlight shivering through a paned window, the last time Leith had seen this man, then a boy.

The Leader flinched and jabbed his finger at Leith. "Arrest him."

General Stewart marched farther into the room and drew his sword.

"No, you don't understand." Shad gripped the hilt of his sword and darted between Leith and the Leader. "Leith saved my father's life and the lives of all the nobility still loyal to you. He may have been a Blade but not anymore."

"Shad, don't." Leith laid a hand on Shad's shoulder. "He has reason to arrest me. I'm the Blade who gave him that scar."

Eyes widening, Shad gaped at him and the Leader. The Leader crossed his arms and glared, his gruesome scar shining in the candlelight.

General Stewart stalked closer, his sword pointed at Leith. A younger, more reckless guard would've charged immediately on the Leader's order, but the general had the experience to approach cautiously. Even though Leith was unarmed, he wouldn't risk Leith fighting back and injuring the Leader before he could be subdued.

Leith wasn't going to fight back.

He took one step forward and knelt in front of the Leader. Or, more accurately, Prince Keevan Eirdon, the second son of King Leon and Queen Deirdre. Leith clasped his fist above his heart in a move he'd done hundreds of times before King Respen. "My king."

Prince Keevan's mouth remained in a thin line, his eyes hard and burning. "How many marks do you have, Blade?"

Leith bowed his head. He might be saved by grace in Heaven, but here on earth his marks still carried consequences. He pushed his right sleeve to his shoulder, exposing the scars marching down his arm. "Thirty-seven."

He touched a mark a little way down from his shoulder. "Killing you was my sixth mark, though it seems I was less successful than either Respen or I realized."

And he couldn't be more thankful. One life not on his conscience.

A cold chill prickled along the back of Leith's neck. What would this mean for Renna? She and Brandi weren't the last of the Eirdon line. Renna wasn't the one the Resistance intended to rally behind.

But surely Prince Keevan wouldn't leave Renna at Nalgar Castle, would he?

Prince Keevan gave a sharp nod, then waved at Leith. "General, take him away."

Leith held his hands up as General Stewart tromped behind him. He yanked Leith's hands behind his back. Leith gritted his teeth as a rope grated against his skin.

Shad adjusted the bundle of Leith's weapons, as if he toyed with the idea of tossing them to Leith. "What do you plan to do with him?"

"Hold a trial. I'm sure I'll be able to find a few eyewitnesses to provide testimony."

The chills settled in Leith's chest. A trial couldn't possibly go in his favor. What would happen to Renna if Leith couldn't return?

Shad glared at Prince Keevan. "You can't do that. He could be sentenced to death. He came here seeking mercy. My father promised him sanctuary in good faith."

"Your father had no right to promise for me."

"He had every right." Shad's hands shook with their white-knuckled grip on his sword's hilt and Leith's knives. "You gave him the authority to lead the Resistance in Acktar in your stead. That gives him the authority to make promises in your stead."

General Stewart jerked Leith by his elbow, wrenching his shoulder painfully.

Leith ignored the pain and held his ground. "A trial won't be necessary. I'm guilty. I'll confess everything, all thirty-seven marks. I have nothing I wish to hide."

It'd be painful, admitting five years of missions for Respen. Not all of them were murders, but some led to deaths or imprisonment.

But he was done with lying. Done with hiding. Even if the truth had consequences.

General Stewart dragged Leith from the room.

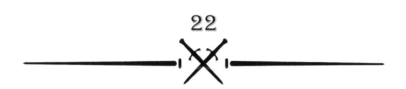

22

Brandi wandered to the big cabin she'd seen Leith and Shad enter. She'd been assigned to share a cabin with Lady Lorraine, Lady Alistair, Jolene, Lydia, and all the rest of the Alistairs. Brandi should've stayed and gotten reacquainted with Abigail Alistair, but Abigail's chatter grated on her.

As Brandi approached, the front door heaved open. That tall man with longish gray hair yanked Leith out the door. Leith's hands were tied behind his back.

What in Acktar was going on? Brandi jumped forward. "Let him go!"

Both of them turned to her. Leith gave her a small smile. "It's all right, Brandi. I'll be fine."

Why had they tied Leith up? Didn't they realize he was a hero? And why wasn't Leith fighting back? "Why are you doing this?"

"Leader's orders." The man hustled Leith away.

Brandi stalked into the big cabin. Whoever this Leader was, he was going to get a piece of her mind. Fists swinging at her side, she marched through the entry and into the first door to her left where she heard raised voices.

Across the darkened room, Shad argued with a blond-haired young man standing near banks of candles. Brandi charged across the room and shoved between them. "How dare you tie Leith up! You let him go!" She swung her fist at him.

Shad lunged, wrapped his arms around her, and dragged her away from the offending young man. "You don't know who this is."

Squirming and wiggling, she shoved at Shad's arms as hard as she could. His arms didn't budge. "I don't care who he is. He had Leith arrested."

The young man turned to her. The light streaked down the scar decorating his cheek and neck. He eyed her, one eyebrow scrunched, the other raised, as if he didn't know what to think.

Shad placed his hands on her upper arms, pinning her arms to her side. "Brandi, this is your cousin Prince Keevan Eirdon. Your Highness, this is Brandiline."

Her cousin was alive? She tried to drag up some memory of him. She remembered his younger brothers, Rorin and Duncan. They'd been nearer to Renna's age and Brandi had done her best to tag along with the three of them whenever her parents visited Nalgar Castle. Prince Keevan and his older brother Aengus were several years older than Renna and far too old to pay attention to their baby cousins, unless it was to pull their hair or tease them.

"It's a pleasure to meet you, Brandiline." Keevan gave her a half-bow. "You look a lot like your mother."

He was trying to get on her good side. Well, it didn't work. Cousin or no, rightful king or no, he'd still arrested Leith. She clenched her fists tighter and glared at him. "Let Leith go. He isn't going to hurt anyone."

A fire sparked in Keevan's eyes. He leaned forward and jabbed at the scar dragging across his face and neck. "Five years ago, he pressed his hand over my mouth, looked me in the eyes, and dragged his knife across my throat. I thought I'd choke on my own blood."

"Leith did that?" Brandi stumbled into Shad. She stared at the horrible scar. Had Leith really done that?

Keevan leaned even closer. "And he helped kill your parents."

She curled over her arms, feeling like Stubborn their mule had accidentally kicked her. Leith had helped kill her parents? He'd been her friend. He'd taken her into the sparkling cavern and let her cry on him. He'd comforted her and acted like a brother to her. All the while he'd carried the guilt of her parents' deaths.

Shad wrapped an arm around her shoulders and pulled her away from Keevan. "That was cruel." After a pause, he added, "Your Highness."

Keevan's shoulders slumped. "I apologize, Brandiline. I didn't mean to take my anger out on you."

She crossed her arms. Maybe Keevan was mistaken. It could've been a different Blade that tried to kill Keevan and helped kill her parents. Leith was probably somewhere else. "I want to talk to Leith."

Keevan nodded. Brandi tapped her foot while he rounded up a guard to take her. After far too many minutes, the guard led her and Shad from the big cabin. She kept her arms crossed and a glare on her face as they hiked across the open space and into one of the canyons twisting through the pillars of rock.

Partway into the canyon, they stopped before a recess in the rock. Three guards paced in front of the opening, as if Leith was a dangerous criminal or something. Their escort talked to the guards a few minutes before waving Brandi to enter.

While Shad remained outside with the guards, Brandi waddled through the rounded hole into a tiny, smooth cave hollowed into the rock. Leith leaned against the far wall, his hands still bound behind his back, one leg bent, the other stretched in front of him.

He glanced up as she entered. "Miss me already?"

She was too brittle to pretend. Plunking onto the stone floor facing him, she stared at her feet and toyed with the hem of her skirt. Now that she was here, did she want to ask him? Once she knew the truth, she'd lose their friendship. She'd never be able to look at him with the same innocent trust again.

Leith went still. When he spoke, his voice was pitched low and gentle. "It's going to be all right. The Leader isn't going to do anything to me. He might want to, but he's too much of a commander not to realize that he needs my skills and my knowledge of the Blades to take back Nalgar Castle and save Renna."

Picking at a thread, she nodded even if that wasn't her concern at the moment. She took a deep breath and forced herself to look at him. "Keevan told me you were the Blade that tried to kill him. That you sneaked into his room and...and..." She hugged her knees to her chest, fighting the shudders coursing down her spine. Leith would tell her Keevan was lying. Surely this was all a mistake.

Leith bowed his head. "I was the Third Blade. I didn't become the Third Blade by refusing to follow Respen's orders. I didn't know anything but darkness. So when Respen ordered me to kill Prince Keevan, I completed my mission."

The words tore at her. Sure, she'd known he'd probably killed a few people, but she'd always believed it had been a kind of self-defense, like how she'd killed that Blade. That was understandable. All fighters had to do it eventually. She hadn't considered that Leith had done something like this.

A part of her begged her tongue not to form the question, but the words popped out anyway. "And my parents? Keevan said you helped killed them."

Leith squeezed his eyes shut and turned his face away. The action stole the last bit of her breath. Everything Keevan had said was true. Leith had helped kill her parents. All this time, he'd pretended to be her friend when he'd really been guilty of her parents' deaths.

She shot to her feet, thunking her head on the cave's ceiling. She needed to get away. Somewhere far away from him.

"Wait." His voice grabbed her. "If you're going to know the truth, you should know all of it."

Fighting to control a heat that prickled in her eyes and shook through her fists, she plopped onto the floor and crossed her arms. She'd listen to what he had to say, then she'd run.

"The First Blade killed your mother. He was supposed to kill you and Renna also, but your aunt and uncle took you from the manor before he could." Leith kept his eyes focused on a patch of floor next to him. "The Second Blade killed your father. I kept your parents' guards from rescuing them."

Brandi clenched her fists. She had such hazy memories of that night. Uncle Abel had been carrying her down the hallway when she woke. There'd been shouting. Her mother had been there, then she'd kissed Brandi's forehead and disappeared behind them. Renna cried while Aunt Mara dragged her down the hallway. Then they'd been outside, running across the prairie, running down the narrow paths in the Spires Canyon, running, running, until Uncle Abel said they could stop.

"I'm so, so sorry, Brandi. So very sorry." Leith's voice cracked, but she couldn't acknowledge the plea. He'd been there that night. He was a part of the shouting and screaming.

"Does Renna know?" Her voice was so hard it sliced at her throat.

"Yes. She asked me that first night in Stetterly while you were tending Blizzard."

Renna knew? And she'd never told her? Renna's fear those weeks while Leith had been stuck in Stetterly healing from an arrow wound finally made sense. Renna had warned her to stay away from Leith, but Brandi hadn't listened. She'd fooled herself into thinking Leith was her friend.

23

Renna scrubbed at the sauce burned onto the bottom of a pan, sharp flakes stabbing under her fingernails. Perhaps if she scrubbed hard enough, she could forget the bustle in the kitchen around her and the ache in her chest. She'd stop thinking. Better yet, stop feeling.

Going numb might be best. Beside her, Martyn seemed to have already mastered it. He stared at the brick wall as if he could see right through it. The drying towel dangled from his fingers as if he'd forgotten where he was. Lucky him.

"My lady." The skinny cook waved one of his bony hands at a table covered with various plates and dishes. "Would you like to approve the dishes for the wedding feast? We have three forms of pheasant and four marinades for the beef for you to choose from."

Her stomach churning, Renna forced herself to approach the table and taste each dish. Another time, the spices might've caused another reaction besides a gag reflex.

A young woman shoved another tray at her. "And the desserts, my lady?"

Renna froze. A pile of maple sugar cookies lay amid the small cakes and candies. Brandi's favorite food, the one she'd wanted Leith to try when he got a chance.

She staggered back from the tray. "I...I need..." She dashed from the kitchen.

Footsteps crunched behind her, but Renna didn't look back as she sprinted across the cobblestone courtyard, through the passageway, and into the Queen's Court.

Pain twinged through her injured leg, and she collapsed onto the grass, gasping breaths between shaking tears. Dirt ground into her palms while grass smeared across the front of her skirt.

Uncle Abel. Aunt Mara. Leith. So many people taken from her. Would it ever end? Even Brandi was far away, hopefully safe at Eagle Heights by now. Would she ever see her again?

Martyn halted a few feet away. He stared at a spot above her head, his hands clasped behind his back.

He was no help. They were both grieving Leith. They should've been some comfort to each other, but no. Martyn had retreated behind cold eyes.

How could she possibly plan her wedding to Respen while mourning for Leith? She might as well stab his memory in the back.

Yet what choice did she have? With Leith dead, Respen had no reason to keep her alive besides his desire to marry her. And if she was going to remain here with no hope of rescue, she should accomplish something worthwhile.

She rubbed the healing bone in her leg and forced the tears back into her chest. The afternoon sun glinted on the gray stones of the castle walls. Respen's banner of black, crossed daggers on a background of blue hung lifeless from the flagpoles jutting from the battlements. The bluestone path around the edge of the Queen's Court shimmered with heat, though the grass and earth beneath Renna's hands remained cool and damp with the water a servant poured onto it each morning.

Marrying Respen was the right thing to do, wasn't it? Then why did it feel so wrong? Perhaps it only felt wrong because she hadn't fully sacrificed herself to the idea yet.

Her emotions were clouding her thinking. That was the problem. She had to stop whining, stop crying, and pull herself together. She'd made her choice. Now she had to face it with all the courage she could muster.

She swiped at her face, drew in a deep breath, and let it out in a few shudders.

Perhaps she could find some healing by talking about Leith. Maybe it'd only make the pain worse, but only one way to find out.

She turned to Martyn. "What was Leith like growing up? How long were the two of you friends?"

Martyn scrubbed a hand through his blond curls. "I met Leith when we were both twelve. He'd already been training under King Respen for three years at that point. Still, he stood up for me. He didn't let Harrison Vane beat me up. Leith was like that. He was always sticking up for the other boys in those days."

"In those days? What changed?" She wrapped her arms around her knees. This was helping, a little.

"There was this one boy. He'd been training for a few years, but he wasn't very good. He just didn't have it in him to be a fighter. Leith helped him when he could." Martyn's square jaw tightened. "When we were thirteen, King Respen was frustrated with Leith. Vane had already killed and so had Hess, even though he'd begun training a year after Leith. A bunch of us were almost ready. One day in training, King Respen handed Leith a knife and told him to kill that boy, or King Respen would kill Leith."

Renna's heart ached. The knowledge of Leith's choice might've sickened her a few months ago, but now all she felt was compassion. In the darkness of Leith's childhood, every choice must've seemed terrible. At least he'd had a few months of peace before...she swallowed and dug her fingers into her palm to stop her tears.

"Something broke in Leith that day. He stopped trying to evade King Respen's orders." Martyn shook his head before he shot a glance in her direction. "Until the day he met you."

"Not me. God." Renna tried to think of a way to explain it to Martyn, but the words jumbled inside her in a disorderly lump.

He snorted. "You still cling to that? After all that happened to you?"

"Yes." She turned her face toward the sun, letting it splash across her face. "I trust *because* of all the things that happened to me."

A few months ago, she wouldn't have said that. But she'd lost everything. She'd been broken. Deep in that dungeon, she'd lost her faith. Only to learn that God wasn't going to let her go even if she let Him go. He wasn't going to forsake her even when she felt forsaken.

It defied all logic and all understanding. That's what made it so precious, so strong.

Even Leith's death couldn't take that away. God had carried her through losing her entire family except for Brandi. He would see her through this too.

Martyn stared at her as if she had lost her mind.

Perhaps she had. But it didn't matter. She had faith. And hope. And Respen wasn't going to take away either of those things no matter how hard he tried.

Boots tromped on the cobbles in the passageway. Martyn stiffened, and his face returned to its blank expression. As the footsteps crunched closer, he thumped his fist across his chest. "My king."

"What is going on, First Blade?"

Renna squared her shoulders, stood, and faced Respen. He glowered at the two of them, a pair of books tucked under his arm. No need for Martyn to get into trouble. "I was in the kitchen arranging the wedding feast, but I needed some air."

"I see." His gaze searched her face. "Why are you smiling?"

She was smiling? She pressed her fingers to her mouth. "I realized today that I have hope. No matter what happens to me, no one can take that away."

"Not even me?"

"Not even you." As much as she wanted to shrink away from his gaze, she gathered her courage and faced him. "You know what I've been through. But God hasn't forsaken me."

Respen dropped his gaze to the grass. "You sound like Clarisse. She spoke about God all the time."

She could hear the note of bitterness in his voice. Had it grated on him all those years ago to pretend Christianity to appease his wife? Would her faith irk him that way? "Clarisse sounds like she was a wonderful person."

He shook himself. "I have something for you." He held out the two books he carried.

She took the books and traced the covers. Uncle Abel and Aunt Mara's Bible. The one with Uncle Abel's neat handwriting in the margins. And her Bible. Vane stole them from Stetterly months ago.

"You're returning these?"

"They are yours, are they not?"

Tears clogged her throat. Perhaps this marriage would work. If Respen would return these Bibles to her, then maybe he'd stop the persecution as he'd promised.

Respen's sharp gaze swept from her dirt-covered palms to the grass stains on her skirt. His mouth curled. "Go make yourself presentable. I have guests arriving. First Blade, see to it that she has no more mishaps between here and her room."

As Respen spun on his heels and stalked away, Martyn took Renna's arm and towed her to the brick staircase. She didn't fight his grip.

Who was coming? They had to be important, so important Respen felt the need to impress them. Who would Respen, King of Acktar, have to impress?

While Martyn waited outside her door, Renna sorted through the dresses in the wardrobe and paused by a deep red dress, a stark contrast to the blue and purple of the rest of the dresses.

She pulled it out and held it against her. Could she pretend enough confidence to pull it off? When she married Respen, she'd be queen. Perhaps it was time to carry herself like one.

After tugging on the dress, she faced the mirror. The bodice hugged her body before sweeping into a flowing skirt of the same rich, floral patterned fabric. Her silver cross necklace rested against the swooping neckline and winked against the bold background.

Renna forced her chin up. She wasn't going to tuck her necklace into hiding once again. Respen had promised he'd stop persecuting her faith. If he was going to keep that promise, he might as well start now.

She swept from her room and held out her arm to Martyn. He gaped at her, blinked, and offered her his arm. Gripping her skirt in one hand, she let Martyn escort her down the corridor and the grand staircase.

As they reached the last few steps, Renna spotted Respen in the center of the Queen's Court conversing with two men. In their silk shirts, fine cotton trousers, and polished boots, they had to be noblemen. That explained Respen's need to impress them. Most likely, they were some of Respen's followers.

While Martyn remained at the bottom of the staircase, Renna held her chin high and glided across the bluestone path to the fountain. Did that look regal enough?

Respen eyes glinted, and a smile spread across his face. He slipped an arm around her, resting his hand against her waist.

She sucked in a breath. Her skin shivered with his touch. It took all her strength not to push his hand away. In a little over two weeks, she'd marry Respen. Somehow, she didn't think it'd be a marriage in name only.

Respen steered her forward. "Lady Faythe, this is Lord Beregern."

The taller of the two noblemen bowed to her. Gray bristled through the blond hair at his temples. When he straightened, his eyes focused on her silver cross necklace. The muscle at the corner of his craggy jaw flexed.

Renna forced herself to smile and give him a half curtsy. Of all the lords in Acktar, Lord Beregern persecuted Christians with the most zeal. More men and women had died in Mountainwood's main square than at Nalgar Castle.

"And this is Lord Norton of Kilm."

Lord Norton bowed as well. Younger than Lord Beregern, his short, brown hair showed no gray above his angular face. He smiled at her, though his gray eyes remained cold as the stones of Nalgar Castle. "A pleasure to meet you, Lady Rennelda."

She struggled to keep her smile in place. Respen had at least given her the courtesy of using her title Lady Faythe, mostly because it suited his purposes to acknowledge her as rightful heir of Stetterly and the throne of Acktar. But Lord Norton only used the title given to every child of a lord.

"Men from Kilm and Mountainwood form the backbone of my army. Their support is invaluable." Respen's grip tightened around her waist.

He must really want her to impress these men. Was Respen's position as king more tenous than she thought? Half the lords in Acktar supported him, but how long would that continue if the Resistance wasn't stamped out quickly? After all, if Respen could claim the throne without a drop of royal blood, what was to stop the others from getting the same idea?

Was that perhaps why he wanted to marry her? Not only would he stop the Resistance, he would also solidify his position with the other lords.

Respen patted her hand. She gritted her teeth and didn't yank her hand away. "Lady Faythe, if you would excuse us. We have a few matters of state to discuss. You will join us for supper, of course."

"Of course." Renna dropped into another curtsy as Respen strode off, leading his two guests.

She frowned. They were probably going to talk about the war. If she could spy on them, perhaps she could learn what was going on. Not that she had any way of telling information to the Resistance, but she'd heard nothing since Respen had told her Stetterly had been overrun and burned.

"Don't even think about it."

Renna turned. Martyn stood a few feet away, his arms crossed.

She sighed. So much for spying.

24

Brandi meandered through the rocks at the base of Eagle Heights. Usually when she was upset, she retreated to the stables. They'd become her refuge after her parents died. The manor seemed too gloomy, and Renna was always on the verge of crying, so it'd been easier to spend time with the mule and goats.

But that wouldn't work in this case. If she went by the horses, she'd see Blizzard, and Blizzard would remind her of Leith and thinking about Leith reminded her that he'd helped kill her parents.

She couldn't go back to the cabin she shared with the others. Lady Alistair or Abigail would notice the look on her face and ask what was wrong. Brandi couldn't tell them. Putting the truth into words would only make it more real and hurtful.

Why had Renna never told her? Didn't she know Brandi could handle the truth?

Brandi stumbled along a path down the north side of the mountain into a thick forest. She smelled smoke and heard people talking in the distance as if another section of the camp lay at the base of the mountain, but she didn't investigate. Curiosity didn't seem all that productive anymore.

Hopping onto a boulder, she hugged her knees. How was Renna surviving at Nalgar Castle alone? Was she still looking for rescue?

Brandi growled and buried her face in her hands. Leith must still plan to rescue her. He wasn't going to let a little thing like Keevan stand in his way. Why did he make it so hard to stay mad at him?

Someone perched on the boulder next to her. She didn't have to look to know that Jamie had found her. "What do you want?"

"Leith told me what he told you." Jamie's quiet voice eased around her, as if asking why she was so angry. Something cracked like he'd picked up a stick and broke it into smaller pieces.

Of course Jamie would be on Leith's side. Brandi rocked back and forth. "He helped kill my parents."

"That doesn't mean he isn't your friend."

She shifted. "Yes, it does."

"Leith wasn't much older than you. He'd spent five years training with King Respen. I know the darkness of that place, how it seeps into you until you aren't sure how to get away, if you had the courage to even try."

Brandi glanced at him as a shudder traveled down his back. His shoulders hunched. "To become a Blade, Respen makes you kill another trainee, someone he deems unworthy. Leith saved me from having to do that, but if he hadn't been there, I would've had to kill or be killed." He heaved a sigh. "The fear of death can make you do a lot of things you don't want to do."

Brandi blinked and turned away. She'd killed someone because she feared he was going to kill her and

Jamie. If she'd been training under Respen, what would she have done? Would she have made the choice to kill or to let Respen kill her? Six months ago, she would've boldly said she'd never follow Respen's orders and never kill. But now? She wasn't sure.

"Will you at least think about forgiving Leith?"

Brandi nodded. As mad as she was now, she'd never stay angry forever. She probably would forgive Leith eventually. Maybe. "I'll think about it."

"Good." Jamie jumped off the boulder. "Now, it's time you did a little exploring."

She slid from the rock. "What else is there to see? It's just more trees, more rocks, and more cabins."

"Come on." Jamie motioned for her to follow him.

She padded after him as he led her away from the base of the mountain. Ahead, the voices from earlier grew louder. As they broke through the tree cover, Brandi caught her breath. They stood on the edge of a lake, the forest dropping away into a rocky shoreline. A few wooden canoes were tied to stumps several yards up the shore. A couple of the canoes floated on the lake, pairs of men throwing nets into the water.

Up the hill from the lake, cabins marched in two rows as if along a street. Several women washed laundry in a tub. A blacksmith pounded on a piece of iron in front of an open-faced shed. Another man laid a fish on a trestle table and deftly fileted it.

"There's a whole village here." She gaped at all the buildings, at the people hustling back and forth with their tasks.

"Respen has no idea something like this exists." Jamie waved at the buildings. "This isn't the only town. There are several more even farther north."

Brandi followed Jamie down the dirt path that could be considered the main street. The rhythmic pounding from the blacksmith's hammer echoed against the mountainside. She paused and watched the blacksmith raise the hammer again. The muscles in his shoulder bulged, but his stocky frame was shorter and leaner than she would've expected for a blacksmith.

Behind him, the open doors of his shed revealed long racks of swords, spears, and pikes arranged in neat rows. Brandi tiptoed closer. On a pair of pegs near the door, a short sword glittered against the log wall. She traced her finger along the hilt. What would it be like to train with a weapon like this? Would she be able to rescue Renna if she could wield a sword along with her knife?

It would mean killing again. Her finger hesitated on the blade. Could she do it?

Most likely, she'd never find out. Leith wouldn't allow her to come along to rescue Renna. He and Shad and Jamie would make her stay here.

The pounding halted. Brandi glanced up. The blacksmith laid his hammer across his anvil and hooked a thumb in one of the pockets on his thick, leather apron. "Can I help you?"

"I was just looking." Brandi drew her hand away from the gleaming sword. "You make weapons for the Resistance?"

"Yep, though I'm not the only one. There are several of us in Eagle Heights." The blacksmith stuck out his soot-stained hand. "I'm Aindre. I was the blacksmith in Mountainwood before the king and queen were killed."

Brandi shook his hand. "I'm Brandi from Stetterly."

"Well, Brandi, I saw you admiring the short sword

there. Why don't you give it a swing?"

She drew the sword and hefted it. She didn't know a whole lot about swords, but they were supposed to be balanced, weren't they? This one felt all right to her. Heavy, but not too heavy.

She swung it. Sunlight glinted along the honed edge and winked on the polished pommel. What could she accomplish with a beautiful weapon like this?

She held it out to Aindre. "It's a good sword."

"Thanks." Aindre took it and hung it back on its pegs. "I'm sure one of the young volunteers will find it useful."

"Thank you for letting me hold it." Brandi forced herself to smile. No one even thought she could fight just because she was a girl. Instead, he was going to hand this gorgeous sword to some stumbling, untrained boy who'd panic the first time he was in the real fight.

She'd been in a real fight, and she hadn't panicked. Perhaps that meant she was a fighter, like David.

Jamie bumped her arm. "Want to see the training?"

With a final glance at the sword, she followed Jamie back up the mountain to a flat spot among the rocks below the cluster of cabins. Several divisions of men ran through maneuvers as their captains called out orders. On the far side, pairs of men sparred with wooden swords.

Brandi tapped her chin. Leith might not allow her to go with him, but it never hurt to be prepared, just in case she got the opportunity to tag along somewhere. "Do you think you could get your hands on a pair of wooden swords?"

"Why?" Jamie eyed her, as if trying to figure out what she was up to.

Brandi widened her eyes and tried to look as innocent as possible. "I'd like to learn. Just in case."

"I learned a little bit of swordplay at Walden. But not much."

"Then we'll have to find someone to teach both of us." With more training, she'd become strong enough to rescue Renna, once she figured out a way to sneak along.

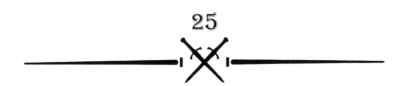

25

Leith flipped the page of the Bible on his lap. He stared at the page. What had he read on the last page? He rested his bound hands on the book.

He should put his time locked in this cave to good use. He had a large chunk of the Bible to read yet. But how could he concentrate when every hour delayed Renna's rescue? Instead of returning with an army, Leith was stuck in here waiting for Prince Keevan to hold a trial. If not for Shad's efforts, the prince would've done so already.

Should he continue waiting for Shad to get through to Prince Keevan? Or should he try something on his own?

What could he do? He could attempt to infiltrate Nalgar Castle, find Renna, and figure out some way to sneak her past Martyn and the rest of the guards without getting both of them killed.

But Renna was Martyn's responsibility. He wouldn't allow Leith anywhere near her again. Would Leith have to fight, and possibly kill, Martyn to rescue Renna?

The guards pacing outside the entrance spoke to someone. A shaggy head of brown hair popped through first. Jamie crawled into the cave and leaned against the wall across from Leith.

"Isn't there a church service this morning?" Leith shut the Bible and set it carefully on the cave floor.

"It doesn't start for another hour yet." Jamie brushed at the dirt on his trousers. "I didn't feel like sitting around waiting."

Leith cleared his throat and steeled himself. "How's Brandi?" He still couldn't banish the look on Brandi's face when she realized her parents' death was his fault, like he'd stabbed her and twisted the knife.

A futile question. She couldn't be good. In the days since he'd told her the truth, she hadn't visited. Not once. The ache in his chest intensified.

"I'm not sure." Jamie hung his head and shrugged. "I don't think she's ready to forgive you, but she will eventually."

Leith shifted his wrists against the rope. What if Brandi didn't forgive him? He couldn't lose her friendship. Not like this.

He shook his head. Best not to dwell on that too long. Brandi would forgive him. She had to. "How are the other trainees we rescued?"

"Lord Shadrach found families who wanted to take them in. From what I could tell, they're adjusting." Jamie drew his knees up to his chest. "He offered to find a family for me too. But I said no."

"No?" Leith straightened so fast he scraped the back of his head on the sloped stone where the cave ceiling met the wall. "Why not?"

"I'm not like the other trainees." Jamie pushed up his right sleeve, revealing the single pink mark across his shoulder. "No one here knows I was the Thirteenth

Blade, besides you and Brandi. People are willing to help orphaned boys captured by Respen. But a Blade? You're proof they don't like Blades here."

"You didn't kill for that mark. You don't have to carry the guilt of being a Blade." Leith twisted his hands again.

"How long would it be before my new family saw my mark? Would they trust me enough to let me explain?" Jamie shook his head. His blue eyes shone wet. "Besides, I am a Blade. Maybe I didn't actually kill anyone, but I planned to. I planned to kill Respen."

Leith raised his eyebrows. "Half the people in Eagle Heights probably plotted to kill Respen at one time or another."

Jamie hugged his knees. "You remember that day at Nalgar Castle when Respen ordered me to kill? And I refused?"

"Yes." Leith tensed. What was Jamie trying to tell him?

"I refused, but when Respen ordered you to kill me, I thought about picking my knife back up. I was scared. If you'd been Vane drawing a knife on me..." Jamie's shoulders shook. "I might've killed. I don't know. That's what makes me a Blade, and it isn't something the people here would understand."

"I understand." Leith leaned his head against the wall. He'd tried to get Jamie out of the Blades, but he'd been too late to prevent damage. Was there a life after the Blades for any of them? Or would their past always bind them? "I'm sorry."

Jamie straightened his shoulders. "It's all right. I already told Lord Shadrach I plan to help the Resistance. They'll need a good scout."

"You're only thirteen. You don't have to go into battle."

Leith glanced toward the cave entrance. From here, all he could see was a circle of bright ground and the guards' boots as they paced in front of the entrance. "How strong is the Resistance army?"

Jamie scratched a toe in the dirt. "The core is really well trained and armed. They've been preparing for years. Most of the old Acktarian army loyal to King Leon fled here shortly after Respen took over. But they're still outnumbered, so they're taking volunteers. There are a lot of boys my age all the way up to old men. A few girls even joined the archers, though General Stewart drew the line at girls in the foot soldiers."

If Leith could only see for himself. He was a Blade. He wasn't used to being blind. "Do they have a chance against Respen?"

Jamie cocked his head. "I think so. Maybe. It'll be tough."

A chance. Slim, but not hopeless. "They're going to need a Blade's help."

"Yes. And since they don't trust you…" Jamie ducked his head. "I guess it'll have to be me."

"Maybe they don't trust me, but Prince Keevan will use me. He and General Stewart spent too long planning this war to waste an asset like me. Or you." Even a Blade trainee could be useful to Prince Keevan and General Stewart.

Leith shouldn't let Jamie carry such a burden. But Jamie had been forced to grow up too fast, and he wouldn't like being told to act like a child when he wasn't one anymore. "So where are you staying?"

"I'm sharing a room with Jeremiah Alistair." Jamie's grimace contorted his nose and mouth. "He's…different. All he does is read. And study. He already knows he wants to be a minister someday, so he knows lots of stuff about the Bible. At least he didn't ask any questions about my mark. And he let me borrow a book to read. Something about famous sermons in history."

Another pair of boots joined the guards, and Shad's voice rang through the opening. After a moment, Shad shuffled inside, his customary bow, arrows, and sword missing from his quiver and belt.

Jamie ducked his head. "I'd better go. I should keep Brandi company."

"Can you tell her..." Leith's throat closed. What did he want Jamie to tell her? What could he say besides sorry? Again?

Jamie nodded. "I'll make sure she knows." He scurried from the cave.

Shad lounged against the wall. "How're you holding up?"

"Except for the lack of a mattress, this is actually nicer than my room at Nalgar Castle." Leith waved his bound hands toward the entrance. "I have light, fresh air, and visitors."

"I've tried everything I can think of, but Prince Keevan won't listen to me. Maybe he would've listened to my father, but not me." Shad's hand closed over the empty space where his sword's hilt normally hung.

"It's fine. I didn't expect much of a welcome. Do you remember how suspicious you were at first? Your father called me a rattlesnake." That's what Leith was to Prince Keevan. A rattlesnake curled in front of his face.

"I remember. Father said he couldn't be sure which side you'd bite." Shad shook his head. "But you've proven you're on our side."

Leith shrugged as much as he could with his hands

tied. "My past isn't easy to forget." Or forgive. Or leave in the past. Would he always carry blood on his hands?

"He agreed to let you attend church services today." Shad's jaw relaxed into a small smile. "He couldn't deny that request no matter how much he wanted to."

Just like Abel Lachlan hadn't been able to refuse that same request months ago. Leith glanced down at his rumpled, black clothes and grimaced. "Hopefully in some out of the way spot where no one will notice that I haven't had a bath in a week."

Shad's smile widened into a grin. "Why do you think I'm here so early? You can't show up to church looking like that."

He helped Leith up and out of the cave. Outside, they were surrounded by ten guards. Leith resisted the urge to laugh. Prince Keevan wasn't taking any chances with the Blade he still deemed dangerous.

They escorted him to a cabin set off to the side. Untying his hands, they pushed him inside and locked the door after him. A tub of water stood along one wall, a chair with a towel and soap next to it. A table held a new set of clothes. Surveying the room, he noted the lack of windows. No way for him to escape other than the door. Not that he had any plans to escape, but he liked to know where he stood.

He hurried through the bath, the water so cold it had most likely been taken from the spring without any effort to heat it. After drying, he pulled on a pair of brown trousers and green shirt. Shad's spare set, if Leith guessed correctly. They'd fit Shad much better than they fit him. The shoulder seams hung partway down Leith's upper arms while the ends of the sleeves dangled a good four inches past his fingertips. His belt did an adequate job of holding the trousers up, but he had to roll the ends several inches so he could walk.

He looked ridiculous. But at least he didn't look like a Blade. Blades didn't get the best reception around here.

When he knocked, the guard unlocked and swung the door open. Shad brushed past the guards and shut the door behind him. He crossed his arms and smirked. "You look like a kid trying on his father's clothes."

Leith grimaced. He'd never done anything like that. His father would've beaten him for such foolishness. Not that he'd want to put on his father's shirt. It had always reeked of alcohol and sweat. He held up the sleeves. "If you weren't such a giant, these would fit better."

Shad pulled out a length of rope. "I'm sorry about this."

"Better you than one of the guards." Leith held out his wrists. Shad tied the rope so loosely Leith would have to be careful he didn't accidentally slip his hands free.

When he was bound once again, Shad strode beside him to the clearing at the top of the mountain. Shad motioned him to a bench set underneath a tree at the back of the clearing. As Leith slid onto the bench, Brandi tiptoed over and slid onto the bench beside him.

Heart in his throat, Leith raised his eyebrows at her.

Scuffing her toes in the dirt, Brandi sneaked a peek his way. "I haven't forgiven you. But keeping you locked in that cave is silly. You're on our side."

It was the best he could ask for at the moment. "Thanks, Brandi." Leith gave her a smile.

Shad and his family gathered on the bench beside and in front of Leith. At first, Leith didn't think anything of it, until he noticed the guards from Walden who had traveled with him to Eagle Heights also sat in the benches surrounding him. Lady Lorraine slipped into the seat next to Brandi, though Jolene sat next to Shad.

Trailed by his general, Prince Keevan strolled into the clearing, a young woman clinging to his arm. He glanced at Leith. Leith gave the prince a nod, the best bow he could do sitting down with his hands tied.

Brandi had her arms crossed as she glared at Prince Keevan. When the prince continued down the aisle to the front row reserved for him, Brandi leaned closer to Leith. "That's his wife, Princess Adelaide. Apparently she was just a servant girl when they met. I heard she saved his life after..." she trailed off, slicing her finger down her cheek and throat.

"After I tried to kill him." Leith shook his head and glanced at the couple. Prince Keevan helped his wife into her seat, the fabric of her dress pulling taut over a rounded figure.

"Oh, and she's pregnant," Brandi added, her voice edging above a whisper. After a few more minutes of silence, she leaned closer once again. "Did you know there are whole villages at the bottom of this mountain? There're several church services being held down there right now because not everyone can fit up here."

"No, I didn't." Leith quirked a smile at her. This was more like the old Brandi. "Locked in a cave, remember?"

She gave him an exaggerated scowl and roll of her eyes. She might've said something more, but the minister strode to the front of the gathering and climbed onto a table, which made him visible even to the back of the clearing.

After a few songs, the minister announced the Bible

passage. Brandi pulled out a Bible and flipped to the passage. She held it out so Leith could see it as well. He steadied it with his bound hands.

As the minister read, the second to last verse caught Leith's attention. The words sparked in his chest. *From henceforth let no man trouble me: for I bear in my body the marks of the Lord Jesus.*

Marks. Leith had marks. Thirty-seven of them. All showing his slavery to Respen and darkness. Even now, those marks still had power over him. They were the reason he'd spent the last three days in a cave. In the eyes of others, he'd always be unworthy of anything besides bound hands and guards.

What about the marks of Jesus Christ? Did Leith have those? His heart felt marked, branded with Christ's ownership. But, as the minister expounded in his sermon, the marks in the verse were the marks of persecution. The physical scars that testified of the inner marks.

Leith shrugged his left shoulder with its two marks for his recent failures. Were they proof enough of his inner marks for him to declare that no one should trouble him about his past?

The writer of that verse was Paul, a betrayer of Christians turned preacher. He had a guilty past. His fellow Christians had feared him because of the things he'd done. But Paul's proof of his sincerity was the scars he'd received for Christ. No one could question him any longer.

Would Leith ever be able to declare the marks of his salvation so boldly? He didn't think so. The thirty-seven marks on his right arm outweighed the two small marks on his left.

Leith stumbled his way through the final song. He

was starting to get a grip on this whole singing thing, but he couldn't belt the songs out as fearlessly as Shad and Brandi.

As the congregation filed from their seats, a dust-covered rider stumbled into the clearing. General Stewart and the rider conversed for a few minutes before the general slapped the man on the back and headed to Prince Keevan.

When General Stewart spoke in the prince's ear, Prince Keevan stiffened, and his wife's grip tightened on his arm. After a few minutes, he patted Princess Adelaide's hand, and she left. General Stewart and Prince Keevan threaded their way through the crowd, trailed by a group of five guards.

As they approached, Leith leapt to his feet. Shad and Brandi stood and all three of them bowed. The guards took positions a few yards back while General Stewart remained beside the prince.

"Lord Shadrach, Lady Brandiline, I have received news about..." Prince Keevan trailed off and eyed Leith. "Lord Shadrach, I believe you said the Blade would be properly secured?"

Leith glanced at his hands. He'd forgotten to keep a grip on the rope. It lay at his feet, leaving his hands free.

Shad crossed his arms. "He's as secured as he needs to be."

Prince Keevan glared. "I believe I've made my policy on this Blade quite clear. He may stay because I wish for him to hear this, but he should be bound."

"You're about as stubborn as a thirsty mule refusing to drink." Brandi heaved a massive sigh, marched between Shad and Prince Keevan, and planted her hands on her hips. "Leith obviously isn't going to do anything. You really think a little rope and three guards were keeping him in that cave? He was the *First Blade*. He could leave anytime he wanted. So stop all your fuss and bother, and say whatever you came all the way over here to say."

Shad rubbed the back of his hand across his face, attempting to hide his grin. Leith had enough trouble keeping his own grin under control. Good thing Brandi was Prince Keevan's cousin. Not that she'd hold back either way, but the prince might take it better.

Prince Keevan's jaw tightened, pulling his scar taut across his face. "General Stewart, please keep an eye on the Blade."

General Stewart rested his hand on his sword's hilt. His dark brown-gray eyes, framed by weathered lines, settled on Leith like shackles.

Prince Keevan turned to Shad. "On his way here, the rider swung past Walden. As of six days ago, it still stands."

Shad's breath whooshed from his chest. Leith clasped his hand over the empty space where his knife usually rested. Somehow, Lord Alistair had held off Respen's army this long. But for how much longer?

Brandi tapped her foot. "What about Renna? You have news, right?"

Renna. Leith stepped closer to Brandi and gripped her shoulders. His heart pounded in his throat. Had Respen hurt her? What if he'd set the trap for Leith, and Leith hadn't shown up? Would Respen have killed her?

Surely not. Respen wouldn't kill her. He couldn't kill her.

Prince Keevan's gaze met Leith's. A challenge hardened his blue eyes. "It appears you aren't as important to Respen as you believe. He has other reasons for keeping her alive."

What was Prince Keevan talking about? What did Respen plan to do to Renna? Leith tightened his grip on Brandi's shoulders. His back muscles cramped with tension. If Prince Keevan didn't stop dancing around the topic, Leith might risk General Stewart's wrath and shake him.

Prince Keevan's mouth twitched like he knew he'd prodded Leith. "She's engaged to marry Respen Felix in two weeks."

Leith stiffened. Renna was getting married? To Respen? The mountain tilted under his feet.

"What?" Brandi gaped at Prince Keevan. "Renna would never marry Respen."

"He must be forcing her." Leith drew in a deep breath, steadying the mountain and his shaking hands. That had to be it. Renna would never willingly marry Respen.

At least they knew Renna was still alive. That was something. He tried to focus on that rather than the thought of Respen touching her, kissing her. Leith's stomach churned as a rush of heat flared along his back. He'd move all of Acktar to prevent that.

"Can he do that?" Brandi glanced over her shoulder at him.

"This is Respen we're talking about. He can do what he wants." Perhaps this was Respen's trap. Not an execution as Leith had expected, but a wedding. Something Respen guessed would provoke Leith as much as an execution without killing Renna.

"We have to do something. We can't let Renna marry Respen. I mean, ewww. Respen would be my brother-in-law." Brandi shuddered and stuck out her tongue. "And what's with the date? Why would Renna want to get married to Respen on her birthday?"

Leith clenched his teeth against the rush of bile on his tongue. He had to stop the wedding. Somehow. The consequences for failure were unimaginable.

Prince Keevan scrubbed at his scar. "My advisors and I will discuss it. Lord Shadrach, please return the Blade to his accomodations." He spun on his heels and strode away. General Stewart marched after him, paused to give instructions to the five guards, and followed the prince.

Brandi crossed her arms and scowled. "Discuss it. That's just another way of saying he has no idea what to do."

"He has more than just Renna to think about." Leith gritted his teeth. How was he going to rescue Renna from this? Especially if he didn't have Prince Keevan's help?

"Then I'll have to make Renna his top priority." That devious twinkle sparked in Brandi's eyes.

She was plotting something, and Leith knew all too well how hard Brandi was to resist. He almost pitied Prince Keevan.

Almost.

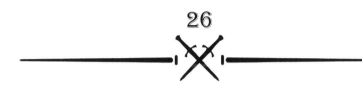

26

Two wo weeks to her wedding. Renna stabbed the fish on her plate. Her dress was almost finished. Most of the details were planned. Many of Respen's guests were arriving. Wasn't a girl supposed to be excited at this point? All she felt was a growing dread. But she didn't have a choice.

Respen's eyes darted to the window. Renna leaned forward, catching sight of a black-clothed rider. Another Blade returning to Nalgar Castle.

Martyn met the rider in the courtyard. His curls bounced as he gripped the other Blade's arm. The Blade handed Martyn something shiny before Martyn clapped him on the back and headed toward the passageway.

Respen turned to Renna. "Lady Rennelda, please return to your room."

What did Martyn have to report to King Respen? Had one of the Blades found Leith's body? She hesistated. Would Respen allow her to stay? She was going to be his queen. Shouldn't she share his secrets?

He turned to her, dark eyes hardening. "I gave an order. Leave."

Heart thumping, she scrambled to her feet and darted from the room, hop-skipping to avoid putting too much strain on her healing leg. Partway down the stairs, she nearly ran into Martyn on his way up. He carried two knives in his hands, but the staircase was too dark for her to make out the initials etched on the hilts. "Sorry, excuse me."

Martyn opened his mouth, like he wanted to tell her something, but he snapped his jaw shut. With a nod, he shoved past her and continued up the stairs.

Renna froze, her foot hovering over the next step. She glanced over her shoulder as Martyn stepped into the king's chambers, the door clicking shut behind him. Did she dare listen even after Respen ordered her to leave?

She needed to know what Martyn had to report. Holding her breath, she tiptoed back up the stairs and pressed her ear to the door. Respen's voice shouted, but the door muffled the words too much for her to hear anything besides the thunder of his tone vibrating the walls.

She eased to the floor, careful of her weak leg, but the door shut too firmly against the carpet of the room above to provide an air gap. Standing once again, she pressed her ear to the door. A faint thwacking sound met her ear. Then silence.

Respen hadn't liked Martyn's report. What was going on? What had Martyn told him?

The door's latch clicked. Renna shrank against the wall, her pulse throbbing in her throat. She couldn't run down the stairs fast enough to avoid detection. What would Respen do to her for trying to eavesdrop on his First Blade's report? He had hit her once. Would he do it again?

174

The door swung open. Martyn stepped from the room. His eyes swung to her and narrowed. He closed the door and steered her down the stairs with a firm grip on her elbow.

When they reached the bottom, he swung her against a wall, his grip painful on her arm. "How much did you hear?" His breath hissed across her cheek, his eyes burning.

"Nothing. The door was too thick. All I could tell was Respen got angry. He didn't like whatever you reported to him." She squeezed her hands together and forced her eyes to swing to his face. A red mark swelled one side of his jaw.

Martyn dragged a hand through his hair. "Get back to your room. You don't want King Respen to catch you here."

She nodded and dashed down the passageway. When she slammed the door to her room behind her, she panted for breath, and shafts of pain shot down her leg. Too much exertion too soon.

She collapsed into a chair by the fireplace, her hands shaking. She would be the one with a bruise on her face if Respen had spotted her.

Squeezing her eyes shut, she tried to find the peace she'd felt when she'd fallen asleep on the fountain wall, but it ghosted away, replaced by the same dark dread she'd harbored for too long.

She'd fought this battle once. After the past four and a half years of living in fear, surely she'd grown past this. Wait on the Lord. Trust.

The door of her room slammed open. Respen charged into her room, his dark eyes raging.

Renna jumped to her feet and clasped her hands

behind her back to hide their trembling. "Is something wrong?"

"There's been a change of plans. We're getting married in two days."

"What? We can't! You agreed—"

"I'm the king. I can do as I please!" He pounded his fist on a nearby end table. Renna leapt backwards, placing her chair between herself and Respen. He looked about ready to hit her next.

Respen drummed his fingers against the end table, a suave look masking the rage she could see still coursing through him. "I have decided I no longer wish to wait that long. Finish your dress. Ready or no, you will marry me in two days." He spun on his heels and marched from the room.

Renna collapsed onto the floor. Two days. Two short, infinitesimal days. Sucking in deep breaths, she curled on the plush rug. The wedding was only the beginning of her misery. She'd be married to King Respen.

Should she go through with this? Respen received bad news, and bad news for him had to be good news for the Resistance. Was the Resistance fighting back? Was rescue on the way?

No, that wasn't it. Martyn had two knives, and he'd carried them like he had to show them to Respen. The Blades who had owned those knives must be dead. It would anger Respen if the Resistance managed to kill two of his Blades. Most likely, the Blades had been killed while trying to find the Resistance or while tracking Shadrach and Brandi. It didn't necessarily mean that help was on the way.

Yet why had Respen changed the date of the wedding? He must be worried about something. Was he worried the Resistance would try to stop the wedding?

Unless he wasn't worried about the Resistance at all. It could be losing two more Blades made his position as king more tenuous. Without the fear of his Blades, how long would some of his allies continue to stay in line?

That must be it. It didn't change her situation. She shuddered, remembering Lord Norton's cold eyes. He wouldn't be any better than Respen. At least if she married Respen, she'd have a chance of stopping the killing.

No one would stop this wedding. Leith was dead. He wasn't going to swoop in to rescue her. As much as she hated it, her wedding to Respen must be God's will. Surely He would give her the courage to endure it.

27

Brandi put her plan into action first thing in the morning.

After a quick breakfast, she marched into the big cabin, ignoring the guards, and burst into her cousin's meeting room. He sat at the head of a long table, General Stewart on his right, Lady Lorraine to his left. Shad sprawled in a chair near the end.

All the better. Brandi could count on Shad to help her, and Lady Lorraine might be an iron lady, but she was a practical sort. She'd listen if Brandi put it right.

Everyone stared as Brandi flounced past the big table, past General Stewart's sword-straight back, past Lady Lorraine's raised eyebrows, and planted her feet in front of Keevan.

She crossed her arms and tried to look as intimidating as possible. "What are you going to do about saving my sister?"

Keevan glanced around the room, as if pleading for someone to save him from her glare. When no one spoke, he turned back to her with the look of someone facing a job he didn't enjoy, like cleaning the privies or something like that. "It's complicated. I can't risk our preparations for one girl, even if she is my cousin. You understand, don't you?"

"No, I don't. What makes us any different than Respen if we weren't going to risk everything for one person?" She cocked her head. How stubborn was Keevan going to be? It'd be so much easier if he caved on her first argument.

"I wish it were that simple. But this is war. The entire picture has to be taken into consideration."

"Such as our supply line." Shad leaned his elbows on the table. He met Brandi's gaze and gave her a nod. She nodded back.

Lady Lorraine pursed her lips. "As we discussed, Walden's siege cuts off our supply line. We can delay, but we will never be more prepared than we are now."

"Perhaps. But that same siege places an army between us and Nalgar Castle." Keevan said the words too quickly, like the words of an argument he'd fought once already.

"Won't it be a bad thing if he marries Renna?" Brandi stuck her bottom lip out farther to make sure her scowl looked as forbidding as possible. She should've known he'd be stubborn. "Everyone back in Acktar thinks you're dead. Respen could claim the throne was rightfully his, and no one would argue anymore."

"Once I return to Acktar and reveal that I'm alive, his claim will no longer be valid. Yes, it'll complicate things, but not for long." Keevan waved her words away like meaningless flies buzzing around his head. "I'm sorry, but it isn't worth the risk. Too much is at stake at the moment. We can't make a reckless move."

Of course too much was at stake. Lord Alistair in Walden. Renna. The country. Why was Keevan dilly-dallying about it?

"A move discussed with a council of wise advisors is

never reckless." Lady Lorraine's slim eyebrow arched.

Shad muttered something under his breath. If he was thinking the same thing as Brandi, then he grumbled that too much discussion made no move at all.

Brandi tapped her foot. She wasn't going to budge until Keevan saw her point one way or another.

Climbing to his feet, Keevan reached for her shoulders, but she side-stepped his grip. He had no right to pretend to be her cousin. Not when he was willing to abandon Renna. He dropped his hands. "Look. I'd like to help Renna. But there's one factor that none of us can change. Even if I rallied the army and we left today, there's no way to get an army large enough to take Nalgar Castle through the Sheered Rock Hills in time to stop the wedding."

Brandi glanced around the room. General Stewart gave her a nod, his mouth framed with deep lines. Shad rubbed the back of his neck and looked away. Even Lady Lorraine's gaze softened.

"One man, riding hard, can reach the edge of the Sheered Rock Hills in six days. An army would take at least twice that long. Then the army has to fight through the line of Respen's army, march the distance to Nalgar, and take the castle." Keevan ran his thumb along his scar. "The cold fact is that we simply can't get to Nalgar Castle in time."

Was it really impossible? Brandi clenched her fists. She couldn't allow Renna to marry Respen. She just couldn't.

Neither would Leith.

"I bet Leith could come up with a plan." Brandi straightened her spine. Yes, Leith had helped kill her family. And he'd given Keevan that scar. But he'd do anything for Renna. And that was good enough for Brandi.

"He's smart that way. He came up with the plan to save eighteen nobles in Acktar without Respen figuring out that he'd been involved. It takes a lot of skill to obviously betray Respen without him actually finding out."

Lady Lorraine shifted. Brandi turned on her. "You were part of that meeting when Lord Alistair set it all up. Renna told me some of it. You know how much Leith helped."

Lady Lorraine's gaze swung to Prince Keevan. "Leith Torren was the First Blade. He knows Respen's strategy better than any of us. It'd be foolish not to listen to his advice."

Brandi tried to add up the times Leith had saved her, but failed. "I think I'd be dead like four or five times already if not for Leith."

"But he nearly killed me." Keevan spun on his heel and paced.

"Exactly. He *nearly* killed you." Brandi couldn't stop her grin. In all her anger at Leith, she'd missed the obvious. Turns out, everyone else had too. "This is Leith we're talking about. When I met him, he had no failures. None. So how does a Blade with no failures manage to mess up so badly on you?"

Silence dropped into the room. Lady Lorraine tilted her head. General Stewart leaned back in his chair, his eyes shadowed as if he had some pondering to do. A grin spread across Shad's face.

Keevan stiffened and faced her. She had him now, and there was nothing he could do about it. She allowed herself to smirk. "Face it. If not for Leith's mistake that night, you'd be dead. It's almost like he saved your life. You owe him."

Keevan's jaw worked for several moments. He turned

to General Stewart. "I've heard everyone else's council. What do you suggest? Should we listen to what the Blade might have to say?"

General Stewart continued his pondering for a few seconds more. Finally, he spoke in his drawly, raw-edged voice. "Yes, I think we should."

"Very well." Keevan straightened his back. "I'll talk to the Blade. But that's all I'll agree to."

"Thank you." With her best I-will-be-back glare, she thrust her head high as she swept from the room. Renna would be proud of how lady like she managed to be.

As soon as she was clear of the big cabin, she hiked up her skirts, threw lady like to the mountain breeze, and dashed across the clearing. Barreling past the guards and their attempts to halt her, she ducked into the jail-cave and skidded to a stop in front of Leith.

His eyes widened at her entrance, but she didn't give him time to comment. "Do you have a plan to rescue Renna?"

He gaped, eyebrows raised. "What?"

"I talked to Keevan and convinced him to talk to you about rescuing Renna, so you'd better have a plan, otherwise he's not going to listen." He might not listen anyway, but she was trying to stay positive. "If you don't have a plan, think up one quick."

Leith's smile only tipped the corners of his mouth. "I have a plan. Don't worry. I'll stop Renna's wedding."

Brandi nodded, but she heard the things that Leith wasn't saying. His plan would stop the wedding, but he couldn't guarantee he'd rescue Renna.

It was the best Brandi could ask for at the moment. That was all right. If Leith couldn't rescue Renna, then Brandi would have to do it, one way or another.

28

Leith didn't resist as four guards tightened the rope on his wrists and yanked him from the cave. After marching him through the camp, the soldiers dragged him into the big cabin. Shad and Lady Lorraine stood in the entry room. Shad gave him a nod.

As before, Prince Keevan stood near the back of the room, flanked by General Stewart. After tying Leith to a chair, the guards left. General Stewart positioned himself by the door.

Prince Keevan paced closer, crossed his arms, and studied Leith. Leith tried not to squirm. He had nothing to hide and no secrets the prince didn't already know.

When Prince Keevan spoke, his raspy voice remained even. "It seems I have you to thank for saving my life."

Leith stared. When had he saved the prince's life? "I tried to kill you."

"Yes, you tried to kill me. Tried, but failed. Why? I know you succeeded in killing before that night and you succeeded many times afterwards. So why did you fail to finish the job with me?" Prince Keevan traced the scar along his cheek and neck. "How did you—a well-trained

Blade—manage to miss by such a wide margin on an unmoving, helpless victim?"

Leith stared at his boots and swallowed at the memories crowding his chest. He'd pressed his hand over the prince's mouth, looked into his frightened eyes, and saw another pair of terrified eyes, the eyes of his first kill. "You were my sixth mark, but my second kill. I panicked. I certainly never intended to let you live, and I resolved after that night never to hesitate again."

And he hadn't, at least, not until that day he'd left Stetterly when he couldn't bring himself to draw his knife on Brandi.

"Still, your failure spared my life. It seems I'm in your debt, as much as I don't wish to be." Prince Keevan grimaced, one finger rubbing the base of his scar.

"I thank God He used my failures for good. It was certainly no doing of mine." Leith shook his head. "How did you survive? Respen paraded your bodies around the courtyard after we took the castle."

"If Addie hadn't found me, stopped some of the bleeding, and kept me calm, I wouldn't have survived." Prince Keevan clasped his hands behind his back and paced. "I had a cousin on my mother's side. No one important to Respen. No one even remembered he was killed that same night defending my father. After General Stewart helped Addie get me out of Nalgar Castle, he and a few of the soldiers loyal to me swapped my cousin's body for mine. In the dark with all the blood across his face and hair, his body looked enough like mine to pass."

Leith glanced at General Stewart. The general hadn't moved from his position near the door, and his expression hadn't changed.

"Soldiers loyal to King Leon snuck the bodies out of

Nalgar Castle later that night and buried them on the hillside. Supposedly to give them a decent burial. But it was more than that, wasn't it? They had to keep people from examining the bodies too closely." Leith turned his gaze back to Prince Keevan.

Prince Keevan nodded. His face remained hard. "I didn't learn all this until later. I was barely conscious and struggling to breathe when Addie, all by herself, managed to get me to Walden. You had missed the vein in my neck and nicked my throat, but it was a full month before I could even make a sound, much less talk."

Leith hung his head. All because of him. It had been hard enough dealing with the guilt when Prince Keevan was nothing but a memory to plague him on dark nights. But facing him in person and seeing the ravages of that night still scarred across his face...nothing Leith said or did would ever make up for it. "I'm sorry."

Prince Keevan's jaw tightened. "Stop the act. You're a Blade. You should be sitting there giving me a bunch of excuses as to why you aren't guilty."

"I don't have an excuse. I am guilty." Leith's chest ached. Would the guilt ever stop haunting him? Perhaps before God his past and guilt were paid, but here on earth, it remained a blood stain across his hands.

Prince Keevan scowled. "I can't seem to find a crack to discover if your sincerity is false. I've tossed you in a cave, kept you prisoner, yelled at you, destroyed Brandi's trust in you, and still I haven't rattled you."

"Have you considered that I might be exactly who I say I am?" Leith met Prince Keevan's gaze. "A Blade saved by the grace of God?"

"There it is again! I've been a Christian all my life, but even I hesitate to talk about my faith in front of others." Prince Keevan blew out a loud breath, as if he hadn't meant to say so much. "So tell me, are your words fake? Whatever it is, you're good at it. You've talked everyone to your side."

Leith understood Prince Keevan's need to lash out at him. Prince Keevan's whole family had been killed by the Blades, yet he'd been given little chance to mourn as he'd been thrust into leading the Resistance. He needed to punish someone for that pain, and Leith happened to be the convenient target.

"I told you. I have nothing to hide. Not my past nor my faith. You wanted the truth, and that's exactly what I'm telling you." Leith gritted his teeth. All this arguing was wasting time.

Something about Prince Keevan's past niggled at him. Leith forced a hard edge to his voice. "If you've been alive this whole time, why were Renna and Brandi left in Acktar? Why weren't they brought to safety at Eagle Heights long ago?"

That cracked Prince Keevan's hard expression for a moment. "Lord Alistair, General Stewart, and Uncle Laurence decided to keep my survival a secret from everyone besides a select few. At the time, they planned a fast strike to drive Respen from Nalgar before he became too entrenched. But the snow came early that year."

"I remember." Leith swallowed. If only he didn't have to say the next words. But while they were being truthful with each other, Leith couldn't hold back. "Respen planned to kill Laurence and Annita Faythe that fall, but the snow delayed him."

"As we learned when the snow let up." The rasp in Prince Keevan's voice deepened. "Uncle Laurence and Aunt Annita were killed. And we all realized that taking back Acktar would take time and patience."

"So why weren't Renna and Brandi brought to safety then?" Leith straightened his shoulders. Heat flashed through his chest. Why had Prince Keevan abandoned his cousins to the dangers of Acktar for four and a half years?

"To protect me." Prince Keevan faced him and planted his feet. "I know what you're thinking. That I'm a coward to let two young girls take the danger meant for me. Perhaps you're right."

He wasn't going to say it out loud, but yes, that's exactly what Leith was thinking.

"At the time, I was an eighteen-year-old boy trying to learn how to talk again and still mourning the loss of my entire family. I did what I was told." He shot a glance at Leith.

Leith raised his eyebrows. He was eighteen. Being young wasn't an excuse. But Prince Keevan would've been raised as the protected and responsibility-free second son. He'd caught a glimpse of the darker side of life the night Leith had tried to kill him. Leith had faced that darkness at six years old.

"I was sent here to Eagle Heights, nothing more than a vacant rock in the forest back then, while Lord Alistair and Lord Lorraine started the Resistance in Acktar on the foundation that a true heir of the Eirdon line remained. To that end, someone from the Eirdon line had to remain in Acktar."

Leith nodded, putting it together. "Since no one knew you were alive, everyone, including Respen, assumed Renna was the Eirdon heir."

"Not only did Respen never suspect I was alive, he also dismissed the Resistance as a true threat. Who would believe the Resistance could have any strength when they placed their hope on a young girl too scared to leave her own manor?" Prince Keevan rubbed at the scar across his cheek. "We were able to quietly build this place, our numbers, our weapons, our skills. Leaving Renna vulnerable bought us the time we needed."

"She shouldn't have to pay for it now." Leith flexed his hands against the ropes that bound him. He had one shot to convince Prince Keevan. He couldn't fail. "Regardless of what you think of me, you can't abandon her. She shouldn't have to pay the price for your crown."

Prince Keevan threw his hands into the air. "The fact of the matter is, there's nothing I can do. I can't even get my army into position fast enough."

"But there's something I can do." Leith leaned forward. The ropes binding him to the chair pressed through his shirt and cut into his skin. "I can buy you time."

"How do you propose do to that?" Prince Keevan crossed his arms again. General Stewart stepped closer.

"If you let me go, I'll ride to Nalgar Castle and turn myself in. My appearance will disrupt the wedding, and Respen will turn his focus on me."

Prince Keevan straightened. "Respen will kill you."

"Yes. But not until after he tortures me." Leith hardened his voice and mind. He couldn't think about it now. He'd already thought this through in the cave. Some might accuse him of committing suicide, but this was Renna's only chance. He'd done as she'd asked and gotten Brandi to safety. Now it was time to return for her.

"I assume you want something from me, unless you're trying to throw your life away."

Leith focused on Prince Keevan. "I'll stop the wedding

and keep Respen's attention focused on me and away from Renna. That'll give you the time to march on Acktar, take Nalgar Castle, and defeat Respen once and for all, which will ultimately save Renna."

"How do I know you won't simply disappear? Or you're on Respen's side, and you'll warn him of our attack?"

Leith raised his eyebrows. "Do you really think Respen would sacrifice ten of his Blades—many of his most experienced Blades—to plant me with the Resistance? Or that I could fool Lord Alistair, Shad, Renna, and Brandi for months? I promise you, my sole aim is to rescue Renna."

Prince Keevan nodded slowly. "General Stewart, please call the rest of the council in. I believe this is a plan we should consider."

General Stewart poked his head out the door, beckoned, and stood aside. Lady Lorraine swept into the room and sat at the far end of the table. Shad strode in and took the seat across from Leith. General Stewart closed the door and took a seat.

Prince Keevan slid into the chair at the head of the table. "The Blade has proposed a plan. If you would explain?" He tipped his head to Leith.

Leith drew in a deep breath. Shad wasn't going to be happy with this idea. "I plan to turn myself in."

"What?" Shad shot to his feet. "You'll be tortured and killed."

"Please hear me out." Leith held Shad's gaze. "Trust me. I know what I'm doing."

Shad returned to his seat and crossed his arms.

"Here's our problem. Walden could be overrun at any time. Renna is set to marry Respen in two weeks, but the army can't get to Nalgar in time." Leith shifted in the seat. The wooden back pressed against his shoulder blades. "Therefore, the army's mission is to free Walden, break through Respen's army, take the castle, and defeat Respen, rescuing Renna in the process."

Lady Lorraine nodded. "That's correct. And turning yourself in will buy us the time to accomplish all that?"

"Yes. I'll stop Renna's wedding. Respen will keep Renna alive while he's torturing me. She's still his best way to control me, and he won't kill me until the next Meeting of the Blades." Leith focused on Prince Keevan and General Stewart at the far end of the table. He didn't dare look at Shad's expression. "When Respen meets with his Blades, the entire castle knows not to disturb him. No one besides the Blades and King Respen are even allowed in that room. If you attack Nalgar Castle while Respen is in a Meeting of the Blades, the soldiers will be in chaos without their leader."

"When is the next Meeting?" Lady Lorraine fixed him with a calculating gaze.

"In three weeks. It'll begin at exactly eight in the morning. You'll want to be in position before then. Respen will enter the Tower when it's about to start."

"Why do you have to be there?" Based on Shad's voice, he was two seconds away from dragging Leith from the room and shaking sense into him. "Yes, the whole army can't stop Renna's wedding, but a small group could. What if we did a quick raid and rescued Renna before the army arrived? Neither of you would be in danger of torture or death."

Such a tempting plan. It'd be safer for Renna, if it succeeded.

But Martyn stood in the way. To rescue Renna, they'd have to fight him. Most likely kill him.

Martyn's life or Renna's. Leith rested his head against the back of the chair. Did he have to choose between them? Did he dare gamble and try to save both?

"A small group might be able to get in, but you'd run into the same problem I had last time. Renna is guarded by a Blade. He'll raise the alarm, and we'd never get her out of the castle." Leith shifted against the ropes to face Shad. "The only way is to conquer the whole castle."

"And at the first sign of trouble, Respen will kill her."

"That's why I have to be there, and you have to attack during the Meeting. Respen might not know what's happening, but if he does, I'll be his first target, buying time for you to rescue Renna."

Shad huffed, crossed his arms, and flopped against the back of his chair. "You're determined to do this."

"Yes." This was their best option, for Renna and Martyn. If only there was some way to get Renna out of there without risking Martyn. But Respen wouldn't let her go, and it'd take something drastic for Martyn to betray his duty to Respen.

Leith turned to Prince Keevan. "If you attack during the Meeting, Respen and his Blades will be in one place.You can capture them all at once. You'll need someone in the Meeting to make sure the door remains unlocked, and Respen doesn't barricade himself inside."

General Stewart cleared his throat. "That's a wise consideration, Your Highness. Unless we wish to fight for every room and tower in the castle, we'll need to capture Respen as quickly as possible in the battle. Once we have him, we can end most of the fighting."

"The Blades will still cause problems." A tiny frown crossed Lady Lorraine's face.

"The current First Blade will be placed in charge of

both me and Renna. Respen might even call back one or two more Blades to help guard me. I flaunted his control. He won't take chances that I'll do it again. You'll face fewer Blades when fighting his army." Leith shrugged. "The Blades are assassins. Most of them aren't the best overall fighters. If you can corner them in the Tower, you'll have the advantage in numbers and the type of battle."

General Stewart faced Prince Keevan. "It's a good plan."

"No, it's not." Shad's square jaw jutted forward. "What if Respen decides to kill you early?"

"I escaped Respen's Blades. I hurt his pride. He has to kill me in front of all his Blades to show he's still in control. He won't kill me early."

"If he moves the Meeting?"

Leith snorted. Respen considered his Meetings a point of pride. He'd sooner surrender than change it. "I doubt it. It'd be difficult to communicate a change of plans to all his Blades. Plus, I think you'd notice if he did. A bunch of confused Blades heading back to the castle a day early would be easy to spot."

"I still don't like it." Shad muttered so quietly only Leith could hear.

Of course he didn't. Leith wasn't thrilled about the prospect of a week of torture either. But to save Renna from marrying Respen, delay and distract Respen long enough for the army to arrive, and protect Martyn from more punishment, Leith had no other choice.

Prince Keevan met General Stewart's gaze. To Leith, he looked young, more like the twenty-three year old boy he was than the Leader he'd been forced to be. "This is it. We have one shot to take back Acktar. If we fail,

Respen will win. Permanently. Are we ready?"

"Yes, you are." General Stewart's tone was gentle.

Leith flexed his fingers as he waited for their answer. If he were to arrive at Nalgar Castle in time to stop Renna's wedding to Respen, he needed to leave soon. He had less than two weeks. The journey from Eagle Heights through the Sheered Rock Hills to the edge of Acktar's prairie would take most of that time.

Prince Keevan drew his back straight. His face hardened. "We have a battle to plan."

29

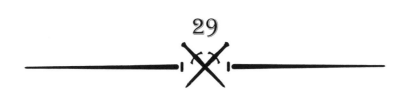

She was getting married today. Renna stared at herself in the full length mirror. The light blue dress hugged her torso, then cascaded from her hips to the floor. The simple embroidery around the hem and neckline gave it an elegant, but understated look. A maid had curled her hair and let it fall around her shoulders and down her back. If not for the frown on her face, she'd look like a princess. Or a queen.

At a knock on her door, she turned, clutching the sides of her skirt. Martyn stepped into the room. He eyed her. "Time to go."

He sounded like he was announcing her execution. He might as well be. Renna stumbled across the room and grasped his arm. She tottered down the hallway and the brick staircase. If not for the strength of Martyn's arm, she would've fallen down the stairs and landed on her face.

As they crossed the Queen's Court, she could hear the strains of music coming from the Great Hall. The wedding had already started. Besides being her escort across the lawn, Martyn had also been assigned the duty of walking her down the aisle. Renna suspected Respen wanted to make sure his bride didn't bolt. Not that she wasn't considering it.

At the broad doors leading into the Great Hall, Martyn paused. She stared at him. Why was he hesitating? Respen wouldn't be happy if Martyn delayed the wedding even by a few minutes. Glancing around, Martyn leaned closer and cleared his throat. "You should know before you go in there. Leith is alive."

His words rang in her ears, roaring, pounding. Alive. How could he be alive? He died in the Waste. Martyn told her he'd died.

Her knees buckled. She gripped Martyn's arm as the whole room spun. "How? You sure?" She couldn't take it if Martyn was lying to her.

"Eighth Blade Harding reported that Leith survived the Waste. He joined Shadrach Alistair and the others and journeyed deeper into the Sheered Rock Hills, presumably to the Resistance's hideout. Leith made sure Harding didn't follow them."

Leith was alive. Her body shook with the force of that one word. *Alive.*

No wonder King Respen had changed the date of their wedding so suddenly. It wasn't due to pressure from Lord Norton and Lord Beregern. Respen had learned Leith was still alive. Leith might've had a chance of stopping the wedding if it had remained on the original date, but he wouldn't know about the change until too late. By the time he could get here, she'd be married to Respen for a week or more.

Martyn had kept this a secret for two days. As a loyal First Blade, he should've let her walk down that aisle believing Leith was dead. She peered up at him,

195

trying to read the expression in his deep, brown eyes. "Why tell me now?"

"I owe Leith that much." Martyn gripped her arm tighter. "It doesn't change anything. He won't stop the wedding."

The wedding. She couldn't walk in now. What was Martyn thinking? What was she thinking?

Martyn knocked on the doors. They swung open, held by liveried footmen, and Martyn dragged her, stumbling, into the Great Hall.

Benches lined the front of the Great Hall. The back rows were filled with soldiers, most of the garrison here at Nalgar Castle. Lord Norton, Lord Beregern, and a few of the other nobles Respen had introduced her to in the last week perched on the front benches.

Respen stood at the front, clothed in a rich, black shirt with a sky blue doublet and black breeches. His black hair lay slicked back while his beard was trimmed to a point sharp enough to draw blood.

Everything wrong about the scene swept through her. The mass of guests she didn't know. The lack of attendants. No parents, friends, or guardians to give their blessing on the marriage. And, most of all, the wrong groom.

Martyn swept up the aisle between the benches. Renna had no choice but to trot to keep up.

Leith was alive. The words pounded in time with the music swelling from the instruments in the corner.

Leith was alive. The words whispered with the silk of her dress and the shuffling of her feet on the velvet rug.

Leith was alive. The words beat in time with her heart, giving life, giving hope.

They'd arrived at the front of the Hall. She found her

arm tucked around Respen's as he led her to her place before a minister. Had Respen scrounged him from a jail cell somewhere? Was he willing to perform this marriage in exchange for his freedom?

The minister's throat bobbed as he began to recite the familiar marriage form Uncle Abel had read for so many weddings back in Stetterly. Renna couldn't concentrate. All she could hear was the tempest of her pulse shouting. *Leith was alive.*

Had she given up too soon? What if marrying Respen wasn't what she was supposed to do? Perhaps her duty was to keep waiting. Waiting for Leith.

How had she thought she could do this?

She couldn't.

Respen hid this information to take away her hope. He wouldn't keep his promise to stop persecuting the Christians. He'd say he'd stopped. But he wouldn't mean it. He'd keep her locked in Nalgar Castle, ignorant of the truth, while he continued to rule Acktar as he pleased. She'd discover his deception somehow, but by then it'd be too late. She'd be his wife, bearing his children and carrying her broken heart.

This sacrifice on her part was pointless. It wouldn't save anyone.

The minister paused. Why was everyone staring at her? Respen's dark eyes swept over her before he stated, "She does."

No, she didn't. She wasn't going to marry him. She ripped her arm from his grasp. "No!"

His face hardened. He lashed forward, gripped her elbow, and dragged her toward him. "You dare defy me?"

"I won't marry you." She lifted her chin and met his gaze. "It isn't the right thing to do."

Respen's eyes glanced toward the row of noblemen. Lord Norton's cold eyes fixed on them. Lord Beregern scowled.

Respen turned to the minister. "Marry us."

The minister's eyes darted between her and Respen. Renna met the minister's gaze. His throat jiggled, his eyes bulging. She knew all too well that faith in God didn't always take away the fear of death. That kind of fear had to be battled. Sometimes it'd be conquered, but it'd slip back through the cracks the moment victory seemed achieved.

She regained her footing and stopped fighting. She needed to remind the minister of the One who fought on their side. "The Lord is my light and my salvation; whom shall I fear?"

The minister's shoulders sagged. He bowed his head and finished the verse. "The Lord is the strength of my life; of whom shall I be afraid?" When he looked up again, his eyes burned as he met Respen's gaze. "Your Majesty, I won't perform this wedding against the lady's will."

It happened too fast. One moment Respen gripped her arm, the next he'd drawn his knife and plunged it into the minister's chest. Renna's throat closed. She couldn't even scream as the minister collapsed in front of her, blood spreading onto the flagstones.

Respen grabbed both of her arms and shoved his face close to hers. His breath scalded her cheeks. "You'll be next. You chose your birthday for our wedding. Fine. Let it be the day of your execution instead."

He shoved her backwards. She stumbled. Hands gripped her elbows as she landed against Martyn.

Execution. She sucked in a breath. She should've expected it. She'd defied Respen in front of his supporters.

He could do nothing less than the harshest punishment possible.

Respen waved them away. "Take her to the Tower."

Martyn dragged her from the hall past Lord Norton's glittering eyes and the soldiers' confused mutterings, across the bridge, and into the dark Blades' Tower. The two Blades sitting at one of the tables stared as he hustled her past them and up the three flights of stairs to the fourth floor.

He tossed her into the black room. She fell against the cot as he locked the door after her. But she didn't care. Leith would be on his way to rescue her as soon as he'd heard the news of the wedding. When he arrived, hopefully he'd be able to stop her execution.

The darkness closed around her. She slid to the floor. That's what Respen was counting on. He knew Leith would try to rescue her from the wedding.

And when he did, Respen would spring his trap.

30

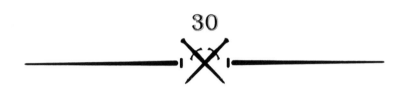

Leith was leaving. Again. As she'd known he would. Brandi watched as he swung a saddle onto Big Brown and tightened its girth. The horse thrust his ears back in an ornery expression.

All around them, the hideout bustled with activity. Resistance soldiers trained with a new fire in their eyes, and Aindre the blacksmith had been busily honing weapons and fixing armor when Brandi had passed his cabin earlier that morning. The women in the camp smoked meat and cooked biscuits that traveled well.

Last she'd heard, the army planned to leave tomorrow, the earliest that all the men could be assembled and the last preparations made. It'd also give Leith and Shad enough time to scout Respen's army around Walden. While Leith continued on to Nalgar Castle, Shad would meet the Resistance army and help tweak their plans to take Walden.

Hefting the saddlebags she'd filled with food, she carried them to Leith. "You're really leaving?"

She sounded like such a child. She was fourteen after all. If she was a boy, she'd be old enough to join the army.

Leith knelt, his face twisting as if she'd stabbed him. His voice pitched low as he gripped her shoulders. "I don't want to leave you behind, but I have to help Renna. She needs me more than you do right now."

She nodded, biting her lip to hold in the scurrying feeling in her stomach. It didn't work. She'd heard rumors around camp about what Leith was planning. He'd never let her come along to help. "You'll keep her safe, won't you?"

"I'll do my best."

He'd be hard pressed to keep that promise. Leith wasn't invincible. He'd do his best, but his best might not be good enough. Both he and Renna might die.

She'd just have to figure out how to do something on her own to stop that from happening.

He patted her shoulder. "Take care of Blizzard for me, won't you?"

"I will." Brandi blinked. He was leaving Blizzard behind. He didn't think he'd come back. A tear trickled down one of her cheeks. She couldn't lose both Leith and Renna.

Leith swiped her tear away with his thumb, his finger warm on her cold cheek. "We'll be all right. We're in God's hands."

Uncle Abel had said that exact same thing, right before he and Aunt Mara left, only to be executed a month later. What good did being in God's hands really do? She should believe it did some good, but it didn't seem like it right now.

"I just..." Another tear dribbled down her cheek. Why was she breaking down now? She didn't want to cry. Not at all. But her tears weren't listening to her. "I don't understand why everything's so hard."

Leith bowed his head. When he looked up at her, his mouth had an odd tilt to it, smiling and yet not. "You remember those Daniel stories you told me all those months ago?"

Blinking, she nodded and scrubbed at her tears. Maybe she could get rid of the evidence before anyone else noticed. "Of course I remember."

"Daniel and his three friends went through a lot of hard things. Just because they believed in God didn't mean their lives were easy. Yes, God saved them from the fiery furnace and the den of lions, but they still were thrown into them. At the time, they didn't know they'd survive. Yet they still trusted God. It always looks hopeless during the middle of the story."

They hadn't known they'd survive. Brandi had never thought about the stories that way. She'd always focused on the ending and its big deliverance. That was the important part, right?

But Daniel and his three friends hadn't known God would give them a big deliverance. They'd faced the same uncertainty she did.

This was Leith's lions' den. He didn't know if God would save him like He'd saved Daniel, but, like Daniel, Leith had to go forward and leave the rest to God.

Biting back her tears, Brandi threw herself forward and hugged Leith as hard as she could. This might be the last time she ever saw him. She didn't want him to leave thinking she was mad at him.

Tightening her grip, she buried her face against his shoulder. Maybe if she hugged him tight enough, he wouldn't have to go. He'd stay here where he was safe. They'd come up with some other plan to rescue Renna.

Wishful thinking didn't solve problems. She knew

that now. With one last squeeze, she pulled away from Leith and put on her most determined face. She dug into her pocket and pulled out the shard of crystal she'd taken from the cave. It was such a small thing compared to everything Leith had given her, but perhaps he'd need the reminder of that sparkling cave more than she would. "Here. You take this."

He took it and dropped it into a pocket. "I'll take care of it." With one last pat on her shoulder, he stood and finished packing the last of his things on Big Brown's back. As Leith led Big Brown to the edge of camp, he halted by Jamie. They spoke for a few minutes. Leith held out his hand, and Jamie shook it, though the handshake turned into a manly, back-slapping sort of hug.

The sight lurched into Brandi's stomach. Guys only hugged if they had a really, really good reason. Like they thought they might never see each other again.

She turned away, only to catch sight of Shad hugging Lady Alistair, his brother Jeremiah, and his sisters Lydia, Abigail, and Esther. He spoke with Jolene for a few minutes. After kissing his mother one last time on the cheek, Shad joined Leith, and together they led their horses out of camp.

Jamie walked over and stood next to Brandi until Shad and Leith disappeared down the trail to the south.

After a few minutes, Brandi drew herself together and faced Jamie. His eyes were wet and red-rimmed, yet his face remained free of tear streaks. "Leith asked you to look after me, didn't he?"

Jamie nodded, but his eyes remained focused on the empty horizon. "Yes, though only until I leave with Prince Keevan's army tomorrow morning. Lady Alistair will look after you then."

It was so unfair. Why did Jamie get to march off to rescue Renna, and probably Leith, while she had to sit here with the children? She'd been practicing knife-fighting and sword-fighting with him. Maybe she wasn't as good as the other boys yet, but she still could fight.

Perhaps she should've taken up archery instead of swordplay. At least then she could've joined the core of archers led by Lady Lorraine. A few girls, including Jolene, had been allowed to go with them since the archers would stay behind the main lines of fighting. And Lady Lorraine hadn't taken no for an answer.

Why did Brandi have to stay behind? Renna was *her* sister. She'd need Brandi to be there when she was rescued. After all this time alone in Respen's dungeon, she'd probably be a broken wreck, and only Brandi knew how to hold her together. She'd been doing it for over four years.

Besides, Brandi was just as old—no, older—than some of the boys going. She shouldn't have to stay behind being bored just because she was a girl.

It really was a bunch of nonsense. If Keevan was so worried about numbers that he allowed fourteen-year-old boys along, then he should've gotten off that traditional high fussiness of his and let girls join.

But, no. Girls were supposed to be weak and helpless and not lift a finger to defend themselves. Well, maybe some girls, like Renna, would be content with that.

But not Brandi.

She'd just have to pretend to be a boy. She could do that. It couldn't be that hard. They weren't complicated. She could get away with being a girl in boy's clothing, couldn't she?

Plastering on her best resigned look, Brandi turned to Jamie. "I need some time alone for a while."

"Oh." Jamie's shoulders slumped. "All right."

He was disappointed. Probably because he thought they had only tonight before he marched off to war as well. But Brandi needed some time alone to see if her plan would work.

She sidled away from him, heading for her cabin. When a few other cabins hid her from view, she scooped a handful of cold ashes from one of the outdoor cook fires and approached the corral where Blizzard and a few other horses were kept.

At her call, Blizzard's head lifted. He trotted to the fence and stuck his head over. She scratched his forehead with her free hand, then slipped between the rails. Still talking soothingly, she smeared the ashes over Blizzard. The ashes lightened his fur so that he looked like a dusty grey instead of a speckled, dark grey.

She grinned. After she finished with Blizzard, even Jamie wouldn't recognize him. When the Resistance army left for Nalgar Castle, Brandi would go with them, and no one would stop her.

Brandi woke before anyone else in the cabin she shared with Lady Lorraine, Lady Alistair, Esther, Abigail, Lydia, and Jolene. Grabbing a set of boy's clothes she'd hidden under her bed, her saddlebags, and a few personal items, she tiptoed down the stairs and eased the door open. Slipping through the camp, she halted in a secluded nook formed of two boulders a few yards away from the corral.

Setting the stuff on the ground, she crouched, drew her knife, and gripped a section of her hair. She loved the way her hair swished and blew in all directions in the wind. Did she really have to sacrifice it?

But she couldn't go along with the army with long

hair. Someone would recognize her. Steeling herself, she closed her eyes and sawed at her hair with the knife. Each strand parted until the whole hank of hair came off in her hand. Gritting her teeth, she did the same to the other side and the back, trimming it as best she could.

The muscles in her neck tightened at the sudden loss of weight. She smoothed the ends frizzing around her ears. It'd grow back. Eventually.

Besides, a few inches—well, a lot of inches—of hair were a small price to pay to save Leith and Renna.

Hurriedly, she dressed in the boy's clothes and hid her dress. The trousers felt different against her legs than her skirt as did the loose fitting shirt against her torso. Much better for adventures.

Thankfully, she didn't have enough of a girl's figure to be too noticeable yet. That would've been a bother.

She strutted in the space between the boulders. She could get used to trousers. Her legs moved freely, without the tangle of fabric clutching at her ankles all the time. Better yet, she wouldn't have to worry about moving the wrong way and exposing more of her leg than was proper. Not that she'd ever worried too much about that anyway.

She pulled the silver cross necklace from under the shirt collar. She fingered the cross, warmed from contact with her skin. It was the last gift Uncle Abel and Aunt Mara had given her. She couldn't part with it. But she also couldn't risk having it fall out from under her collar at the wrong moment.

After cutting a square of fabric from her dress, she took off the necklace, wrapped it in the fabric, and tied the bundle with another strip of fabric. She buried it in the bottom of one of her saddlebags.

After packing the rest of her things, she retrieved the

bowl of ashes she'd hidden in the nook. Blizzard   slept near the fence, head drooping toward the ground. His ears flicked sleepily as she slipped through the rails next to him and rubbed the ashes over his coat. He glanced at her a couple of times but went back to sleep once she'd held up her hand to show she didn't have an apple for him.

Brandi finished covering Blizzard in ashes as the sun peeked up the slope of the mountain and the rest of the camp stirred. Eating a quick breakfast, she joined the line of boys and men claiming their supplies. The line snaked past Aindre's blacksmith shop where he handed out weapons, through a leather worker's station, and on to several army lieutenants.

It took forever. She rocked back and forth as the line inched forward. All the good stuff would be taken by the time she arrived. She glanced behind her. It stretched into the forest farther than she could see. At least she wasn't last.

At last, she reached the blacksmith shop. Holding her breath, she peered at the pegs on the wall. There on its peg, that gorgeous short sword glittered in the early morning sunlight.

Aindre tromped to her. The head of a battle ax peeked over his shoulder from its sheath across his broad back. "What weapons do you need?"

She ducked her head to keep him from seeing her face and deepened her voice. "A sword. I have a knife." She patted the knife Leith had given her.

Aindre took the short sword down from its pegs. "This should suit you."

She took it from him. The sword was just as beautiful today. No, more beautiful.

"And, here's a dagger and another knife. It never

hurts to have a few extra weapons." Aindre piled the weapons in her arms and pointed at the leather worker's. "You can get your sheaths and armor over there."

At the leather worker's, she found a sheath for each of her new weapons along with a belt to hold all of them. One of the workers fitted her with a vest, made from layers of hardened leather, and a helmet made from the same tough leather and reinforced with strips of iron.

Brandi strutted to the next section of the line. She had a sword, heavy leather vest, and helmet. Just like a real warrior.

The boy in front of her finished with the army lieutenant. The lieutenant glanced over his paper and motioned Brandi forward. "Name?"

She'd been up half the night figuring out a name she'd remember but also wouldn't be recognized by anyone. "Randy David of Stetterly."

"Age?"

"Fourteen." She drew herself up as tall as she could.

"Really?" The lieutenant's gaze swept up and down her small frame. "All volunteers younger than sixteen need parental permission."

That could be a problem. She caught herself before she flashed her smile and big blue eyes. That wasn't a tactic a boy could use. Instead, she hung her head and scuffed the dirt as she'd seen Jamie do. "Well you see, sir, I don't got parents. Respen killed them. And my guardians were executed at Nalgar Castle. I want to fight, sir. Respen killed my family. He destroyed my town."

She held her breath. The lieutenant could try to check her story with someone from Stetterly, and he'd discover that no family by the name of David existed. But so few survivors from Stetterly made the journey to Eagle Heights that he'd be hard pressed to find them in the bustle.

"I see." The lieutenant nodded, as if he understood. "Do you have a horse?"

She'd made it in. "Yes."

"You're one of the lucky ones. You'll be able to ride instead of march." The lieutenant scanned the papers in his hand. "You'll be in Captain Stewart's Riders."

Did she dare push farther? "Which division is the Blade trainee, Jamie Cavendish, in? He's a friend of mine, sir."

The lieutenant consulted his lists. "He's assigned to Captain Alistair's Riders."

Brandi chewed on her lip. It'd be risky to ride in the same division as Shad and Jamie. But, there was something about going into battle surrounded by friends. "Do you think I could join Captain Alistair's Riders instead?"

"I don't see why not." The lieutenant marked her name on a list. "You're all set. You can claim whatever supplies you need over there. We're a little short on tents, so there aren't any more available. If you want a roof over your head, you'll have to find someone in your division who wants to share."

"Thank you, sir." Brandi hurried to the tables of supplies. She grabbed a thick blanket and oil skin, a canteen, and a sack of rations.

Saddling Blizzard, she strapped on her saddlebags and bedroll. When the men assembled, she slipped into a spot towards the rear of the formation.

She caught a glimpse of Jamie also slipping into the army a few rows ahead of her. He scanned the crowd of women and children waving and blowing kisses toward their husbands, fathers, and brothers. After a few minutes, his face fell.

He'd been looking for her. He'd hoped she'd see him off. He probably thought she was mad at him or something. A pang shot through her. She'd hurt him. Hopefully he'd forgive her when she had a chance to apologize, whenever that would be.

Keevan strode from the big cabin, dressed in shiny new leather armor with a bright green tunic draped over it. Even with the scar marring his face, he still looked regal. He strolled to his pale palomino horse and mounted gracefully.

Brandi's chest swelled. Of course, the magnificent horse and rigmarole were all staging, but it still managed to be impressive.

General Stewart called them into formation. At the head of her division of riders, Shad passed along the order. Brandi lined up with the other men and boys. When the entire line of soldiers had assembled, Keevan gave the order to move out.

The women and children cheered. A few broke into songs while others blared on a variety of instruments. Brandi ducked as she passed Lady Alistair and Abigail. Her entire plan would be wrecked if Abigail recognized her.

Once she'd safely passed the Alistairs, Brandi held her head high as she rode along with the others. Blizzard's ears pricked forward, as if he was eager to be traveling once again.

For as far as she could see, the line of soldiers stretched down the mountain and into the forest, swords glinting, leather armor and saddles creaking, banners flying.

It was time to reclaim Acktar. It was time to rescue Renna.

31

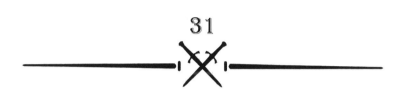

Renna twisted her fingers together, held them up to the candle, and cast a strange, misshapen shadow on the wall. Maybe if she squinted, it'd look like a horse head.

She sighed and flopped back onto the cot. After the freedom she'd enjoyed, sitting in a tiny cell grew old fast. At least Martyn had been kind enough to give her the divided skirt and ragged blue shirt she'd been wearing when captured, thankfully washed by the castle staff. Sitting in the layers of dress she'd worn to her almost-wedding would've been even more uncomfortable.

A knock rattled her door.

She sat up. "Come in." Not that she had a choice. The lock was on the outside. But at least Martyn gave her that much dignity.

When the door opened, a slim young man with straight, brown hair and blue eyes slipped inside.

Renna bolted to her feet and backed against the far wall. He was dressed in black. A Blade. What did he want with her? She reached for the candlestick. The wax pooled at the bottom of the wick would burn painfully if she threw it into the young man's face. "What do you want?"

He held up his hands. "I'm not here to hurt you."

That's when she spotted the belt around his waist, empty except for a single knife. He was nearly unarmed, though that didn't mean he couldn't hurt her. "Why are you here? Where's Martyn?"

Martyn was a loyal, dutiful Blade who'd do anything Respen ordered him to do, but at least he'd never gone out of his way to harm her.

The Blade swallowed. "The First Blade doesn't know I'm here. He's meeting with the king, so I only have a few minutes. I talked to Leith."

Which Blade had reported that Leith was alive? Renna scrunched her fingers in her skirt. "You're Eighth Blade Harding."

"Yes, I'm Ranson Harding." The Blade bobbed his head. How old was he? With his thin shoulders and lanky legs, he couldn't be more than fifteen, maybe sixteen years old. His eyes met hers. "He asked that I check on you, if I could."

Warmth surged through Renna's fingers. Leith was doing his best to watch out for her, even from so far away.

Why had this Blade done as Leith asked? He risked punishment if caught being friendly to her. "Thank you. Why'd you do it for Leith?"

"He helped me when he didn't have to. I was wounded, and he stitched it up. He said he did it because you helped him once. Something about forgiveness and God." Ranson's head dipped, and his shoulders shook. "I still don't understand."

So lost, like all the Blades she'd met here. Martyn, Ranson, even Respen wallowed in a blackness so thick she couldn't imagine the choking awfulness of it. She could only try to comprehend the hurt she saw in their eyes.

She remembered the cold blue eyes of Harrison Vane,

the former First Blade who'd tried to kill her. If she'd looked harder, deeper, would she have seen the same hurt? If she'd been less afraid, could she have reached out to him too? That's what Leith had tried and failed to do with Vane. He'd tried again with Ranson.

Not everyone could be helped. Some, like Vane, wouldn't hear even at the end. But that didn't mean she had to give up trying. She had a little over a week left. She had to make that count for something.

First things first. Renna squared her shoulders. "You said Leith stitched a wound? That must've been a week or more ago. Those stitches have to come out, unless you pulled them out already."

"No, I didn't. I..." Ranson swallowed.

Based on the gray cast to his face, he was squeamish. Not a good quality in a Blade. Renna pointed at her cot. "Sit. I'll take the stitches out. I'm a trained healer. Where were you wounded?"

He eyed her as if debating whether risking punishment was worth her help. "You're going to help me?"

The look in his eyes, like he'd been kicked too many times yet still wanted to trust someone, tore at her. Until Leith, how many people had ever offered him a kindness? She gave him a gentle smile. "Yes, I'll help. Leith told you I would, didn't he? You trusted him. You can trust me."

For a long moment, he didn't move as his gaze searched her face. The set of his jaw relaxed. He eased onto the cot, unbuckled his belt, and set it next to him. With one hand still on his sheathed knife, he pulled up one side of his black shirt with the other. A six-inch scab ran along the last rib. Jagged stitches laced through the scab and healing skin.

Renna shook her head. What a mess. No wonder Leith

had once cauterized his wound rather than pass off her stitching as his own. Aunt Mara would've barred him from ever touching a wound again.

Aunt Mara. Execution.

No, she mustn't think about that now.

Renna knelt and inspected the wound. "Looks like it's healing all right. But those stitches have to come out. Leave them in there any longer, and they'll be stuck permanently."

Ranson's face turned a shade whiter. "Take them out. Please."

She drew in a deep breath. She didn't have her medical kit with its small knife to cut the stitches. "I'll need to borrow your knife."

He bolted to his feet, lines cutting across his face. "I knew you and Leith were being too nice. This was all a set up to get me here and give you a knife. You want to escape."

Respen planned to execute her in a little over a week. Of course she wanted to escape.

But she had promised Respen she wouldn't try to escape on her own. Perhaps she could argue that he'd broken his part of the promise by taking away her freedom to roam the castle. She could take Ranson's knife and attempt it.

Yet something held her back. She was needed here, in this room right now. Ranson needed her. As did Martyn. Even Respen still needed her here. Maybe she didn't want to marry him, but she had to reach out and try to touch that hurting part of him somehow and, perhaps through her, God would touch Respen too.

All that was more important than escaping her execution.

"I'm not going to escape, and I'm not going to hurt you. I promise all I'm going to do with your knife is cut the stitches." Renna held his gaze. "Look at me. Even if I managed to get a hold of your knife, do I look like I could overpower you?"

She could stab him in the stomach while taking out the stitches, and he'd have to have inhumanly fast reflexes to stop her. But, she was a healer. She wasn't about to stab him.

His wariness remained. She couldn't blame him. If she escaped because of him, Respen would torture him, maybe even kill him.

"I'm a healer. It's my duty to place the wellbeing of my patient above my own."

Duty. The one creed that resonated with a Blade.

He drew his knife and held it out to her, hilt first. She took it. When she didn't move, he returned to his seat on the cot and pulled up the corner of his shirt again.

That act of trust must've cost him dearly. She couldn't waste it.

Renna knelt and eased the tip of the knife under the first stitch. Ranson flinched. Probably preparing for her to gut him where he sat.

The knife parted the thread easily. Trust a Blade to keep his knives well-sharpened. Instead of pulling out each thread as she cut them, Renna sliced through all the stitches and handed the knife back to Ranson. He sheathed it but kept a hand gripped around the leather sheath.

"You said you didn't understand why Leith would help you." Renna tugged on the first stitch. After a moment of resistance, it slid free of Ranson's skin.

He sucked in a breath and nodded.

"Our faith calls us to kindness. To share the love we've been given with those God places in our path." She tugged a few more pieces of thread free. "I never was very good at doing that. Not until Leith came along and showed me how to have courage to share my faith and give kindness freely."

Ranson's fingers flexed against the blanket. His jaw worked. Would he ask more questions? Or would he shut her words out the same way Martyn had?

She yanked at another thread. Only one more to go. She leaned in closer to pinch the tiny end.

"What's going on here?"

The rock-hard voice whipped through the tiny room. Ranson bolted to his feet so fast his knee came close to smacking Renna's nose. He thumped his fist across his chest. "First Blade."

"What were you thinking? The door was open. You have a knife right there. What do you think the king would do to you—and to me—if she escaped?" Martyn jabbed Ranson in the chest with a finger. "Get out."

Renna stood, rested a hand on Ranson's arm to stop him, and faced Martyn. "I was removing Ranson's stitches. I still have one left, so if you'll let him sit back down, I'll take care of it."

Martyn glared at Ranson. "Leave."

"But there's one stitch left!"

"He'll pull it out himself." Martyn shoved Ranson toward the door. When Ranson caught his balance, he dashed from the room and down the hallway.

"And you—" Martyn whirled toward Renna and shook his finger at her nose. "Don't you dare turn him like you did Leith. Don't talk to him. Don't even get close to him. Ranson is too young. Leith at least knew the consequences of listening to you. Ranson doesn't. He can't handle pulling out his own stitches. How do you think he'd handle torture?"

Renna took a step back. A tremble wiggled through her fingers. But she drew herself straight. "He came to me. He was looking for help. I gave it."

"Well, don't give it." Martyn's eyes blazed. His body shook with the force of his words.

"I know you're just trying to protect him. And I know you were trying to protect Leith. But maybe they don't need protecting. Maybe they need courage more." She raised her chin. She wouldn't back down. Not this time.

Martyn cursed and raked a hand through his hair. When he turned back to her, his face had smoothed into the same, hard lines he always wore. "Duty motivates just as well as courage. Now, we've delayed long enough. Come."

Renna followed Martyn from her room. Instead of dragging her down three flights of stairs and over to the king's apartments, he turned the other way and hauled her up the set of stairs to the final floor of the Blades' Tower.

The Blades' meeting room. She'd been there once before when Respen had ordered Leith to kill her and Brandi during the last Meeting of the Blades.

Yanking the door open, Martyn shoved her into the black room lit with only a single candle at the head of a long table. Renna swallowed. Shadows stalked the corners, slinking around the chairs and slithering beneath the table.

Martyn released her arm. She walked the length of the table, running her hand along the top of the chairs. She paused as she reached the chair to the right of the throne. This had been Leith's seat as the First Blade and

Harrison Vane's before that. Now it was Martyn's.

She crept to the other side of the room and touched the chains bolted to the wall. Dark stains marred the stones of the wall and floor. Dried blood. If not for Leith, her blood would've joined the stains on this wall.

"Seven failed Blades have died chained to that wall." Respen's deep voice rumbled from the darkness behind her.

She whirled. He stood near the head of the table, the shadows dancing through the candlelight across his face. That explained Martyn's anger. If he hadn't stumbled on them first, Respen would've seen Ranson talking to her.

Her heart vibrated a shuddering rhythm in her chest. "Are you going to kill me here?"

Was that how she'd die? Chained against the wall like one of the failed Blades? Only this time, Leith wouldn't be able to save her.

His chuckle thrummed along the stones. "I want the whole kingdom to watch your execution. No, this is where I will kill Leith Torren when he comes to rescue you."

She wasn't supposed to know Leith was still alive. She forced herself to jump as if in surprise. "Leith's alive?"

"Yes. It seems the Waste was not enough to kill him." Respen trailed his fingers along the arms of the throne-like chair at the head of the table. "But he will not escape me for long. He will come to stop your execution, and when he does, I will catch him. He will beg for death before he dies."

Renna shivered and glanced at the chains behind her. Would Leith's blood stain this wall? Squeezing her eyes shut, she drew in several deep breaths. She couldn't let Respen's words, the darkness of this place, get to her head. She straightened her shoulders. "God is with me, and He is with Leith."

Respen drummed his fingers on the tabletop. When he spoke, his voice was low and almost gentle. "You still surprise me. After all I have put you through, you still cling to your faith. Just like Clarisse. Even in the end, she died praying."

"Then she is with Jesus." Renna tiptoed to the table. She gripped the back of the nearest chair. "I look forward to meeting her there after my execution."

Respen's fingers stopped tapping. He glanced up at her, his eyes shadowed. "I suppose you believe I will not join her when I die."

She hesitated. What was she supposed to tell him? Could she reach Respen's heart? "At the moment, your actions indicate that you won't. But even you aren't beyond the hope of salvation. God can work in any heart, no matter how black and hard. He can change you."

"Only if I admit I am weak and helpless, is that it?" Respen snorted.

"When God touches your heart, you'll see your own weakness. You'll see how helpless you are. And that will make you long for His strength."

"I am the most powerful man in Acktar. I am far from weak." Respen waved his arms at the dark room, as if to encompass the whole country.

Of all the emotions she thought she'd feel toward King Respen, pity wasn't one of them. Yet that's exactly what she'd call the squeezing, hurting pressure in her chest. Respen was proud. He was like the wicked kings in the Bible stories Brandi loved so much, so proud and hard-hearted that they wouldn't—couldn't—bow to God.

She faced him. "Only when you're weak will God make you strong."

In the months she'd spent at Nalgar Castle, she'd learned that lesson over and over again. She was weak. She wasn't courageous like Leith or hopeful like Brandi. Still, God had given her the strength to survive when she'd needed it. She hadn't denied her faith. She hadn't given in to Respen's smooth lies. And that defied all expectation, including her own.

Respen strolled toward her. The look in his dark eyes might've been tender as he reached a hand toward her, as if to touch her. "Renna. We could have been powerful together. We could have ruled Acktar side by side with everyone at our feet. You could have been my queen."

For a moment, she was almost taken in by the ache in his eyes. If she'd married him, would she have eventually loved him? Was what she saw in his eyes love? Could he even love?

Perhaps he could, but not the way the Bible instructed a man to love his wife. He could never do that as long as he didn't love God.

How had she become so blinded? She'd thought that if she tried to love Respen, she could eventually change him. But that was backwards. Hadn't she learned that with Leith? She'd only been able to love him after God had already changed him.

Renna forced her chin up. "I'd rather be God's servant than your queen."

Respen's eyes darkened, washing away whatever gentleness may or may not have been there. "Then you'll die."

If he thought those words would send her back to the cowering girl she'd been for the past four and a half years, then he was mistaken. That girl was long gone. God was on her side.

"So be it." She spun on her heels and marched to the door. She flung it open, nearly running into Martyn as he stood guard on the landing. "Martyn, return me to my cell."

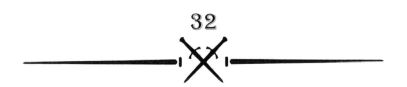

32

Leith and Shad lay at the edge of a promontory, the maze of boulders at their backs. From their vantage point, the dusty brown expanse of prairie stretched away to the horizon, broken only by the black disease of Respen's army gathered along a roll of the foothills. Beyond them, the shapes of Walden Manor and its defenses darkened one patch of prairie.

"Walden's still standing." Shad craned his neck and pushed onto his elbows to get a better view. "Can you spot any Blades?"

Leith pointed at a spiked section of stone thrusting through the carpet of pines, keeping his hand low. "See that wisp of smoke by those rocks? Someone has a campsite there. I'm guessing one of the lower Blades. The more experienced Blades would know better than to make a fire while on lookout."

Shad squinted towards the rock. After several minutes, he shrugged. "I think I see something."

"There're several places the other Blades could be, but I haven't seen any definite signs." Leith inched back

DEFY

from the rim. "The foothills will be crawling with Blades no matter where we are. Respen will want to know the moment anyone from the Resistance sets a toe in Acktar."

Shad crawled on his belly until he was out of sight of the land below. When he was clear, he stood and brushed his trousers off. "So what do we do now? Sneak past them?"

Leith slid to his feet and scrubbed at the dust covering his black clothes. "I'll scout the area tonight. You'll stay up here." When Shad opened his mouth to protest, Leith held up his finger. "While your sneaking skills are excellent for a lord's son, you aren't good enough to scout out the positions of all the Blades down there and the army around Walden. I'm a Blade. This is what I do."

When darkness closed around the Hills, Leith slipped from their campsite. Skittering down the cliff side, Leith dropped to the ground. He padded through the pines and cedars, moving the branches as little as possible. Circling a spine of rock, he peeked around the edge.

Ninth Blade Altin slept next to a small fire. His dusty brown horse dozed beyond him. Its head raised, and it looked at Leith. But it didn't give a warning nicker. It must not see him as a threat.

Leith frowned. Altin had been sent to aid the army attacking the western towns. If Altin was here, it meant the western towns had fallen and that division of Respen's army now reinforced the army around Walden.

Not good. When Prince Keevan arrived with the Resistance army, he'd have to face the full brunt of Respen's army instead of facing it one division at a time as they'd hoped.

Fading into the darkness, Leith explored the rest of the foothills between the cliff and the prairie. He discovered

223

Third Blade Crossley and Fourth Blade Tooley on either side of Altin's position. Far enough apart that a small group might be able to slip through, but an army would be noticed.

Skirting the Blades, Leith hiked out of the foothills. At the bottom, he reached an open stretch of ground between him and the army. He crouched and eased through the long grass, moving with a sliding, weaving motion. Near the rise, he spotted the first sentry yawning and stamping his feet. Leith sneaked past him easily.

The camp sprawled along the high ground. Leith slipped through the shadows, counting tents and the number of men trudging about. He spotted the horses and bedrolls of two more Blades near General Wentle's command tent.

When he'd noted the size of this section of the army, he wandered toward Walden. Ranks of tents surrounded the dry moat and dirt fortification Leith had helped build weeks ago. Torches lit the top of the fortifications, preventing the Blades from sneaking too close.

Lord Alistair's sentries peeked between wooden barricades, alert and wary. Even Leith didn't stand a chance of getting past them. Still tempting to try, if only to reassure Lord Alistair that help was coming.

Leith crept past the army sentries and into the foothills. As dawn burst across the eastern horizon, he dropped from a rock into the camp he and Shad had set up.

At the scuffling of his feet, Shad startled awake and reached for his dagger. Leith held out his hands. "Easy. It's just me."

Shad yawned and sat up. "What did you find?"

Leith shrugged. "The Blades are stationed along the foothills. I spotted the campsites for three of them, but there might be another one or two in the Hills to the west. Two Blades are the camp below. But we have a bigger problem."

"Bigger problem than the Blades?" Shad scrubbed at his eyes.

"I spotted a couple of the Blades that had been with the division attacking the western towns. That means the western towns have fallen, and Respen's entire army is now positioned between us and Nalgar Castle." Leith drew the positions in the dust.

Shad studied the crude dust map. "We can't go around them?"

"This route through the Hills is the best one for a large army. Respen knows it, which is why he has his army positioned here. But even if we could go around them, our army has to face them before taking on Nalgar Castle to prevent being pinned between the castle and Respen's army. It's best to drive down from the Hills here to push them back toward Nalgar."

Shad scowled and nodded. "Respen planned his position well. How many men does he have?"

"Roughly ten thousand. I spotted the banners for the towns of Kilm, Surgis, Mackton, Mountainwood, Deadgrass, and Dyman. The men from the other towns supporting him are stationed farther west."

"Ten thousand? And we can scrape together maybe six thousand. That's including old men and young boys who won't be as strong or as skilled as Respen's soldiers." Shad's shoulders slumped. "And they've dug in on the high ground."

Leith swallowed at the weight in his stomach. They had hoped Respen's army would remain divided, which would put the numbers facing them roughly equal to their own.

They couldn't back down from this fight now. "If you can drive Respen's army from this position, you'll get a few reinforcements from Walden."

"We don't know what kind of shape they'll be in after defending Walden for this long." Shad's eyes strayed toward the direction Walden lay. "It's possible Prince Keevan's return could prompt the towns of Calloday and Dently to send reinforcements and some of Respen's men might even defect when they see the Eirdon banner. Maybe a few men survived the attacks on Arroway and Flintley. If we can contact them, they'll help."

Long shots, all of them. But that's all they had.

Shad met Leith's eyes, his expression sober. "A tough battle here will delay our army. If we take too much time..."

"Then you won't arrive at Nalgar Castle in time to save me. I know." Leith shook his head. "I have to stop the wedding regardless. No matter what happens to me, I'll make sure Renna gets out."

Whatever it took, he'd get her away from Respen somehow. He couldn't let Respen marry her or hurt her in any way.

Shad rubbed the hilt of his sword. "You don't have to turn yourself in. Yes, having you on the inside might be helpful when we try to take the Blades' Tower, and, yes, it might take a few of the Blades away from this front. But those benefits aren't worth your life. We still can send a small group into Nalgar Castle and attempt a rescue that way."

Leith leaned against a boulder, the long night of scouting pressing into his skull. "A long time ago, I told you Martyn Hamish was a friend. He's the Blade guarding Renna, and he won't let her go without a fight."

"A small raid would be comprised quickly, wouldn't it?"

"Yes. The only way to prevent Martyn from raising the alarm would be to assassinate him." Leith rested his hands on the boulder. The gritty surface scratched at his palms. "I'm the only one with the skills to do it."

"And you can't. Not even for Renna." Shad's voice remained even.

Leith shook his head. He couldn't meet Shad's gaze. "Is that wrong? Shouldn't I be willing to do anything for her?"

"No. There are some lines you shouldn't cross, not for anyone." Shad's boots crunched, and the next moment, the weight of his hand rested on Leith's shoulder. "You're currently planning to give yourself to a week of torture to save her from marriage to Respen. No one doubts the lengths you are willing to go."

When Shad put it that way, Leith's plan sounded downright suicidal. But to save both Renna and Martyn, he had to risk it.

"Martyn can't be persuaded to help?"

"He knows I betrayed him. It's going to take something more drastic than talk to make him help me." Leith sucked in a deep breath of the morning air, rich with pine and earth.

"Like seeing you tortured?" Shad scowled. "What if that isn't enough?"

"I'm betting it is."

Shad stepped back and crossed his arms. His scowl deepened the lines across his forehead. "You don't have to throw your life away like this. We need you."

Leith smiled, though the action felt tight and strained. "You don't need me. With this information, you'll be able to guide Prince Keevan to the best position to attack the army. The Blades won't pose a threat to your numbers." He clapped Shad on the shoulder. "Besides, you're going to save me."

"You can't be sure of that."

"Yes, I am." Leith put as much confidence in those words as possible. "You're going to rescue your father, then you'll rescue me and Renna when you conquer Nalgar. That's what lord's sons do."

One week of torture. Leith had to survive it. No matter how much Respen tortured him, the king wouldn't let him die before the Meeting. But if Prince Keevan was delayed and didn't attack during the Meeting, Leith would be long dead by the time Shad arrived at Nalgar Castle.

At that point, Leith had better hope Martyn had a change of heart.

Shad huffed a sigh. "You're the most insane Blade of the lot, aren't you?"

"Most likely." Leith shrugged and forced a grin. After a moment, his grin faded. "I'll be all right. I trust God with my life. Respen can't hurt me a hair beyond what God has already planned for me."

"Then the Lord's will be done." Shad bowed his head. After a few moments of silence, he straightened his shoulders. "I'll report what we've seen to Prince Keevan. He and General Stewart will come up with a plan. We'll get to the castle on time."

"I know."

In the end, it didn't matter whether Shad got there in time or not. Renna needed Leith there. He couldn't abandon her.

Not this time.

33

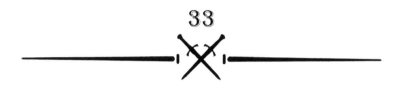

After three long days travelling with the army, Brandi had learned more about what guys did when they didn't think a girl was looking than she'd ever wanted to know.

The latrines, if the pits dug at the end of camp could be called that, were in plain sight with no privacy whatsoever. Not that all the guys took the time to walk to that end of the camp. She'd learned that one the hard way. Guys also had no inhibitions against changing in the open air, comparing chest hair, and making a variety of rude noises and laughing about it.

Not *all* of them were that crude, and, to their credit, most of them tried to be a little more civilized when any of the women archers were nearby.

But Brandi looked like one of the boys. If any of them stumbled across her at the moment, that wouldn't last long. After finding a secluded spot behind a fallen tree, she hurried to take care of some personal business after the day's ride.

Footsteps crunched on the dead leaves and sticks.

Shoot. Of course someone would decide to wander in this direction. Brandi hurriedly straightened her clothes, buckled her belt, and stepped around the fallen tree.

A young man skidded to a halt, his short brown hair flying around a slim face. His hazel eyes widened. "Oh!" The word came out in a high-pitched squeak. The young man coughed, and his voice deepened. "I mean, sorry."

The voice did it. Brandi grinned. Not a young man. A young woman. A fellow masquerader. Brandi spoke in her normal voice. "I see you're also looking for a bit of privacy. There's a nice spot back there. Would you like me to stand guard?"

The woman's shoulder's relaxed. When she spoke, she made no attempt to disguise her voice either. "Thanks."

Brandi leaned her back against a tree, keeping an eye on the men bustling around the fires. None of them made any move into the forest.

After a few minutes, the young woman joined Brandi by the tree. She stuck out her hand. "Thanks again."

Brandi shook her hand. "I'm Brandi with Captain Alistair's Riders. Glad to see I'm not the only girl in disguise here. What's your name?"

The young woman frowned, leaning away from Brandi as if she wanted to bolt. "I'm Kay."

That sounded more like her fake army name than her real name, but Brandi wasn't going to be picky. "Nice to meet you."

Kay nodded and tromped away, headed in the direction of the main mass of foot soldiers.

With a shrug, Brandi strolled in the other direction. The Riders were stationed on the outskirts of the camp to have room for their horses, one division of Riders for each side. Brandi had left her bedroll and saddle in a heap since she'd been in such a hurry to find a quiet spot in the woods.

She could go set up a small campsite by herself.

That's what she'd been doing the past two nights. But the near miss convinced her. She couldn't keep doing this on her own. There were too many guys and too little privacy. She needed an ally to keep watch.

At the outskirts of the Alistair Riders, Jamie perched on a log by a small fire by himself. He turned a small carcass on a spit. His bedroll lay a few feet away. Apparently he missed out on a tent too.

She plopped to the ground across from him. "Hi."

His eyes flicked up then returned to the carcass. He froze, and his gaze inched back to her. "Brandi? What in Acktar are you doing here?"

"I joined the army. What does it look like I'm doing?" Brandi crossed her arms and glared at him. She wasn't going to back down. She'd come too far to have Jamie try to talk her out of this.

"That's ridiculous." Jamie jumped to his feet. "We're going to report this to Prince Keevan. He'll arrange to have someone take you back to Eagle Heights."

"Don't you dare!" She grabbed his shirt sleeve. She couldn't go back yet. "I have to do this. Leith and Renna are in trouble. I can't run and hide. Not this time. Surely you understand."

His shoulders sagged as he slumped onto his log. "You know Leith's going to kill me if he finds out I let you join the army."

"And Renna's going to kill me when she finds out, but that isn't going to stop me." Brandi clenched her fists and her jaw. "If you try to send me back, I'll just slip out and follow the army on my own. Then I'd be unprotected, and that'd be worse, wouldn't it?" She cocked her head as she looked up at him, trying to add a note of innocence to those last words.

Jamie's sigh contained a growl. He scowled at her. "This isn't a game. We're headed to war. There's going to be killing and deaths."

"I know." She met his gaze. Of course she knew that. She wasn't stupid. But this was the middle of the story. If Leith was Daniel meekly walking into the lions' den, then she was David grabbing a sling on the way to slay a giant. Yes, there'd be bloodshed. Yes, she'd see death and even cause a few deaths herself. But she had to face this fight. "I can handle it."

She'd killed once. For Leith's and Renna's sakes, she could face doing it again in battle. That's what warriors did.

She studied the expression flashing across Jamie's face. He turned the spit, staring at the fire as if it held all the answers to his problems. She raised her eyebrows. "You haven't killed before, have you?"

He shook his head, still focused on the spitted meat. "Leith took me out of Nalgar Castle before Respen had a chance to force me to kill. I haven't had too many fights since then."

And she'd killed instead of him in the one attack they'd suffered.

Jamie's eyes flashed upward. "But this is what I've trained for. You've had a few lessons, but I've spent over two years with the Blades. I haven't killed yet, but I'll be able to fight when the time comes."

"And I proved I can hold my own in a fight." Brandi gripped the hilt of the knife Leith had given her. "Look around. I'm hardly the only fourteen-year-old here. I have about as much training as some of them. Besides, I'm older than you."

"By three months. I'll turn fourteen soon." Jamie

waved at her. "Besides, you're a…"

"A girl?" Brandi grimaced at him. "So I've noticed. Do you realize how disgusting boys are when they think a girl isn't watching?"

Jamie's eyebrows shot up. "You're just realizing this?"

"All I had was a sister. Not much time spent around boys."

"That explains a few things." He pulled the spit from the fire. After waving it in the air for a few minutes, he ripped off a chunk of meat and handed it to her. "Dig in."

After praying, she blew on the meat for several minutes before she took a bite. The juice dribbled onto her chin. She swiped it away with her fingers.

Jamie chomped into his piece, chewed, and swallowed. "If this army wasn't so big, someone would've noticed you're a girl. You have no idea how to act like a boy."

She watched his movements, the way he gripped the meat in his fist, the big bites. She shoved as much of the meat as she could in her mouth, chewed with her mouth partly open, and said with her mouth still full, "How's this?"

"Better. If you want everyone to think you were raised by wolves." He rolled his eyes and kept eating.

She copied him, taking a bite when he took a bite, chewing as long as he chewed, wiping her mouth on her sleeve when he did. Based on the twinkle in his eyes, she wasn't getting it right. This whole being a boy thing was harder than she'd thought.

"So are you going to report me?" She chomped her bite and slurped on her fingers to clean them.

"Guess not." His fingers tightened. "It wouldn't stop you from doing anything crazy, and I'd rather have you here where I can keep an eye on you than doing something reckless where I can't."

She grinned and reached for another chunk of meat. She'd known he'd agree with her when she put it to him the right way. Most people did.

As dawn broke in the distance, Leith had hiked west through the edge of the Sheered Rock Hills. After allowing himself a few hours of rest, he continued hiking until he'd passed the far western flank of Respen's army.

Toward evening, he approached the town of Flayin Falls. Smoke trickled from a few of the buildings while a line of people snaked from the town headed north into the Hills. If Leith were to guess, Respen's army had raided the town looking for supplies.

Leith watched the people. Should he talk to them? He needed information. Without it, he'd walk into Respen's trap blind. But if he questioned someone, Respen might discover his whereabouts and capture him before he had a chance to stop the wedding.

Lord Westin was one of the Christian noblemen killed by Blades a few months ago. The odds were high that the people fleeing northwest were Christians escaping into the Sheered Rock Hills. It was unlikely one of them would report Leith to Respen.

If Leith managed to get them to talk. He glanced down at his black clothes. He might frighten them to silence dressed as he was.

He had to risk it. Waiting until darkness dropped around them, Leith slithered through the grass toward a man lagging behind the others. His wife and children trudged into the foothills ahead of him, already weary with the burden of the possessions they carried on their backs.

Ghosting behind the man, Leith drew a knife and pressed the flat of the blade against the man's throat. "I'm not going to hurt you. I just need information."

The man stiffened and remained silent.

"I heard King Respen plans to marry Lady Rennelda. When and where is the wedding taking place?" Leith kept his voice low but friendly. No need to scare the man more than he had to.

"The wedding was several days ago." The man's throat bobbed.

He was too late. Leith's stomach burned. Respen must've moved it. He'd known Leith would try to interfere and had fooled him into thinking he'd still had time.

"But the king didn't marry the lady." The man swallowed again. "I heard she refused him. So he's having her executed."

An execution. Not a wedding. Should he be relieved or worried? "When's the execution?"

The man made a gargling sound. Leith winced. He'd pressed the knife harder against the man's neck than he'd realized. Since the man was cooperating, Leith released him. "Please. I need to know. When is Lady Rennelda's execution?"

Cautiously, the man turned around. His eyes flicked over Leith, taking in the knives and the black clothes. "You're that Blade King Respen is hunting, aren't you?

There were other Blades here asking about you."

Too late to deny it now. "Yes."

The man's tense shoulders eased as he glanced at his family. They'd stopped trudging down the road and now huddled in a group as if numbers would protect them. "The lady's execution is a week from today."

Leith's shoulders sagged. He had time.

The man waved a hand at the knife Leith still held. "You know, you could've just asked."

Leith glanced at the knife, grimaced, and sheathed it. It hadn't even occurred to him that he could go up to the man and ask. Questioning always involved knives. "Sorry. Let me give you some provisions for your trouble."

He dug in his pack and pulled out half of his dried meat and biscuits. If only he could tell the man that the Resistance army was on its way. But he couldn't risk word reaching Respen's army.

The man took the supplies. "I hope you rescue her."

Leith nodded. "Your prayers would be appreciated." He spun on his heel and headed for Nalgar Castle.

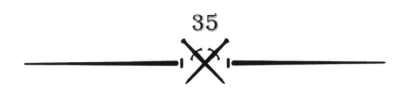

35

Brandi craned her neck to see what was causing the commotion at the front of the army. Blizzard flicked his ears, as if he could hear and understand the words being said.

She caught a glimpse of dark hair and the shine of chestnut fur. "Shad's back." As she settled back into the saddle, the order barked along the column to halt and make camp.

"Must have some crucial information." Jamie dismounted and tugged Buster in the direction their lieutenant indicated. "Prince Keevan and General Stewart need to plan."

Brandi undid the girth on her saddle and hauled it off Blizzard's back. She brushed the sweat coating the fur under the saddle. When she'd finished, she took a few handfuls of dust and rubbed it over Blizzard's distinctive grey, speckled coat.

Since she'd told Jamie, she hadn't bothered, but with Shad back in camp, she needed to keep Blizzard hidden. Jamie might be willing to let her ride into this battle, but she didn't think Shad would be as lenient. He might tolerate Lady Lorraine and Jolene with the archers, but he wouldn't allow her to continue with the Riders. He'd personally escort her all the way to Eagle Heights and see to it that Lady Alistair kept Brandi tied in her room until this war was over.

Brandi couldn't let that happen. She needed to be here.

Several soldiers erected a tent for the commanders, complete with Prince Keevan's light green banner flying from the tallest pole. Shad, General Stewart, Prince Keevan, and Lady Lorraine disappeared inside.

Brandi caught Jamie eyeing the tent. He had to be thinking the same thing she was. After all, what was the use of being a Blade and a sort of Blade trainee if they didn't use their sneaking skills? "Want to listen in?"

With a sly smile, he eased to his feet. Brandi followed him on tiptoes as they skirted the edge of the camp. Sticking to the shadows, they sidled up to the side of the tent and crouched by a tree.

"...Blades here, here, and here." Shad's voice filtered through the canvas.

"Can we slip past them?" Prince Keevan's voice rasped.

"No. They're spaced far enough apart that a small group could slip through, but not the whole army." Paper rustled. "Respen has his army stationed here with their eastern flank anchored against Walden and their western flank on this ridge in the foothills. The rest of the line curves between those two points. If we try to bypass them through Flayin Falls, they'll swing around and squeeze us against Nalgar Castle."

"So a costly frontal assault is our only option." General Stewart's growl cut through the air. "Hit them in the center and try to break the line."

Brandi bit her lip. She didn't understand much about

military planning, but that didn't sound good. Especially if she was going to be a part of this "costly frontal assault."

"I wouldn't advise it." Shad's voice accompanied a tapping sound. "Several of the Blades Leith spotted had been with the division attacking the western towns. We're facing Respen's entire army. There are about ten thousand men down there."

"Not a pleasant prospect." Lady Lorraine's voice cut through the tent's thick fabric. "Is there any way to hit their flanks?"

"They have sentries watching the Spires Canyon behind Walden, and there's too much open space to sneak from that side." More rustling paper accompanied Shad's words. "On the other end, a Blade is stationed on this cliff overlooking the ridge. It's the highest elevation in the area, and he'll see our army coming. But, this canyon here is hidden from view. It's too small for our entire army, but a hundred of my Riders could circle around from the west and come out on this steep slope. The Blade wouldn't see us until we were between him and Respen's army."

"That Blade Leith Torren could've been an asset." Keevan's tone sounded almost guilty. "His scouting expertise could've been useful."

Brandi grimaced. Her cousin's stubbornness had forced Leith to choose the path he had. If Leith wasn't here now, then Keevan had no one to blame but himself.

"Leith isn't here, but Jamie, his trainee, came along. He's a part of my division. He has all the training of a Blade."

Beside her, Jamie eased a hand to touch the top of his right shoulder. He was probably thinking about how close to the truth Shad was. Shad didn't know Jamie was a full-fledged Blade. Perhaps not as skilled as Leith, but still sneaky.

Brandi would have to be just as sneaky to join those hundred riders when Shad picked them out of their division of two hundred and fifty. No way was she going to be left out of that adventure.

"Their flank should crumble, and their line shatter." General Stewart sounded satisfied with that thought.

Crumbling and shattering sounded like good things to Brandi.

"I say we do one better." Something tapped, like a finger on paper, as Lady Lorraine spoke. "General Wentle will expect a flank attack since it's the best option for assailing his position. So let's give him two flanking attacks. As we've discussed, Captain Alistair will take a hundred of his Riders on this circular route to hit the western flank. To divert General Wentle's attention, we'll send Captain Stewart with the rest of the three hundred and fifty Riders down the Spires Canyon. They'll hit the eastern flank stationed around Walden. General Wentle will be forced to reinforce his eastern flank when his sentries report the attack."

Brandi leaned closer to Jamie. "Captain Stewart?"

"General Stewart's son."

One guess as to how he got his position as captain.

"When my father sees what's happening, he'll rally Walden's defenders and hit that flank as well."

"If your father is still alive." Keevan rasped.

Brandi rolled her eyes. Of course her cousin had to be the sour apple in the basket.

"He is. No one else could've kept Walden standing this long."

"Precisely." Lady Lorraine's tone chided the others

into silence. "With such a strong attack from the east and the foot soldiers and archers attacking the center, General Wentle will weaken his western flank to reinforce the rest of his line. That's when Captain Alistair should make his move."

Brandi tilted closer to the tent as everyone inside lapsed into silence. Probably mulling over the plan and looking for problems. She didn't see any, but she wasn't a military planner.

General Stewart's gruff voice broke the silence first. "I'll instruct Captain Stewart to proceed cautiously. If he's observed, he should look like he's attempting a sneak attack. If he isn't seen, we'll have two sneak attacks, which would be all the better."

"It is imperative, Captain Alistair, that your sneak attack proceeds without detection." Lady Lorraine's voice had the sharp quality of a commander instructing a captain rather than a future son-in-law. "The Blades will give General Wentle warning of the rest of our movements. We're depending on yours to be a surprise."

"With Jamie's help and a hundred of the best Riders, it'll work."

Jamie drew his shoulders straight, as if preparing himself for the burden of the sneak attack's success to rest on him. Brandi squeezed his shoulder. Now she had to make sure she was one of the hundred. No way would she let Jamie face all that pressure alone.

"Your Highness, do we have your approval of this plan?" General Stewart's tone softened into a deferential, yet fatherly timbre.

"Yes, please proceed with the arrangements." Keevan's voice changed into a stuffily official tone. "See to it that messengers are sent to Calloday and Ably. It's possible that they might send reinforcements once they hear I've returned to Acktar. I'll write the messages for you to give them. I'll instruct them to rendezvous with our army at Aven."

"Yes, Your Highness." The pitch of General Stewart changed, as if he was bowing. "Do you wish to send a rider to Dently?"

"Not yet. It's too close to Nalgar Castle, and thus at greater risk of the rider being intercepted."

Jamie climbed to his feet and waved for her to follow him. Brandi staggered to her feet and followed him back the way they'd come. When they returned to their bedrolls at the edge of camp, Jamie sprawled on his blanket. "Don't need to listen to more. Captain Alistair will be looking for me before long."

She lay back on her blanket and pulled her leather helmet down over her eyes. "I'll just be sleeping. No reason for him to notice me."

"Except to pick you for the mission." Jamie scowled, like he wanted to try to talk her out of it but realized it'd do no good.

"Yes, except that." It might be a bit tricky, trying to impress Shad without him recognizing her or Blizzard. Then again, how hard would it be? Shad didn't expect to see Renna's little sister strutting around in boys' clothes and leading Blizzard. All he'd see would be a skinny fourteen-year-old boy with an ash gray horse.

But no matter what it took, Brandi would ride into that battle on Blizzard with Jamie at her side

36

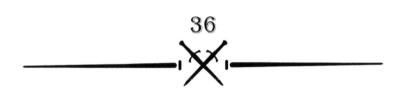

Today was her eighteenth birthday and the day she'd die.

Renna pinned her hair up as best she could without a mirror. Eighteen. What had she done in those eighteen years? She'd spent so much of the last few years hiding. And recently, what had she accomplished?

Perhaps if she'd married Respen, she could've done something. Or maybe her purpose now was to die as bravely as she could.

She stared at the flickering candlelight, praying away the seconds. Soon she'd join Mother, Father, Aunt Mara, Uncle Abel, Aunt Deirdre, Uncle Leon, and her cousins in Heaven.

Brandi. Who would look after her now? Surely Leith would take care of her. If he couldn't, then Lord and Lady Alistair would.

Leith. Would he try to rescue her? What if he was killed in the attempt?

If only she'd had a chance to tell Brandi and Leith a better good bye.

Her door creaked open. Martyn stood in the doorway, his eyes a swirling, liquid brown. "Renna, I..." His voice broke, and he swallowed.

It was time. Renna climbed to her feet. As she walked out the door, she held her head high. A bolt of dread pierced her stomach, but she refused to give in to it.

Martyn gripped her elbow as he led her down the flights of stairs. She could feel a tremble in his grip, a tightening in his fingers.

As they reached the bottom of the stairs, Renna halted. When Martyn glanced towards her, she laid a hand on his arm. "God is with me."

He looked like he wanted to snort in derision, but the imminence of her execution halted him. When he stared at her through his blond curls, he seemed young. Small. She was tempted to give him a hug. Without the faith she clasped so tightly, Martyn didn't have any comfort. Nothing she said could give him the comfort she felt pouring through her.

Was this how Uncle Abel and Aunt Mara felt in the moments before their execution? Was that how they'd been able to sing on their way to death?

She'd be all right. Her chest warmed, even though the tips of her fingers and the pit of her stomach remained blizzard cold. If Leith came to save her or if she died, she'd be all right. God was with her.

As they crossed the common room, two Blades joined them, one on either side. The one, a dark-haired Blade Renna didn't recognize, swept his gaze over her, a sneer tugging at the corner of his mouth. The other, Ranson, ducked his head as soon as she glanced at him.

Martyn tugged her from the Blades' Tower and across the bridge to the passageway that connected the cobblestone courtyard with the Queen's Court. Ranson and the other Blade kept pace, hands on their knives.

As they turned toward the cobblestone courtyard, Renna spotted the block and axman framed in the light at the end of the passageway. Her heart beat in her ears. Her stomach skittered, and the hairs on the back of her neck prickled with the sensation of the ax slicing down.

She couldn't let herself think about it. She wasn't going to let fear be her last emotion.

Uncle Abel and Aunt Mara had sung on their way to their execution. They'd sung for her, but they'd also sung for themselves to place their focus on God instead of the death waiting them. Perhaps she could do the same. Would it distract her from the ax waiting for her?

The words of Aunt Mara's favorite song breezed through her mind. Renna opened her mouth and sang. "In doubt and temptation I rest, Lord, in Thee."

The words coated her tongue with a bittersweet honey, filled with memories of Aunt Mara singing her and Brandi to sleep with this song in the long nights following their parents' deaths. Renna closed her eyes, trusting Martyn to guide her to the block. "My hand is in Thy hand, Thou carest for me."

She could tell by the echoes that they'd left the passageway and stepped into the open courtyard. She cracked her eyes open. There, beyond the block, a crowd of people stood by. Mostly soldiers, but a few of the castle staff as well. The skinny cook shook, his eyes wide. The old woman was being held back by a soldier, her face moist.

A few of the soldiers shouted, but the rest remained silent. Eerily silent.

All she could do was walk forward and sing away her final moments of life. Her voice echoed in the hot, quiet courtyard. "My soul with Thy counsel through life Thou wilt guide."

Martyn halted her. The wooden block crouched in front of her, brown with bloodstains, rough with the slices of the ax. Her voice faltered. Her knees buckled on their own, sending her crashing painfully to the cobblestones. The pain didn't matter. It'd all be over in a matter of moments.

Her hands and body shook. This was it. Tears built in her eyes. Her breathing changed into a ragged gasp.

No. She would not panic. God would grant her courage to face even this.

She laid her neck in the groove on the block. The wood scraped against her throat, the back of her neck exposed to the ax.

Squeezing her eyes shut and her fingers into fists, she poured her breath into the last line of the song. "And afterward make me in glory abide."

Glory. Focus on glory. God. Jesus. No pain. No tears. Just glory.

37

Leith vaulted over the battlements and landed in a crouch on top of the North Tower. With the two guards focused on the courtyard below, no one noticed him.

Someone was singing. A glance at the courtyard showed Renna falling to her knees and placing her neck on the block. His heart froze. Too late.

Not too late. Perfect timing. He slipped behind the guards and brought the hilt of his knife down on the backs of their unprotected heads. First one, then the other, crumbled. The clanking of their swords hitting the stones drew the attention of the guards on the walls on either side of the tower. Leith stepped onto the battlements with a knife in each hand. He glared at the soldiers and held the knives as if he were prepared to throw them.

The soldiers had no way of knowing that he couldn't throw knives to save his life. But as long as he fooled them, they wouldn't take a step toward him.

"Lord Respen Felix!"

In the courtyard below, the executioner halted. The crowd, already silent, gaped upward. The Blades Harding and Daas reached for their knives. Martyn stared, a look that might've been pain twisting his features. Renna's white face tipped upward, her eyes wide. With hope? With fear? He couldn't tell from this distance.

The window of Respen's chamber creaked open. Sunlight washed across Respen's face and glinted on his beard as he stepped closer to the window. "I knew you would return, my traitorous Blade. Your foolish sentiment has made you weak." Respen's deep voice rang loud enough to carry, but soft enough to appear bored.

"Perhaps. But you need my foolishiness to keep me here." Leith brandished the knives. The sun shot daggers of light along their blades. "I evaded the five Blades you sent after me. I survived the Waste. If you kill her, I'll leave, and you'll never catch me."

He had done what no Blade had ever managed to do: outrun Respen's punishment. Respen couldn't afford to let him leave again. He held his Blades under his control because they knew they couldn't escape the punishment. But if Leith proved it was possible, some of the others would be tempted to try as well.

If only Leith could bargain for Renna's freedom, but Respen wouldn't let her go. All Leith could do was buy time with his surrender. Respen would keep Renna alive as a tool to break him.

Respen mulled Leith's ultimatum over for only a few seconds before he twitched his hand. Martyn darted forward and dragged Renna to her feet. Even with the distance of the courtyard separating them, Leith could see Respen's nonchalant shrug. "I can wait to kill her until after you are dead. It makes no difference to me to delay her death by a few more days. I will make her watch me break you."

He couldn't focus on Respen's words. He'd known what he'd face. He'd known it from the first moment he'd stepped into Lord Alistair's study with the intention of joining the Resistance. All the months of hiding and running, they'd all led to this.

The inevitable.

"I'll surrender. But first I have a message for you." Leith drew in a deep breath, gathering the words of the formal proclamation that Prince Keevan had him memorize before he'd left. "Lord Respen Felix of Blathe, you are hereby charged with high treason against His Majesty King Leon Eirdon as well as the murders of King Leon, Queen Deirdre, and three of their sons. You are ordered to surrender yourself to justice. If you do not do so, you will be hunted and arrested by the order of His Royal Highness Prince Keevan Eirdon, true heir and prince of Acktar."

Respen's face mottled. He pounded the windowsill. "Prince Keevan's dead. You killed him yourself."

Leith tipped his head, unable to resist a smile. "It seems I was a failure as a Blade even then."

Respen gripped the windowsill, his knuckles white. "First Blade, return Lady Rennelda to her cell and see to it that Torren is brought to the Tower." With a final glare at Leith, Respen slammed the window closed so forcibly the panes rattled.

Leith had done what he'd set out to do. He'd shaken the king. Badly. Hopefully Respen would remain off balance and blind to Prince Keevan's plan.

More than that, Prince Keevan's return took away Respen's one main reason for killing Renna. She wasn't a threat to his throne, and once again, she'd be worth more alive to use against her cousin than she would dead.

In the courtyard below, the lines of soldiers milled about. A captain shouted orders and began herding his men back to their barracks. Martyn grasped Renna's arm and hustled her from the courtyard, Daas and Harding following. Instead of heading for the North Tower and the dungeons, Martyn steered her toward the passageway between the two courtyards.

Where was Renna's cell? Leith craned his neck and watched until they disappeared in the passageway. Respen's chambers lay in that direction, as well as the guest apartments and the bridge to the Blades' Tower. Had Renna been locked in the Tower these past weeks?

With Renna safely away from the block, Leith stepped down from the battlements and dropped his knives. They clattered against the stones, sounding like the clanking of the chains that would soon clamp around his wrists. He laced his fingers together and placed them on top of his head. He glanced at the soldiers lining the wall top.

The soldiers stared back. Leith resisted the urge to grin. Even now, the soldiers feared him. He might be a disgraced Blade, but he'd once been the First Blade.

Swallowing, one soldier drew his sword. He motioned to the trap door set in the top of the tower.

Leith raised his eyebrow. Surely the soldier didn't want him taking his hands off his head to open the trap door himself.

Another soldier scurried to the trap door, opened it, and drew his sword. Leith eased past him and trudged down the spiral staircase, two of the soldiers following close behind him.

They marched him across the cobblestone courtyard, into the passageway between courtyards, and turned left to the wooden bridge spanning the dry moat to the Blades' Tower.

As Leith stepped onto the end of the bridge, Martyn exited the door of the Tower and strode toward him. The soldiers remained at the far end.

Leith and Martyn halted a few paces from each other. A silence stretched between them. What could Leith say? He'd done too much. Betrayed Martyn. Tore their friendship apart.

Martyn's face remained as hard as the stones of the Blades' Tower behind him.

Leith walked ahead of Martyn into the Tower. Its darkness swallowed him. He glanced over his shoulder and caught one last glimpse of sunlight before the door shut behind them. Would Leith ever set foot outside this Tower again?

After crossing the empty common room, Leith marched up the spiraling stairs. His boots scuffed against each stone tread. By the time they reached the fourth floor, the muscles in Leith's calves burned. His heart thundered, though he couldn't blame it all on exertion.

One more flight of stairs.

Leith climbed the last set of steps and strode into the meeting room. Candles glowed on the two candlesticks spaced along the table. Fifth Blade Daas glared, his mouth twisting into a sneer. Eighth Blade Harding ducked his head.

At the far end of the table, Respen lounged in his throne, his fingers stroking the end of the armrest.

Martyn closed the door and slid the bolt into place, locking them in. Leith fought the shiver traveling down his arms. Could he hold his steel during the coming torture?

Slowly, Leith undid the buckles of the leather straps crossing his chest, the belt around his waist, and the sheaths of his boot knives. The chip of rock Brandi had given him remained safely hidden in the toe of his boot. Even if Martyn decided to search him, he probably wouldn't deem it a threat. Leith handed his weapons to Martyn.

Martyn set them aside and pulled out a length of rope. Leith held out his wrists. This was now the second time in less than a month that one of his friends had tied his hands. Though unlike Shad, Martyn tied the rope plenty tight.

Martyn shoved Leith forward and forced him to kneel in front of Respen. The familiar stone floor pressed against Leith's knees. He'd knelt like this too many times over the years. Too many times, Respen pronounced him successful.

Lunging forward, Respen's fingers jabbed into Leith's chin and dragged his head up. Leith met Respen's burning gaze. As a submissive Blade, he'd never spoken to Respen unless bidden, but this time he didn't wait for Respen to speak first. "When you kill me, I want you to know that I don't fear you. My God is stronger than fear."

Respen's fingers tightened like a hawk's talons digging into its prey. "Even now, you still cling to your drivel."

Leith didn't flinch. Didn't look away.

Respen leaned back and drew one of his knives. Switching his grip, he smashed the pommel into Leith's face.

Pain burst along Leith's jaw. The room tilted. His shoulder smashed against the floor. Sucking in a breath past the pain, he worked his jaw. Not broken.

A hand on his shirt yanked him back to his knees.

Martyn tugged up Leith's left sleeve, exposing the two white lines already marring the top of his shoulder.

"My traitorous Blade, you have failed." Respen sliced the knife across Leith's shoulder below the other two marks.

Three failures. The mark of death.

"First Blade, prepare him for a whipping."

Martyn hauled Leith to his feet and dragged him across the room to the pair of manacles dangling from the wall. He locked the manacles around Leith's forearms beside the rope that bound his wrists together.

As he checked the tightness of the rope, Martyn held something out to Leith's face, the movement shielded from the other Blades by Martyn's body. "Bite."

Leith bit the piece of leather. Why was Martyn giving him that much courtesy? He should've let Leith either grind his teeth together or cry out at the pain that was coming. But Martyn's hard face and eyes gave nothing away.

Martyn gripped the collar of Leith's shirt. The cold steel of his knife whispered against the back of Leith's neck and spine as Martyn sliced downward. Cold air prickled along Leith's exposed skin.

Leith craned his neck to see over his shoulder as Martyn returned to his seat on Respen's right. Would Respen order Martyn to do the whipping? Or perhaps Fifth Blade Daas, who leaned forward and flexed his fingers. Maybe he'd force Ranson to do it.

Respen held out a coiled whip. "First Blade, execute his punishment."

Of course it'd be Martyn. Leith would have to take this whipping at the hand of his former best friend. A cruelty for both of them.

For a moment, Martyn stared at the whip. Was he thinking about refusing? Then his back and shoulders stiffened as if reinforced with an extra layer of stone. He stood and took the whip. "How many lashes, my king?"

"The same number given to you as your punishment."

A bitter taste rose in Leith's throat. Martyn had been whipped. That had been his punishment when Leith had escaped with Brandi. No wonder Martyn didn't refuse this duty now. This whipping was no more than Leith deserved for abandoning Martyn.

His expression as icy as a winter wind, Martyn strode forward and stopped a few feet behind Leith. The whip uncoiled. The three braided and knotted ends slapped the floor.

Leith turned his face away and pressed his forehead to the wall. If Martyn could take a whipping, then he could too. Whatever pain the next moments brought, he wouldn't scream. He couldn't make this any harder on Martyn than it already was.

The whip cracked. Half a heartbeat later, lines of pain seared Leith's back. His muscles cramped. A cry built in his chest. He clamped his teeth on the piece of leather so tightly the bruise on his jaw throbbed.

Another lash. Then another. He didn't bother counting. He could trust Martyn to give him no more and no less than the amount ordered.

The knotted ends tore like the claws of a mountain lion, shredding the skin from his back. Agony lanced deeper into his body with every blow, searing, tearing.

He mustn't cry out. No matter how much pain bottled inside his chest begging for release, he wouldn't give in. It was all he could do to remember to drag in another breath.

Another lash. Another. Lines of pain tore away his skin.

How much longer could this go on? Leith trembled. How many lashes had Martyn suffered?

His head spun. Blackness filled his vision. Was it from squeezing his eyes shut or unconsciousness threatening to take him?

Martyn was there beside him, undoing the chains that cut into his wrists. Leith's legs buckled. He fell onto his hands and knees.

His hands. He stared at his fingers splayed against the floor. When had his hands been untied? Martyn must've done it. Had Leith blacked out there at the end?

Leith spat the piece of leather onto the floor. Dents marred the leather from each of his teeth. He glanced around the room. Respen's chair and the long table were empty.

Martyn knelt and tugged one of Leith's arms over his shoulders. He half-dragged, half-carried Leith across the room and down the stairs. Leith tried to force his feet to keep up, but his spinning head couldn't seem to get his muscles to cooperate. Something hot and wet trickled down his arms. Blood.

As they passed the door to the First Blade's room, the door rattled and thumped. "Let me see him!"

Renna was here. Alive. Leith should call out to her, but he wasn't sure words or a cry of pain would escape if he opened his mouth. Martyn opened the door to the Second Blade's room and hauled him inside.

Leith collapsed into a sitting position on the cot. Pain shot through each limb and nerve. If only he could lie down and rest, but he had to remain strong for a little longer. How was he ever going to survive a week of

Respen's torture? Not that he had a choice at this point. He had to bear it until rescue or death, whichever came first.

Martyn paced to the far side of the room, cursed, and slapped his hand against the wall. "Why? Why didn't you just stay away? Then neither of us would be forced to go through this."

"I'm sorry." Leith gripped the edge of the cot to hold himself upright. He choked in a breath. "I couldn't abandon Renna. Or you. I'm sorry for the pain I caused you."

"You have no idea what I've gone through." Martyn clenched his fists. "I was alone. When Respen finished the whipping, he unchained me and left. He didn't even send the one remaining trainee to help. I had to crawl down the stairs to my room. I had no one."

Leith squeezed his eyes shut. The pain in Martyn's voice ached worse than the agony crackling across his back. He'd betrayed his friend. Stabbed him in the back. Abandoned him.

And in Martyn's eyes, that abandonment cut worst of all.

Leith couldn't take away that pain or undo it. "I'm sorry."

Martyn leaned against the wall, his back rigid.

Renna's continued pounding filled the room. "Martyn Hamish, you let me see him. You owe me that much."

Leith tipped his head at the wall separating the Second and First Blades' rooms, nearly falling over with the dizziness that slight action caused. His voice sounded far away in a passageway of pain. "What's Renna doing in the Tower?"

257

"Respen had me move her shortly after you left. He feared you'd find rescuing her from the dungeon too easy." Martyn shook his head and drew his fingers through his hair. "She noticed I was injured. She tended my back."

Warmth curled in Leith's chest. Even though Martyn was the reason she'd been forced to stay behind, Renna had still helped him. Respen hadn't managed to steal her compassion from her.

Renna's door banged so loudly Leith felt the vibration through the floor stones. Had Renna thrown herself against the door?

Martyn straightened. "I'd better go fetch her before she draws any more attention to herself."

"You'll let her help me?"

Martyn paused with his hand on the door. "I am your friend. Even if it counts for very little at the moment."

Leith let his shoulders sag. As bad as the torture would be, he wouldn't want to be in Martyn's boots for anything.

With a deep breath, Leith pushed himself to his feet, only to collapse. His knees struck the stone floor, sending shafts of pain into his toes. He nearly retched at the agony burning through every inch of his back.

He couldn't stay on the floor. He needed to be strong for Renna, if only for the first few moments. She'd see him weak and broken later.

Pushing himself to his feet took all he had. He rested a hand against the wall, gasping. He straightened the remains of his shirt to hide the blood trickling down his arms. Surely he could stand for a few minutes.

Renna flew into the room. Her hair frizzed from its

coil on her head, and she wore the same blue shirt and buckskin skirt she'd worn last time he'd seen her. He searched her face but didn't see any cuts or bruises. She stood steadily on her feet and didn't move like someone recovering from a beating. He let out a shuddering breath. Thankfully, it didn't look like Respen had hurt her.

Though there were other, deeper ways she could've been hurt that Leith wouldn't be able to tell at a glance.

"Leith." She touched his jaw, her finger brushing the bruise left by Respen's knife. "How bad are you hurt?"

"I'm fine." He caught her hand and gave her fingers a gentle squeeze. The trickle of blood coursed around his elbow and down his arm. He lifted their clasped hands to keep the blood hidden under his shirt. He wasn't quite ready to admit how wounded he was. "I promised I'd return for you. Are you all right?"

"Yes." She met and held his gaze.

He searched her eyes. He saw steel there, stronger than it had been before. Whatever she'd gone through, he wasn't looking at the same Renna he'd left behind. He forced his sore jaw into a smile. "Happy birthday. I'm sorry I didn't bring any cake or maple sugar cookies or presents."

"I don't care about that. I'm just glad you're here." She wrapped her arms around his neck and hugged him.

His breath seized at her touch, her nearness, and the pain spasming across his back when her arms brushed the torn skin. He couldn't swallow his moan.

She stiffened and held up her hands. Blood shone on her sleeve and fingers. With a firm hand on his shoulder, she turned him and peered at his back. "What are you doing still standing? Lie down."

Based on the black spots gathering at the corners of

his eyes, Leith's body was going to do that in a moment whether or not he wanted to. He eased onto the cot, collapsing the last few inches when his strength gave out. So much for being strong.

"What do you need?" Martyn set a candle on the nightstand next to the one already burning. The light flickering on his face left deep shadows below his eyes.

Renna's shoulders straightened. "I'll need water. Both boiling water and cold water, as cold as you can get it. Clean linen for bandages. Some kind of salve."

Martyn slipped from the room. Had he taken the time to lock the door? Leith couldn't remember hearing the lock, but he didn't have the strength to escape. Nor was that part of the plan.

Renna knelt next to the cot. The candlelight played across her face, highlighting her round cheeks and the faint shadows beneath her eyes. "I have so much to tell you."

What had she been through? Leith threaded his fingers through hers. Her hands were cold. A little damp. The contact felt strange and new, like the first hint of green after the snow melts. Once before he'd dared hold her hand like this, and that had been right before he'd been forced to leave her behind.

He cleared his throat. "Listen, before Martyn gets back. There's a loose stone in the wall between our rooms. There's a shard of rock holding it in place. You'll have to take it out so we can talk after Martyn leaves."

She nodded. "I found it when I was first brought to the room."

"Good." Had she found the knife he'd hidden in that room months ago when he'd become First Blade? They could talk about knives and plans later. Right now, while he had the opportunity to hold her hand and see her face, he had other things to say.

If only he didn't have to place more of a burden on her. Zed Burin, the last failed Blade, had been reduced to a whimpering, bleeding mess by the time Respen finished with him. That's what Respen would try to do to Leith.

He squeezed her hand. "Respen will torture me, and I don't know if I can be strong enough for both of us. I'm going to need you to be strong, all right?"

Renna held his gaze, her back straight. "God will be strong enough for both of us."

Leith waited for some sign of crumbling, but he didn't see it. The strength he'd seen in her all those months ago had been refined and hardened. Perhaps she would be strong enough to face this next week alongside him.

A good thing, since he wasn't sure he'd have the strength to face it on his own.

He shoved those thoughts aside. He had another pressing question to ask. "You nearly married Respen?"

She ducked her head and toyed with the end of her blouse with her free hand. "He promised he'd stop the persecution. I thought he might change, and you were dead. I didn't know what to do." She blinked and pressed their linked fingers to her cheek.

Respen had hurt her. Lied to her. If Leith got the chance, he might smash his fist into Respen's jaw for that.

He struggled to shove the heat deep into his chest. Renna didn't need his anger. "I'm glad you didn't."

"I know. I just..." She rested her forehead on the edge of the cot. Her voice dropped until Leith could barely hear her. "Sometimes I wonder if I should've married him. If maybe that's what I was supposed to do. Maybe I could've made a difference."

"No." Leith tightened his grip on her hand. He drew in a deep breath to steady his heartbeat. Renna needed him to come up with something comforting, not harsh. "Respen is deceptive. He twists the truth until you aren't sure what to believe. You've already made a difference by showing kindness to those around you. That's what you're supposed to do."

"Really?" Renna lifted her face. Her eyes were wet.

"Yes." Leith leaned forward, bit back a cry of pain, and pressed a kiss into her hair. "Thank you for helping Martyn after his whipping."

Her eyes rounded, and her jaw dropped open, like she couldn't believe he'd just done that. He couldn't either.

Footsteps sounded in the corridor outside. Two sets of footsteps. Leith raised his head as Martyn stepped into the room, carrying a pitcher in each hand. Ranson followed him, balancing a tray laden with several bowls, stacks of bandages and rags, and a jar of salve.

Ranson glanced toward Leith before he ducked his head, set the tray on the bedside table, and hurried from the room.

What would've happened if Leith had stopped Ranson Harding and Blane Altin from becoming Blades the way he'd rescued Jamie? If he'd had the courage to step in and prevent that first kill?

Renna tugged her hand free from Leith's and stood. "Thanks, Martyn." She filled a cup with water from one of the pitchers and held it out to Leith. "You must be thirsty."

He reached for it. Pain tore across his back. He cried out and pressed his mouth against his arm to stifle the sound. The cup clattered to the floor. Darkness wavered across his sight.

"Here. Let me help." Renna's soft hand slid against his cheek.

Cold metal pressed against his mouth. Water soaked into his dry mouth. He tried to swallow, but his stomach and throat rebelled. He coughed. More pain stabbed his back.

"Take it easy. A little bit more."

With her help, he managed to finish most of it. When he was done, she tucked a cold, damp rag against his throbbing jaw. "For your bruise. Ice would've been better, but I have a feeling the ice room is off limits."

Martyn crossed his arms. "Yes."

Leith pressed the cloth to the swollen spot on his jaw. The cool water eased some of the ache.

Renna picked up a bottle. "This will hurt. Would you like some laudanum first?"

"No." The laudanum will dull the pain, but it'd also dull his senses. By the time Renna finished and Martyn returned her to her room, Leith wouldn't be able to talk beyond a few mumbled words. He could always sleep and talk to her later, but she'd been alone and abandoned for three weeks. She couldn't wait any longer. "I'll manage. Save the laudanum for later."

They'd need it later. A whipping was the least of the torture Respen would inflict.

Leith squeezed his eyes shut and braced for the pain. A cool liquid splashed onto his back a moment before fire scorched his skin. He writhed away from it, all his senses burning. Iron hands on his upper arms pinned him down as the torment scoured his back from his shoulders to his hips.

"There. All done." Renna's voice dragged him from the edges of the beckoning darkness.

He was moaning and shaking. He tried to swallow back a groan but choked. He had to be stronger than this. If he couldn't even take this much pain, how would he ever manage a week of it?

Martyn released his grip on Leith's forearms. When Leith peeled his eyes open, Martyn leaned against the door, his expression hard once again.

Leith let his eyes fall closed. Renna muttered something. Her boots scraped against the stone next to Leith. Water dribbled, probably as she wrung out a rag.

Something warm and wet touched one of Leith's shoulder blades. Pain sizzled into his skin and muscle. He pressed his face into the crook of his arm and concentrated on breathing.

The hot water seared the open wounds and, when Renna spread the salve across the lacerations, her fingers caught on the rough edges of what was left of his skin.

Leith ground his teeth and tightened his fists. If only he could beg for laudanum, to slip into oblivion and sleep away the pain. All he'd have to do is ask. Renna wouldn't keep him in pain a moment longer.

But he couldn't ask. He had to remain alert. For her.

Someone tapped his shoulder. "Do you think you can sit up?"

The quaver in Renna's voice stung as much as the rag. If just for that, he had to get up.

He sucked in a breath, gathered his strength, and pushed himself upright. Pain shot down his back, but he swung his legs to the floor anyway. He had to grip the edge of the cot as his head spun. His stomach heaved, and it took all his effort to keep it down.

When he finally had the strength to raise his head, Martyn stood across the room, arms crossed, face hard. Renna stared at Leith, her fingers fisted into her skirt so tightly her knuckles shone white. If she'd been anyone else, he would've told her he was fine. But she'd just patched up his back. She wouldn't be fooled. "I'm sure it looks worse than it is."

"I doubt it. Now hold still."

He tried to follow her order as she wrapped his torso with bandages. When she finished, she stood and helped him drink another cup of water. The shock of the cold water in his mouth helped his dizziness.

"All right." Martyn straightened and reached for Renna's elbow. "That's enough. I've given you more than enough time already."

Renna glanced over her shoulder, but she didn't struggle as Martyn steered her out the door. Leith didn't call after them. He and Renna would be able to talk once Martyn left.

After a few minutes, Martyn returned and paced along the far wall, his black clothes shifting with candlelight. After several minutes, he pressed his palm against the wall. "Why did you do it, Leith? What do you have now that you didn't have as the Third Blade?"

What did he have? From Martyn's standpoint, it probably didn't look like much. He had a failed friendship, a bleeding back, and a week of torture to look forward to.

But Martyn couldn't see the other things. The blood of Christ that washed away the blood Leith had spilled. The peace that swelled his chest and pushed away the fear that had chained him. The forgiveness that had cooled the anger he'd harbored toward his father for so long.

Leith met Martyn's gaze. "I have hope."

Martyn pounded the wall. "What do you have to hope for? Look around you. You're going to die very slowly and very painfully, probably by my hand. Renna will die shortly afterwards. What do you have to hope for? And don't give me some nonsense about a place called Heaven you've never seen."

Leith tried to remember the words Shad and Brandi had used to reach him all those months ago. He wouldn't have believed in talk of Heaven either. Like Martyn, he'd been taught to only believe in things he could see and touch.

"I have the hope of God's strength so that no matter what I face He will make me strong enough. I have the hope of God's courage so that no matter what Respen does to me, he won't break me. I know you don't believe in things you can't see, but I hope you can see those things in me."

Martyn dragged his fingers through his curls. Leith understood that frustration. It was the same frustration he'd felt after meeting Renna, Brandi, and Shad. He could see something different about them and that difference had no apparent explanation besides the one he hadn't wanted to consider.

Martyn headed for the door. "I'll be back later with food."

"Respen is actually feeding me?" The words felt light on Leith's tongue, like he was joking with his best friend instead of his guard.

"Whether King Respen wants it or not, I'm feeding you." Martyn strode to the door.

Leith shook his head. "You can't try to play both sides. Respen will make you choose."

Martyn halted in the doorway. "Why do I have to choose? We should be on the same side. If you'd stayed loyal to King Respen, none of this would've happened."

Perhaps, but Leith would still be a Blade. Renna and Brandi would be dead. "I'm sorry, but I couldn't."

Martyn huffed a breath and dragged the door closed. The lock clicked into place.

As soon as he was gone, Leith groaned and reached for his boot. He was shaking and breathing hard by the time he managed to tug it off. Dumping the chip of stone Brandi had given him onto the floor, he found a hole in the straw tick, widened it, and tucked the stone inside.

That done, he eased onto the floor at the head of the cot and located the loose stone. He couldn't remove it from this side, thanks to the rock chip he'd jammed into the other side when he'd been the First Blade.

He leaned his head and shoulder against the wall, unable to hold himself upright. Now all he had to do was wait.

38

Renna sank to the floor and leaned against the door. Leith was here. She wasn't alone.

Not that she'd been alone here. God had been with her. Still, it'd be nice to no longer have to face Respen all by herself.

Should she be relieved or scared that Leith had come? Respen would torture and kill him. What good would that do?

Surely Leith had a plan. He always did.

She dug her fingernails into her palms. She'd tried to tell Leith what had happened with her and Respen. But what could she say? How could she admit she'd almost believed she could eventually love Respen when Leith looked at her like that? When he'd walked into torture for her?

This—the look on Leith's face, the way he clasped her hand and asked her to be strong for him—this was what she'd been waiting for. Not someone to rescue. Not someone to simply rescue her.

A partner. A friend. Someone to walk next to her even in the darkest places.

She touched the spot on her hair where he'd kissed her. *Kissed* her. She gave herself a shake. Now was not the time to dissolve into mush.

She pressed her ear to the door and listened to Martyn's footsteps. When she heard Martyn exit Leith's room and lock the door, she set to work on the stone chip she'd spotted wedged in the wall. Digging her fingernails against the stone, she yanked at it. Her first few attempts resulted in nothing but skinned knuckles and broken fingernails.

Gritting her teeth, she tightened her grip and threw her whole body into yanking it out. The wedge shifted, then popped free. She crashed backwards and bashed her elbows against the stone floor.

Rubbing her elbows, she crouched next to the stone once again. It stuck out from the rest of the wall enough for her to pry at it with her fingertips. She inched it out of the wall, slowly at first, then faster.

Something pushed it from the other side. It fell through her hands, bounced against her foot, and clumped onto the floor.

"Are you all right?" Leith's voice carried clearly through the opening.

"Just dropped the stone on my foot." She wiggled her toes. "Nothing broken. I'm all right. Now get back into bed before you pass out there on the floor."

Groans and shuffling sounded through the hole. Leith's cot creaked. "There. I'm lying down."

If he wanted to pretend he wasn't in pain, she could play along. "What's this loose stone doing in the wall anyway?"

"First Blade Vane used to spy on Second Blade Hess to make sure the Second Blade wasn't plotting against him. Hess knew Vane was doing it, so he used the hole to spy right back."

Renna peeked through the hole. She couldn't see much of the room besides the far wall and the legs of the washstand. The cot rested against the same wall as the hole, hidden from sight. "Will Martyn be able to listen through a loose stone in the other wall?"

"No. Vane and Hess didn't bother spying on me. They knew I had no ambitions to become the First or Second Blade. So no loose stones in the walls."

She nodded, even though Leith couldn't see her. Did Martyn know about this loose stone? Probably.

So why had he placed them in two rooms where he knew they'd be able to talk to each other? Was he still trying to be Leith's friend even now?

Was that why he was still staying in the Third Blade's room, even though he'd been the First Blade for the past several weeks?

"They probably searched that room before they locked you in there, but there might be one hidden knife yet." Leith's voice was pitched loud enough for her to hear, but low enough that it wouldn't carry through his door. "I hid a knife in there when I became the First Blade. I never knew when I might be discovered."

"Where would it be?" Renna glanced around the room. "I searched under the mattress and behind the bedside table. I didn't find anything."

"Crawl under the cot. There should be a knife strapped to the front post next to the wall."

Renna studied the cot. It was formed of thick, metal bars, too heavy for her to lift. Twine laced between the two sides and supported the straw tick.

Grimacing, she lowered herself onto the floor. The

stones under the cot fuzzed with a layer of dust. "Didn't you ever clean under here?"

From the other side of the wall, Leith chuckled. "No. I was a Blade, remember? Cleaning anything other than my knives wasn't one of my skills."

She pressed her palms against the dust and tried to ignore the grit grinding against her skin. Inch-worming forward, she reached the cot's far post. The light from the candle didn't penetrate this corner, shrouding her in dusty darkness. She reached for the iron post and felt leather straps winding around it. Unbuckling them, she tugged what felt like a leather sheath with a knife from its place wedged between the wall and the post.

When it inched free, she wiggled from under the bed. "Got it."

"Good. Keep it on you and don't let anyone know you have it. Not even Martyn."

"All right." Standing, she hiked up her skirt and strapped the knife and sheath around her thigh. It was uncomfortable, but couldn't be seen if her divided skirt fluttered while she walked. After considering it for a moment, she drew the knife and cut off the bottom of the dress's pocket on that side. Now she could draw the knife through the pocket without hiking up her skirt.

Not that she could do much with a knife. But she might be able to hide it for Leith until he needed it, for whatever he was planning.

She sprawled on her cot with her head facing the missing stone in the wall. "So what's the plan?"

"Does there have to be a plan? Maybe I just turned myself in to be with you."

No plan? She just assumed Leith would have a plan. "Sorry, I expected..." Her voice trailed off as his tone registered. He was teasing. "Empty romantic gestures are fine and all, but I expect a sensible plan too."

"I'm not sure how sensible you'll consider my plan, but I do have one." Leith's sigh filled the space between them. "It all depends on Prince Keevan."

Keevan. She squeezed her eyes shut as she tried to picture her cousin. The only image she got was a gangly teenager with flyaway blond hair and impish blue eyes. She'd had cause to shriek his name whenever he'd pulled her hair or poked her in the side. "He really is alive?"

"Yes." The word held a weight of guilt that Renna felt even through the stone wall. For nearly five years, Leith had believed he'd killed Keevan.

Renna drew in a deep breath. What was so shocking about that? This wasn't anything she hadn't already known. "Respen told me how you killed him. Or thought you killed him."

"I sliced down his face and neck, but I didn't stay to watch him die." Leith's tone lowered further. "He survived, but he still has a scar across his face and a rasp to his voice. And he probably would've executed me for attempted murder if I hadn't offered to turn myself in to Respen to stop what I thought would be your wedding."

Leith's mission was basically a suicide mission? Renna swallowed.

"Prince Keevan is leading an army from the Sheered Rock Hills. He intends to attack Nalgar Castle. I'm here to keep Respen distracted, pull some of the Blades from the front, prevent him from killing you, and be Prince Keevan's inside man when he attacks during the Meeting of the Blades."

The things Leith wasn't saying echoed in the room.

When the Resistance army arrived, Leith would be the first person Respen killed. Their only hope was speed on Keevan's part. "Will he get here in time?"

"Maybe. Respen's army is stationed between here and the Hills. Prince Keevan will have to push them back before he can approach the castle."

An army between them and rescue. Renna swallowed down the warmth bubbling inside her ever since Leith had halted her execution. He might've prolonged her life, but neither of them was safe. Not by a long shot.

She needed to change the subject. "How's Brandi?"

Silence greeted her question.

Her body clenched. "What happened to Brandi? Is she all right?"

"She wasn't hurt, but..." Leith's voice grew so quiet she barely picked out the next words. "She killed a Blade."

Brandi had killed a Blade? Renna gripped the blanket, her head spinning. How had Brandi even known enough about fighting to kill someone, much less a Blade?

"I'm sorry, Renna. I wasn't there. I was in the Waste at the time."

"What were you doing in the Waste? Respen told me you'd died there." Renna folded her arms on the cot. "I think you'd better start at the beginning."

It took all morning for them to catch each other up on what had been going on. Renna told him everything that had happened to her while he described the events she'd missed while locked in Nalgar Castle.

Renna pressed her fingers against her chest as if she could hold in her tears. She should've been there for her sister. Brandi had gone through the hardest time of her life, and Renna wasn't able to be there for her.

"She seemed better when I left this time, but I'm not

sure." Leith's voice held a note of worry. "I'm not sure what she might've been planning.

"You did the best you could. Thank you."

Leith had done everything in his power to keep Brandi safe. He couldn't do more than that. Thanks to Leith, Brandi was all right, for now. Renna could only hope that wherever she was, Brandi remained safe and didn't decide to do something crazy.

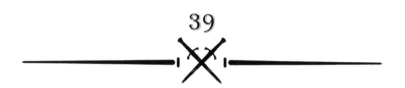

39

This was the craziest thing she'd ever done. Brandi strapped the last of her gear onto Blizzard's back and tugged him into the line of Riders forming along one side of the encampment.

She checked the knife Leith had given her, her short sword, dagger, and the knife she'd strapped to her ankle. Packing so many weapons, she felt powerful.

Powerful was good. Powerful would rescue Renna and Leith.

Brandi flexed her arms. Strength rippled through her muscles. While she wasn't as strong as a boy her age would've been, she was stronger than she'd ever been in her life. And she was quick. She wasn't in the awkward growing stage like the teenage boys, so she wasn't tripping over her own feet whenever she tried to walk.

Shad approached, leading his chestnut gelding. Jolene dashed from the group of archers and wrapped her arms around Shad's waist. They talked quietly for a few minutes before Shad leaned forward and kissed her.

A few of the assembled men hooted. Brandi rolled her eyes. Of course Shad and Jolene were kissing. They weren't going to see each other again before marching into battle. Why were all the guys making such a big deal out of it?

With one last kiss on her forehead, Shad turned away, straightened his shoulders, and faced them. His mouth moved as if he silently took a head count. Brandi kept her head down, peeking through a fringe of bangs. She couldn't risk him recognizing her now, not when she was so close to being a part of this adventure.

Seemingly satisfied, Shad took his place at the head of the column and motioned for Jamie to join him. With a glance in her direction, Jamie led Buster to Shad. Of course she'd be on her own while they traveled. Jamie was their scout, and he'd work closely with Shad. She didn't have the skills to help, nor could she spend that much time near Shad. He'd notice her for sure then.

She dropped into line beside a boy who looked like he couldn't be too much older than her fourteen years. He was a good foot taller than her. Lanky, like a scrawny buck no self-respecting hunter would take down. A dark brown horse with a star on its forehead followed him.

Gripping Blizzard's reins, Brandi tried out her tough-boy voice and nonchalant swagger. "I'm Randy. Where are you from?"

"Uh, Deadgrass." His head bobbed in time with his strides. "Though my family has lived in Eagle Heights for over two years. I'm Ian McCrae by the way."

"Deadgrass. That's not too far from Stetterly. That's where I'm from." Brandi fought to stop her smile. Ian wasn't looking at her strangely, so her acting was passing. "Think we'll get through?"

"Don't know. I heard this Blade trainee is good. But he's only a trainee. The other Blades will be better." Ian glanced at her. "I saw you talking to him. You know him? Is he any good?"

"I stayed in Walden for a while. Got to know him." She bit her lip. She couldn't reveal which Blade had trained Jamie. Or that Jamie was actually a full-fledged Blade. "Pretty good. You got to be to get away from the Blades."

A sharp whistle called them to attention. Shad swung onto his horse. "Mount up!"

Brandi placed her foot in the stirrup, grabbed the saddlehorn, and pulled herself onto Blizzard's back. Her stomach flipped. This was it.

She was riding off to war.

The whistle pierced Brandi's head. She dragged her eyes open. Ugh. Her muscles were so sore. Why had she thought this would be an adventure? All they did was hike and ride all day. Nothing more exciting than a new ridge to climb or a new ravine to travel around. Thanks to their circuitous route, they'd had to go through some of the roughest country in the Sheered Rock Hills.

Rolling to her feet, she scrubbed her eyes, straightened her grubby clothes, and reached into her saddlebag for a hardtack biscuit. While she chewed, trying not to break a tooth, she blinked at the waking camp. The pre-dawn, grey haze obscured the trees at the edges of their camp. Several of the men checked weapons or brushed their horses.

A few yards away, Ian groaned and tugged his blanket over his head. He'd joined their little circle, and so far, Brandi hadn't had too much difficulty convincing him she was a boy. Lack of baths and no changes of clothes helped.

She tossed a stick. It smacked Ian on the head. "Stop lazing about. Even I'm up."

Ian rubbed the back of his head and sat up. "Wouldn't be so tired if not for your snoring. Kept me up half the night."

"Your teeth crunching and lip smacking kept me up the other half." She grinned. "Did you dream about eating beef roast all night?"

"My mama's cookies." He pulled out a biscuit and chomped on it. "Wish she was here now. She makes the best buttermilk biscuits. My brothers and sisters are probably stuffing themselves with them right now."

"You have a lot of siblings?" Brandi worked to keep her smile on her face. How she missed Aunt Mara's maple sugar cookies, her biscuits, the way she bustled around Stetterly's kitchen, smelling of flowers and food. Ian at least had his mother waiting for him at Eagle Heights. Brandi had only Renna.

"Two brothers and four sisters. All younger." The grin died on Ian's face. He stared at the hard biscuit in his hand. "Father got us all out of Deadgrass, but he didn't make it."

Another life Respen had taken. Brandi ground her teeth into the stale crumbs in her mouth. They had to win this war. Respen couldn't get away with this.

Jamie slumped to the ground beside her. Dark splotches encircled his eyes. Ian snapped his mouth shut, his eyes wide. Not fearful, exactly. More like awe.

"Did you get any sleep last night?" She handed Jamie a biscuit. When she'd collapsed into her bedroll, he'd still been scouting the area ahead of them.

"Some." He turned the biscuit over in his fingers rather than biting into it right away. "We're going to sneak past the Blade today. I located his lookout post last night."

She gulped her bite of biscuit. Then today was it. By that afternoon, their group of a hundred Riders would slip past the Blade and attack the army's flank. "And we'll be attacking Respen's army after that?"

He nodded, stared at his biscuit pensively, then bit into it. After a moment, he grimaced. "These biscuits just keep getting worse."

She grimaced also and forced herself to eat the rest of hers. After she finished, she gathered and checked her weapons. When her knives and short sword were sharp and ready, she strapped her bedroll to Blizzard's back, taking care to make sure nothing would rattle.

Shad called them into order. "Men, this is it. Today, we're going to sneak past a Blade and surprise Respen's army."

A bunch of the guys gave low cheers.

Shad fixed them with a look. "We have to be quiet and inconspicuous. Blacken any shiny objects now, if you haven't done so already. Strap your canteen and pot in your bedroll so they don't rattle. I have strips of buckskin to tie around your horse's hooves. Prince Keevan is depending on us. We cannot make a mistake."

Brandi joined the line and snatched her four squares of buckskin. Blizzard remained still while she tied the buckskin over his hooves. He'd probably done this before. He was a Blade's horse, after all.

When Blizzard was ready, she fell into line behind Ian. Ian grinned, though the corners of his mouth remained tense.

Jamie led Buster over to her. "I'll need my hands free while scouting. I'll tie Buster's lead to Blizzard's saddle. They won't give you any trouble."

"All right." Brandi held Blizzard while Jamie tied

Buster's lead rope around the saddlehorn. True to Jamie's word, Buster fell into line behind Blizzard. Jamie scrambled back to the front of the line. When he disappeared into the forest ahead of them, Shad waved them forward.

A strange silence enveloped them. Everyone remained silent, not even whispering. The leather of their saddles creaked, but the bridles and stirrups had been wrapped in cloth. Blizzard's hooves clumped on the ground with the same rhythm, but without the sharp clatter of hoof on stone.

Brandi led Blizzard and Buster directly in the footsteps of Ian's horse. Jamie led them along a path to stay out of sight of the Blade, but one move out of line could ruin all of it.

They reached the head of the canyon. Brandi gulped. Jamie had assured Shad that he'd found a game trail leading to the bottom, but looking at the cliffs falling away below them, Brandi wasn't sure the horses would make it, especially not with their hooves made slick with the leather padding.

At the head of their column, Shad and his horse disappeared into the canyon.

One man and horse after another descended over the rim. Ian's horse balked at the edge. Brandi swatted the horse on the rump. It jumped, getting halfway over before it realized what it was doing. Bracing its legs, it skidded downward and reached a wider ledge a few feet down.

Her turn. Brandi tightened her grip on Blizzard's reins. Thankfully, Blizzard didn't hesitate. He placed each hoof carefully as he navigated down the incline. Buster followed with the same unfazed care.

As they eased down the side of the cliff, Brandi

scowled. Jamie had a strange definition of the word *path*. At times, the rocky ledge became barely wide enough for their horses to place one hoof in front of another. At other times, the path disappeared altogether into a gravelly slope that the horses slid down one at a time. Dust billowed into the air, coating Brandi's face and throat. Hopefully the dust wouldn't billow above the rim of the canyon where the Blade could see it.

At last, they reached the bottom. Shad allowed them a short rest by the trickling creek that meandered through the canyon's bottom. While Blizzard and Buster grazed on the tufts of green grass growing beside the stream, Brandi splashed water on her face and tried to rinse the dust from her mouth. A few bites of dried meat silenced her stomach.

The sun stabbed down from the sky and poked at their backs. Sweat trickled down Brandi's spine in a hot, sticky river. As she led Blizzard, the reins grew slick in her fingers.

She would've loved to roll in the stream to cool off, but she had to keep moving and stay in line. Even though the initial dousing would feel amazing, hiking in itchy, drying clothes would be even more miserable than the sweat.

The afternoon crawled along with her aching feet. Apparently a sneak attack involved a lot of boredom.

As the sun dipped toward the horizon, Jamie led them up another winding trail out of the canyon. The horses slipped and skidded on the gravel slopes, but they lunged upward without too much trouble. Brandi lost her footing several times, but her grip on Blizzard's reins kept her from falling.

Crossing over the top of a rise, they followed a long

ridge that sloped down from the Hills into the prairie below, sticking to the eastern side below the top to remain out of sight. Silence still reigned. Brandi's tongue hurt from clenching it between her teeth to stop herself from talking. A whole day of silence was seriously torture.

Blizzard's head shot upward, jerking her arm. His ears pricked as he stared forward and across the ridge. Shad halted the column as his horse's head also lifted. Jamie dropped from a line of trees in front of them and whispered something to Shad.

A breeze drifted up and over the ridge in front of them. Brandi heard it now too. Clanging. Yelling. Drumming hoof beats.

The battle. Her boredom galloped away on pounding heartbeats. A tingle rushed from her stomach into her fingers and toes. In minutes, she'd ride into battle.

The man in front of Ian turned around and whispered something to Ian. Ian nodded, turned, and leaned closer to Brandi. "Captain Alistair has ordered everyone to prepare for battle. Pass the word."

Brandi nodded her understanding and whispered the message to the man in line behind her. When he nodded, she turned her attention to Blizzard. With shaking fingers, she untied the strips of cloth from the bridle and the buckskin from Blizzard's hooves.

As she redid the straps on her pack and checked the placement of her weapons, Jamie appeared at her side. He untied Buster's lead rope and quickly divested him of the buckskin and cloth strips. He opened his mouth but snapped it shut.

"God is with us." Brandi had to believe that. Her faith still felt shaky as a cliff face, but she couldn't let that stop her from trusting. David trusted God when he

marched into battle against a giant. Today, she was
going to be David. Strong. Courageous. Fearless.

Shad motioned them into formation in the line of
trees. Brandi swung onto Blizzard and rode between Ian
and Jamie into the clumps of trees at the crest of the
ridge. A few feet from Blizzard's hooves, the ridge fell
away into rolling grassland. Respen's army clumped on
a series of hills below, dirt fortifications ringing their
positions. Their line curved into the distance, ending at
the black dot of Walden Manor.

On the field below the fortifications, the Resistance
army streamed away from recent battle, motionless forms
dotting the prairie between the two armies. One attack
already failed.

If their sneak attack didn't work, the Resistance
could be broken on that hill. She fisted her hands in
Blizzard's mane. This wasn't a game. This wasn't an
adventure. This was war. Life and death. Blood and battle.

She'd have to kill again in a few minutes. Something
inside her shook, yet she forced it down. She was a
warrior. Like David. Perhaps there was a cost for those
who shed blood in war. But someone had to pay it.

Keevan's shiny palomino whirled and faced the hill
again. The army formed behind him, preparing for
another charge. Behind them, the line of archers raised
their bows.

Now or never. Brandi glanced along their line. Each
face wore the same look. Determination, but more than
that. Resolve. Courage. Fear. Clenching her jaw, she
faced the battle below. No turning back.

Keevan's army broke into a march and charged across
the prairie. The riders that had remained with the main
army galloped in a wedge ahead of the foot soldiers.

Brandi tightened her legs around Blizzard. A few horses along the line stomped their hooves. Blizzard remained steady.

The Resistance army charged closer. Brandi leaned forward. Any moment now. Her tongue dried like a fall cornstalk.

"Get ready, men." Shad's voice, while low, cut through the evening.

Brandi drew her short sword. Beside her, Jamie and Ian pulled out their weapons.

Keevan's palomino galloped in the lead, its mane and tail streaming like golden banners. Black slivers streaked past her cousin and the front runners. Arrows. The Resistance archers answered with a volley of their own.

A crash sounded behind them. Brandi craned her neck. A horse and a rider dressed in black burst from the trees above them and pelted down the hill.

The Blade had spotted them. But he was too late.

"Now." Shad's voice sliced the stillness. He kicked his horse into a gallop. It plunged down the ridge. All around her, the men kicked their horses. Brandi dug her heels into Blizzard's sides. Blizzard leapt into a gallop in two jumps, Jamie's horse matching him stride for stride.

Brandi leaned low in the saddle, swaying in time with Blizzard's movements. Her right hand remained steady, gripped around her sword.

The Blade ahead of them shouted and motioned over his shoulder.

With a yell, Keevan's army crashed into the fortifications. Even with the drumming of hoof beats around her, she could hear the clash of blades.

The men in the fortifications closest to them turned. Before the men had a chance to react, Shad and the front runners smashed into them. Blizzard gathered himself and jumped over the fortification, Buster hurdling beside them. Ian's horse leapt the barricade a moment later.

Brandi swiped at a man lunging for her. He jumped back, and Ian plunged his knife into the man's back. Blood spattered. Brandi gulped down her heaving stomach. She wasn't going to be sick.

The next fortification bristled with soldiers, all of them braced for the Riders' attack.

Shad spurred his horse forward and smashed into the line of men. Brandi only had a moment before Blizzard shoved his way between two of the soldiers. She didn't have time to search for her friends or watch Shad. She could only watch for the next stab, the next thrust. Dropping the reins, she drew her knife. She slashed a man with her knife and thrust at another soldier. Kicking a soldier in the shoulder, she stabbed him.

Blizzard swerved. Brandi gripped with her knees and leaned low to keep her seat. A sword sliced the air where she'd been a moment before. She swiveled in the saddle and plunged her knife into the soldier. She didn't have time to think. Didn't have time to regret.

Soldiers piled into the fortifications in front of them. The Riders around Brandi wavered. Their charge faltered.

She couldn't let that happen. Respen's army had to break. Not just for Renna. Not just for Leith. But for Acktar. For the children waiting at Eagle Heights, waiting for the opportunity to grow up, live, and worship God in the freedom Brandi barely remembered.

"Forward!" She yelled the word and urged Blizzard onward. Blizzard plowed into two men, staggered a beat, and shoved them out of the way. Jamie and Buster plunged into the gap on one side, Ian and his horse on the other.

Others took up the shout. Shad's voice roared something at them above the din. Brandi couldn't make out his words. It didn't matter. Her arms hurt with the weight of her sword and dagger. She'd lost one of her knives somewhere along the way. She didn't remember where.

The soldier in front of her wavered and took a step back. The soldiers on either side of him stumbled as well. In a wave, the line of soldiers crumbled before them as men turned and ran. Soldiers tripped over each other as they dashed away from the melee.

"Onward, men!" Shad's chestnut horse shimmered in the sunset. "Keep them on the run!"

More slashing. Hacking. Stabbing. Blood. Screams.

Then the battle ended. One moment she was fighting, the next there was no one left to fight. She blinked at the nighttime darkness that had descended around her. In the haze, Prince Keevan claimed the top of the hill they'd fought all evening for. A ragged cheer rose from the foot soldiers gathered around him. They'd won.

Weariness poured into her body. She sat on Blizzard, not sure what to do or where to go and too weary to find out. She could feel Blizzard trembling beneath her. She should at least give him a rest.

When she slid from Blizzard's back, her legs buckled. Her whole body shook. Somewhere behind her, a man retched. Moans and cries filled the air along with the stench of blood. Men shouted, trying to locate friends and family among the living. The shouts turned to wails at finding those loved ones among the dead.

Where was Jamie? Ian? She peered into the darkness,

but all she could see were staggering, black forms moving among mounds of bodies. A stench fouled the air, one she recognized all too well from the courtyard after Respen executed Uncle Abel and Aunt Mara. Fresh death. Musty blood. Sour body.

Her teeth chattered. Her fingers trembled with an intense cold. Bile gathered in her throat, but she choked it back into her heaving stomach. No, she wasn't about to lose her stomach. She had to be tougher than that.

"Shad!"

Brandi dragged her head up. That was Lord Alistair's voice. But could that gaunt figure staggering up the hill really be him?

A man dropped from his horse and dashed forward. "Father!"

Lord Alistair sagged to his knees as if too weak to stay standing. Shad crashed to the ground, and the two embraced. At least Lord Alistair was alive. But she couldn't go near him.

Brandi tottered a step forward. Where were Jamie and Ian? She searched the upright silhouettes for a pair of slim, small frames. They had to be among the living.

"Randy!"

Jamie's voice. She gripped Blizzard's reins to keep herself standing. Her voice croaked. "Over here!"

Jamie appeared at her side. He reached out, as if to grip her shoulders, before he halted and dropped his arms. "You're alive. When we got separated, I—never mind. Come on. I found Ian. Captain Alistair's Riders are gathering down the hill."

Nodding, Brandi turned to follow him. As she tugged on Blizzard's reins, he lurched forward. Frowning, she halted and patted Blizzard's neck. When she swiped her hand down his damp fur, her hand encountered a wet patch of something thicker than sweat.

Her stomach catapulted to her toes. Blizzard couldn't get hurt. She'd promised Leith. What would Leith think when he learned she'd recklessly injured his horse? "Jamie, can you bring a light over here?"

He must've heard the wobble in her voice because he jumped to do as she asked. Returning with a torch, he held it up. The light fell across Blizzard's sweat-soaked frame and illuminated the deep gash running along the base of the horse's neck and across the upper muscles of his front leg.

Brandi gulped at a rush of tears. Blizzard had been hurt, but he'd kept going into the battle. He'd carried her forward even bleeding as he was.

"Let's get him to our camp. We can help him there." Jamie's blue eyes, glowing with the torchlight, steadied her.

Patting Blizzard's neck, Brandi coaxed him down the hill. They had to take a winding path around motionless and writhing bodies.

She stepped on something both hard and squishy. She glanced down. A hand, all by itself, lay under her boot.

Jerking her foot, she jumped away. A shudder violently shook her shoulders and traveled all the way down into her toes. Must. Not. Scream.

"Water..." Something scrabbled at her trouser leg.

She tore away from the bloodstained hand and pulled Blizzard forward as fast as the injured horse could. They had to get away from the carnage before she gave in to the shriek tearing through her chest.

Jamie halted and waited for her to catch up. Together,

they skirted the last of the dead and dying. Up ahead, the dry moat and dirt fortifications of Walden Manor loomed black against the cloudy, dark gray sky.

At the edge of the cluster of Riders, Ian tied a rope between his horse's front hooves. Buster already wore a hobble and cropped at the grass. Ian clambered upright when he spotted them. "Good. You found him. Glad to see you're both in one piece."

"Yes, but Randy's horse was hurt." Jamie headed for his pack. "Fetch a bucket of water. There's a well by Walden's stables."

Ian dashed into the darkness toward Walden. Jamie pulled medical supplies from his pack.

Squaring her shoulders, Brandi faced the gash across Blizzard's chest. If Renna was here, she could've taken care of it with no problem. Brandi had watched her several times. Surely she could copy Renna's movements.

When Ian returned, he held the torch while Jamie gripped Blizzard's bridle. Jamie's weight wouldn't do any good if Blizzard really spooked, but hopefully the nonsense words Jamie was mumbling would be enough to keep Blizzard calm.

After dipping a rag into the bucket of water, Brandi cleaned the wound. Blizzard flinched and raised his head, jerking Jamie off his feet.

Brandi smoothed her hand across Blizzard's shoulder. "It's all right, Blizzard. Stay still."

Digging her fingers into the jar of salve, she spread the thick paste over the wound. If she let herself feel the slimy muscle, the slippery flap of skin, the sticky blood, she'd fall apart.

How did Renna do this all the time? Brandi's stomach heaved at the sight of blood and pain. The times she'd offered to help Renna, she'd done what she could to keep the patient comfortable and distracted. But the stitching and mending? She was more than happy to leave that part to Renna.

Blizzard kepts his hooves planted, skin quivering, nostrils flaring.

Long ago, Aunt Mara had told her that animals usually fared better with their wounds left open than stitched and bandaged. After she had filled the gash with salve, Brandi swiped her fingers against her blood-spattered trousers. "There. That's the best I can do."

Kneeling, she scrubbed the blood from her fingers as best she could. Not that it mattered. Blood had infiltrated the cracks in her skin and dried beneath her fingernails. Blizzard's blood or blood from someone she'd wounded or killed, she didn't know. She didn't want to know. The stench of blood hovered over the entire hill. The grass reeked with death.

A lieutenant strolled by, a sheaf of papers in his hand. He glanced at Blizzard. "Better put that one out of its misery."

"No!" Brandi hugged Blizzard's head. She couldn't let them kill Blizzard. "He'll heal."

"Not fast enough. Either put him down now or be prepared to leave him when we move out tomorrow."

She crossed her arms.

"Look, I heard the men from Walden are too weak to join us. They're staying behind to bury the dead and tend the wounded too hurt to travel. Leave the horse with them. Now what're your names and whose division are you with?"

While Jamie answered for her, Brandi gripped Blizzard's mane. She'd have to leave him tomorrow. Her legs shook with the effort of holding back her tears. She was pretending to be a boy at the moment. Boys didn't cry.

The lieutenant checked off their names on a list. He glanced over at them. "Prince Keevan exempted Captain Alistair's Riders from the detail gathering the wounded. Get some rest. I heard you guys earned it."

He stalked away to find the next group of survivors.

Brandi glanced over her shoulder at the battlefield. Moans and screams still echoed into the night, replacing the crickets' nighttime lullaby. Sleep? How would any of them sleep after this?

40

Leith cracked his eyes open when Martyn stepped into his cell. Groaning, he pushed himself upright and tugged off the bandages Renna had so carefully wrapped around his torso. As much as he appreciated Renna's help, it probably didn't make much of a difference. What little healing his body accomplished each night was torn apart each morning.

After he dumped the last bandage on the floor, Leith held out his wrists. Martyn tied the rope firmly around Leith's wrists and hauled him to his feet. "Ninth Blade Altin returned with news that the Resistance sent an army down from the Hills. King Respen wasn't happy."

Leith nodded. Whatever Respen had in store for Leith today would be even more unpleasant than before.

When they reached the meeting room, Leith glanced at the assembled Blades. Altin had joined Daas and Ranson around the long table. Respen lounged in his chair at the head of the table. His fingers drummed against the armrests.

Martyn chained Leith's hands above his head. Spinning on his heels, Martyn saluted Respen and slipped into the

First Blade's seat at the king's right.

Leith flexed his fingers and pressed his back against the cool stone wall. The smell of smoke wrapped around him from a fire burning in an iron brazier set a few feet to his right, iron pokers sticking out of the glowing coals. Leith swallowed and tried to keep his breathing steady. Those pokers were for him.

Respen's fingers halted. "It seems I underestimated you. I assumed that sentimental weakness drove you to surrender. Instead your surrender was a distraction to draw my attention away from the real threat."

Leith remained silent. He couldn't give away the thrill thumping in his chest. Prince Keevan had rallied the army, and he was on his way to attack Nalgar Castle.

Respen slid to his feet and pointed at Daas. "Fifth Blade, come."

Daas followed as Respen stalked around the table and approached Leith. Daas's eyes glittered. His mouth slid into a rattlesnake's smile.

Behind Daas, Ranson curled in his seat, head bowed, as if he fought to hold his stomach in place. Blane Altin's hands clutched the edge of his chair. Something broke through Martyn's hard eyes before he turned his gaze away.

Leith would find no help there.

He clamped his jaw shut. Could he endure this torture? Months ago, he'd pressed a heated knife to his shoulder to cauterize a knife wound. That pain would be small compared to what was coming. Respen would make Leith an example for any other Blade thinking about turning traitor.

Respen pointed at Daas. Daas wrapped a thick cloth around his hand and pulled one of the iron pokers from the fire. The end pulsed orange.

Clenching his jaws, Leith squeezed his eyes shut and focused on breathing. He felt the pressure of the poker against the soft skin of his stomach a moment before the searing pain registered. He choked on the agony burning into his body. He tried to squirm away, but Daas shoved the poker harder against his skin.

He couldn't breathe. His chest seized. His muscles refused to move.

When Daas pulled back the cooling poker, Leith had only a moment to gasp a few breaths before Daas drew the second poker from the fire and touched the end to one of Leith's ribs.

The pain crackled across Leith's skin, flaming into his chest. He fought for breath as the agony raged inside him like a living beast, curling, growing, howling, until he couldn't fight it in silence anymore. Renna would hear, but he couldn't help it. The force of the pain drove the screams from him.

As Daas raised the glowing poker again, Respen held up a hand. "Wait." He leaned closer. "What is Prince Keevan's plan to take Nalgar?"

Leith ran his dry tongue across his teeth. Apparently his pain wasn't enough. Nor his screams. Respen had to break him. Humiliate him. Prove that no Blade was strong enough to resist him.

Respen waved at Daas. The red-hot poker raked across Leith's stomach. The smell of burning skin filled his lungs. His throat ached from screaming.

"What is the plan?" Respen's voice curled through the smoke.

Another poker. More screams. More pain twisted under his skin. He slumped against the wall, sweat pouring down his body, the salt flaming against the burns that covered his stomach and chest. He couldn't fight it. He wasn't strong enough.

He clamped his teeth on his tongue. No. He wouldn't give in to this torture.

Respen halted Daas. "He is not going to break. Fetch Lady Rennelda. We will see how long he lasts when she is the one screaming."

Not Renna. Please not Renna.

"Wait!" Leith pulled himself straighter against the wall. "Do whatever you want to me but don't hurt her."

Respen stepped closer and held his gaze. "You cannot stop me. Give me what I want to know or..." He trailed off and waved at the fire heating the pokers.

What could he do? Leith closed his eyes and leaned his head against the wall. Either he betrayed Prince Keevan and the entire Resistance or he let Respen torture Renna.

His heart would die if he had to listen to her screams.

But Shad, Jamie, Lord Alistair. They'd all die if Leith betrayed them. So would Renna.

Leith met Respen's gaze. As Respen stared back, something flickered in his eyes. Not fear. Reluctance?

Respen was bluffing.

What had happened during those weeks Renna was imprisoned? Had Renna somehow managed to touch Respen's heart? Leith wouldn't go so far as to guess that Respen cared for her, but he didn't want to hurt her. Kill her, maybe. But not torture her.

Leith did the only thing he could do. He called Respen's bluff. "I won't tell you anything."

Respen's dark eyes sparked. He gripped Leith's chin and growled in a low voice. "Beg. Don't force me to torture her."

Leith gasped past Respen's fingers digging into his face. Respen couldn't back down without losing face in front of the Blades. Either Leith gave in, or Respen had to torture Renna.

His pride—the part that knew he was strong enough—rebelled. But he was willing to sacrifice his life for Renna. Why not his dignity too?

"Please. Don't hurt her." Leith's voice cracked. "Please."

Respen released Leith and paced. He clasped his hands behind his back. "For Renna's sake, you should be grateful I have already figured out your plan."

Leith's stomach sank. It was possible. Respen wasn't stupid, and their plan wasn't complicated.

"You told them I always meet with my Blades on Sunday morning, and that I would kill you during that Meeting. It would be the perfect distraction for their attack." Respen's voice rang with a mocking tone.

He motioned to Daas. Daas drew one of the pokers from the fire. Leith barely had time to gasp a breath before the agony clawed into his skin.

When Daas pulled away the poker, Respen's gaze flicked briefy at the door. "Is that the plan?"

"Yes." Leith sagged against the chains. For Renna's sake, he had to break.

A thin smile slithered onto Respen's face. "You never were going to win. You have proven yourself to be a failure, just like your father."

Leith gritted his teeth. Those words couldn't hurt him anymore.

Respen waved toward the fire and the waiting Blade once again. Leith steeled himself. More punishment. Respen wouldn't stop until Leith truly broke.

Respen's smile leered through the smoke. "You are

marked for death, my failed Blade."

Leith sucked in a breath as the pain seared again. He choked on the agony and the stench of burning flesh. His head swirled. The patches of candlelight and shadows blended together with the dark shapes of the Blades, shimmery ghosts in the haze.

Marks. Respen had marked Leith a total of forty times. Thirty-seven successes and three failures.

For I bear in my body the marks of the Lord Jesus.

These were the marks of Christ. The gentle touch of fire. The tender caress of the knife's edge. Each mark echoing with the words of God saying *Well done, my good and faithful servant.*

He was blessed. Each blow, each burn, was a blessing raining down from heaven. He didn't have to doubt his salvation. He'd been counted worthy to suffer for Christ.

Worthy. Blessed. Heir of Heaven.

He didn't realize he'd been talking out loud until Respen's laugh wrapped around him. Fingers dug into his cheeks and forced his head up. Respen's eyes burned inches away, his breath mingling with the smoke. "Blessed? You think you're blessed?"

"God is with me." Those words soaked into Leith like a cooling stream. God was with him. Even though he'd been a Blade. Even though he'd shed blood. For the sake of Christ, the Almighty God was with him.

Respen shoved Leith's face away. "You're a fool."

The iron poker pressed into his skin yet again. Agony stole his words. He tried to drag in a breath, but his throat closed.

Darkness slammed around him.

41

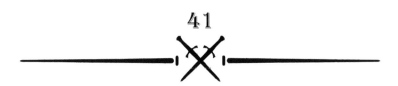

Renna pressed her cheek to the floor. Her tears formed a puddled around her face as she peered under the door. She couldn't help but hear Leith's screams. She'd sunk to the floor, covering her ears and sobbing. She'd been helpless to do anything but pray that God granted Leith the courage to survive this.

She eased her hand off her ear. No more screams. Had Leith passed out? Was Respen finished?

Or was he dead?

Footsteps ground on the stairs. Respen's polished, black boots strode into view. He paused outside her door.

Renna held her breath. Would Respen taunt her? What else did he want with her?

He turned away and strolled down the corridor toward the stairs. A few minutes later, a Blade's black boots swaggered past.

She pressed her fingers against the stone floor. Leith had to be all right. Any moment now, she'd spot his and Martyn's boots. Leith would be leaning on Martyn, but he'd be walking. That's how he'd been the last two days.

A scuffing sound came from the stairs to the meeting room.

"Harding, get the door." Martyn's voice called through the passage.

A pair of boots dashed past, and the door to Leith's room creaked open. Two more pairs of boots shuffled into view. One man walked backwards as if—Renna clapped a hand over her mouth—as if they carried a body between them.

What had they done to Leith? Tremors shook her arms as she pushed herself upright.

When Martyn opened her door, she shoved him aside and dashed into Leith's room, skidding on the stone floor.

Leith lay crumpled on the cot, his chest rising and falling slowly. Black and red marks charred the skin of his stomach and chest. Burns. Raw, oozing burns.

She dropped to her knees beside the cot. Each gasp for breath rasped through her tightening throat, faster and faster. Her hands trembled as she brushed a sweat-soaked lock of hair from Leith's forehead. Tears pricked her eyes.

"I'm sorry. I couldn't stop it. I..." Martyn leaned against the wall, his face a pale glow against the shadows. His hands shook violently.

Heat seared white in Renna's chest. She surged to her feet and whirled. "You could've stopped this weeks ago. If you'd come with us back then, none of this would've happened. I would've escaped. Leith wouldn't have turned himself in. Don't blame anyone else. This is your fault."

Martyn staggered away from her words, small and broken.

"Renna." Leith's cold fingers closed around her wrist. "It's all right."

She glanced over her shoulder. He could barely crack

his eyes open, but their vibrant green still pierced her. "If not for Christ, I would've made the same choice."

Drawing in a deep breath, she let it out slowly. Martyn didn't have the courage God provided her and Leith. Fear and a sense of duty made Martyn loyal to Respen.

"Fine. If you want to help, fetch lots of cold water. If you can scrounge up any laudanum, get it." Renna couldn't keep the bite out of her words.

"I sent Ranson and Blane for supplies. I'd better help." Martyn bobbed his head and stumbled from the room.

Renna retrieved the basin, pitcher, and pewter cup from their stand. Pouring some of the water into the basin, she tested it with her finger. Cold. At least Martyn had done a decent job of bringing Leith fresh water every day.

Filling the tin cup, she slid a hand under Leith's head. "Here. Take a few sips. You must be thirsty."

He gulped at the water but coughed after a few swallows.

"Easy. Not so fast." She soaked one of the few cloths leftover from yesterday and placed it still dripping across one of the burns.

Leith cried out and turned his face away from her. He sucked ragged breaths between his teeth. Tears leaked from the corners of his eyes, mingling with the trails of sweat on his face. He probably didn't even realize the tears were there. "Sorry. I shouldn't..."

"Ssh." Renna drew in a deep breath and willed away her trembling. She couldn't break. Not now. Placing her hand on Leith's cheek, she tipped his head toward her. "You've been strong enough. It's my turn now. I can handle it. Now I need you to take deep breaths, all right?"

He nodded, squeezed his eyes shut, and drew in several deep breaths until his breathing steadied.

She dipped the cloth back in the water and placed it on another burn. Leith flinched but didn't cry out this time.

He slitted his eyes open and laid his hand over hers. "Respen knows. He figured out our plan."

She let out a slow breath. Shouldn't she be scared at hearing those words? But she wasn't. Maybe she'd faced death too many times already. Perhaps she'd always known they wouldn't live long enough to be rescued.

She threaded her fingers through his. "At least neither of us is going to die alone."

Leith squeezed her hand. "You might survive. I'm not sure if it'll be enough to spare you, but I saw something in Respen today. He could've tortured you to make me talk, but he didn't."

"I remind him of Clarisse, his wife. She died years ago."

She had made an impression on Respen after all. It probably wouldn't be enough to prevent Respen from killing her. He'd come close to having her beheaded.

Or had he? Had he counted on Leith saving her? What would he have done if Leith hadn't shown up? Would Respen have stepped in before the ax fell?

Whatever his motives, Respen wouldn't subject her to the same torture as Leith. Small comfort, but at least she'd be whole enough to care for Leith until the end came for both of them.

She rubbed the back of Leith's hand. Death wasn't far away. Respen would kill them before Keevan's army arrived. If Leith's estimates were correct, then they had only days. Even if Respen didn't kill her, he'd force her to watch him kill Leith.

She couldn't waste a minute, especially not with fear. She'd rejoice in the little moments, like this one now, that she had left to enjoy.

Perhaps it was the knowledge of death that gave her a heady sense of boldness. Maybe it was the longing for the things she'd never have. Resting a hand against Leith's cheek, she leaned over and kissed him. His mouth was still swollen from his beating the day before, his breath hot with the fire that had eaten at his skin. His fingers tangled in her hair, shooting tingles down her back.

He pulled away first, gasping. "Can't...breathe..."

"Sorry." She straightened. She'd accidentally leaned an elbow on his chest. What was she thinking? Here he was, barely conscious, and instead of tending to the burns, she kissed him.

He dragged in several gulps of air before he turned back to her. With a hand on the back of her neck, he tugged her down for another kiss. This time, Renna kept her elbows planted on the bed.

By the time she leaned back again, she was breathless and light headed. Leith glanced over her shoulder, and his smile widened. "We're making Martyn uncomfortable."

Renna huffed and sat back on her heels. "He deserves to be uncomfortable."

She turned to Martyn, who hesitated in the doorway like he couldn't decide if he wanted to bolt or interrupt or just lose the contents of his stomach right there on the floor. He carried a bucket in one hand and a bundle of clean cloths in the other.

Behind him, Ranson gripped the handle of another bucket while the other Blade, Blane, held a tray with medical supplies. Both of the younger Blades gaped like they'd never seen anyone kiss before.

Red-faced, Martyn tiptoed into the room and dropped the bucket and cloths next to Renna. "I...forgot something." He pelted from the room like she might start kissing *him* in a minute.

Ranson shuffled forward and set his bucket next to Martyn's. His hands trembled. He opened his mouth but snapped it closed again. Apparently he was still following Martyn's orders not to speak with her.

"Thank you." Renna soaked several cloths in the bucket of cold water and placed them on Leith's burns.

Leith closed his eyes. His body sagged into the cot. "That feels good."

Blane set the tray on the end table. Unlike Ranson, his hands remained steady. "Is there anything I can do to help?"

"Can you give him the laudanum? Just a spoonful."

Blane nodded, knelt, and reached for the vial. After pouring a spoonful, he lifted Leith's head and gave him the medicine. Blane grabbed the cup Renna had set aside and held it to Leith's mouth.

Leith gulped several times. Some of the water dribbled around the edge of the cup and over his chin.

When Leith had finished, Blane laid him back down. "Would you like more?"

"No." Leith tipped his head toward Blane. "I should've gotten you and Ranson out like I did Jamie. I'm sorry I didn't."

Renna glanced over her shoulder and caught sight of Ranson's wet eyes a moment before he slid to the floor and wrapped his arms around his knees.

"I'm glad you got Jamie out." Blane reached for

another cloth, soaked it in the bucket, and placed it across one of the burns.

"Look out for Ranson. Watch each other's backs." Leith's eyes fluttered closed. His muscles relaxed beneath Renna's hand as the drug took effect. "If you get a chance, you get Ranson out. Shadrach Alistair will help you."

Renna swallowed at the lump in her throat. Leith was saying goodbye, giving Blane and Ranson last instructions. Would they listen?

Blane froze and shot a glance at Ranson. "I'll keep that in mind."

Leith didn't move in response. His chest rose and fell in a steadier rhythm than before.

Renna kept replacing the cloths with wet, cold ones. After half an hour, she took stock of the burns. Some of them had formed red, puffy blisters. Painful, but as long as the blister didn't burst, she wouldn't need to tend them further.

The rest—the deeper burns—were pale with dead skin and splotched red. Pale liquid oozed from the open wounds.

After some convincing, she managed to borrow a knife from Martyn after he cleaned it with alcohol for her. She cut away the dead skin, filled the burns with salve, and placed bandages over them.

Standing, she rubbed her knees and glared at Martyn. "He's going to need lots of fresh water. And the bandages will need to be changed several times today. Not that it really matters. Respen is going to just hurt him worse again tomorrow."

Martyn scrubbed his hand through his hair. "We'll take care of it. I'll fetch you when it's time to change the bandages." He drew in a deep breath, and his face hardened back into that of the First Blade. "Eighth and Ninth Blades, the trainee could use some practice. See to it."

"Yes, First Blade." Blane thumped his fist across his chest. Ranson did the same a moment later. They hurried from the room, though both of them glanced at Leith before they left.

"I guess I'd better return to my room." Renna rested her hand on Leith's shoulder for a moment. His skin still flared hot, sticky with sweat. A tear trickled down one of his cheeks.

She turned away and strode into her room. As soon as Martyn locked the door behind her, she leaned against the wall separating her and Leith. She removed the loose stone and listened to the steady sound of Leith's breathing.

As long as she could hear him breathe, he was all right. It wouldn't last, but for now, it was enough.

42

As morning broke over the battlefield, Brandi cracked her eyes open. Her muscles groaned. Aching her way to her feet, she stared at the hill above Walden. Bodies still sprawled where they had fallen. In the flat area at the base of the hill, a few tents had been set up in the middle of rows of men. How many of them were still waiting for someone to tend them?

She shivered and rubbed her upper arms. Sunlight didn't make death look any better.

Shaking herself, she grabbed breakfast and checked on Blizzard. The wound remained hot and swollen. He stood on three legs with his injured leg resting on a hooftip.

Jamie stopped next to her and scrubbed Blizzard's neck. "You know we'll have to leave him. He'd never keep up, and he'd hurt himself worse if we forced him to try."

She nodded, biting back tears, while she slid her hand over the horse's nose. She'd known it the moment she'd seen the wound, as much as she'd wanted to deny it. When the army moved out, she'd have to abandon Blizzard here.

Would Blizzard heal? Or would he die? Horses couldn't live on three legs. They needed to move to stay healthy.

If she left him, would he die all alone?

Brandi leaned her face against Blizzard's neck, soaking in the warmth of his sleek fur. The scent of horse, normally a sweet smell, held a sour taste today. The smell of a horse in distress.

Blizzard swiveled his head, nibbled on the edge of her shirt, and stared at her with his big, liquid eye.

"Are you telling me it's all right to go, boy?" She scrubbed his neck. His ears twitched.

A bugle sounded, calling the army to assemble. Brandi straightened her clothes and lined up with Jamie and Ian in Shad's division.

Shad called them to attention as General Stewart strode from the command tent and eyed the army. "Men, we gained a victory yesterday, but that's one battle in this war. Mourn the friends we lost, then move on. Gather your things. We move out in an hour. Lord Alistair and the survivors of Walden have agreed to stay behind to finish burying the dead and tend those too wounded to continue."

General Stewart waved at a figure standing a few feet behind him. Lord Alistair stepped forward. His gray-streaked beard straggled across his gaunt cheeks. He leaned on a cane, and one arm rested in a sling. But his eyes still burned.

If Lord Alistair and his men could hold out for weeks against Respen's army, maybe Leith and Renna could survive too.

General Stewart clasped his hands behind his back. "Riders have already been sent to Ably and Calloday to see if those lords would join us once they realize that the true king of Acktar has returned. We should hear their responses shortly. Now that we have entered Acktar, riders must be sent to Dently. Captain Alistair, please select a pair of boys from your division and have them step forward."

Shad spun on his heels. Scanning the assembled men, he pointed at Jamie and then at Brandi. "You two, step forward."

Brandi kept her eyes facing forward as she strode to the front of the group with Jamie. As the smallest "boy" in the division, she'd be the lightest. Her weight wouldn't tire the horse out as quickly as one of the larger boys. Jamie was also slim of build and his experience as a Blade trainee would get them through safely and quickly.

"Do you both have fast horses?" Shad stood straight and expressionless, all commanding and whatnot. Of course, in front of all the men, Shad couldn't be anything less than official.

Brandi shot a glance towards Jamie before facing forward. Her dirty face and short hair might fool Shad since he wasn't looking at her too closely, but her voice would be difficult to disguise, even talking deeper.

Jamie cleared his throat. "My horse is fast, sir, but Randy's horse was injured yesterday."

Shad nodded. "You'll be issued a new one. We captured several in the battle yesterday." He handed a folded and sealed paper to Jamie. "Give this letter to Lady Emilin."

Jamie and Brandi nodded. Lord Emilin had been killed by a Blade a few months ago when he'd refused to take any sort of action against King Respen, even to safe his own life from assassination. Perhaps his widow would be more willing now.

"Yes, sir." Jamie tapped two fingers against his forehead. Brandi did the same a second later.

"Gather your things. Dismissed."

Jamie and Brandi returned to their camp and rolled their bedrolls. Brandi glanced at Jamie. "You didn't object to me being placed on this assignment."

He shrugged. "You're a good rider. And I think you'll be safer on this mission than sticking with the army. They'll be fighting for every mile on the way to Nalgar Castle."

She swallowed and tied her bedroll with the leather straps. Respen's army wouldn't make it easy. Keevan wouldn't be sending out riders to ask for more allies if he didn't think he'd need the extra men to take the castle.

Ian strolled over and slapped both their backs. "Be careful. Don't run into any Blades."

"You too." Jamie returned the gesture.

Brandi swallowed. Would Ian be all right? He'd ride into battle without Jamie and Brandi to watch his back. Would he survive by himself?

Two soldiers walked up leading three horses. Brandi threw her saddle onto a slim, brown mare and picked a small black horse for her spare. Jamie tied the lead of the second spare horse to his saddle.

As the soldiers began to walk away, Jamie held out a hand. "Wait. Can you take this horse to Lord Alistair?" He pointed at Blizzard.

One of the soldiers raised his eyebrows, but he nodded.

Brandi checked Blizzard's wound one last time and hugged him around the neck. "You take care of yourself, Blizzard."

The horse nudged her, as if telling her to go. He'd be all right.

Blinking at tears, Brandi handed Blizzard's lead to the soldier, swung onto the brown horse, and nudged it into a trot, Blizzard's parting whinny echoing in her ears.

43

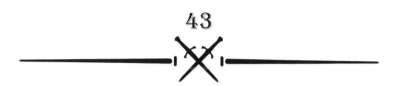

Pain throbbed through Leith's skull. He groaned and shifted. Shafts of pain slashed through his chest. Spots of stabbing agony seared across his stomach and chest. He ground his teeth and tried to draw in a deep breath, but more pain choked his lungs.

Something cold pressed against the side of his head. Achingly cold. He tried to turn his head away, but the cold stayed.

"Sssh. Lie still." A soft touch stroked his forehead.

Leith peeled his eyes open. Colors swirled above him. He blinked several times until the forms solidified into shapes that remained blurry around the edges.

Renna sat with her back to the wall, one hand on his forehead, the other pressing something cold and wet to the side of his skull. Only then did he realize she cradled his head on her lap. He worked his tongue free from the roof of his mouth. "What happened?"

"You took a nasty beating, including a blow to your head that knocked you out. You've been out for half an hour." Renna shifted the cold and wet rag from the side of his head. Her fingers trailed over the spot. "You have a large lump on the side of your head. Martyn even fetched ice for me."

Leith sucked in a breath and winced as pain shot through his head and chest. He tried to remember, but his head slogged through mush. "I don't remember much."

It must've been bad, though, to make Martyn trek all the way from the Blades' Tower, through the castle, into the kitchens, and beg for ice from the cook, who had the key to the iceroom.

Renna frowned. "Do you have a headache? Is your vision blurry?"

"Yes. Both." Leith squeezed his eyes shut and tried to draw in a deep breath. Agony tightened his chest.

"A mild head injury." She pressed the cold cloth back to his head. "And a few cracked ribs. I think with a little rest your blurry vision and headache should fade."

He tried to move, but weakness filled every inch of his body. A moan built in his chest and slipped out his teeth before he could bite it back.

"I'm sorry. You've had too much laudanum in the last few days as it is. I can't give you any more. Blane is making willow bark tea." Renna stroked his forehead. "Martyn, can you hand me a cup of water?"

Leith could barely hear the scuffing of footsteps over the ringing in his ears. A few minutes later, Martyn entered Leith's line of sight. Even with Leith's blurry sight, Martyn's face appeared pale. He handed Renna a cup. She raised his head and pressed the cup to Leith's mouth.

His throat tightened with thirst. But his stomach knotted until he wasn't sure he could even hold water down. After a few swallows, he turned his face away.

"Come on, Leith. Just a little more. With those burns,

you need lots of water."

For Renna, he'd do about anything. His stomach churned, but he forced each mouthful down until the cup was empty.

"I'll fetch the tea." Martyn straightened.

"Let Blane and Ranson know Leith's awake."

If Martyn replied, Leith didn't hear it. He closed his eyes and concentrated on breathing past the haze of pain.

He shouldn't lie here like this. He should sit up. He should be the one comforting Renna and being strong for her.

But he was broken. His energy drained out of him. He didn't know how much strength he had left.

Renna laced her fingers between his. The touch sent tingles through his arm. He shouldn't, but he drew on her strength.

"How did Ranson become a higher Blade than Blane?"

Talking. A distraction from the pain. Leith struggled to gather his thoughts, scattered with the ringing and throbbing and the feel of her hand in his. It'd been a year ago. Two fifteen-year-olds, neither one ready. But when Respen had handed Ranson a knife, Blane had offered to kill too to give Ranson the courage to do it.

Leith squeezed his eyes shut tighter. The looks on their faces after they'd done it. He should've stepped in. He should've done something. Instead, he stood by and let them become Blades.

"They killed at the same time. Ranson is two months older, so he became the higher Blade." Leith laid his free hand against one of the bandages on his chest as if that action could stop the pain from grinding deeper.

Once, he'd feared death. He'd feared it enough to kill over and over again to avoid Respen's knife. But now, he felt almost ready. Did that mean this was God's time for his death?

He'd never had a chance to read the whole Bible. He could count the number of sermons he'd heard on his hands. He trusted God, but the gaps in his knowledge still gnawed at him.

He gathered enough breath to speak. "What is Heaven like?"

The silence stretched. Had she heard him? He drew in another painful breath when her voice drifted through the shadows. "The Bible says it's a place of light. No darkness there. No suffering. No tears. The souls of God's people are there, already rejoicing in the presence of Jesus and waiting for their bodies to be raised from the dead at the end of time."

No darkness. He savored that thought. No suffering. He couldn't imagine a place without blood and pain.

"I've heard some people say that we won't remember our past, but I'm not sure."

"I hope I remember everything." Leith pressed a hand against one of his cracked ribs. If only he could hold the pain back, push it into a corner, so he could force the words out. "When I get to Heaven, I want to remember every sin so I can thank Christ for saving me from each one of them."

"I never thought of it that way." She shifted, jostling his head. "We can't truly be thankful if we don't have something to be thankful for."

A thought struck him, painful and sharp as his cracked ribs. "Will your parents have forgiven me? And the others I killed?"

What would it be like, meeting his victims in Heaven? If hatred no longer existed, what would they feel spending eternity with their killer?

Her sigh was a whisper in the darkness. "I suspect that in Heaven, they'll have the perspective to be able to rejoice in your salvation." She paused for a moment, her voice lowering until he could barely hear her. "Uncle Abel once said that in Heaven, we'll all be part of the family of Christ. We'll be brothers and sisters, but we'll know each other better than we knew even our closest brother or sister or friend on this earth. I could never imagine it."

Leith couldn't imagine it either. The thought of meeting Renna's parents and have them welcome him or greeting Daniel from the Bible as a long lost friend. Perhaps there was a reason the Bible didn't speak about Heaven too much. He couldn't fathom the little Renna had told him.

Without being asked, she began singing. He didn't recognize the words or the tune, but it was soft and slow. He closed his eyes, letting the light of the words shiver into his skin and dull the pain for a few moments.

44

Brandi could've cried in relief when the town of Dently poked above the horizon. Her legs, back, shoulders, and pretty much her entire body ached. She and Jamie had ridden almost nonstop for two days after leaving the Resistance army, only pausing for a few hours of sleep each night. Would she even be able to walk when she dismounted?

As they rode into town, the townsfolk peeked out of doors and shuttered windows at them. Fear strolled through the town, stalking around the buildings with gusty footsteps. A squad of armed men casually surrounded Brandi and Jamie, drawing the circle tight before they reached the manor house.

Lady Emilin might claim to be sitting out of the fight, but she wasn't exactly standing down.

Jamie held up the sealed letter. "I have a message for Lady Emilin."

"Dismount. Leave your weapons here." One of the soldiers commanded them, his hand clasped around the hilt of his sheathed sword.

Brandi slid from the horse's back and removed her

daggers and short sword. She placed them in a pile on the ground and stepped away from them. She held her breath. Hopefully the guards wouldn't feel the need to frisk her for additional weapons. Her baggy shirt and leather vest disguised her figure, but it wouldn't do anything if someone searched her.

Jamie eyed her as he placed his weapons on the pile, as if he were wondering the same thing. She gave a small shrug. If it came down to it, she'd just have to confess who she was. What would they do? Maybe they'd think Keevan had allowed girls in his army.

"Come with me." The spokesman waved them forward. Brandi huffed. Apparently they looked innocent enough.

The guard led them into the manor house, four of the other guards trailing behind them. Inside, the spokesman ordered them to wait in what looked like the study while he fetched Lady Emilin.

Brandi rocked back and forth on her feet, studying the small bookcase and the honeyed pine paneling. Lord Alistair's study in Walden had been lavish, all dark paneling and so many books no one person could ever read them all. This study was understated. Functional. She rather liked the look of it.

Lady Emilin swept into the room. Her brown hair curled in a loose bun at the back of her head, accentuating her pale face. Shadows ringed her eyes and tightened her mouth.

Jamie gave a half bow, and Brandi hurried to do the same. As Brandi straightened, Jamie held out the letter. "I have a message from the Leader of the Resistance."

Lady Emilin stiffened. "I won't take communication from the leader of that rebellion. My husband died for his refusal to aid the rebellion. I will do no less."

"I understand, my lady." Jamie extended the letter again. "But you'll want to read this one." He turned the letter so the seal caught the afternoon sunlight dazzling through the windows.

Lady Emilin blinked and paled to the same color as the letter. With trembling fingers, she took the letter and broke the seal. Her brown eyes flicked back and forth as she read it quickly.

If she wasn't pretending to be a boy, Brandi would've given the lady a hug. Lord Emilin had died because he'd refused to fight against King Respen. He'd seen the Resistance as a rebellion against the king God had placed over them. He'd had no way of knowing that the Resistance was trying to restore the true king to the throne. As Lord Alistair had maintained all along, Respen was the one rebelling. It'd be hard for a widow to come to terms with that.

Lady Emilin swallowed. When she raised her head from the letter, her face had smoothed into a calm mask, her eyes flinty. "Captain, assemble our men. We'll be joining the Resistance. We move out as soon as possible."

Her captain nodded, his eyes full of questions that Brandi could tell he was too disciplined to ask in front of his men. "Shall I arrange for quarters for these messengers?"

Jamie shook his head. "We need to return to the Leader to report, my lady. A pair of fresh horses and provisions is all we ask."

As Lady Emilin nodded her assent and commanded her captain to see to it, Brandi bit back her groan. So much for a good night's sleep in a soft bed.

※

As the evening shadows lengthened, Jamie wheeled

his horse. "Let's swing by Nalgar Castle."

Brandi nodded. They'd have to circle around it to reach her cousin's army anyway. They might as well stop and scout the area. It might come in handy when Keevan's army attacked in the morning.

Brandi and Jamie left their horses in a stand of trees and stalked through the prairie grass to a hill overlooking Nalgar Castle. At the top, they crawled on their stomachs and parted the strands of grass. To their left, the sun hung low, a ball of gold in hills of orange fire. Nalgar's towers stood dark against the blazing sky.

Men streamed over the hill from the north and darted through the open gate. Jamie gave a small nod of his head in their direction. "Our army must have them on the run."

"Good. To rescue Leith and Renna, Keevan has to attack tomorrow morning." Brandi peered north as if she could spot the advancing army. "They can't be that far away."

"It looks like these men ran for several miles to get here. Look at how they're staggering. At this time of night, Prince Keevan will probably give the order to halt and camp several miles away from the castle." Jamie scowled and tipped his head again. "One of the Blades."

A figure dressed in black galloped his horse past the tottering soldiers, shoved a few aside, and cantered through the gate. A moment later, Brandi spotted the Blade exiting the wall of the castle and crossing the wooden bridge across the moat to enter the Blades' Tower.

For an hour, they watched Respen's army retreat into the castle walls. More Blades galloped into the castle and entered the Tower. Brandi leaned over and whispered to Jamie. "How many is that? Are all the Blades there?"

Jamie bobbed his head. "I think so." He wiggled backwards. "We'd better report to Captain Alistair."

Brandi began to crawl backwards, but movement in the castle halted her. She peered through the descending darkness at the bridge to the Blades' Tower. A tall, dark-haired figure strode across the bridge dressed in what looked like dark blue clothing. She swallowed. Even at this distance, she could recognize King Respen. "Jamie, look."

Jamie's jaw tightened. "Something's gone wrong. I think Respen called a Meeting of the Blades."

"Tonight? But he isn't supposed to have one until tomorrow morning." Her heart twisted and tumbled into her stomach. "He isn't just going in there to..." She didn't want to say torture Leith, but torture was better than death.

Jamie shook his head. "Respen likes to do that kind of stuff in the morning. That's why he always calls a Meeting of the Blades in the morning. Always. I've never known him to enter the Blades' Tower after dark. Ever."

The evidence clanged like a blacksmith's hammer hitting the anvil, shaping her thoughts. "Respen knows our army's attacking in the morning. He's going to kill Leith before they arrive." They would be too late. "We have to do something. We can't just let him kill Leith and Renna."

Jamie tugged her below the crest of the hill. "Listen. I'll sneak into the castle and try to delay them. Ride to Prince Keevan as fast as you can. Tell him what's happening. You have to convince him to attack tonight. Got that?"

She nodded as a weight fell onto her shoulders. "I'll be back with the army before you know it."

Without a glance backwards, she slid down the hill and raced for the horses. Divesting the small, brown mare of everything except for the saddle and reins, she swung onto the horse and kicked it into a gallop.

The mare flared her nostrils and ran. If the mission hadn't been so urgent, Brandi would've enjoyed the thrill. She'd sensed the mare longed to be given her head and run.

She was running now. Floating, almost flying over the prairie. Brandi crouched low, the ends of the horse's mane lashing her face with sharp strands. She didn't care. All that mattered was speed.

45

Leith woke from a fitful sleep to the sound of voices. He blinked at the ceiling. Why were so many Blades tromping up the stairs at this time of night? And why the talking? Blades didn't usually talk to each other on the way to the meeting room.

The meeting room. With a deep breath, Leith pushed himself onto his elbows. Respen had called a Meeting of the Blades. Tonight. He planned to kill Leith tonight, well before Prince Keevan's army ever spotted the castle walls on the horizon.

Not too unexpected, but Leith had hoped Respen would wait until early the next morning.

Groaning, he swung his legs over the side of his cot and forced himself to sit upright. The room tilted, but he didn't have time to wait for it to stop spinning. Thankfully, his blurry vision and headache had faded yesterday.

He tore at the bandages covering his torso. Tears pricked his eyes as cool air brushed the open burns. "Renna."

"I know." Her voice broke.

If only he could say something, anything, to take away

the starkness of this moment. He dropped the last of the bandages on the floor and kicked them under the cot. Each painful breath felt special with the knowledge that he had so few left. "Our lives are in God's hands."

Her sigh whispered through the gap in the wall. "I know. But I'm still scared."

He'd leaned on her too often in the last couple days. Now, Leith had to be strong for her. One last time.

He slid onto his knees by the hole in the wall and reached his hand into the space. Her hand fumbled for a second until their fingers linked.

Leaning his head against the stones, Leith tried to breathe past the pain of his broken ribs and breaking heart. "No matter what happens, we'll be all right."

If he survived or if he arrived in Heaven, he'd be all right. Respen could do nothing to his soul, no matter how hard he tried.

"Leith." Her sobs echoed through the wall. "When I met you, I would've been happy to watch you die. But now...I can't do it, Leith. I can't."

He squeezed her hand. If only he could wrap his arms around her and let her sob onto his shoulder one last time. Their linked fingers would have to be enough. "Then don't. You have my knife. I'll make sure the door isn't locked. They'll be distracted watching me die. When you get the chance, you run."

"And leave you to die alone? I couldn't."

"I didn't have the courage to die for you back then. I do now. So please let me. I'll die easier knowing I'm buying you time to escape." Leith wrapped his free arm around his waist. Several of his burns seeped a clear liquid.

Steeling his mind, he forced himself to go through

his death step by step. He'd seen this death—he'd caused this death—too many times. He could count the seconds it'd take to die, either by suffocating or bleeding out, depending on how his throat was slit.

"No matter what happens, no matter what you hear, you run. Promise me you'll run."

"I...I promise." She was crying so hard her words wobbled.

"Find a place to hide until morning. Prince Keevan will attack Nalgar Castle then. You should be able to find an opportunity to escape."

"I will."

He sagged against the wall. As long as Renna escaped, he could die content.

"I want to tell you...before..." Renna's voice dropped to a hoarse whisper. "I love you."

Her words punched his stomach. What was he supposed to say to that? Words piled in his throat, but nothing squeaked from his mouth. Somehow, saying it was a promise he couldn't keep. He cleared his throat. "Me too."

He heard footsteps pause outside his door. Footsteps must've halted outside Renna's door because she sobbed harder.

Leith rubbed the back of her hand with his thumb. "I need you to put the stone back in place."

With one last squeeze, he pulled his hand free of hers. The loss tugged all the way to his bones. The stone grated into the hole, separating them permanently.

As his door lock rattled, Leith dug into the straw tick and pulled out the chip of stone he'd hidden there. He gripped it in his fist.

The door creaked open, and Second Blade Offen and

Third Blade Crossley strode in, hands on the hilts of their knives. Renna's door also groaned open.

Leith held out his wrists. Even if he wanted to, he didn't have the strength to fight them. Nor could he risk dropping the stone.

After tying his wrists, the Blades yanked him to his feet. Leith moaned as his cracked ribs shifted and the motion tore at his burns. They hauled him out his door and past the open door to Renna's empty room.

At the stop of the stairs, Leith faked a stumble and fell against the door jamb to the meeting room. He pushed the stone into the opening where the bolt would slide when locked.

The Blades jerked him upright and dragged him forward. Crossley turned and slid the bolt to lock the door. It clicked as if locked, but it didn't slide all the way.

In the meeting room, Martyn huddled in his seat to the king's right. Renna fidgeted in a chair near the end of the table, a rope around her waist tying her to the chair and her hands hidden under the table. Their eyes met, and she tipped her chin. Her tears were gone, except for the faint sheen on her face. She was ready.

Respen lounged in his throne at the head of the table. "Chain him."

The Blades lugged him to the end of the room where they chained his hands above his head.

Leith leaned against the wall and gasped a few breaths. This was it. This was how he'd die.

"The Blades have been dishonored and betrayed. When the rebels arrive in the morning, I want them to see their spy's body hanging from the battlements." Respen held his knife out to Martyn. "My loyal First Blade, kill the traitor."

Martyn's hand only bobbled a fraction as he took the knife and slid to his feet. Leith watched his friend approach. He didn't feel fear. Only a resigned sadness.

Martyn halted in front of him, his brown eyes a swirl of pain, the knife clutched in a white-knuckle grip. "Back when we were trainees, I always thought you'd be the one ordered to kill me."

"Back then, I feared the same thing." Leith closed his eyes and rested his head against the wall, exposing his neck to the blade. He'd gambled to save both Renna and Martyn, but he'd failed. Martyn couldn't be swayed. "It's all right, Martyn. I don't blame you."

Cold steel shivered against his neck. The edge grazed the ridge of his throat, nipping at his skin.

Martyn heaved in a deep breath. The knife pressed harder against Leith's neck in preparation to slice his throat.

46

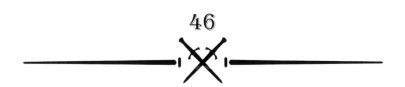

Brandi spotted the pinprick glows of the Resistance army's camp. She urged the mare faster. The mare stretched her neck, ears pressed flat against her skull. Her nostrils flared wide, the insides pink. Sweat splattered into the air and onto Brandi's face.

They blew by the sentry so fast he didn't have time to raise his bow and nock an arrow. Brandi cupped her hands around her mouth and hollered, "Rider coming in! Captain Alistair's rider reporting in!"

She kept shouting as she neared the large tent flying Keevan's banner of prairie-green silk with a silver cross. The mare's hooves skidded. Dust rattled into the air. Brandi launched herself from the horse even before it stopped.

Keevan stepped from the tent, General Stewart at his heels. Shad hurried from the darkness. "Randy, what is it? Where's Jamie?"

Brandi caught her breath, hoping the dust would add enough gravel to her voice to disguise it. "Lady Emilin pledges aid. Her men are moving toward Nalgar Castle as we speak. On our way back, Jamie and I swung by the castle. Respen entered the Blades' Tower. Jamie says he never enters there after dark. He must've called a Meeting of the Blades. Tonight. Jamie stayed behind to see what he could do to delay him."

Keevan rubbed his scar, as if he was undecided about changing their plans. "The men are tired. We had a long march today."

Shad stepped in front of Keevan. "We have to move out tonight. He'll kill Leith and Renna if we don't hurry."

Keevan turned to General Stewart. "What do you advise?"

"The men are tired. But this is our opportunity to corner Respen and his Blades in the Tower. And Respen's men will be just as tired as ours."

"His army is unorganized. It was still retreating while we watched. If we hurry, they won't have time to get organized, especially with Respen busy in the Tower." Brandi curled her fingers into fists. Couldn't Keevan see how urgent this was? Yes, the men were tired. She was too. But so was Respen's army. They couldn't miss this chance. Leith's and Renna's lives depended on it.

Keevan gave a nod. "All right. We'll attack tonight. Captain Alistair, gather your division. General Stewart, rouse the divisions and gather the additional riders and archers aiding Captain Alistair."

"Yes, sir." Shad saluted and spun on his heels. He waved for Brandi to follow him.

Brandi trotted to keep up, leading the huffing mare. At their section of the camp, Shad barked orders. He arranged for someone to take care of the mare and fetch a new horse for Brandi. In minutes, Shad had gathered his division. Brandi fell into line next to Ian, her aches forgotten. She was headed back to save Renna and Leith.

As they trotted from the camp, more riders joined them, reinforcements from Captain Stewart's Riders. One of the riders wore a cloak and hood over his head. Brandi caught sight of a scar running across the man's face. Keevan? What was he doing joining them?

The prairie rumbled with four hundred hooves as they galloped to Nalgar Castle. Brandi's heart pounded with each hoofbeat. They had to get there in time. Respen couldn't kill Leith and Renna. He simply couldn't.

Shad signaled a halt at the base of the hill overlooking the castle. They dismounted and dropped their reins to ground hitch their horses.

Gathering them into three groups, two small groups and one larger group that comprised the bulk of the men, Shad pointed at each of the small groups. "You'll go with me to attack the Blades' Tower, and you'll take the front gate. The rest of you will reinforce them once the gate is open."

Brandi frowned. She'd been set aside as part of the large group.

"No." The figure in the black cloak stepped forward. He tossed his hood back. Brandi rolled her eyes. Of course it was Keevan. He did have a taste for the dramatic, and that scar just helped the whole impression.

Keevan waved at the top of the Blades' Tower peaking over the crest of the hill. "I'll take the group of men into the Tower. Captain Alistair, you'll lead the men at the gate."

Shad clenched his sword's hilt, as if he wanted to protest.

Keevan speared Shad with a look. "Respen's mine to face. You'll help your friend more by taking and holding the gate. You'll have to hold it longer than we originally planned. Your men will need their leader with them. If we lose at the gate, none of us will get out alive."

Shad gave a sharp nod and whirled. "Let's go."

The two groups of men followed Shad and Keevan toward Nalgar. Brandi moved to join the group following Keevan. No way was she letting them leave her behind.

Ian grabbed her arm. "Where do you think you're going? We've been ordered to stay here."

Brandi glanced from him to the men disappearing over the crest of the hill. They were getting farther away. She was missing her chance to save Leith and Renna.

But what had Keevan said? If they didn't hold the gate, no one was leaving Nalgar alive. Not Jamie. Not Leith. Not Renna. No one.

For all the practice she'd had, Brandi wasn't the trained fighter like the men going with Keevan. She might even get in the way as Keevan's men fought the Blades.

Perhaps she'd do more good by staying here. She'd help hold the gate until the rest of the Resistance army arrived. For once in her life, she'd follow orders.

She nodded at the top of the hill. "Someone has to keep watch."

"Good idea." Ian followed her as they reported what they were doing to Shad's lieutenant.

Stalking up the hill, Brandi and Ian wiggled to the top on their stomachs, much the way she and Jamie had less than half an hour before.

In the time since Brandi left, Nalgar's gates had swung closed. Soldiers milled in the courtyard, as if they weren't sure where to go.

Shad, Keevan, and the men were nearly to the castle. They stuck to the shifting shadows as they crept to the base of the low wall by the dry moat surrounding the Blades' Tower. The guards on the wall tops seemed too busy staring at the bustle inside the castle to notice, and the torchlight blinded them to the darkness at the base of the walls.

As Brandi watched, the sentries walking the perimeter of the low wall crumpled, probably struck down by Shad's arrows. Though Brandi and Ian could see them, the Blades' Tower hid the fallen sentries from the view of the rest of the castle.

Several of the men tossed grappling hooks over the wall and snugged them tight. They scaled the walls quickly and disappeared.

"Yes." Ian pumped his fist against the sand. "They're in."

"Now we wait." Brandi tapped her fingers against the sand. How she hated waiting. Hated it.

Down below, Nalgar Castle remained still. The guards patrolled. The soldiers in the courtyard tried to get organized.

"How long is this going to take?" Brandi tried not to squirm.

"Look."

Brandi peered into the darkness. There was a commotion at the front gate. The guards patrolling the wall fell. The gates swung open.

"They did it!" Brandi jumped to her feet. She waved toward the men "The gate is open!"

The lieutenant straightened. "Come on! Charge!"

They charged down the hill. Brandi pelted along next to Ian, her smaller legs barely keeping up with all the longer legs around her. As they reached the gates, they filled the opening shoulder to shoulder.

Shouts echoed in the courtyard as Respen's soldiers noticed the intrusion at the gate. Boots clapped against the cobblestones. Swords swished from their sheaths.

Shad placed himself in the center of the line of men. A few yards away, Aindre the blacksmith hefted his double-bladed battle ax. Brandi glanced between them and the guards charging toward them.

Shad brandished his sword. "Stand steady, men! No matter what, we will hold this gate."

Brandi gripped her short sword in one hand and a dagger in the other. Chills bolted through her, but she planted her feet against the cobbles. No going back. No running. They'd hold this gate or die trying.

If they failed, she wouldn't mind dying. At least she and Renna would die together.

47

The edge of the knife nicked his neck. Leith breathed out for the last time. As much as he thought he'd regret his past, he didn't. His past was gone in the blood of Christ. The only thing he could regret was that his blood would stain Martyn's hands.

The pressure against his throat eased. Steel clanged against the stone next to his ear. Leith cracked his eyes open. Martyn's head hung. He peered at Leith with tortured, brown eyes. "I can't do it. I thought I could, but I can't."

Leith blew out a long breath and flexed his fingers. Martyn wasn't going to kill him. "All right. What are you going to do?"

Martyn gripped his knife tighter, his eyes hardening. "Fight until the king kills us."

He reached up, and Leith felt something cold and hard press into his palm. The key to the manacles.

Martyn turned and faced Respen. "No."

"No?" Respen rose to his feet, glowering.

A chair scraped against stone. Blane pushed to his feet. A moment later, Ranson stood as well. Blane raised his chin. "We won't kill him either."

Renna's eyes widened. She moved just enough for Leith to see that her hands were free. She was ready to bolt the moment fighting broke out.

"Leith is my friend." Martyn gripped his knife. "I won't kill him."

Respen slowly drew a knife from his dark blue clothes. "I am surprised at you, my First Blade. I expected such foolishness as friendship out of Torren. But you have always placed your duty above such frivolities."

Leith's stomach clenched. He knew something no one else but Respen knew.

Respen had taught Harrison Vane how to throw knives.

Once Vane had mastered knife throwing, he'd taught the rest of the Blades. Only Leith, Vane, and Hess had known that Respen was the best of all of them.

Switching the grip on his knife, Respen raised his arm and swiped it forward. Leith wrapped his fingers around the chains and yanked himself off his feet. Gritting his teeth at the agony shooting through his chest, he kicked Martyn in the back with both feet. Martyn sprawled on the floor.

A sharp pain blossomed in Leith's leg.

Respen raised his hand again. "Kill them."

Blane and Ranson lunged away from the other Blades while the Blades supporting Respen scrambled toward the hooks along the wall holding their weapons. Leith tried to ignore the chaos as he twisted his hand and fitted the key into the lock. He'd do little good to anyone with his hands chained above his head.

Martyn was on his feet, facing two of the Blades. Ranson and Blane joined him a moment later, though they lacked weapons.

Then Renna was there, handing her knife to Blane and pressing her hands to the blood dribbling around the knife in Leith's leg.

Leith gritted his teeth as one manacle clacked open. "I told you to run."

"I did. I ran to you." She gripped the knife's hilt and yanked it from his leg.

He groaned and re-focused on unlocking the second manacle with his free hand. It clicked open, and he sagged against the wall.

Renna stopped him from sliding all the way to the floor. He leaned on her shoulder, fighting the burn of his cracked ribs and the cramping in his thigh. She slid the knife between his wrists and sawed on the rope still holding his wrists together. The rope parted.

Sixth Blade Uldiney charged past Martyn and Blane. Leith lunged and gripped Uldiney's knife wrist, stopping his stab.

Renna pressed the hilt of the knife that had been in Leith's leg into his hand. He swiped upward with it, catching Uldiney across the forearm of his free hand. Uldiney stumbled backwards.

The door slammed open. Jamie burst into the room, knife in his hand. He swiped a set of knives off their hook on the wall, vaulted onto the table, and jumped off the other side. Dodging the other Blades, he landed near Martyn and placed his back to Leith. "Would've been here sooner, but ran into a little trouble. Help's coming. We just have to stall."

Prince Keevan was on his way. Shad would be coming, and he'd stop at nothing to breach this Tower. Leith gritted his teeth and limped forward as Jamie handed two knives to Ranson and gave another one to Martyn and Blane.

When Leith swayed, Renna's hands pressed against his back, holding him upright. He reached behind him, and she clasped his hand.

Together, they faced King Respen and his Blades.

Brandi shoved a dead soldier off her sword and swung to face the next man charging her. The Resistance soldier to her right fell to the ground. She stepped sideways to fill the gap. All along their line, others fell, pierced by arrows or run through with swords.

"Hold the line!" Shad shouted, kicking a man away from him and stabbing his sword at another.

Brandi's arms and shoulders ached. She staggered as she swung at the next man charging her. The cacophony of screaming wounded, clanging swords, and shouting men pounded against her ears. The stench of blood sliced into her nose. Her own hands and clothes bore splatters of blood. She didn't have time to dwell on it. The ranks of soldiers charged them in an endless stream.

They'd be overrun in a few more minutes. She didn't have the time to worry about her coming death. She dodged a sword thrust and whacked it away with her knife.

Hoofbeats sounded behind them. She glanced over her shoulder to spot a stream of riders coming down the hill from the west. Dently's banner, white with a blue tree, flapped above them.

She whirled back to face the battle. Reinforcements. Not Keevan, yet. But Lady Emilin had kept her word.

The riders from Dently dismounted and dashed to defend the gate.

For a few minutes, the reinforcements steadied the line. Brandi was able to step back and catch a breath.

But only for a minute. Then the crush of Respen's army shoved against them. Brandi raised her sword again and joined the line. Blood drenched the cobblestones beneath her boots. Bodies piled before the gate. Each time she moved, she nearly tripped on the dead and dying.

Ian cried out and crumpled to the ground.

Brandi's stomach lurched at the sight of the blood pumping from his chest. "Ian!"

"Rand..." He weakly pointed at something past her shoulder.

She whirled in time to see a man rushing at her, sword raised. She threw herself sideways. Something crashed into her leather helmet.

Pain burst in her skull. A rioting, searing pain.

She blinked. She was lying on the ground. How had she gotten here?

The ground seemed to be humming. Drumming.

A horse leapt over her. Several more followed it, leaping over her along with the other dead and wounded lying in the gateway. A green and silver banner streamed over her head.

The army had arrived. They'd held the gate long enough. She let her eyes flutter closed and gave in to the crushing darkness.

48

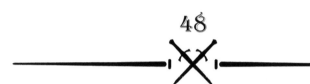

Renna bit her tongue to stop her shriek as Leith stumbled backwards into her, a Blade plunging a knife at his chest. The clash of steel, the grunts of fighting men, and the scuffing of scrambling boots filled the room. Bodies moved in a chaotic tumble, and it was all Renna could do to stay out of the way.

Maybe she should've fled the room when she'd had the chance. She wasn't a fighter. She wasn't doing a whole lot of good here.

No. She wasn't going to doubt herself. Not this time. Her place was here, doing what she could to help Leith fight. If only she could figure out how best to help.

The Blade fighting Martyn crumpled to the floor. Martyn leapt his fallen body and slammed a shoulder into the Blade trying to stab Leith. That Blade tottered backwards, fending off Martyn's thrusting knife.

Leith's grip on her hand tightened as his leg buckled. She staggered but managed to keep them both upright.

"You doing all right?" Leith gasped as he steadied himself against her shoulder.

She nodded. No way would she admit her muscles

ached with his weight and a shriek was building in her chest. She wasn't going to turn into a screeching, hysterical mess.

Leith limped a step, probably to help Blane, Ranson, and Jamie, who were trying to hold off three more experienced Blades, but he halted. Renna froze next to him as Respen strode forward.

Respen raised his hand, a knife flashing in the candlelight. Leith pressed her against the wall, shielding her.

But the knife wasn't for them. Blane cried out and dropped to the floor, Respen's knife in his stomach.

"Blane!" Ranson froze, gaping. He would've been killed then and there if Blane, wounded as he was, hadn't stabbed the Blade attacking Ranson in the foot.

Renna peered around Leith's shoulder. Respen stalked toward them, knives in both of his hands. She bit her lip. How many knives did he have left? Surely he couldn't have too many more, not with the one he'd given Martyn, the two he'd thrown into Leith and Blane, and the two he held.

Leith limped two steps forward. Respen strode to meet him. Their knives clashed.

Renna clenched her fists. Leith wasn't strong enough to fight Respen, not after the week of torture he'd suffered. She glanced to Martyn, but he, Jamie, and Ranson struggled to hold back the four remaining Blades. They couldn't help.

Respen slammed Leith against the wall. Leith cried out. The veins in his neck pulsed as he strained to keep Respen's knife away from his throat.

No. She would *not* stand by and watch Leith die.

She threw herself at Respen and yanked his arm

away from Leith. Respen whirled and tossed her to the ground. Her shoulder smashed against the stone floor.

Leith swiped his knife at Respen's neck. Respen staggered backward to avoid the cut. He and Leith grappled again.

But Leith was losing. His body shook with each ragged gasp for breath. Sweat rolled from his hairline and between his shoulder blades. Respen's knives inched closer to his skin, one aimed at his chest, the other at his stomach.

Renna grabbed Respen's arm and threw her weight backwards. This time she held on as he tried to shake her off.

Respen shoved her into Leith. She let go as both of them tumbled to the floor.

Leith struggled to get up but only had the strength to raise his head. He flopped back to the ground, gasping between clenched teeth. He was spent. Done.

Respen lifted a knife, gripping it by the blade in preparation to throw.

Renna faced Respen and shielded Leith, one hand braced on the other side of his body. "No. You will not harm him. You'll have to kill me first."

"No..." Leith's hands pressed against her waist as if he was trying to move her out of the way. "Renna, don't."

She refused to budge. Leith had been willing to sacrifice himself for her. Shouldn't she be just as willing to sacrifice herself for him?

Leith didn't want her to do it. She could feel his desperation through his struggle behind her.

But for once in her life, Renna had the same courage as her mother. Her mother had turned around to face death at the hands of First Blade Vane. Renna could do nothing less facing Respen now.

She met Respen's dark eyes. Would Respen kill her? A few days ago, Leith had believed Respen didn't want to torture her. And she'd sensed something in him when they'd talked about Clarisse.

But would it be enough? Would it stay his hand?

"You couldn't prevent Clarisse's death." Renna searched Respen's hard face for the glimmer of softening that name normally caused. "Do you really want to be responsible for mine?"

Respen hesitated, the knife poised to throw.

A man in green and silver vaulted into the room, sword drawn. Renna had only time to capture an impression of a scarred face and blond hair before more men piled into the room behind him, some with swords drawn, others with arrows nocked.

The scar-faced man pointed his sword at Respen. "Drop your knife, Respen Felix. You are under arrest."

Respen eyed the man and the bowmen standing behind him. As one, the bows creaked as the bowmen drew them back.

Turning his gaze to Renna, Respen gave her a slow nod, almost a bow.

He dropped the knife.

49

Renna sagged as the knife clattered on the floor. The war was over. The killing. The torture. The fighting. All over.

The scar-faced man twitched his hand, and four men rushed Respen. Two tied his hands behind his back while two others searched him for more weapons. Respen stood straight, not like a man defeated.

As soon as he was secure, Renna turned to Leith. He lay on the floor, gasping in short stabs. Both arms wrapped around his stomach. His eyes squeezed shut so tightly his whole face twisted. Blood soaked his trousers all the way to his left boot.

She cradled his head. "It's all right now. Deep breaths."

"Can't." Leith's body shook. "Rib. Broke."

She ran her fingers over his lips. Her fingers came away streaked with blood, though she couldn't tell if the blood came from a punctured lung or his split lip. She leaned closer, but she didn't hear a gurgle in Leith's pained gasps. She felt along Leith's chest until she located the sharp lump formed by the fractured rib. Leith cried out and knocked her hand away by reflex.

"Calm down. I didn't yank two knives and an arrow out of you to have you die on me now. Deep breaths. I need you to fight the pain." She gripped one of Leith's hands and rested her other hand against his cheek. "Can you do that for me?"

For a moment, she wasn't sure he'd heard her. Then he nodded. His chest shuddered as he tried to steady his breathing.

A commotion across the room yanked her head up. Several of the soldiers dragged Ranson to his feet. He was shouting and struggling to free himself. Blane lay on the floor, still and pale.

Renna eased Leith's head back to the floor. "I'll be back in a minute. Our friends need help."

She clambered to her feet and dashed across the room. Ranson met her gaze. "Please help him."

She knelt and pressed her fingers to Blane's neck. Tears gathered in her throat. "I'm sorry. There's nothing I can do. He's dead."

"No." Ranson sagged in the soldiers' grasp. Tears leaked down his face.

Had her and Leith's words reached Blane? Had God given him hope before he'd died? She didn't know. And that was the worst ache of all.

She swallowed back her tears and looked around. One of the other Blades sprawled lifeless. The other five had their hands bound, and soldiers herded them to the door.

A few feet away, a soldier bound Martyn's hands behind his back. Martyn's head hung. His shoulders sagged like he was one of the defeated Blades.

Jamie stood in front of the scar-faced man, saluting and pointing toward Ranson and Martyn. That must be the man in charge. A captain or something. Renna had better explain that Ranson and Martyn were on their side before they got locked in the dungeon. And she needed help to carry Leith to someplace where she could tend him.

She marched over to him. "Sir, what are you going to do with these two Blades?" She pointed at Ranson and Martyn. "They fought Respen. They're on the side of the Resistance."

"They're still Blades." The man's voice rasped, as if he struggled to talk. "They'll be locked in a cell until a proper inquiry can be held."

Of all the...she huffed a breath. She didn't have time to argue. Not with Leith as hurt as he was. "Please, at least lock them in a separate cell from the other five Blades. They'll kill Martyn and Ranson if they are locked up together."

"Very well. I'll instruct my men." The man studied her. His head cocked slightly, tipping the scar away from her and highlighting his angular cheeks and nose with candlelight. He looked to be in his mid-twenties, with clear, blue eyes and straight, blond hair. His eyebrows scrunched. "You don't recognize me, do you?"

Should she? She peered closer at him. He didn't look familiar.

"I'm your cousin Keevan."

Keevan. She saw it then. The scraggle-legged boy who'd teased her at every chance, who'd made things so difficult for her and Brandi that her parents had stopped visiting Nalgar Castle. Once, she'd overheard her father muttering something about how Uncle Leon could rule a country, but he couldn't rule his sons.

The silence had stretched too long. She managed a

weak smile. "I'm glad you're alive. Now, could you spare two of your men? Leith needs to be carried to somewhere I can tend him."

Keevan waved to two soldiers. "Please stay with the lady and aid her as she requires."

Spinning on his heels, Keevan pointed at the soldiers guarding Respen. "Bring him along. Time to stop this war."

Oh, of course. The battle in this Tower was only a fraction of the fighting. The whole castle was crawling with Respen's soldiers.

No matter. The rest of the battle was Keevan's concern. Hers was Leith.

The two soldiers stared at her, still as mountains. Jamie rocked back and forth, waiting for her instructions. She drew her back straight. "You two, fetch one of the cots from the room down below."

They both nodded, wheeled, and marched down the stairs.

Jamie bounced on his toes. "Are you going to tend him in the common room? I'll go start the water boiling and laying out bandages and other supplies."

"Yes, please do."

Jamie pelted from the door. Hopefully he wouldn't tumble into the soldiers on their way up with a cot.

Renna returned to Leith's side. His breaths came steadier, though every muscle remained tense with pain. She touched his hand. "Hold on a little longer."

His fingers curled around hers. She held his hand until the two soldiers returned with the straw tick from one of the cots. They lifted Leith onto the tick and carried him from the room. Renna trailed behind them as they navigated down the four flights of stairs.

In the common room, Jamie had lit every candle and

lamp and clustered them around one of the tables. Renna directed the soldiers to set Leith on the table. Leith shuddered with the force of his gasps, but at least he was still breathing.

Jamie hurried from the kitchen nook and set a tray of supplies on the table next to Leith's head. "What can I do?"

Renna reached for the small knife on the tray. "Clean the burns and spread the open ones with balm."

She cut away the fabric around the knife wound. The knife had sliced the muscles of his upper thigh and nicked the bone, but it had missed the major blood vessels. He'd bled a lot, but he wouldn't bleed to death. She bit her lip. He might have a limp for the rest of his life. How would Leith handle that?

No time to worry about that now. She uncorked the brandy and dumped it over his wound. Leith groaned.

The Tower door flew open, showing a patch of black castle wall and deep blue sky pinpricked by stars. Shadrach dashed inside, still carrying his bloodstained sword. Blood spattered the front of his trousers, boots, and shirt, and more blood dribbled from a tear on his left sleeve.

He skidded to a halt by the table. His sword clattered to the floor as he gripped the table's edge. His square jaw tightened. "What did Respen do to him?"

Renna could only imagine how Leith looked to Shadrach. Thin. Beaten. Burned. "Torture."

"He looks...dead." Shadrach's voice cracked.

"I'm also awake and can hear you." Leith didn't open his eyes, but his mouth quirked. The laudanum Renna had given him was working. "And if I was dead, it'd hurt less."

Shadrach hung his head. "I never should've let you go."

"Wasn't your choice." Leith eased one eye open. "I told you. You'd rescue us."

Renna handed Shadrach a roll of bandages. "If you're going to stand there, you'd better help."

Together, she, Shadrach, and Jamie tended Leith's wounds and bandaged his leg, burns, and broken rib. When they finished, Renna turned to Shadrach. "I can tend your arm now."

He glanced down at the tear in his sleeve. "It's just a scratch. There are others more wounded."

As much as she wanted to stay at Leith's side, others needed her more. Once she would've stayed in the Tower, waiting for someone else to step in first. But now, she was strong enough.

She pointed at the soldiers Keevan had assigned to her. "Stay with this man until I can locate a place to let him rest."

The soldiers nodded and positioned themselves on either side of the table.

Jamie and Shadrach led the way from the Tower and across the wooden bridge. Both of them kept their weapons drawn. Renna gripped a saddlebag she'd stuffed with supplies from the Tower. Was the battle over? Or was it still raging somewhere in the castle?

As they entered the passageway and headed toward the cobblestone courtyard, cheering echoed around them. When they entered the courtyard, she spotted the Eirdon banner, a silver cross over a light green background, flying over the battlements against the dome of stars.

Rows of soldiers stood in the courtyard, staring at the king's window. Renna craned her neck. Keevan stood framed in the window, a knife to Respen's neck.

That explained the cheering.

Still, the evidence of the battle remained in the courtyard. Bodies lay strewn over the cobbles. Blood pooled around them like the aftermath of a grotesque rain. Renna squeezed her fingers into fists. So many people needed help. Where did she even begin?

A soldier stepped over to Shadrach and saluted with two fingers pressed to his forehead. "Captain Alistair, we've set up a temporary infirmary in the Great Hall as you requested."

"Gather the men and search for the wounded." Shadrach returned the soldier's salute. When Jamie took a step to follow, Shadrach rested a hand on his shoulder. "Stay with Renna. She'll need the extra pair of hands."

"Shad!"

A body with a head of blond hair slammed into Shadrach. He wrapped his arms around her and kissed her.

Must be Jolene. Renna glanced away. Should she head to the Great Hall now or should she wait?

Shadrach stepped back and turned Jolene around. "Look who I found."

"Renna!" Jolene crushed Renna's ribs with her hug. "You're safe. When that Blade arrived with only Brandi and told us you'd been left behind, I was so worried for you."

"I'm fine, thanks to Leith." Renna held up the saddlebag. "I was on my way to help the wounded."

Shadrach squeezed Jolene's hand. "I need to report to General Stewart."

"Go on. I'll help Renna." Jolene swatted his arm and turned back to Renna. "Let's go."

They hurried to the door of the Great Hall. Renna

halted in the doorway. Wounded men lay in rows. Some lay on blankets, others had simply been set on the ground as they were. The castle healer knelt by a man, trying to tend to a gaping wound in the man's stomach while also shouting out orders to the other men and women who had volunteered to help. Renna spotted most of Nalgar Castle's kitchen staff and a few of the other maids in the light cast from the torches and lamps.

Where should she start? The wounded needed help, yet someone needed to organize this mess.

Jolene placed her hands on her hips, scanned the room, and gave a nod. "I'll fetch my mother. She'll get this straightened out."

While Jolene dashed off, Renna found the castle healer and explained. The healer gave a relieved look and pointed toward the near end of the Hall. "The worst of the wounded are on that side, the least on the other end. What supplies I have are on that table over there."

Nodding, Renna gathered a stack of supplies and handed most of them to Jamie to carry. If only she had her medical kit. But she'd manage. Heading to the far end of the Hall, she started on the first patient in a long row lined across the hall. She fell into a rhythm, cleaning, stitching, bandaging.

Lady Lorraine swept into the hall and barked orders. Some of the tension in Renna's shoulders relaxed. With Lady Lorraine in charge, these poor men would finally get some water and some blankets to lie on.

As they approached their next patient, Jamie made a strangling noise in the back of his throat, dropped his armload, and crashed to his knees. "No, no, no."

Renna knelt. A layer of blood coated the patient's

face. Based on the skinny body and short height, the boy couldn't be older than thirteen. He'd taken a sword to the skull, resulting in a deep gash that had peeled the skin away from the bone. Must've been a glancing blow, and the boy's leather helmet must've slowed some of the force. From what she could see, it hadn't cracked the skull. A good sign, but she couldn't tell what sort of damage the blow had done to the boy's brain.

Easing off the helmet, she brushed a lock of red-blond hair away from the boy's face. And shrieked.

It was Brandi. Her hair had been chopped short and blood covered half her face, but Renna knew her sister's face better than she knew her own.

She turned to Jamie, her voice and hands shaking. "What's Brandi doing here?"

"She refused to be left behind. She sneaked along with the army and didn't tell anyone until three days after we'd left. By then, it was too late to send her back, and she threatened to sneak away by herself if I tried." He hung his head, a tear leaking out of the corner of his eye. "I should've tried harder. I should've stopped her. I..."

Renna laid a hand on his arm. "We don't have time for this now." She'd get mad at Jamie later. Right now she had to save Brandi's life. "Get me fresh water."

Jamie hurried to do her bidding while she studied the wound once again. "Please be all right, Brandi." She stroked the hair away from Brandi's temple. She'd have to cut away most of it along one side of Brandi's head. Pulling a knife from her supplies, she sliced away the short strands of Brandi's hair.

When the wound was free of hair, she poured the last of the brandy over it before cleaning it with the water Jamie brought her. Threading her needle, she steeled herself and pushed the first stitch through Brandi's scalp.

She never imagined this, never in her wildest nightmares. Whatever possessed Brandi to dress as a boy and join the army? Brandi must've been determined—desperate—to go to such lengths.

Each stitch became a prayer for healing, each tug of the thread another petition at the Lord's feet. Renna's hands grew steadier the longer she prayed. Aunt Mara told her once that she always prayed while she worked. It steadied her hands and placed the burden of healing where it belonged.

After she tugged the last stitch through and tied it off, she spread salve over the wound and wrapped a bandage around it. With the blood cleaned from her face, Brandi appeared pale and drawn. Renna traced Brandi's cheek and turned to Jamie. "Don't leave her side."

"I won't. I promise." Jamie sat cross-legged on the floor with a look that said only a tornado could move him away from that spot.

Her heart aching, Renna moved on to the next patient. The wounded men also had mothers, sisters, wives, daughters, and families waiting for them to return. She couldn't neglect them to stay by Brandi's side any more than she could to remain by Leith.

But as soon as the last of the wounded was tended, she'd plop herself by their sides and nothing would drag her away.

50

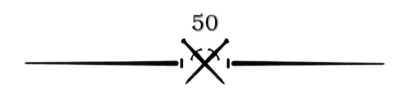

As Leith drifted awake, he became aware of the sharp pain in his leg, the ache of his ribs, and the throb of his burns. He forced his eyes open.

He lay on a cot in an opulent room. Rugs covered the floor while wood paneling and thick drapes covered the walls. A set of chairs clustered around a fireplace a few feet away, but a tall screen prevented him from seeing the rest of the room.

The sound of footsteps and fabric rustled on the other side of the screen. Should he call out? Why was his cot screened off from the rest of the room?

The rustling drew closer until a slim figure in a blue dress bustled around the edge of the screen. The candlelight glinted off her blond hair.

"Renna." Her name rolled off his tongue, rasping through his dry throat.

She looked up and smiled, though her eyes remained shadowed. "You're awake! I didn't think you'd sleep too much longer, but it's a relief that at least one of you woke up..." She trailed off, her smile dying as she glanced at the screen as if she could see what lay on the other side. She slipped into one of the chairs and drew it closer to the head of his cot. "How do you feel?"

"Better." He was tempted to close his eyes and go back to sleep, but he couldn't give in to the impulse. Not with her hollow eyes looking at him. "Have you slept?"

"Not yet. I've been busy tending the wounded in the Great Hall and looking after you and..." Renna's braid fell over her shoulder as she shook her head.

Something was going on, but his head still felt too fuzzy to figure it out. "Martyn?"

"He's locked in the Tower until Keevan can decide what to do with him and the other Blades. Ranson is with him." Renna frowned and rubbed her thumb along the back of his hand.

He stared at her thumb moving back and forth, sending tingles up his arm. He'd been about to say something else, but he couldn't seem to remember it at the moment. Something about Martyn. He roped his thoughts. "Martyn saved our lives. That should be taken into account."

"It will be." Renna squeezed his hand. "Leith, there's something I have to—"

Somewhere beyond the screen, the door creaked open. Jamie's voice called, "How are they?"

"Leith's awake. Can you fetch him some water?"

Moments later, Jamie slipped around the screen. He held out a glass. Renna took it and held it to Leith's mouth.

The water helped. By the time Leith drained the glass, some of the haze in his head cleared. He noted the lines around Renna's mouth and the wrinkles puckering Jamie's forehead. "What aren't you telling me?"

Renna's shoulders heaved with a deep breath. She stared at the screen, and her grip tightened on Leith's hand. "It's about Brandi."

Brandi. She was safe at Eagle Heights. Wasn't she?

Jamie toyed with the edge of the blanket. "I tried to stop her. Honestly, I did. But I didn't know until we were on the trail what she'd done. And by then it was too late to send her back."

"Send her back?" Leith blinked at both of them. His head must still be fuzzy. Jamie wasn't making sense.

"She sneaked along with the army. She cut her hair and dressed as a boy. I didn't find out what she'd done until she showed up by my fire and told me." Jamie scrubbed a hand along his face.

"And you didn't tell Shad?" The room tilted. Brandi, his Brandi, had joined the army. Leith blinked and tried to focus.

"I thought about it, but it wouldn't have done any good." Jamie hunched on the chair, hands digging into his hair. "She threatened to run away from Eagle Heights and make the journey on her own. And she'd do it, too. Her sneaking skills are almost as good as mine."

Leith was crumbling from the outside in. If Brandi was all right, then she would've been bouncing by his side when he woke up. Instead, Jamie and Renna wore identical, grave expressions.

"Please tell me she's still alive." His heart was breaking already, and he didn't even know if she was dead.

A tear traced the length of Renna's nose. "She's alive, but she was hurt taking the castle. A sword glanced along her skull. I sewed up the wound, but she's still unconscious." She waved at the room on the other side of the screen. "I had her moved to the bed in this room where I could tend her better, and I had a cot brought in so I could watch you both. Neither of you could be tended properly with the rest of the wounded in the Great Hall. Too many people would notice your secrets."

Their secrets. The secret that Brandi was a girl, and he was a Blade. He glanced at the rows of scars marching down his right arm. Until someone scrounged a shirt for him, he couldn't leave the room.

He stared at the screen that gave him and Brandi a little privacy and tried to push himself onto his elbows. "I'd like to see her."

Renna laid a hand on his shoulder and pushed him down. "Rest. Your wounds need to heal before you can start moving about."

He scowled. She'd had no trouble pinning him down.

Jamie fidgeted in his seat. "There's more."

Surely not more bad news. Wasn't victory supposed to be an occasion to celebrate, not mourn? "Respen escaped?" He couldn't think of anything else that would cause the grim expression on Jamie's face.

"No. He's safely locked in the dungeon." Jamie stared at the floor. "When she joined the army, Brandi rode Blizzard. He was hurt one of the times we fought Respen's army, and we had to leave him behind. I don't know if he survived or not."

The words punched Leith, but they didn't hit the vital spots that Brandi's injury had. He'd rather lose Blizzard than lose Brandi. But the thought of losing both...he forced himself to nod. "Thanks for telling me. When Brandi wakes up, she'll feel bad about it." He didn't let himself consider that she'd never wake. She'd wake up. She had to.

Renna and Jamie must've understood how he felt,

because neither of them tried to correct him.

Good. He wasn't going to lose hope. And he wasn't going to let them give up either.

The door groaned open again. "Renna, the room next door is ready if you'd like to rest."

"Leith's awake."

Shad stepped around the screen and leaned against the wall near the foot of the cot. His face wore the same, tired shadows as Jamie and Renna, and his clothes still bore the spatters of battle. He crossed his arms. "Took you long enough."

"First decent rest I've had in a week." Leith started to put his hands behind his head but stopped when the movement tweaked his ribs.

"And you ought to go back to sleep." Renna patted his shoulder and stood. "I'd better get back to the Great Hall. I only stopped by to check on Leith and Brandi for a minute."

"I'll stay with them." Shad raised his eyebrows. "You should get some sleep yourself."

"I will once the wounded are all resting comfortably." Renna's skirt swirled as she bustled around the screen and disappeared.

When Leith heard the door shut behind her, he pushed onto his elbows. He gritted his teeth. Was there any part of his body that didn't throb with weakness?

Shad straightened. "What do you think you're doing? You're supposed to stay in bed."

"I have to see Brandi." Leith managed to sit most of the way up. Jamie jumped to his feet, glancing at the door like he considered fetching Renna. Leith held a hand to him. "Help me up."

"Stubborn Blade." Shad grasped Leith's other arm,

and he and Jamie hauled Leith to his feet.

Leith sucked in a breath as his vision narrowed. He couldn't pass out. That'd have him back in bed and tied down so fast he'd never be allowed back up. Pain wracked through his bones, but he could push through it. This was the worst the pain would get. No more torture. No additional wounds. It'd only get better from here.

Thankfully, he still wore his trousers. Or, at least, what was left of them. The left leg had been cut open partway down his thigh to expose his bandaged wound. The ragged end flopped around his knee.

He managed a few hobbling steps, leaning most of his weight on Shad and Jamie. As they turned the corner of the screen, Leith focused on the four poster bed. A small form lay still and white in the blankets.

When they reached the bedside, Jamie let go long enough to drag one of the large, plush chairs from beside the fire to a spot next to the bed. Leith sank into it, groaning. Jamie handed him a pillow, which he propped against his side to ease his aching ribs.

Brandi lay so still, her face as white as the bandages layered across her head. The short ends of her hair spiked in all directions.

Leith propped his elbows on the edge of the bed. Shad rested a hand on Leith's shoulder. "I'm sorry. I should've recognized her. I never would've sent her into battle if I'd known."

The raw edge in Shad's voice matched the lump in Leith's throat. "I know."

Why? After everything he'd done to protect her and Renna, why had this happened?

He rested his head in his hands. Something hot and wet trickled against his palm. He'd been whipped. Burned.

Beaten. And he'd faced it all with the knowledge that no matter what Respen did to him, the king couldn't break him.

But this could.

51

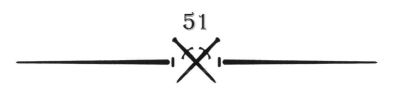

Her head pounded like a horse was kicking it from the inside. Her eyes felt like they were rolling about in her skull.

Somewhere above her, someone was talking. No, not just talking. Telling a story. Something about David. And the giant. For the first time, she sympathized with the giant. Being hit in the head was horrible. The stories didn't mention how much it hurt or the headache afterwards. She groaned.

The story stopped. The voice called to her. "It's all right, Brandi. Wake up."

She tried to obey. Her eyelids stuck together as if Renna had sewn them shut. If only she could explain, but her mouth refused to move. She curled her fingers into fists. At least that worked. Gathering all her strength, she peeled her eyes open.

A hazy shape leaned over her. She gave two slow blinks. The figure focused into Leith, his dark hair falling into his green eyes, both cheeks dark with yellow and purple bruises. The room behind him remained a blur.

He smiled. "I knew you'd wake up."

She inched a hand to her galloping head. "Ugh! My head hurts."

"A sword to the head will do that."

She had a vague memory of the sword swinging down before everything went black. "So we won?"

He nodded, picked up something from the bedside table, and held it out to her. "Yes. You toppled a giant with your pebble."

She took the shard of rock from him. It was the same chip of crystal she'd taken from the sparkling cave and had given to him before he'd left. But now, one side of it was crushed flat, like it'd been pounded against something. "How did I do that?"

"I jammed that rock into the lock of the meeting room door. If I hadn't, Jamie and Prince Keevan couldn't have gotten in to help fight Respen." Leith shifted in the chair, as if sitting up was uncomfortable. "Respen is locked in the dungeon. His trial starts in a couple of days once the rest of the nobles get here. Prince Keevan's official coronation will be in a few weeks."

At least they'd won. It'd be awful if she'd gotten this headache all for nothing. "What about Renna? And Jamie?" A flash of memory speared her, Ian falling to the ground, blood pouring from his chest. "And Ian?"

"Renna's fine. She's checking some of the other wounded." Leith hesitated and glanced at the window.

The pink haze of dawn creased the horizon. At least, Brandi assumed it was dawn. It might be sunset for all she knew, but sunsets were usually more orange.

"Jamie left. He volunteered to carry a message to Walden. If he'd known you were going to wake up so soon, he would've stayed. He'll be back in a few days." Leith paused again. His shoulders hunched. "Jamie told me Ian died of his wounds."

She blinked. She didn't want to cry. She'd known friends would die. She hadn't been naïve about that when she'd ridden into battle. But it still stabbed at her. Ian hadn't even known she was a girl. He'd died thinking she was only Randy, a peasant boy from Stetterly. She wouldn't have a chance to tell him the truth.

And somehow, that seemed rather important. Like he'd only known a part of her or a pretend her or something. Because she wasn't Randy, a peasant boy. She was Brandi, a girl desperate to rescue her sister.

What about his brothers and sisters? His mother? They'd already lost so much.

Another thought sliced at her. She had to confess about Blizzard. "Leith, I got to tell you, I...Blizzard..."

"Jamie told me about Blizzard."

"I'm sorry. I shouldn't have ridden your horse into battle. I should've left him at Eagle Heights where he would've been safe." This time, her voice did break. She couldn't help it. It all felt like too much. Ian. Blizzard. The memories of battle.

Leith patted her shoulder. "Listen, Brandi. I'm not angry. I'm glad you rode him. As much as you and I love that horse, in the end he's still just a horse. A horse can be replaced. You can't."

She blinked away a tear. It crawled down her face and under her chin. Leith leaned over and tucked his arms around her as best he could while she was lying down. She had enough strength to lift her arms, wrap them around Leith's neck, and hug him back. She buried her face against his shoulder. What would she have done without Leith these last few months? "Thank you."

As Leith pulled away, the door opened. Renna's eyes

darted to her and widened. "Brandi!" She dropped the tray she'd been carrying. It crashed to the ground, spilling water and food onto the floor. Hiking her skirts, Renna leapt over the debris and dashed across the room.

Brandi barely had time to grit her teeth before Renna shoved past Leith and hugged her. Brandi wrapped her arms around Renna and squeezed as tightly as she could manage. Her head pounded, but she didn't care. They'd survived. For all that Brandi had been determined to rescue Renna, her sister had been rescued without her help. God had protected her even though Brandi had doubted.

As Renna pulled back, Brandi studied her. She seemed...different. She didn't hunch her head as if trying to become invisible but met Brandi's gaze with a confident tilt of her chin. That same confidence strengthened her blue eyes.

She wasn't broken. Somehow, Renna had not only survived being alone at Nalgar Castle, she'd gotten stronger.

Brandi hadn't believed Renna had strength. Worse, Brandi had scorned Renna's lack of strength. She'd assumed Renna would break into a sobbing mess by the time Brandi rescued her.

But perhaps Renna was the strong one. There was strength in waiting.

Brandi lifted her own chin, ignoring the spinning in her skull. She'd faced death and survived battle. She'd faced doubt for the first time in her life. While she missed the child-like naiveté of the faith she'd had a year ago, the faith she had now was stronger, mature, and something that couldn't be quenched by her own doubt or despair. It would survive.

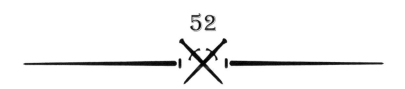

52

Brandi pressed a cold cloth to her head. It dulled the pain a bit. If her head didn't hurt so much, she'd find something to do to break her boredom. She fingered the silver cross once again hanging around her neck. Toying with her necklace was about the only thing she could do while stuck in bed.

Jamie hadn't visited her at all since she'd been awake. Leith had told her he had left the castle, but she couldn't help the churning in her stomach in time with her pounding head. Wasn't he concerned at all for her? After all they'd been through, weren't they friends? Didn't he care even a tiny bit if she survived?

Bustling to the side of the bed, Renna leaned over, her silver cross necklace nearly whacking Brandi's nose, and kissed her forehead. "I'll be back as soon as the Gathering is over."

"I hope they vote in favor of executing Respen. He deserves it."

A strange expression wrinkled Renna's forehead. "I'm sure they will."

Someone knocked on the door.

"Come in." Renna turned back to Brandi. "While I'm gone, Leith has a surprise for you."

Leith tapped inside using a cane to ease the weight on his injured leg. The shoulder seams of the shirt he wore hung partway down his upper arms and the ends of the sleeves were rolled up around his wrists.

Brandi crossed her arms. Traitor. While she'd been stuck in bed thanks to one—one!—dizzy spell, Leith had refused to rest. Yet he'd taken Renna's side in insisting that Brandi stay in bed.

Renna paused by Leith's side. He clasped her hands and whispered something to her.

Brandi rolled her eyes. Now that Leith and Renna had *finally* realized they liked each other, they insisted on lots of hand holding. Lots and lots of hand holding. It was kind of cute, in its own way. If a person was into all that mushy stuff.

Renna swept from the room, the layers of her blue, silk dress swishing in a lady-like fashion.

Leith limped to Brandi's bed. "I have a surprise for you, but it's outside. I have Renna's permission to let you out of bed, but you'd better not pass out. I'm not sure I'll be able to catch you."

Brandi shot upright and swiveled her feet to the ground. Her head spun in a most annoying fashion. "I'm finally getting out of bed. Of course I'm not going to faint."

She kept pace with Leith out of the room, through the hallway, and down the grand, brick staircase.

Near the bottom, Leith halted. "Close your eyes."

She raised her eyebrows. "Do you want me to trip and fall to my death?"

"You won't fall."

"Fine." Brandi squeezed her eyes shut. Leith rested

a hand on her shoulder. She reached up and gripped his arm to keep herself steady as they strolled down the last few steps.

Leith steered her around a corner. Sunlight fell across Brandi's face.

"All right, Brandi. Open your eyes."

Blizzard stood next to the fountain in the center of the Queen's Court, munching on a patch of grass. Brandi tottered across the courtyard and wrapped her arms around Blizzard's neck. He smelled of horse and sunshine. "Where'd you get him? We left him at Walden."

"I fetched him."

Brandi peeked over Blizzard's shoulder and noticed Jamie standing on the other side of the horse, shifting his feet. He patted Blizzard's neck. "I volunteered to carry a message to Lord Alistair. Since I was there, I thought I'd bring him back to you."

She ran her fingers along Blizzard's neck, then along the puckered ridge of his healing wound.

Leith joined her and rubbed Blizzard's nose. "He still limps. He'll probably never run like he used to, but, then again, neither will I."

She glanced at Leith, but he didn't seem concerned about either his limp or Blizzard's. It probably didn't matter. Leith's skills as a Blade wouldn't be needed any more, and Blizzard could be put out to pasture to enjoy a leisurely life. After what both of them had been through, they'd earned it.

Brandi wrapped an arm around Leith's waist but didn't squeeze too hard because of his healing ribs. "Thanks, Leith." She met Jamie's gaze across Blizzard's back and grinned. "Thanks."

He grinned back at her. She could read his forgiveness

in his eyes, and something else. Something deep and lasting. No matter where the two of them went, Jamie would always be her friend.

As Renna entered the Great Hall, she clenched her fists into her skirts. Hopefully no one would notice her sweaty palms. She'd never attended a Gathering of Nobles. They'd been discontinued when Respen had taken the throne.

Keevan already sat on the throne at the end of the hall, a tall wooden staff in his hand. In front of him, two rows of tables with chairs had been set up on either side of the room with a single chair set between them facing the throne.

Straightening her shoulders, she lifted her chin as she swept to her seat near the head of one of the tables. She was Lady Faythe. She could do this.

More nobles filed into the room. Lady Lorraine slipped into a seat a few chairs away. Shadrach took the seat next to her.

Renna leaned closer to him. "Why didn't your father come? I thought Brandi said he was all right?"

"He is. He's wounded but healing." Shadrach bobbed his head toward Keevan. "But he decided it'd be best to stay away from this Gathering. Some of the nobles were already suspicious of his motives for leading the Resistance. If he took part in this Gathering, some might accuse him of setting up Prince Keevan as a puppet king. Better if I fill in as his representative and make it clear that Prince Keevan is a king in his own right."

Renna nodded. Politics. She'd had her fill of it. How would she ever have managed if Keevan hadn't been alive? She could've been the one sitting on that throne.

Just the thought sent her stomach skittering.

No, she never wanted to be queen. She'd much rather return to Stetterly and rebuild a life there. With Leith, hopefully. If that's what he wanted.

Would he want that? Would he be content with a quiet life?

All around the room, the remnants of the nobles of Acktar found their seats. Not all the nobles were there. The heirs for some towns were too young to sit in a Gathering. Others, like Lord Alistair, were too wounded to come. In those cases, representatives took their places along the tables.

As Renna stared around the room, she noted the nobles that had been loyal to Respen, including Lord Norton and Lord Beregern. Lord Beregern had his arms crossed, while Lord Norton's eyes remained as cold as a prairie blizzard. Of all the nobles that supported Respen, only they didn't appear fazed by the proceedings. Perhaps that had been their plan all along. They allowed Respen to have the power of the throne because he also took the fall when it came.

When the last noble found a chair, Keevan tapped the wooden staff against the floor. His rasping voice rang through the room. "Quiet. I call this Gathering to order."

Renna tried not to squirm as the Gathering plodded through all its proper procedure. First they had to recognize all of the nobles or their representatives as the legal voice of their town. Only Blathe didn't have a representative since Respen was still its lord. Then they had to vote to recognize Keevan as the rightful lord and heir of Acktar with the power of an acting king. After that, several of the representatives presented requests to Keevan to have him decide on matters of succession.

A whole lot of rigmarole, as Brandi would've called it. Worse, Renna would have to attend this Gathering once a year from now on. At least, until she married and her husband became Lord of Stetterly.

She frowned. Could she really see Leith sitting here, putting up with the politics and procedure? If the other nobles knew he was a former Blade, would they even recognize him as a lord?

All worries for the future. Right now, she had to get through this Gathering.

Finally, Keevan waved to General Stewart. "Bring in the prisoner."

General Stewart stepped to the door and called outside. Four guards led Respen into the room, chains clanking around his wrists and ankles. The guards shoved him into the chair in the center and wrapped another set of chains around him.

As they took positions along the walls, Respen cast a glance around the room until he met Renna's eyes. She held his gaze, refusing to be cowed by him now. His unbowed defiance shone back.

Prince Keevan picked up a piece of paper. "Lord Respen Felix, you are charged with high treason against His Majesty King Leon, his murder, and all the murders committed by your Blades, including that of Queen Deirdre, Prince Aengus, Prince Rorin, and Prince Duncan. How do you wish to plead to these charges?"

Respen held his head high. "I have no wish to waste time denying the charges. You have already decided I am guilty. Let us skip to the sentencing."

Renna clenched her fingers below the table. By now, she understood Respen all too well. By pleading guilty, Respen had momentarily shifted the control of the proceedings to himself rather than Keevan. Instead of making everyone sit through a long litany of offenses that would sway everyone to vote against him, Respen had forced the vote to be cast quickly, while everyone was still off balance and, possibly, willing to vote in his favor.

Keevan tilted his head. "Very well. Lord Respen Felix of Blathe, I sentence you to death by beheading two days hence. Nobles, please cast your vote either in favor of or against this sentence."

Renna reached for the single sheet of paper laid on the table in front of her. Her hand shook as she drew the quill from the ink bottle and let the ink drip from the tip into the bottle for a moment. Respen's eyes fixed on her, daring her to vote against him. She could almost hear his taunting words, as if he hissed in her ear. *Do it. Vote for my death. Let my blood be on your hands.*

Could she really vote in favor of his death? Her hands shook harder. All around her, the other nobles scratched their votes on their papers and folded them in half. Next to her, Shadrach scrawled his vote and folded his paper. She knew his vote. He didn't hesitate to hand out justice to the man who'd nearly killed his father.

Justice. She swallowed and stared at her blank paper. This wasn't about revenge. This was about justice. Justice was the reason Keevan hadn't killed Respen outright that day in the Blades' Tower. If he'd killed Respen, some might've argued that he'd taken the throne in the same way Respen had. By calling the Gathering and asking for justice, Keevan proved he was the restoration, not a rebellion.

Blood shed in justice wasn't murder. God gave the sword to the government to punish wrongdoers. Everything about this Gathering had been held according to the law.

Gulping in a breath, she wrote her answer on the paper, folded it, and pushed it to the edge of the table. As she placed her quill in the ink, she winced. She'd been nearly the last one to write her vote.

After Lord Doughtry of Calloday wrote his vote, General Stewart collected the sheets of paper and brought them to a far corner to verify them.

Keevan pointed his staff at Lord Caren. "Please state your vote."

Lord Caren stood. "My vote is yes."

His face impassive, Lord Norton rose to his feet. "My vote is yes."

Respen glared at him. He switched his glare to Lord Beregern when he also voted yes.

As he regained his seat, the next lord stood. Also a yes. Renna squeezed her hands together as one by one each lord or lady gave their vote. Each vote was a yes. Lady Lorraine stood. She voted yes.

Shadrach rose. He scowled at Respen. "My vote is yes."

Renna swallowed. Hers was the last vote. For Keevan's sentence to be affirmed and carried out, the Gathering's vote must be unanimous. She pushed herself to stand on shaking legs. Respen's dark eyes glared at her. She refused to look away. "My vote is yes."

Respen's eyebrows went up. He gave her a small nod. She'd surprised him. Again.

As she slipped into her seat, General Stewart nodded that the votes written on the papers matched the votes cast verbally, thus confirming that none of the nobles had changed their minds once they'd heard what everyone else was voting.

Keevan pounded his staff on the ground. "The sentence is confirmed. Lord Respen Felix, I suggest you seek the forgiveness of your Maker because you will meet Him in two days."

Renna sagged in her seat, her stomach tight. She'd made the right decision, but that wouldn't make it easier to watch Respen die.

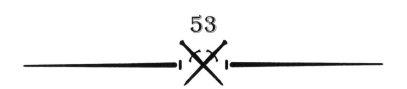

53

Renna tiptoed down the stairs and peeked around the corner into the Queen's Court. She didn't see Shadrach, Jamie, or Leith around. They wouldn't like what she was going to do. That didn't matter. She had to do this. She slipped across the Court and hurried through the passageway to the cobblestone courtyard.

Approaching the North Tower, she took a deep breath and strode to the soldiers guarding the door into the dungeons. "Lady Rennelda Faythe to see Respen Felix."

The guards stared at her. "He isn't allowed any visitors."

"Prince Keevan is my cousin. I'm not about to free Respen. I merely wish to talk to him about the state of his soul." She drew herself up straight. If she had to, she'd come back after she'd gained Keevan's permission, but she'd rather not go through all the trouble trying to secure it. She had a feeling Keevan, Leith, and Shadrach would fight her every step of the way.

The guards glanced at each other in a silent debate. Finally, one shrugged. "All right. But you have to be searched for weapons."

She held herself still as the guard, flushing red, hurriedly patted her down. She'd taken off the knife she'd had hidden under her skirt, so he found nothing. When he was satisfied, he unlocked the door and beckoned for her to follow him.

It was strange walking down these stairs under her own power. The last time she'd been in the dungeons, she'd been unable to walk because of her broken leg.

The guard halted at the bottom of the stairs. "You may speak with him."

She nodded and inched to the barred window set into the wooden door. She'd seen it so often from the other side that it felt unreal approaching it from the side of freedom. Was the blood from the mass execution of the citizens of Stetterly still staining the wall and floor?

"Respen?"

His dark silhouette moved along the far wall. As her eyes adjusted, she could see he paced below the ventilation window set high in the wall. He clasped his hands behind his back. "I knew you'd come."

She never would've guessed, when this moment came, that she'd hurt for him the way she did. Perhaps she should be here gloating or at least taking pleasure in justice for her parents' murders. Instead, all she saw was a lonely, lost man. "There's still time, Respen. You can still repent and ask God for forgiveness. Nothing you've done is beyond His power to forgive."

"Is that what Torren did? Beg?" Respen snorted and continued pacing. "I have never bowed to anyone, and I am not about to start now. I am not like Torren. I will not debase myself. I still have my pride."

"Leith isn't weak. He's found true strength and courage in God." She leaned her forehead against the bars. Tears squeezed at the corners of her eyes. All these weeks she'd been trying so hard to reach Respen, but all her efforts died against his hardened heart. She prayed that maybe this time God would use her words to reach him. "Humility isn't weakness. Surely Clarisse tried to tell you that."

Respen paused beneath the window looking out into the courtyard. "Yes, she did. But humility means a loss of control. I am not willing to part with that. Besides, I have what I wanted."

He'd wanted this? A dungeon and an execution? "What do you mean?"

He spun on his heels to face her, his hands still clasped behind his back. "I shall be remembered. Years from now, children will have to be taught about me. I am forever etched into the history of Acktar, and no one can remove that."

"You'll be remembered as a villain." Renna gripped the bars. "Why would you want that?"

"Fame. Infamy. They both have the same result." Respen shrugged. "I do not believe I will be remembered with the hatred you think I will. Why do you think I could claim the throne the way I did? Your uncle Leon was a weak king. He allowed the Rovers to overrun Acktar. Trade suffered. The country needed a strong king, and that is exactly what I gave them."

Renna bit her lip. She'd been too young to care about politics when her parents had died. Had the country really been that bad off? "If all you wanted to be was a strong king, then persecuting your Christian subjects wasn't necessary."

"It was a weakness that needed to be purged." He raised one eyebrow at her. "The churches were filled with self-righteous hypocrites who only attended the church services to be seen by others. I exposed that hypocrisy for what it was. But now, that exposure will tear Acktar apart. Neighbors can no longer hide behind their lies. The bitterness will linger. Your so-called Christians will shout for blood and vengeance. Your cousin will either give in to their demands or risk angering the very people who placed him on the throne. I predict Acktar will tear itself apart within a year."

Was Respen right? Would Acktar tear itself apart with bitterness? She'd thought the war was over, but was it really? She swallowed. "What good does it do you? You'll be dead."

"And so will you, eventually. Death comes the same for both of us." Respen's eyes burned into her. "But the difference is that I will be remembered, perhaps even fondly, while you will not. Who will know that the infamous King Respen surrendered, not to the warriors or heroes, but to the insignificant girl whose name will not even be recorded in history?"

Renna flinched. As she'd suspected, Respen had surrendered to her. Not to Keevan. Not to Leith. But to her, for the sake of the love he'd once had for Clarisse.

His tone sharpened. "You will be forgotten. Or worse, you will be scorned as the girl who helplessly remained captured while waiting for her hero to rescue her. Your part will be overshadowed by Prince Keevan as history gives him the heroic deeds when, in truth, he did little more than accidentally survive and eventually return to claim the spoils that others won for him. No one wants to remember a useless hero any more than they want to remember strength in those who are not."

It finally made sense to her why Respen had

surrendered instead of fighting to the death or even committing suicide. If he'd gone down fighting, it would've been an easy, clean ending for Keevan. He could've claimed the throne with Respen fully out of his way.

If Respen had killed himself, he would've been branded a coward for not facing the consequences of his actions. It would've tainted the image he wanted written into Acktar's history.

But surrendering and facing his execution without fear? That was brave. Noble, even. His death would be on Keevan's hands for the rest of his reign. It'd begin to drive the wedge between Keevan and the nobles who'd supported Respen.

In an odd way, it gave Respen some sort of control over his circumstances. He'd forced Keevan into executing him. Respen, not Keevan, had chosen this death.

She shook her head. "Being remembered isn't important. Not really. Not compared with eternity."

"Perhaps." His back remained straight as one of Shadrach's arrows. "But I am no coward."

Perhaps not. But he was arrogant. So sure of his own strength that he believed he could defy his Maker.

He was so blind. So hard. Couldn't he see that only the weak gained true strength? Renna shook her head. There was nothing in this world more pitiable than a man whose heart was so hard that he wouldn't—couldn't—be saved.

"Then I'm very sorry for you." She blinked at tears, refusing to let him see her cry. She whirled and dashed from the dungeons.

As the morning sunlight bathed the castle in gold, the executioner placed the block in the center of the courtyard. A ring of guards prevented the crowd from interfering, though the soldiers could do nothing to still the angry shouting.

Renna paced by the window in the king's chambers. Once before she'd witnessed an execution from this window. Her stomach churned. She wasn't enjoying it any more this time either.

Keevan leaned against the wall, calmly staring out the window and rubbing the scar along his face. Brandi sat in one of the plush chairs by the fireplace, close enough to hear what was happening in the courtyard below, but not close enough to see. Both she and Jamie beside her had their arms crossed.

Shadrach paced the far end of the room, hand on his sword hilt. Nearby, Martyn and Ranson sat on the floor, wearing clean, nondescript brown clothing. Ranson had his arms wrapped around his knees, like he feared Keevan would order his neck to the block next. Martyn stared at the floor, as if he knew he should be joining Respen in death but didn't trust the mercy that had been extended to him so far.

A hand slipped into hers. Renna turned to Leith, who leaned against the wall on the other side of the window from Keevan. So far, Keevan hadn't said a word to Leith beyond the order to join him in his chambers for the execution.

Renewed shouting drew her attention to the courtyard. Two guards led Respen from the North Tower and escorted him toward the block set in front of the castle gates. As he passed below the window, he looked up. His dark, proud eyes met hers. He gave her a half nod before he continued, head high, to the block.

Renna pressed her hand to her mouth to hold back

her tears. Leith's arm wrapped around her and drew her to him. "You don't have to watch."

She buried her face against his shoulder, stifling her sobs against his shirt. No one else in the room would understand her tears. Not even Leith. But he held her anyway, rubbing her back and whispering soothing sounds into her ear.

The all too familiar thud of the ax chopping down flinched against her skin. She gasped a sob.

Keevan gave a long sigh. "It's done." His boots scuffed against the rugs. "Captain Alistair, I'd like you and General Stewart to ride out tonight to bury the body. Take it deep into the Hills where no one will ever find it. I don't want any supporters he might have left to make a shrine out of his resting place."

"Wait!" Renna pushed herself away from Leith and forced herself to face the rest of the room. She scrubbed the tears from her face. "Could you bury him in Blathe next to his wife? They should be together." It seemed right, somehow, even though no one else would understand.

After a moment's consideration, Keevan nodded. "All right. I'll send General Stewart and his men on a decoy trip into the Hills. If we plant the rumor that we buried in him in the Hills in the right ears, no one will question the addition of an unmarked grave in Blathe."

"Thank you." She sagged. It really was over. Behind her, the others started to chatter. She should join them, but she couldn't at the moment.

Leith held her close and swiped a thumb over her cheek. "You've always had a kind heart. It was the first thing I noticed when I met you."

She smiled and slipped her arms around his neck. "And I noticed that you were humble. It confused me, coming from a Blade." She studied the way his black hair fell across his forehead and his green eyes danced above the fading bruises on his cheekbones. She loved him. Her imagination spun into dreams for the future.

"I'm sorry about Stetterly Manor." Leith hung his head, a fringe of his hair hiding his eyes. "You and Brandi won't have much to return to."

"It's all right. Too many memories in that house." The loss of the manor didn't give her the pang it once had. Starting over without the burden of the past hanging over them held a certain appeal. "I think we should build a cabin, something small, with a view overlooking the Spires Canyon."

"We?" Leith raised his eyebrows.

If he couldn't figure it out on his own, she wasn't going to explain it to him. But she would give him plenty of hints.

54

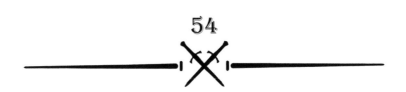

If his leg wasn't aching so much, Leith would've pressed Renna until she admitted what had her grinning like a hawk that had swooped down on a plump prairie dog. But he needed to sit down before he passed out.

His hand tucked in Renna's, he limped forward, spasms of pain shooting down his leg and into his chest with every step. As he reached the nearest chair, he leaned against it and glanced at Prince Keevan. "May I, Your Highness?"

Prince Keevan waved a hand. "Please do before you fall over. I don't think my cousins would appreciate me forcing you to stand on formality."

Leith collapsed into the chair. His cracked ribs ached. His burns throbbed. Renna fetched a footstool, propped it under his bad leg, and slid a chair next to him.

Prince Keevan picked up a folded piece of paper from his desk. "After much discussion with my advisors, I have decided not to pursue punishment for the remaining Blades. Acktar has seen enough bloodshed to last for years, and I don't want to spend the first months of my reign conducting trial after trial. The blame for those deaths will remain on Respen's head."

Leith nodded. Too many executions would resemble the first months of Respen's reign. "What do you plan to do?" He twined his fingers through Renna's once again. Keevan had once told him he had no intention of letting Leith go free.

"The Blades locked in the Tower will be banished on pain of death should they ever try to return."

"They'll cause trouble." Leith clenched his fist.

"I know. Hopefully whatever trouble they cause can be dealt with quietly." Prince Keevan ran the paper through his fingers.

Leith swallowed. When that trouble came, he'd have to deal with it. They'd come hunting their former First Blade, the one who'd betrayed them and Respen.

But that was a problem for tomorrow.

"Besides, I couldn't conduct their trials without your name coming up and forcing me to hold a trial for you as well." Prince Keevan paced closer and extended the paper. "My cousins are the only family I have left. I cannot afford to lose them."

Leith took the paper and opened it. He scanned a few words. "A pardon? You're pardoning me?"

"Yes, however the pardon isn't going to be made public. It'd cause too much resentment. Perhaps someday Acktar will be ready for the truth, but for now, it's best left a secret. As far as the official records will show, the Blade Leith Torren died in the final battle." Prince Keevan strode back to his desk. "You'll be able to choose a new name and start over with a new life. The pardon is only a security measure in case anyone should discover your past."

More secrets. Leith released a slow breath. Could he

ever live without secrets? Was a new name the only way he could make a new life?

Prince Keevan returned and dumped a bundle onto Leith's lap. "And these are in case someone ignores the pardon."

Leith pushed aside the cloth and found all his knives in their sheaths. He touched the initials *LT*

carved into the hilt. Secrets had a way of coming out. How long would it be before someone discovered his past as a Blade? "And Martyn and Ranson?"

Prince Keevan held up two more folded papers. "They've been granted clemency. Not a complete pardon, but they'll be able to start over, should they decide to remain in Acktar."

Ranson rose to his feet. Leith hadn't seen him or Martyn since the battle. Leith hadn't had the strength to climb the stairs to the rooms in the Tower where they were being held and, until today, Keevan hadn't let them out. Ranson's eyes were ringed with red, and his hands trembled as he took the paper from Prince Keevan.

He turned to Leith. "Did you mean what you said? About forgiveness?"

Leith couldn't help the smile that warmed his face. "Yes." He glanced at Renna. He thought he understood her meaning earlier, but he didn't dare assume.

She squeezed his hand. "We're going to need a lot of help rebuilding Stetterly. You're welcome to come, as long as you don't mind a little hard work."

Ranson's face broke into a smile. Perhaps, Leith wasn't too late to help Ranson adjust to life outside of the Blades. If only he hadn't been too late for Blane.

Martyn inched from the wall and took the paper as if he was afraid it might turn into a snake and bite him.

His brown eyes stayed on the ground before swiveling to the door. "I guess this is goodbye. I'll be leaving shortly."

Leaving? Leith shook his head. "You can't leave now, Martyn. Where would you go?"

Martyn shrugged. "I don't know. Perhaps I'll go south to the Great Mountains. Or I'll join the Surana to the west."

"You don't have to leave."

Martyn finally met his gaze. "You can't want me here. Not after what I did to you."

"You saved my life. You refused to kill me." Leith swiped his free hand against his trousers. Martyn did have a point. Would Leith be able to trust Martyn? Whatever friendship they'd had, it was broken. Could it be fixed?

"I captured Ladies Rennelda and Brandiline. I stopped you from rescuing both of them. I whipped you. I stood by and watched Respen torture you within an inch of your life." Martyn dragged a hand through his curls.

Brandi scowled and narrowed her eyes at Martyn. Shad jerked, and his eyes widened. Leith gritted his teeth. Brandi and Shad hadn't known the details of how Leith had been tortured. Shad flexed his fingers, crossed his arms, and glared at Martyn like he was contemplating punching him.

Leith waved around the room. "I helped kill Renna and Brandi's parents. I tried to kill Prince Keevan. I understand the guilt you're feeling. But running away from guilt doesn't make it go away. You have to face the ones you hurt. If they've experienced the forgiveness of Christ, they'll extend that same forgiveness to you." As Renna and Brandi had done to him. Prince Keevan hadn't fully forgiven him, but he was working on it.

Martyn groaned and tugged at his hair. "I still think you're chasing fantasies with all this God talk of yours, but fine. I'll try to stick around."

"Thanks." He and Martyn had a long way to go to repair their friendship, but at least they'd have a chance now.

Sitting across from Leith, Brandi swung her feet a few inches above the floor. "What're you going to pick for your new name?"

Shad leaned a shoulder against the wall. "He should go with Daniel for a first name. He already has a backstory and everything set up for that name already. If anyone asks, he can truthfully say he was a farm laborer in Walden before joining the Resistance where he was wounded in the Battle of Nalgar Castle."

"I like the name Daniel." Brandi grinned. Jamie stood over her, as if making sure she couldn't do anything reckless.

Leith grinned back. Brandi had started all this with her Daniel stories. If he was going to carry a new name for the rest of his life, Daniel was better than most.

He turned to Renna. The look in her eyes stole his breath away. He cleared his throat. "I'll need a last name too, and I'd like you to share it someday. Eventually. Not right away. If you'll have me. I—"

She put her finger over his mouth. "Whether you go by Daniel or Leith Torren, it doesn't matter to me. You're a Blade saved by God's grace, and I'll be proud to carry your name someday."

Grace. The word wrapped around him. Cleansing from the blood of his past in the blood of Christ. All undeserved. He never wanted to forget the wonder of it. He clasped both of Renna's hands. "How does Daniel Grayce sound?"

"Perfect." She leaned forward and kissed him.

He tugged one of his hands free so he could pull her closer. He could get lost in this moment, the feeling of loving and being loved.

Someone coughed. He pulled away but couldn't stop grinning, especially when he spotted Martyn, red-faced and uncomfortable, rocking on his heels. "We're making Martyn uncomfortable again."

Her grin matched his. "As well as everybody else in the room."

A quick glance told him she was right. Prince Keevan looked like he wanted very much to punch Leith. He couldn't be happy knowing his cousin would eventually marry the Blade that tried to kill him. Ranson and Jamie both stared at the ceiling like they wished he and Renna had waited for a more private setting.

The only one who didn't look uncomfortable was Brandi. She smirked like this had been her plan all along. Leith wouldn't put it past her.

He bent to kiss Renna again. Might as well let Brandi enjoy her victory.

THE BLADES OF ACKTAR

BOOK FOUR

DELIVER

Coming Winter 2016

Don't Miss the First Part of the Adventure

THE BLADES OF ACKTAR

BOOK ONE

DARE

Courage could cost him everything.

Third Blade Leith Torren never questions his orders or his loyalty to King Respen until an arrow wound and a prairie blizzard drive him to the doorstep of the girls whose family he once destroyed.

Their forbidden faith and ties to the Resistance could devastate their family a second time.

Survival depends on obedience, but freedom beckons. How far does he dare go to resist the king and his Blades?

No matter what Leith chooses, one thing is certain. Someone will die.

ACKNOWLEDGEMENTS

This past year has been such a crazy, amazing journey! Thank you to all the readers who stuck through the cliffhanger at the end of *Deny* to pick up *Defy*. You guys are the best!

Thank you especially to those who submitted names for this book, especially Emily Drown, Addyson Huneke, Amy K., and Valerie S for submitting the names Uriah, Stewart, Ian, and McCrae. Honorable mention to Chloe L., C.B. Cook, Jesseca Wheaton, Josie Ophoff, and Sierra Faith for submitting names I loved but weren't quite right for the book.

To all those who participated in the fan art contest. It was amazing to see all your talent and enthusiasm!

Thank you to the students and teachers of Eastside Christian School in Grand Rapids MI, who made me so welcome during my first ever school visit.

Also thanks to the students and teachers at the Protestant Reformed School and Heritage Christian High School of Dyer IN for being so enthusiastic about these books! You have made my day more than once!

To my family for once again being supportive and enthusiastic. My mom for spreading the word. My dad for being an early reader. My brothers Ethan and Josh for helping me with the guys' perspective. My brother Andy for being the real Aindre the blacksmith. My sister-in-law Alyssa and my soon-to-be sister-in-law Abby for being the most amazing sisters a girl could ask for.

And of course, my friends Bri, Paula, and Jill. You're the best street team and early readers ever.

My author friends (Angie, Jaye, Shantelle, Kim, and many, many others) who keep me sane and help pray these books into existence.

To Nadine Brandes, whose edits once again made all the difference in the world. I don't know what I'd do without you!

Thanks, Sierra, for once again making time to critique *Defy* and give lots and lots of comments. I can't wait for the day when I'll be able to return the favor on your books!

To Mindy Bergman, who stepped up and offered to proofread *Defy*. Thanks for helping anhililate those pesky typos!

Thank you also to a few of my early readers who also found a few missing words and typos.

And Ashley, for once again putting together a vibrant cover that captures the book perfectly!

All praise and glory be to God. He is my Light and my Salvation each and every day.

ABOUT THE AUTHOR

Tricia Mingerink is a twenty-something, book-loving, horse-riding country girl. She lives in Michigan with her family and their pack of pets. When she isn't writing, she can be found pursuing backwoods adventures across the country.

To learn more about Tricia Mingerink and get a behind-the-scenes peek her books, visit triciamingerink.com.

73004680R00223

Made in the USA
Columbia, SC
02 July 2017